STORIES, ESSAYS, & POEMS

G. K. CHESTERTON

INTRODUCTION TO EVERYMAN

In this Everyman volume, one of an adventurous set of modern authors, G. K. C. (he will pardon the initials) is represented as essayist, story-teller, poet, critic, humorist—an 'omnibus' volume in short, as the saying is. But it does not reveal him in all his aspects, for he has been a dramatist, a novelist, a biographer, and a brilliant journalist, too. A personal legend has grown up about him, indeed, and if its yet unwritten record can be trusted, he was observed one day when riding in a London omnibus to rise and courteously give up his seat to three ladies who had just got into the vehicle. The incident may seem casual, but it is characteristic, even symbolic, of his courtesy to literature and its three muses. Because of that genial, eclectic spirit, he has every right to a place as a link between the old literature and the new that figure in Everyman's Library. He is modern but medieval; contemporary yet reminiscent; and as we read his prose or his poetry that follows, we recall that he has dipped deep in Chaucer as well as Browning, Dickens, and the last Victorians, while retaining his own alert and paradoxical pen. I may add that he has kindly co-operated in making this selection.

E. R.

The following is a list of the chief works of Chesterton with the date of their first appearance in book form. A large proportion of them are collections of essays first contributed to various journals.

Greybeards at Play, 1900; *The Wild Knight*, 1900 (new ed. 1914); *The Defendant*, 1901; *Twelve Types*, 1902; *Robert Browning*, 1903; *G. F. Watts*, 1904; *The Napoleon of Notting Hill*, 1904; *The Club of Queer Trades*, 1905; *Heretics*, 1905; *Charles Dickens*, 1906; *The Man who was Thursday*, 1908; *All Things considered*, 1908; *Orthodoxy*, 1908; *George Bernard Shaw*, 1909; *Tremendous Trifles*, 1909; *The Ball and the Cross*, 1910; *What's Wrong with the World*, 1910; *Alarms and Discursions*, 1910; *William Blake*, 1910; *Appreciations and Criticisms of the Works of Charles Dickens*, 1911; *Innocence of Father Brown*, 1911; *The Ballad of the White Horse*, 1911; *Manalive*, 1912; *A Miscellany of Men*, 1912; *The Victorian Age in Literature*, 1913; *Magic*, 1913; *The*

Flying Inn, 1914; *The Wisdom of Father Brown*, 1914; *The Crimes of England*, 1915; *Poems*, 1915; *Wine, Water, and Song*, 1915; *A Shilling for my Thoughts*, 1916; *A Short History of England*, 1917; *Irish Impressions*, 1919; *The New Jerusalem*, 1920; *The Superstition of Divorce*, 1920; *The Uses of Diversity*, 1920; *The Ballad of St. Barbara*, 1922; *Eugenics and Other Evils*, 1922; *The Man who knew Too Much*, 1922; *What I saw in America*, 1922; *Fancies versus Fads*, 1923; *Saint Francis of Assisi*, 1923; *The End of the Roman Road*, 1924; *The Everlasting Man*, 1925; *The Superstitions of the Sceptic*, 1925; *Tales of the Long Bow*, 1925; *The Catholic Church and Conversion*, 1926; *The Incredulity of Father Brown*, 1926; *The Queen of Seven Swords*, 1926; *The Outline of Sanity*, 1926; *William Cobbett*, 1926; *The Judgment of Dr. Johnson*, 1927; *Robert Louis Stevenson*, 1927; *The Secret of Father Brown*, 1927; *Generally Speaking*, 1928; *The Sword of Wood*, 1928; *Do we agree?* (a debate with Bernard Shaw), 1928; *The Poet and the Lunatics*, 1929; *The Thing*, 1929; *Four Faultless Felons*, 1930; *The Resurrection of Rome*, 1930; *Come to think of It*, 1930; *All is Grist*, 1931; *Christendom in Dublin*, 1932; *Chaucer*, 1932; *Sidelights on New London and Newer York*, 1932; *All I survey*, 1933; *St. Thomas Aquinas*, 1933; *Avowals and Denials*, 1934; *The Scandal of Father Brown*, 1935.

Collected editions of the poems were published in 1927 and 1933, and a volume of introductions was published under the title of *G. K. C. as M.C.* in 1929. Although Chesterton's work has brought forth from time to time appreciations—though, more often, rejoinders—no full and serious estimate of it has yet been made.

ACKNOWLEDGMENTS

Permission to include material other than *The Defendant* essays, the Dickens essays, and *The Wild Knight* poems is due to Mr. Chesterton and the following publishers: Cassell and Co. Ltd. (the Father Brown Stories); Elkin Mathews and Marrot Ltd. (*The Sword of Wood*); Methuen and Co. Ltd. (essays from *All Things Considered, A Miscellany of Men, Tremendous Trifles, Come to think of It, The Outline of Sanity*); Sheed and Ward (essays from *The Thing* and *Sidelights on New London and Newer York*); Burns, Oates and Washbourne Ltd. (*Lepanto*).

CONTENTS

ix

* 913

CONTENTS

CONTENTS

CONTENTS

STORIES

THE BLUE CROSS

BETWEEN the silver ribbon of morning and the green glittering ribbon of sea, the boat touched Harwich and let loose a swarm of folk like flies, among whom the man we must follow was by no means conspicuous— nor wished to be. There was nothing notable about him, except a slight contrast between the holiday gaiety of his clothes and the official gravity of his face. His clothes included a slight, pale grey jacket, a white waistcoat, and a silver straw hat with a grey-blue ribbon. His lean face was dark by contrast, and ended in a curt black beard that looked Spanish and suggested an Elizabethan ruff. He was smoking a cigarette with the seriousness of an idler. There was nothing about him to indicate the fact that the grey jacket covered a loaded revolver, that the white waistcoat covered a police card, or that the straw hat covered one of the most powerful intellects in Europe. For this was Valentin himself, the head of the Paris police and the most famous investigator of the world; and he was coming from Brussels to London to make the greatest arrest of the century.

Flambeau was in England. The police of three countries had tracked the great criminal at last from Ghent to Brussels, from Brussels to the Hook of Holland; and it was conjectured that he would take some advantage of the unfamiliarity and confusion of the Eucharistic Congress, then taking place in London. Probably he would travel as some minor clerk or secretary connected with it; but, of course, Valentin could not be certain; nobody could be certain about Flambeau.

It is many years now since this colossus of crime suddenly ceased keeping the world in a turmoil; and when he ceased, as they said after the death of Roland, there was a great quiet upon the earth. But in his best

3

days (I mean, of course, his worst) Flambeau was a
figure as statuesque and international as the Kaiser.
Almost every morning the daily papers announced that
he had escaped the consequences of one extraordinary
crime by committing another. He was a Gascon of
gigantic stature and bodily daring; and the wildest tales
were told of his outbursts of athletic humour: how he
turned the *juge d'instruction* upside down and stood
him on his head, 'to clear his mind'; how he ran down
the Rue de Rivoli with a policeman under each arm.
It is due to him to say that his fantastic physical strength
was generally employed in such bloodless though undignified scenes; his real crimes were chiefly those of
ingenious and wholesale robbery. But each of his
thefts was almost a new sin, and would make a story by
itself. It was he who ran the great Tyrolean Dairy
Company in London, with no dairies, no cows, no carts,
no milk, but with some thousand subscribers. These
he served by the simple operation of moving the little
milk-cans outside people's doors to the doors of his own
customers. It was he who had kept up an unaccountable and close correspondence with a young lady whose
whole letter-bag was intercepted, by the extraordinary
trick of photographing his messages infinitesimally
small upon the slides of a microscope. A sweeping
simplicity, however, marked many of his experiments.
It is said he once repainted all the numbers in a street
in the dead of night merely to divert one traveller into
a trap. It is quite certain that he invented a portable
pillar-box, which he put up at corners in quiet suburbs
on the chance of strangers dropping postal orders into
it. Lastly he was known to be a startling acrobat;
despite his huge figure, he could leap like a grasshopper
and melt into the tree-tops like a monkey. Hence the
great Valentin, when he set out to find Flambeau, was
perfectly well aware that his adventures would not end
when he had found him.

But how was he to find him? On this the great
Valentin's ideas were still in process of settlement.

There was one thing which Flambeau, with all his

dexterity of disguise, could not cover, and that was his singular height. If Valentin's quick eye had caught a tall apple-woman, a tall grenadier, or even a tolerably tall duchess, he might have arrested them on the spot. But all along his train there was nobody that could be a disguised Flambeau, any more than a cat could be a disguised giraffe. About the people on the boat he had already satisfied himself; and the people picked up at Harwich or on the journey limited themselves with certainty to six. There was a short railway official travelling up to the terminus, three fairly short market-gardeners picked up two stations afterwards, one very short widow lady going up from a small Essex town, and a very short Roman Catholic priest going up from a small Essex village. When it came to the last case, Valentin gave it up and almost laughed. The little priest was so much the essence of those eastern flats: he had a face as round and dull as a Norfolk dumpling; he had eyes as empty as the North Sea; he had several brown-paper parcels which he was quite incapable of collecting. The Eucharistic Congress had doubtless sucked out of their local stagnation many such creatures, blind and helpless, like moles disinterred. Valentin was a sceptic in the severe style of France, and could have no love for priests. But he could have pity for them, and this one might have provoked pity in anybody. He had a large, shabby umbrella, which constantly fell on the floor. He did not seem to know which was the right end of his return ticket. He explained with a moon-calf simplicity to everybody in the carriage that he had to be careful, because he had something made of real silver 'with blue stones' in one of his brown-paper parcels. His quaint blending of Essex flatness with saintly simplicity continuously amused the French-man till the priest arrived (somehow) at Stratford with all his parcels, and came back for his umbrella. When he did the last, Valentin even had the good nature to warn him not to take care of the silver by telling everybody about it. But to whomever he talked, Valentin kept his eye open for someone else; he looked out steadily for any one, rich or poor, male or female, who was well up to six feet; for Flambeau was four inches above it.

He alighted at Liverpool Street, however, quite conscientiously secure that he had not missed the criminal so far. He then went to Scotland Yard to regularize his position and arrange for help in case of need; he then lit another cigarette and went for a long stroll in the streets of London. As he was walking in the streets and squares beyond Victoria, he paused suddenly and stood. It was a quaint, quiet square, very typical of London, full of an accidental stillness. The tall, flat houses round looked at once prosperous and uninhabited; the square of shrubbery in the centre looked as deserted as a green Pacific islet. One of the four sides was much higher than the rest, like a dais; and the line of this side was broken by one of London's admirable accidents — a restaurant that looked as if it had strayed from Soho. It was an unreasonably attractive object, with dwarf plants in pots and long, striped blinds of lemon yellow and white. It stood specially high above the street, and in the usual patch-work way of London, a flight of steps from the street ran up to meet the front door almost as a fire-escape might run up to a first-floor window. Valentin stood and smoked in front of the yellow-white blinds and considered them long.

The most incredible thing about miracles is that they happen. A few clouds in heaven do come together into the staring shape of one human eye. A tree does stand up in the landscape of a doubtful journey in the exact and elaborate shape of a note of interrogation. I have seen both these things myself within the last few days. Nelson does die in the instant of victory; and a man named Williams does quite accidentally murder a man named Williamson; it sounds like a sort of infanticide. In short, there is in life an element of elfin coincidence which people reckoning on the prosaic may perpetually miss. As it has been well expressed in the paradox of Poe, wisdom should reckon on the unforeseen.

Aristide Valentin was unfathomably French; and the

French intelligence is intelligence specially and solely.
He was not 'a thinking machine'; for that is a brainless
phrase of modern fatalism and materialism. A machine
only *is* a machine because it cannot think. But he was
a thinking man, and a plain man at the same time. All
his wonderful successes, that looked like conjuring, had
been gained by plodding logic, by clear and commonplace French thought. The French electrify the world
not by starting any paradox, they electrify it by carrying out a truism. They carry a truism so far—as in
the French Revolution. But exactly because Valentin
understood reason, he understood the limits of reason.
Only a man who knows nothing of motors talks of
motoring without petrol; only a man who knows nothing
of reason talks of reasoning without strong, undisputed
first principles. Here he had no strong first principles.
Flambeau had been missed at Harwich; and if he was
in London at all, he might be anything from a tall
tramp on Wimbledon Common to a tall toastmaster at
the Hôtel Métropole. In such a naked state of nescience,
Valentin had a view and a method of his own.

In such cases he reckoned on the unforeseen. In such
cases, when he could not follow the train of the reasonable, he coldly and carefully followed the train of the
unreasonable. Instead of going to the right places—
banks, police-stations, rendezvous—he systematically
went to the wrong places; knocked at every empty
house, turned down every cul-de-sac, went up every
lane blocked with rubbish, went round every crescent
that led him uselessly out of the way. He defended
this crazy course quite logically. He said that if one
had a clue this was the worst way; but if one had no
clue at all it was the best, because there was just the
chance that any oddity that caught the eye of the
pursuer might be the same that had caught the eye of
the pursued. Somewhere a man must begin, and it had
better be just where another man might stop. Something about that flight of steps up to the shop, something
about the quietude and quaintness of the restaurant,
roused all the detective's rare romantic fancy and made

him resolve to strike at random. He went up the steps, and sitting down by the window, asked for a cup of black coffee.

It was half-way through the morning, and he had not breakfasted; the slight litter of other breakfasts stood about on the table to remind him of his hunger; and adding a poached egg to his order, he proceeded musingly to shake some white sugar into his coffee, thinking all the time about Flambeau. He remembered how Flambeau had escaped, once by a pair of nail scissors, and once by a house on fire; once by having to pay for an unstamped letter, and once by getting people to look through a telescope at a comet that might destroy the world. He thought his detective brain as good as the criminal's, which was true. But he fully realized the disadvantage. 'The criminal is the creative artist; the detective only the critic,' he said with a sour smile, and lifted his coffee-cup to his lips slowly, and put it down very quickly. He had put salt in it.

He looked at the vessel from which the silvery powder had come; it was certainly a sugar-basin; as unmistakably meant for sugar as a champagne-bottle for champagne. He wondered why they should keep salt in it. He looked to see if there were any more orthodox vessels. Yes, there were two salt-cellars quite full. Perhaps there was some speciality in the condiment in the salt-cellars. He tasted it; it was sugar. Then he looked round at the restaurant with a refreshed air of interest, to see if there were any other traces of that singular artistic taste which puts the sugar in the salt-cellars and the salt in the sugar-basin. Except for an odd splash of some dark fluid on one of the white-papered walls, the whole place appeared neat, cheerful, and ordinary. He rang the bell for the waiter.

When that official hurried up, fuzzy-haired and somewhat blear-eyed at that early hour, the detective (who was not without an appreciation of the simpler forms of humour) asked him to taste the sugar and see if it was up to the high reputation of the hotel. The result was that the waiter yawned suddenly and woke up.

'Do you play this delicate joke on your customers every morning?' inquired Valentin. 'Does changing the salt and sugar never pall on you as a jest?'

The waiter, when this irony grew clearer, stammeringly assured him that the establishment had certainly no such intention; it must be a most curious mistake. He picked up the sugar-basin and looked at it; he picked up the salt-cellar and looked at that, his face growing more and more bewildered. At last he abruptly excused himself, and hurrying away, returned in a few seconds with the proprietor. The proprietor also examined the sugar-basin and then the salt-cellar; the proprietor also looked bewildered.

Suddenly the waiter seemed to grow inarticulate with a rush of words.

'I zink,' he stuttered eagerly, 'I zink it is those two clergymen.'

'What two clergymen?'

'The two clergymen,' said the waiter, 'that threw soup at the wall.'

'Threw soup at the wall?' repeated Valentin, feeling sure this must be some Italian metaphor.

'Yes, yes,' said the attendant excitedly, and pointing at the dark splash on the white paper; 'threw it over there on the wall.'

Valentin looked his query at the proprietor, who came to his rescue with fuller reports.

'Yes, sir,' he said, 'it's quite true, though I don't suppose it has anything to do with the sugar and salt. Two clergymen came in and drank soup here very early, as soon as the shutters were taken down. They were both very quiet, respectable people; one of them paid the bill and went out; the other, who seemed a slower coach altogether, was some minutes longer getting his things together. But he went out at last. Only, the instant before he stepped into the street he deliberately picked up his cup, which he had only half emptied, and threw the soup slap on the wall. I was in the back room myself, and so was the waiter; so I could only rush out in time to find the wall splashed and the shop empty. It didn't do any particular damage, but it was confounded cheek; and I tried to catch the men in the street. They were too far off though; I only noticed they went round the corner into Carstairs Street.'

The detective was on his feet, hat settled and stick in hand. He had already decided that in the universal darkness of his mind he could only follow the first odd finger that pointed; and this finger was odd enough. Paying his bill and clashing the glass doors behind him, he was soon swinging round into the other street.

It was fortunate that even in such fevered moments his eye was cool and quick. Something in a shop-front went by him like a mere flash; yet he went back to look at it. The shop was a popular greengrocer and fruiterer's, an array of goods set out in the open air and plainly ticketed with their names and prices. In the two most prominent compartments were two heaps, of oranges and of nuts respectively. On the heap of nuts lay a scrap of cardboard, on which was written in bold, blue chalk: 'Best tangerine oranges, two a penny.' On the oranges was the equally clear and exact description: 'Finest Brazil nuts, 4d. a lb.' M. Valentin looked at these two placards and fancied he had met this highly subtle form of humour before, and that somewhat recently. He drew the attention of the red-faced fruiterer, who was looking rather sullenly up and down the street, to this inaccuracy in his advertisements. The fruiterer said nothing, but sharply put each card into its proper place. The detective, leaning elegantly on his walking-cane, continued to scrutinize the shop. At last he said: 'Pray excuse my apparent irrelevance, my good sir, but I should like to ask you a question in experimental psychology and the association of ideas.'

The red-faced shopman regarded him with an eye of menace; but he continued gaily, swinging his cane. 'Why,' he pursued, 'why are two tickets wrongly placed in a greengrocer's shop like a shovel hat that has come to London for a holiday? Or, in case I do not make myself clear, what is the mystical association which connects the idea of nuts marked as oranges with the idea of two clergymen, one tall and the other short?'

The eyes of the tradesman stood out of his head like a snail's; he really seemed for an instant likely to fling himself upon the stranger. At last he stammered angrily: 'I don't know what you 'ave to do with it, but if you 're one of their friends, you can tell 'em from me that I 'll knock their silly 'eads off, parsons or no parsons, if they upset my apples again.'

'Indeed?' asked the detective, with great sympathy. 'Did they upset your apples?'

'One of 'em did,' said the heated shopman; 'rolled 'em all over the street. I 'd 'ave caught the fool but for havin' to pick 'em up.'

'Which way did these parsons go?' asked Valentin.

'Up that second road on the left-hand side, and then across the square,' said the other promptly.

'Thanks,' said Valentin, and vanished like a fairy. On the other side of the second square he found a policeman, and said: 'This is urgent, constable; have you seen two clergymen in shovel hats?'

The policeman began to chuckle heavily. 'I 'ave, sir; and if you arst me, one of 'em was drunk. He stood in the middle of the road that bewildered that——'

'Which way did they go?' snapped Valentin.

'They took one of them yellow buses over there,' answered the man; 'them that go to Hampstead.'

Valentin produced his official card and said very rapidly: 'Call up two of your men to come with me in pursuit,' and crossed the road with such contagious energy that the ponderous policeman was moved to almost agile obedience. In a minute and a half the French detective was joined on the opposite pavement by an inspector and a man in plain clothes.

'Well, sir,' began the former, with smiling importance, 'and what may——?'

Valentin pointed suddenly with his cane. 'I 'll tell you on the top of that omnibus,' he said, and was darting and dodging across the tangle of the traffic.

When all three sank panting on the top seats of the yellow vehicle, the inspector said: 'We could go four times as quick in a taxi.'

'Quite true,' replied their leader placidly, 'if we only had an idea of where we were going.'

'Well, where *are* you going?' asked the other, staring.

Valentin smoked frowningly for a few seconds; then, removing his cigarette, he said: 'If you *know* what a man's doing, get in front of him; but if you want to guess what he's doing, keep behind him. Stray when he strays: stop when he stops; travel as slowly as he. Then you may see what he saw and may act as he acted. All we can do is to keep our eyes skinned for a queer thing.'

'What sort of a queer thing do you mean?' asked the inspector.

'Any sort of queer thing,' answered Valentin, and relapsed into obstinate silence.

The yellow omnibus crawled up the northern roads for what seemed like hours on end; the great detective would not explain further, and perhaps his assistants felt a silent and growing doubt of his errand. Perhaps, also, they felt a silent and growing desire for lunch, for the hours crept long past the normal luncheon hour, and the long roads of the North London suburbs seemed to shoot out into length after length like an infernal telescope. It was one of those journeys on which a man perpetually feels that now at last he must have come to the end of the universe, and then finds he has only come to the beginning of Tufnell Park. London died away in draggled taverns and dreary scrubs, and then was unaccountably born again in blazing high streets and blatant hotels. It was like passing through thirteen separate vulgar cities all just touching each other. But though the winter twilight was already threatening the road ahead of them, the Parisian detective still sat silent and watchful, eyeing the frontage of the streets that slid by on either side. By the time they had left Camden Town behind, the policemen were nearly asleep; at least. they gave something like a jump

THE BLUE CROSS   13

as Valentin leapt erect, struck a hand on each man's shoulder, and shouted to the driver to stop.

They tumbled down the steps into the road without realizing why they had been dislodged; when they looked round for enlightenment they found Valentin triumphantly pointing his finger towards a window on the left side of the road. It was a large window, forming part of the long façade of a gilt and palatial public-house; it was the part reserved for respectable dining, and labelled 'Restaurant.' This window, like all the rest along the frontage of the hotel, was of frosted and figured glass; but in the middle of it was a big, black smash, like a star in the ice.

'Our cue at last,' cried Valentin, waving his stick; 'the place with the broken window.'

'What window? What cue?' asked his principal assistant. 'Why, what proof is there that this has anything to do with them?'

Valentin almost broke his bamboo stick with rage.

'Proof!' he cried. 'Good God! the man is looking for proof! Why, of course, the chances are twenty to one that it has *nothing* to do with them. But what else can we do? Don't you see we must either follow one wild possibility or else go home to bed?' He banged his way into the restaurant, followed by his companions, and they were soon seated at a late luncheon at a little table, and looking at the star of smashed glass from the inside. Not that it was very informative to them even then.

'Got your window broken, I see,' said Valentin to the waiter, as he paid his bill.

'Yes, sir,' answered the attendant, bending busily over the change, to which Valentin silently added an enormous tip. The waiter straightened himself with mild but unmistakable animation.

'Ah, yes, sir,' he said. 'Very odd thing, that, sir.'

'Indeed? Tell us about it,' said the detective with careless curiosity.

'Well, two gents in black came in,' said the waiter; 'two of those foreign parsons that are running about.

They had a cheap and quiet little lunch, and one of them paid for it and went out. The other was just going out to join him when I looked at my change again and found he'd paid me more than three times too much. "Here," I says to the chap who was nearly out of the door, "you've paid too much." "Oh," he says, very cool, "have we?" "Yes," I says, and picks up the bill to show him. Well, that was a knock-out.'

'What do you mean?' asked his interlocutor.

'Well, I'd have sworn on seven Bibles that I'd put 4s. on that bill. But now I saw I'd put 14s., as plain as paint."

'Well?' cried Valentin, moving slowly, but with burning eyes, 'and then?'

'The parson at the door he says, all serene: "Sorry to confuse your accounts, but it 'll pay for the window." "What window?" I says. "The one I'm going to break," he says, and smashed that blessed pane with his umbrella.'

All the inquirers made an exclamation; and the inspector said under his breath: 'Are we after escaped lunatics?' The waiter went on with some relish for the ridiculous story:

'I was so knocked silly for a second, I couldn't do anything. The man marched out of the place and joined his friend just round the corner. Then they went so quick up Bullock Street that I couldn't catch them, though I ran round the bars to do it.'

'Bullock Street,' said the detective, and shot up that thoroughfare as quickly as the strange couple he pursued.

Their journey now took them through bare brick ways like tunnels; streets with few lights and even with few windows; streets that seemed built out of the blank backs of everything and everywhere. Dusk was deepening, and it was not easy even for the London policemen to guess in what exact direction they were treading. The inspector, however, was pretty certain that they would eventually strike some part of Hampstead Heath. Abruptly one bulging and gaslit window broke the blue twilight like a bull's-eye lantern; and

Valentin stopped an instant before a little garish sweetstuff shop. After an instant's hesitation he went in; he stood amid the gaudy colours of the confectionery with entire gravity and bought thirteen chocolate cigars with a certain care. He was clearly preparing an opening; but he did not need one.

An angular, elderly young woman in the shop had regarded his elegant appearance with a merely automatic inquiry; but when she saw the door behind him blocked with the blue uniform of the inspector, her eyes seemed to wake up.

'Oh,' she said, 'if you 've come about that parcel, I 've sent it off already.'

'Parcel!' repeated Valentin; and it was his turn to look inquiring.

'I mean the parcel the gentleman left—the clergyman gentleman.'

'For goodness' sake,' said Valentin, leaning forward with his first real confession of eagerness, 'for Heaven's sake tell us what happened exactly.'

'Well,' said the woman, a little doubtfully, 'the clergymen came in about half an hour ago and bought some peppermints and talked a bit, and then went off towards the Heath. But a second after, one of them runs back into the shop and says: "Have I left a parcel?" Well, I looked everywhere and couldn't see one; so he says: "Never mind; but if it should turn up, please post it to this address," and he left me the address and a shilling for my trouble. And sure enough, though I thought I 'd looked everywhere, I found he 'd left a brown-paper parcel, so I posted it to the place he said. I can't remember the address now; it was somewhere in Westminster. But as the thing seemed so important, I thought perhaps the police had come about it.'

'So they have,' said Valentin shortly. 'Is Hampstead Heath near here?'

'Straight on for fifteen minutes,' said the woman, 'and you 'll come right out on the open.' Valentin sprang out of the shop and began to run. The other detectives followed him at a reluctant trot.

The street they threaded was so narrow and shut in by shadows that when they came out unexpectedly into the void common and vast sky they were startled to find the evening still so light and clear. A perfect dome of peacock-green sank into gold amid the blackening trees and the dark violet distances. The glowing green tint was just deep enough to pick out in points of crystal one or two stars. All that was left of the daylight lay in a golden glitter across the edge of Hampstead and that popular hollow which is called the Vale of Health. The holiday makers who roam this region had not wholly dispersed: a few couples sat shapelessly on benches; and here and there a distant girl still shrieked in one of the swings. The glory of heaven deepened and darkened around the sublime vulgarity of man; and standing on the slope and looking across the valley, Valentin beheld the thing which he sought.

Among the black and breaking groups in that distance was one especially black which did not break—a group of two figures clerically clad. Though they seemed as small as insects, Valentin could see that one of them was much smaller than the other. Though the other had a student's stoop and an inconspicuous manner, he could see that the man was well over six feet high. He shut his teeth and went forward, whirling his stick impatiently. By the time he had substantially diminished the distance and magnified the two black figures as in a vast microscope, he had perceived something else; something which startled him, and yet which he had somehow expected. Whoever was the tall priest, there could be no doubt about the identity of the short one. It was his friend of the Harwich train, the stumpy little *curé* of Essex whom he had warned about his brown-paper parcels.

Now, so far as this went, everything fitted in finally and rationally enough. Valentin had learned by his inquiries that morning that a Father Brown from Essex was bringing up a silver cross with sapphires, a relic of considerable value, to show some of the foreign priests at the congress. This undoubtedly was the 'silver with blue stones'; and Father Brown undoubtedly was the little greenhorn in the train. Now there was nothing wonderful about the fact that what Valentin had found out Flambeau had also found out; Flambeau found out everything. Also there was nothing wonderful in the fact that when Flambeau heard of a sapphire cross he should try to steal it; that was the most natural thing in all natural history. And most certainly there was nothing wonderful about the fact that Flambeau should have it all his own way with such a silly sheep as the man with the umbrella and the parcels. He was the sort of man whom anybody could lead on a string to the North Pole; it was not surprising that an actor like Flambeau, dressed as another priest, could lead him to Hampstead Heath. So far the crime seemed clear enough; and while the detective pitied the priest for his helplessness, he almost despised Flambeau for condescending to so gullible a victim. But when Valentin thought of all that had happened in between, of all that had led him to his triumph, he racked his brains for the smallest rhyme or reason in it. What had the stealing of a blue-and-silver cross from a priest from Essex to do with chucking soup at wallpaper? What had it to do with calling nuts oranges, or with paying for windows first and breaking them afterwards? He had come to the end of his chase; yet somehow he had missed the middle of it. When he failed (which was seldom), he had usually grasped the clue, but nevertheless missed the criminal. Here he had grasped the criminal, but still he could not grasp the clue.

The two figures that they followed were crawling like black flies across the huge green contour of a hill. They were evidently sunk in conversation, and perhaps did not notice where they were going; but they were certainly going to the wilder and more silent heights of the Heath. As their pursuers gained on them, the latter had to use the undignified attitudes of the deer-stalker, to crouch behind clumps of trees and even to crawl prostrate in deep grass. By these ungainly ingenuities the hunters even came close enough to the quarry to hear the murmur of the discussion, but no word could be distinguished except the word 'reason' recurring frequently in a high and almost childish voice. Once, over an abrupt dip of land and a dense tangle of thickets, the detectives actually lost the two figures they were following. They did not find the trail again for an agonizing ten minutes, and then it led round the brow of a great dome of hill overlooking an amphitheatre of rich and desolate sunset scenery. Under a tree in this commanding yet neglected spot was an old ramshackle wooden seat. On this seat sat the two priests still in serious speech together. The gorgeous green and gold still clung to the darkening horizon; but the dome above was turning slowly from peacock-green to peacock-blue, and the stars detached themselves more and more like solid jewels. Mutely motioning to his followers, Valentin contrived to creep up behind the big branching tree, and, standing there in deathly silence, heard the words of the strange priests for the first time.

After he had listened for a minute and a half, he was gripped by a devilish doubt. Perhaps he had dragged the two English policemen to the wastes of a nocturnal heath on an errand no saner than seeking figs on thistles. For the two priests were talking exactly like priests, piously, with learning and leisure, about the most aerial enigmas of theology. The little Essex priest spoke the more simply, with his round face turned to the strengthening stars; the other talked with his head bowed, as if he were not even worthy to look at them. But no more innocently clerical conversation could have been heard in any white Italian cloister or black Spanish cathedral.

The first he heard was the tail of one of Father Brown's sentences, which ended: '. . . what they really meant in the Middle Ages by the heavens being incorruptible.'

The taller priest nodded his bowed head and said:

'Ah, yes, these modern infidels appeal to their reason; but who can look at those millions of worlds and not feel that there may well be wonderful universes above us where reason is utterly unreasonable?'

'No,' said the other priest; 'reason is always reasonable, even in the last limbo, in the lost borderland of
things. I know that people charge the Church with
lowering reason, but it is just the other way. Alone
on earth, the Church makes reason really supreme.
Alone on earth, the Church affirms that God Himself is
bound by reason.'

The other priest raised his austere face to the spangled
sky and said:

'Yet who knows if in that infinite universe——?'

'Only infinite physically,' said the little priest, turning
sharply in his seat, 'not infinite in the sense of escaping
from the laws of truth.'

Valentin behind his tree was tearing his finger-nails
with silent fury. He seemed almost to hear the sniggers
of the English detectives whom he had brought so far
on a fantastic guess only to listen to the metaphysical
gossip of two mild old parsons. In his impatience he
lost the equally elaborate answer of the tall cleric, and
when he listened again it was again Father Brown who
was speaking:

'Reason and justice grip the remotest and the loneliest
star. Look at those stars. Don't they look as if they
were single diamonds and sapphires? Well, you can
imagine any mad botany or geology you please. Think
of forests of adamant with leaves of brilliants. Think
the moon is a blue moon, a single elephantine sapphire.
But don't fancy that all that frantic astronomy would
make the smallest difference to the reason and justice
of conduct. On plains of opal, under cliffs cut out of
pearl, you would still find a notice-board: "Thou shalt
not steal."'

Valentin was just in the act of rising from his rigid
and crouching attitude and creeping away as softly as
might be, felled by the one great folly of his life. But
something in the very silence of the tall priest made him
stop until the latter spoke. When at last he did speak,
he said simply, his head bowed and his hands on his
knees:

'Well, I still think that other worlds may perhaps rise

higher than our reason. The mystery of heaven is unfathomable, and I for one can only bow my head.'

Then, with brow yet bent and without changing by the faintest shade his attitude or voice, he added:

'Just hand over that sapphire cross of yours, will you? We're all alone here, and I could pull you to pieces like a straw doll.'

The utterly unaltered voice and attitude added a strange violence to that shocking change of speech. But the guarder of the relic only seemed to turn his head by the smallest section of the compass. He seemed still to have a somewhat foolish face turned to the stars. Perhaps he had not understood. Or, perhaps, he had understood and sat rigid with terror.

'Yes,' said the tall priest, in the same low voice and in the same still posture, 'yes, I am Flambeau.'

Then, after a pause, he said:

'Come, will you give me that cross?'

'No,' said the other, and the monosyllable had an odd sound.

Flambeau suddenly flung off all his pontifical pretensions. The great robber leaned back in his seat and laughed low but long.

'No,' he cried; 'you won't give it me, you proud prelate. You won't give it me, you little celibate simpleton. Shall I tell you why you won't give it me? Because I've got it already in my own breast-pocket.'

The small man from Essex turned what seemed to be a dazed face in the dusk, and said, with the timid eagerness of 'The Private Secretary':

'Are—are you sure?'

Flambeau yelled with delight.

'Really, you're as good as a three-act farce,' he cried. 'Yes, you turnip, I am quite sure. I had the sense to make a duplicate of the right parcel, and now, my friend, you've got the duplicate, and I've got the jewels. An old dodge, Father Brown—a very old dodge.'

'Yes,' said Father Brown, and passed his hand through his hair with the same strange vagueness of manner. 'Yes, I've heard of it before.'

The colossus of crime leaned over to the little rustic priest with a sort of sudden interest.

'*You* have heard of it?' he asked. 'Where have *you* heard of it?'

'Well, I mustn't tell you his name, of course,' said the little man simply. 'He was a penitent, you know. He had lived prosperously for about twenty years entirely on duplicate brown-paper parcels. And so, you see, when I began to suspect you, I thought of this poor chap's way of doing it at once.'

'Began to suspect me?' repeated the outlaw with increased intensity. 'Did you really have the gumption to suspect me just because I brought you up to this bare part of the Heath?'

'No, no,' said Brown with an air of apology. 'You see, I suspected you when we first met. It's that little bulge up the sleeve where you people have the spiked bracelet.'

'How in Tartarus,' cried Flambeau, 'did you ever hear of the spiked bracelet?'

'Oh, one's little flock, you know!' said Father Brown, arching his eyebrows rather blankly. 'When I was a curate in Hartlepool, there were three of them with spiked bracelets. So, as I suspected you from the first, don't you see, I made sure that the cross should go safe, anyhow. I'm afraid I watched you, you know. So at last I saw you change the parcels. Then, don't you see, I changed them back again. And then I left the right one behind.'

'Left it behind?' repeated Flambeau, and for the first time there was another note in his voice beside his triumph.

'Well, it was like this,' said the little priest, speaking in the same unaffected way. 'I went back to that sweet-shop and asked if I'd left a parcel, and gave them a particular address if it turned up. Well, I knew I hadn't; but when I went away again I did. So, instead of running after me with that valuable parcel, they have sent it flying to a friend of mine in Westminster.' Then he added rather sadly: 'I learnt that,

too, from a poor fellow in Hartlepool. He used to do
it with handbags he stole at railway stations, but he 's
in a monastery now. Oh, one gets to know, you know,'
he added, rubbing his head again with the same sort
of desperate apology. 'We can't help being priests.
People come and tell us these things.'

Flambeau tore a brown-paper parcel out of his inner
pocket and rent it in pieces. There was nothing but
paper and sticks of lead inside it. He sprang to his feet
with a gigantic gesture, and cried:

'I don't believe you. I don't believe a bumpkin like
you could manage all that. I believe you 've still got
the stuff on you, and if you don't give it up—why, we 're
all alone, and I 'll take it by force!'

'No,' said Father Brown simply, and stood up also;
'you won't take it by force. First, because I really
haven't still got it. And, second, because we are not
alone.'

Flambeau stopped in his stride forward.

'Behind that tree,' said Father Brown, pointing, 'are
two strong policemen and the greatest detective alive.
How did they come here, do you ask? Why, I brought
them, of course! How did I do it? Why, I 'll tell you
if you like! Lord bless you, we have to know twenty
such things when we work among the criminal classes!
Well, I wasn't sure you were a thief, and it would never
do to make a scandal against one of our own clergy. So
I just tested you to see if anything would make you
show yourself. A man generally makes a small scene
if he finds salt in his coffee; if he doesn't, he has some
reason for keeping quiet. I changed the salt and sugar,
and *you* kept quiet. A man generally objects if his bill
is three times too big. If he pays it, he has some motive
for passing unnoticed. I altered your bill, and *you*
paid it.'

The world seemed waiting for Flambeau to leap like
a tiger. But he was held back as by a spell; he was
stunned with the utmost curiosity.

'Well,' went on Father Brown, with lumbering
lucidity, 'as you wouldn't leave any tracks for the

police, of course somebody had to. At every place we went to, I took care to do something that would get us talked about for the rest of the day. I didn't do much harm—a splashed wall, spilt apples, a broken window; but I saved the cross, as the cross will always be saved. It is at Westminster by now. I rather wonder you didn't stop it with the Donkey's Whistle.'

'With the what?' asked Flambeau.

'I'm glad you've never heard of it,' said the priest, making a face. 'It's a foul thing. I'm sure you're too good a man for a Whistler. I couldn't have countered it even with the Spots myself; I'm not strong enough in the legs.'

'What on earth are you talking about?' asked the other.

'Well, I did think you'd know the Spots,' said Father Brown, agreeably surprised. 'Oh, you can't have gone so very wrong yet!'

'How in blazes do you know all these horrors?' cried Flambeau.

The shadow of a smile crossed the round, simple face of his clerical opponent.

'Oh, by being a celibate simpleton, I suppose,' he said. 'Has it never struck you that a man who does next to nothing but hear men's real sins is not likely to be wholly unaware of human evil? But, as a matter of fact, another part of my trade, too, made me sure you weren't a priest.'

'What?' asked the thief, almost gaping.

'You attacked reason,' said Father Brown. 'It's bad theology.'

And even as he turned away to collect his property, the three policemen came out from under the twilight trees. Flambeau was an artist and a sportsman. He stepped back and swept Valentin a great bow.

'Do not bow to me, *mon ami*,' said Valentin, with silver clearness. 'Let us both bow to our master.'

And they both stood an instant uncovered, while the little Essex priest blinked about for his umbrella.

THE SECRET GARDEN

ARISTIDE VALENTIN, Chief of the Paris Police, was late for his dinner, and some of his guests began to arrive before him. These were, however, reassured by his confidential servant, Ivan, the old man with a scar and a face almost as grey as his moustaches, who always sat at a table in the entrance hall—a hall hung with weapons. Valentin's house was perhaps as peculiar and celebrated as its master. It was an old house, with high walls and tall poplars almost overhanging the Seine; but the oddity—and perhaps the police value— of its architecture was this: that there was no ultimate exit at all except through this front door, which was guarded by Ivan and the armoury. The garden was large and elaborate, and there were many exits from the house into the garden. But there was no exit from the garden into the world outside; all round it ran a tall, smooth unscalable wall with special spikes at the top; no bad garden, perhaps, for a man to reflect in whom some hundred criminals had sworn to. kill.

As Ivan explained to the guests, their host had telephoned that he was detained for ten minutes. He was, in truth, making some last arrangements about executions and such ugly things; and though these duties were rootedly repulsive to him, he always performed them with precision. Ruthless in the pursuit of criminals, he was very mild about their punishment. Since he had been supreme over French—and largely over European—police methods, his great influence had been honourably used for the mitigation of sentences and the purification of prisons. He was one of the great humanitarian French freethinkers; and the only thing wrong with them is that they make mercy even colder than justice.

When Valentin arrived he was already dressed in

black clothes and the red rosette—an elegant figure, his dark beard already streaked with grey. He went straight through his house to his study, which opened on the grounds behind. The garden door of it was open, and after he had carefully locked his box in its official place, he stood for a few seconds at the open door looking out upon the garden. A sharp moon was fighting with the flying rags and tatters of a storm, and Valentin regarded it with a wistfulness unusual in such scientific natures as his. Perhaps such scientific natures have some psychic prevision of the most tremendous problem of their lives. From any such occult mood, at least, he quickly recovered, for he knew he was late and that his guests had already begun to arrive. A glance at his drawing-room when he entered it was enough to make certain that his principal guest was not there, at any rate. He saw all the other pillars of the little party: he saw Lord Galloway, the English Ambassador—a choleric old man with a russet face like an apple, wearing the blue ribbon of the Garter. He saw Lady Galloway, slim and threadlike, with silver hair and a face sensitive and superior. He saw her daughter, Lady Margaret Graham, a pale and pretty girl with an elfish face and copper-coloured hair. He saw the Duchess of Mont St. Michel, black-eyed and opulent, and with her her two daughters, black-eyed and opulent also. He saw Dr. Simon, a typical French scientist, with glasses, a pointed brown beard, and a forehead barred with those parallel wrinkles which are the penalty of superciliousness, since they come through constantly elevating the eyebrows. He saw Father Brown of Cobhole, in Essex, whom he had recently met in England. He saw—perhaps with more interest than any of those—a tall man in uniform, who had bowed to the Galloways without receiving any very hearty acknowledgment, and who now advanced alone to pay his respects to his host. This was Commandant O'Brien, of the French Foreign Legion. He was a slim yet somewhat swaggering figure, clean-shaven, dark-haired, and blue-eyed, and as seemed natural in an officer of that

famous regiment of victorious failures and successful
suicides, he had an air at once dashing and melancholy.
He was by birth an Irish gentleman, and in boyhood
had known the Galloways—especially Margaret Graham.
He had left his country after some crash of debts,
and now expressed his complete freedom from British
etiquette by swinging about in uniform, sabre, and
spurs. When he bowed to the Ambassador's family,
Lord and Lady Galloway bent stiffly, and Lady
Margaret looked away.

But for whatever old causes such people might be
interested in each other, their distinguished host was
not specially interested in them. No one of them at
least was in his eyes the guest of the evening. Valentin
was expecting, for special reasons, a man of world-wide
fame, whose friendship he had secured during some of
his great detective tours and triumphs in the United
States. He was expecting Julius K. Brayne, that multi-
millionaire whose colossal and even crushing endowments
of small religions have occasioned so much easy sport
and easier solemnity for the American and English
papers. Nobody could quite make out whether Mr.
Brayne was an atheist or a Mormon, or a Christian
Scientist; but he was ready to pour money into any
intellectual vessel, so long as it was an untried vessel.
One of his hobbies was to wait for the American Shakespeare — a hobby more patient than angling. He
admired Walt Whitman, but thought that Luke P.
Tanner, of Paris, Pa., was more 'progressive' than
Whitman any day. He liked anything that he thought
'progressive.' He thought Valentin 'progressive,'
thereby doing him a grave injustice.

The solid appearance of Julius K. Brayne in the room
was as decisive as a dinner-bell. He had this great
quality, which very few of us can claim, that his presence
was as big as his absence. He was a huge fellow, as fat
as he was tall, clad in complete evening black, without
so much relief as a watch-chain or a ring. His hair was
white and well brushed back like a German's; his face
was red, fierce, and cherubic, with one dark tuft under

the lower lip that threw up that otherwise infantile visage with an effect theatrical and even Mephistophe-lean. Not long, however, did that *salon* merely stare at the celebrated American; his lateness had already become a domestic problem, and he was sent with all speed into the dining-room with Lady Galloway upon his arm.

Except on one point the Galloways were genial and casual enough. So long as Lady Margaret did not take the arm of that adventurer O'Brien, her father was quite satisfied; and she had not done so; she had decorously gone in with Dr. Simon. Nevertheless, old Lord Galloway was restless and almost rude. He was diplomatic enough during dinner, but when, over the cigars, three of the younger men—Simon the doctor, Brown the priest, and the detrimental O'Brien, the exile in a foreign uniform—all melted away to mix with the ladies or smoke in the conservatory, then the English diplomatist grew very undiplomatic indeed. He was stung every sixty seconds with the thought that the scamp O'Brien might be signalling to Margaret somehow; he did not attempt to imagine how. He was left over the coffee with Brayne, the hoary Yankee who believed in all religions, and Valentin, the grizzled Frenchman who believed in none. They could argue with each other, but neither could appeal to him. After a time this 'progressive' logomachy had reached a crisis of tedium; Lord Galloway got up also and sought the drawing-room. He lost his way in long passages for some six or eight minutes: till he heard the high-pitched, didactic voice of the doctor, and then the dull voice of the priest, followed by general laughter. They also, he thought with a curse, were probably arguing about 'science and religion.' But the instant he opened the *salon* door he saw only one thing—he saw what was not there. He saw that Commandant O'Brien was absent, and that Lady Margaret was absent, too.

Rising impatiently from the drawing-room, as he had from the dining-room, he stamped along the passage once more. His notion of protecting his daughter from the Irish-Algerian ne'er-do-weel had become something central and even mad in his mind. As he went towards the back of the house, where was Valentin's study, he was surprised to meet his daughter, who swept past with a white, scornful face, which was a second enigma. If she had been with O'Brien, where was O'Brien? If she had not been with O'Brien, where had she been? With a sort of senile and passionate suspicion he groped his way to the dark back parts of the mansion, and eventually found a servants' entrance that opened on to the garden. The moon with her scimitar had now ripped up and rolled away all the storm-wrack. The argent light lit up all four corners of the garden. A tall figure in blue was striding across the lawn towards the study door; a glint of moonlit silver on his facings picked him out as Commandant O'Brien.

He vanished through the french windows into the house, leaving Lord Galloway in an indescribable temper, at once virulent and vague. The blue-and-silver garden, like a scene in a theatre, seemed to taunt him with all that tyrannic tenderness against which his worldly authority was at war. The length and grace of the Irishman's stride enraged him as if he were a rival instead of a father; the moonlight maddened him. He was trapped as if by magic into a garden of troubadours, a Watteau fairyland; and, willing to shake off such amorous imbecilities by speech, he stepped briskly after his enemy. As he did so he tripped over some tree or stone in the grass; looked down at it first with irritation and then a second time with curiosity. The next instant the moon and the tall poplars looked at an unusual sight—an elderly English diplomatist running hard and crying or bellowing as he ran.

His hoarse shouts brought a pale face to the study door, the beaming glasses and worried brow of Dr. Simon, who heard the nobleman's first clear words. Lord Galloway was crying: 'A corpse in the grass—a blood-stained corpse.' O'Brien at least had gone utterly from his mind.

'We must tell Valentin at once,' said the doctor, when

the other had brokenly described all that he had dared to examine. 'It is fortunate that he is here'; and even às he spoke the great detective entered the study, attracted by the cry. It was almost amusing to note his typical transformation; he had come with the common concern of a host and a gentleman, fearing that some guest or servant was ill. When he was told the gory fact, he turned with all his gravity instantly bright and business-like; for this, however abrupt and awful, was his business.

'Strange, gentlemen,' he said, as they hurried out into the garden, 'that I should have hunted mysteries all over the earth, and now one comes and settles in my own backyard. But where is the place?' They crossed the lawn less easily, as a slight mist had begun to rise from the river; but under the guidance of the shaken Galloway they found the body sunken in deep grass—the body of a very tall and broad-shouldered man. He lay face downwards, so they could only see that his big shoulders were clad in black cloth, and that his big head was bald, except for a wisp or two of brown hair that clung to his skull like wet seaweed. A scarlet serpent of blood crawled from under his fallen face.

'At least,' said Simon, with a deep and singular intonation, 'he is none of our party.'

'Examine him, doctor,' cried Valentin rather sharply. 'He may not be dead.'

The doctor bent down. 'He is not quite cold, but I am afraid he is dead enough,' he answered. 'Just help me to lift him up.'

They lifted him carefully an inch from the ground, and all doubts as to his being really dead were settled at once and frightfully. The head fell away. It had been entirely sundered from the body; whoever had cut his throat had managed to sever the neck as well. Even Valentin was slightly shocked. 'He must have been as strong as a gorilla,' he muttered.

Not without a shiver, though he was used to ana-tomical abortions, Dr. Simon lifted the head. It was

slightly slashed about the neck and jaw, but the face
was substantially unhurt. It was a ponderous, yellow
face, at once sunken and swollen, with a hawk-like nose
and heavy lids—the face of a wicked Roman emperor,
with, perhaps, a distant touch of a Chinese emperor.
All present seemed to look at it with the coldest eye of
ignorance. Nothing else could be noted about the man
except that, as they had lifted his body, they had seen
underneath it the white gleam of a shirt-front defaced
with a red gleam of blood. As Dr. Simon said, the man
had never been of their party. But he might very well
have been trying to join it, for he had come dressed for
such an occasion.

Valentin went down on his hands and knees and
examined with his closest professional attention the
grass and ground for some twenty yards round the body,
in which he was assisted less skilfully by the doctor, and
quite vaguely by the English lord. Nothing rewarded
their grovellings except a few twigs, snapped or chopped
into very small lengths, which Valentin lifted for an
instant's examination, and then tossed away.

'Twigs,' he said gravely; 'twigs, and a total stranger
with his head cut off; that is all there is on this lawn.'

There was an almost creepy stillness, and then the
unnerved Galloway called out sharply:

'Who's that? Who's that over there by the garden
wall?'

A small figure with a foolishly large head drew waver-
ingly near them in the moonlit haze; looked for an
instant like a goblin, but turned out to be the harmless
little priest whom they had left in the drawing-room.

'I say,' he said meekly, 'there are no gates to this
garden, do you know.'

Valentin's black brows had come together somewhat
crossly, as they did on principle at the sight of the
cassock. But he was far too just a man to deny the
relevance of the remark. 'You are right,' he said.
'Before we find out how he came to be killed, we may
have to find out how he came to be here. Now listen
to me, gentlemen. If it can be done without prejudice

to my position and duty, we shall all agree that certain
distinguished names might well be kept out of this.
There are ladies, gentlemen, and there is a foreign
ambassador. If we must mark it down as a crime, then
it must be followed up as a crime. But till then I can
use my own discretion. I am the head of the police;
I am so public that I can afford to be private. Please
Heaven, I will clear every one of my own guests before
I call in my men to look for anybody else. Gentlemen,
upon your honour, you will none of you leave the house
till to-morrow at noon; there are bedrooms for all.
Simon, I think you know where to find my man, Ivan,
in the front hall; he is a confidential man. Tell him to
leave another servant on guard and come to me at once.
Lord Galloway, you are certainly the best person to tell
the ladies what has happened, and prevent a panic.
They also must stay. Father Brown and I will remain
with the body.'

When this spirit of the captain spoke in Valentin he
was obeyed like a bugle. Dr. Simon went through to
the armoury and routed out Ivan, the public detective's
private detective. Galloway went to the drawing-room
and told the terrible news tactfully enough, so that by
the time the company assembled there the ladies were
already startled and already soothed. Meanwhile the
good priest and the good atheist stood at the head and
foot of the dead man motionless in the moonlight, like
symbolic statues of their two philosophies of death.

Ivan, the confidential man with the scar and the
moustaches, came out of the house like a cannon-ball,
and came racing across the lawn to Valentin like a dog
to his master. His livid face was quite lively with the
glow of this domestic detective story, and it was with
almost unpleasant eagerness that he asked his master's
permission to examine the remains.

'Yes; look, if you like, Ivan,' said Valentin, 'but don't
be long. We must go in and thrash this out in the house.'

Ivan lifted his head, and then almost let it drop.

'Why,' he gasped, 'it's—no, it isn't; it can't be.
Do you know this man, sir?'

'No,' said Valentin indifferently; 'we had better go inside.'

Between them they carried the corpse to a sofa in the study, and then all made their way to the drawing-room.

The detective sat down at a desk quietly, and even with hesitation; but his eye was the iron eye of a judge at assize. He made a few rapid notes upon paper in front of him, and then said shortly: 'Is everybody here?'

'Not Mr. Brayne,' said the Duchess of Mont St. Michel, looking round.

'No,' said Lord Galloway in a hoarse, harsh voice. 'And not Mr. Neil O'Brien, I fancy. I saw that gentleman walking in the garden when the corpse was still warm.'

'Ivan,' said the detective, 'go and fetch Commandant O'Brien and Mr. Brayne. Mr. Brayne, I know, is finishing a cigar in the dining-room; Commandant O'Brien, I think, is walking up and down the conservatory. I am not sure.'

The faithful attendant flashed from the room, and before any one could stir or speak Valentin went on with the same soldierly swiftness of exposition.

'Every one here knows that a dead man has been found in the garden, his head cut clean from his body. Dr. Simon, you have examined it. Do you think that to cut a man's throat like that would need great force? Or, perhaps, only a very sharp knife?'

'I should say that it could not be done with a knife at all,' said the pale doctor.

'Have you any thought,' resumed Valentin, 'of a tool with which it could be done?'

'Speaking within modern probabilities, I really haven't,' said the doctor, arching his painful brows. 'It's not easy to hack a neck through even clumsily, and this was a very clean cut. It could be done with a battle-axe or an old headsman's axe, or an old two-handed sword.'

'But, good heavens!' cried the Duchess, almost in

hysterics; 'there aren't any two-handed swords and battle-axes round here.'

Valentin was still busy with the paper in front of him. 'Tell me,' he said, still writing rapidly, 'could it have been done with a long French cavalry sabre?'

A low knocking came at the door, which for some unreasonable reason, curdled every one's blood like the knocking in *Macbeth*. Amid that frozen silence Dr. Simon managed to say: 'A sabre—yes, I suppose it could.'

'Thank you,' said Valentin. 'Come in, Ivan.'

The confidential Ivan opened the door and ushered in Commandant Neil O'Brien, whom he had found at last pacing the garden again.

The Irish officer stood disordered and defiant on the threshold. 'What do you want with me?' he cried.

'Please sit down,' said Valentin in pleasant, level tones. 'Why, you aren't wearing your sword! Where is it?'

'I left it on the library table,' said O'Brien, his brogue deepening in his disturbed mood. 'It was a nuisance, it was getting——'

'Ivan,' said Valentin: 'please go and get the Commandant's sword from the library.' Then, as the servant vanished: 'Lord Galloway says he saw you leaving the garden just before he found the corpse. What were you doing in the garden?'

The Commandant flung himself recklessly into a chair. 'Oh,' he cried in pure Irish; 'admirin' the moon. Communing with Nature, me bhoy.'

A heavy silence sank and endured, and at the end of it came again that trivial and terrible knocking. Ivan reappeared, carrying an empty steel scabbard. 'This is all I can find,' he said.

'Put it on the table,' said Valentin, without looking up.

There was an inhuman silence in the room, like that sea of inhuman silence round the dock of the condemned murderer. The Duchess's weak exclamations had long ago died away. Lord Galloway's swollen hatred was satisfied and even sobered. The voice that came was quite unexpected.

'I think I can tell you,' cried Lady Margaret, in that clear, quivering voice with which a courageous woman speaks publicly. 'I can tell you what Mr. O'Brien was doing in the garden, since he is bound to silence. He was asking me to marry him. I refused; I said in my family circumstances I could give him nothing but my respect. He was a little angry at that; he did not seem to think much of my respect. I wonder,' she added, with rather a wan smile, 'if he will care at all for it now. For I offer it him now. I will swear anywhere that he never did a thing like this.'

Lord Galloway had edged up to his daughter, and was intimidating her in what he imagined to be an undertone. 'Hold your tongue, Maggie,' he said in a thunderous whisper. 'Why should you shield the fellow? Where 's his sword? Where 's his confounded cavalry——'

He stopped because of the singular stare with which his daughter was regarding him, a look that was indeed a lurid magnet for the whole group.

'You old fool!' she said, in a low voice without pretence of piety; 'what do you suppose you are trying to prove? I tell you this man was innocent while with me. But if he wasn't innocent, he was still with me. If he murdered a man in the garden, who was it who must have seen— who must at least have known? Do you hate Neil so much as to put your own daughter——'

Lady Galloway screamed. Every one else sat tingling at the touch of those satanic tragedies that have been between lovers before now. They saw the proud, white face of the Scotch aristocrat and her lover, the Irish adventurer, like old portraits in a dark house. The long silence was full of formless historical memories of murdered husbands and poisonous paramours.

In the centre of this morbid silence an innocent voice said: 'Was it a very long cigar?'

The change of thought was so sharp that they had to look round to see who had spoken.

'I mean,' said little Father Brown, from the corner of the room: 'I mean that cigar Mr. Brayne is finishing. It seems nearly as long as a walking-stick.'

Despite the irrelevance there was assent as well as irritation in Valentin's face as he lifted his head.

'Quite right,' he remarked sharply. 'Ivan, go and see about Mr. Brayne again, and bring him here at once.'

The instant the factotum had closed the door, Valentin addressed the girl with an entirely new earnestness.

'Lady Margaret,' he said, 'we all feel, I am sure, both gratitude and admiration for your act in rising above your lower dignity and explaining the Commandant's conduct. But there is a hiatus still. Lord Galloway, I understand, met you passing from the study to the drawing-room, and it was only some minutes afterwards that he found the garden and the Commandant still walking there.'

'You have to remember,' replied Margaret, with a faint irony in her voice, 'that I had just refused him, so we should scarcely have come back arm-in-arm. He is a gentleman, anyhow; and he loitered behind—and so got charged with murder.'

'In those few moments,' said Valentin gravely, 'he might really——'

The knock came again, and Ivan put in his scarred face.

'Beg pardon, sir,' he said, 'but Mr. Brayne has left the house.'

'Left!' cried Valentin, and rose for the first time to his feet.

'Gone. Scooted. Evaporated,' replied Ivan, in humorous French. 'His hat and coat are gone, too; and I 'll tell you something to cap it all. I ran outside the house to find any traces of him, and I found one, and a big trace, too.'

'What do you mean?' asked Valentin.

'I 'll show you,' said his servant, and reappeared with a flashing naked cavalry sabre, streaked with blood about the point and edge. Every one in the room eyed it as if it were a thunderbolt; but the experienced Ivan went on quite quietly:

'I found this,' he said, 'flung among the bushes fifty yards up the road to Paris. In other words, I found it just where your respectable Mr. Brayne threw it when he ran away.'

There was again a silence, but of a new sort. Valentin took the sabre, examined it, reflected with unaffected concentration of thought, and then turned a respectful face to O'Brien. 'Commandant,' he said, 'we trust you will always produce this weapon if it is wanted for police examination. Meanwhile,' he added, slapping the steel back in the ringing scabbard, 'let me return you your sword.'

At the military symbolism of the action the audience could hardly refrain from applause.

For Neil O'Brien, indeed, that gesture was the turning-point of existence. By the time he was wandering in the mysterious garden again in the colours of the morning the tragic futility of his ordinary mien had fallen from him; he was a man with many reasons for happiness. Lord Galloway was a gentleman, and had offered him an apology. Lady Margaret was something better than a lady, a woman at least, and had perhaps given him something better than an apology, as they drifted among the old flower-beds before breakfast. The whole company was more light-hearted and humane, for though the riddle of the death remained, the load of suspicion was lifted off them all, and sent flying off to Paris with the strange millionaire—a man they hardly knew. The devil was cast out of the house—he had cast himself out.

Still, the riddle remained; and when O'Brien threw himself on a garden seat beside Dr. Simon, that keenly scientific person at once resumed it. He did not get much talk out of O'Brien, whose thoughts were on pleasanter things.

'I can't say it interests me much,' said the Irishman frankly, 'especially as it seems pretty plain now. Apparently Brayne hated this stranger for some reason; lured him into the garden, and killed him with my sword. Then he fled to the city, tossing the sword away as he went. By the way, Ivan tells me the dead man had a Yankee dollar in his pocket. So he was a

countryman of Brayne's, and that seems to clinch it.
I don't see any difficulties about the business.'

'There are five colossal difficulties,' said the doctor
quietly; 'like high walls within walls. Don't mistake
me. I don't doubt that Brayne did it; his flight, I
fancy, proves that. But as to how he did it. First
difficulty: Why should a man kill another man with a
great hulking sabre, when he can almost kill him with
a pocket-knife and put it back in his pocket? Second
difficulty: Why was there no noise or outcry? Does a
man commonly see another come up waving a scimitar
and offer no remarks? Third difficulty: A servant
watched the front door all the evening; and a rat cannot
get into Valentin's garden anywhere. How did the
dead man get into the garden? Fourth difficulty:
Given the same conditions, how did Brayne get out of
the garden?'

'And the fifth,' said Neil, with eyes fixed on the
English priest, who was coming slowly up the path.

'Is a trifle, I suppose,' said the doctor, 'but I think
an odd one. When I first saw how the head had been
slashed, I supposed the assassin had struck more than
once. But on examination I found many cuts across
the truncated section; in other words, they were struck
after the head was off. Did Brayne hate his foe so
fiendishly that he stood sabring his body in the
moonlight?'

'Horrible!' said O'Brien, and shuddered.

The little priest, Brown, had arrived while they were
talking, and had waited, with characteristic shyness, till
they had finished. Then he said awkwardly:

'I say, I 'm sorry to interrupt. But I was sent to tell
you the news!'

'News?' repeated Simon, and stared at him rather
painfully through his glasses.

'Yes, I 'm sorry,' said Father Brown mildly. 'There 's
been another murder, you know.'

Both men on the seat sprang up, leaving it rocking.

'And what 's stranger still,' continued the priest,
with his dull eyes on the rhododendrons, 'it 's the same

disgusting sort; it's another beheading. They found the second head actually bleeding in the river, a few yards along Brayne's road to Paris; so they suppose that he——'

'Great Heaven!' cried O'Brien. 'Is Brayne a monomaniac?'

'There are American vendettas,' said the priest impassively. Then he added: 'They want you to come to the library and see it.'

Commandant O'Brien followed the others towards the inquest, feeling decidedly sick. As a soldier, he loathed all this secretive carnage; where were these extravagant amputations going to stop? First one head was hacked off, and then another; in this case (he told himself bitterly) it was not true that two heads were better than one. As he crossed the study he almost staggered at a shocking coincidence. Upon Valentin's table lay the coloured picture of yet a third bleeding head; and it was the head of Valentin himself. A second glance showed him it was only a Nationalist paper, called *The Guillotine*, which every week showed one of its political opponents with rolling eyes and writhing features just after execution; for Valentin was an anti-clerical of some note. But O'Brien was an Irishman, with a kind of chastity even in his sins; and his gorge rose against that great brutality of the intellect which belongs only to France. He felt Paris as a whole, from the grotesques on the Gothic churches to the gross caricatures in the newspapers. He remembered the gigantic jests of the Revolution. He saw the whole city as one ugly energy, from the sanguinary sketch lying on Valentin's table up to where, above a mountain and forest gargoyles, the great devil grins on Notre Dame.

The library was long, low, and dark; what light entered it shot from under low blinds and had still some of the ruddy tinge of morning. Valentin and his servant Ivan were waiting for them at the upper end of a long, slightly sloping desk, on which lay the mortal remains, looking enormous in the twilight. The big black figure and yellow face of the man found in the garden confronted them essentially unchanged. The second head, which had been fished from among the river reeds that morning, lay streaming and dripping beside it; Valentin's men were still seeking to recover the rest of this second corpse, which was supposed to be afloat. Father Brown, who did not seem to share O'Brien's sensibilities in the least, went up to the second head and examined it with his blinking care. It was little more than a mop of wet, white hair, fringed with silver fire in the red and level morning light; the face, which seemed of an ugly, empurpled and perhaps criminal type, had been much battered against trees or stones as it tossed in the water.

'Good morning, Commandant O'Brien,' said Valentin, with quiet cordiality. 'You have heard of Brayne's last experiment in butchery, I suppose?'

Father Brown was still bending over the head with white hair, and he said, without looking up:

'I suppose it is quite certain that Brayne cut off this head, too.'

'Well, it seems common sense,' said Valentin, with his hands in his pockets. 'Killed in the same way as the other. Found within a few yards of the other. And sliced by the same weapon which we know he carried away.'

'Yes, yes; I know,' replied Father Brown, submissively. 'Yet, you know, I doubt whether Brayne could have cut off this head.'

'Why not?' inquired Dr. Simon, with a rational stare.

'Well, doctor,' said the priest, looking up blinking, 'can a man cut off his own head? I don't know.'

O'Brien felt an insane universe crashing about his ears; but the doctor sprang forward with impetuous practicality and pushed back the wet, white hair.

'Oh, there's no doubt it's Brayne,' said the priest quietly. 'He had exactly that chip in the left ear.'

The detective, who had been regarding the priest with steady and glittering eyes, opened his clenched mouth and said sharply: 'You seem to know a lot about him, Father Brown.'

'I do,' said the little man simply. 'I 've been about with him for some weeks. He was thinking of joining our Church.'

The star of the fanatic sprang into Valentin's eyes; he strode towards the priest with clenched hands. 'And, perhaps,' he cried, with a blasting sneer: 'perhaps he was also thinking of leaving all his money to your Church.'

'Perhaps he was,' said Brown stolidly; 'it is possible.'

'In that case,' cried Valentin, with a dreadful smile, 'you may indeed know a great deal about him. About his life and about his——'

Commandant O'Brien laid a hand on Valentin's arm. 'Drop that slanderous rubbish, Valentin,' he said, 'or there may be more swords yet.'

But Valentin (under the steady, humble gaze of the priest) had already recovered himself. 'Well,' he said shortly, 'people's private opinions can wait. You gentlemen are still bound by your promise to stay; you must enforce it on yourselves—and on each other. Ivan here will tell you anything more you want to know; I must get to business and write to the authorities. We can't keep this quiet any longer. I shall be writing in my study if there is any more news.'

'Is there any more news, Ivan?' asked Dr. Simon, as the chief of police strode out of the room.

'Only one more thing, I think, sir,' said Ivan, wrinkling up his grey old face; 'but that 's important, too, in its way. There 's that old buffer you found on the lawn,' and he pointed without pretence of reverence at the big black body with the yellow head. 'We 've found out who he is, anyhow.'

'Indeed!' cried the astonished doctor; 'and who is he?'

'His name was Arnold Becker,' said the under-detective, 'though he went by many aliases. He was a wandering sort of scamp, and is known to have been in America; so that was where Brayne got his knife into him. We didn't have much to do with him ourselves, for he worked mostly in Germany. We 've communicated, of course, with the German police. But, oddly

enough, there was a twin brother of his, named Louis
Becker, whom we had a great deal to do with. In fact,
we found it necessary to guillotine him only yesterday.
Well, it 's a rum thing, gentlemen, but when I saw that
fellow flat on the lawn I had the greatest jump of my
life. If I hadn't seen Louis Becker guillotined with my
own eyes, I 'd have sworn it was Louis Becker lying
there in the grass. Then, of course, I remembered his
twin brother in Germany, and following up the clue——'

The explanatory Ivan stopped, for the excellent
reason that nobody was listening to him. The Commandant and the doctor were both staring at Father
Brown, who had sprung stiffly to his feet, and was
holding his temples tight like a man in sudden and
violent pain.

'Stop, stop, stop!' he cried; 'stop talking a minute,
for I see half. Will God give me strength? Will my
brain make the one jump and see all? Heaven help me!
I used to be fairly good at thinking. I could paraphrase
any page in Aquinas once. Will my head split—or will
it see? I see half—I only see half.'

He buried his head in his hands, and stood in a sort
of rigid torture of thought or prayer, while the other
three could only go on staring at this last prodigy of
their wild twelve hours.

When Father Brown's hands fell they showed a face
quite fresh and serious, like a child's. He heaved a
huge sigh, and said: 'Let us get this said and done with
as quickly as possible. Look here, this will be the
quickest way to convince you all of the truth.' He
turned to the doctor. 'Dr. Simon,' he said, 'you have
a strong head-piece, and I heard you this morning
asking the five hardest questions about this business.
Well, if you will now ask them again, I will answer them.'

Simon's pince-nez dropped from his nose in his doubt
and wonder, but he answered at once. 'Well, the first
question, you know, is why a man should kill another
with a clumsy sabre at all when a man can kill with a
bodkin?'

'A man cannot behead with a bodkin,' said Brown,

calmly, 'and for *this* murder beheading was absolutely necessary.'

'Why?' asked O'Brien, with interest.

'And the next question?' asked Father Brown.

'Well, why didn't the man cry out or anything?' asked the doctor; 'sabres in gardens are certainly unusual.'

'Twigs,' said the priest gloomily, and turned to the window which looked on the scene of death. 'No one saw the point of the twigs. Why should they lie on that lawn (look at it) so far from any tree? They were not snapped off; they were chopped off. The murderer occupied his enemy with some tricks with the sabre, showing how he could cut a branch in mid-air, or what not. Then, while his enemy bent down to see the result, a silent slash, and the head fell.'

'Well,' said the doctor slowly, 'that seems plausible enough. But my next two questions will stump any one.'

The priest still stood looking critically out of the window and waited.

'You know how all the garden was sealed up like an air-tight chamber,' went on the doctor. 'Well, how did the strange man get into the garden?'

Without turning round, the little priest answered: 'There never was any strange man in the garden.'

There was a silence, and then a sudden cackle of almost childish laughter relieved the strain. The absurdity of Brown's remark moved Ivan to open taunts.

'Oh!' he cried; 'then we didn't lug a great fat corpse on to a sofa last night? He hadn't got into the garden, I suppose?'

'Got into the garden?' repeated Brown reflectively. 'No, not entirely.'

'Hang it all,' cried Simon, 'a man gets into a garden, or he doesn't.'

'Not necessarily,' said the priest, with a faint smile. 'What is the next question, doctor?'

'I fancy you're ill,' exclaimed Dr. Simon sharply;

'but I 'll ask the next question if you like. How did Brayne get out of the garden?'

'He didn't get out of the garden,' said the priest, still looking out of the window.

'Didn't get out of the garden?' exploded Simon.

'Not completely,' said Father Brown.

Simon shook his fists in a frenzy of French logic. 'A man gets out of a garden, or he doesn't,' he cried.

'Not always,' said Father Brown.

Dr. Simon sprang to his feet impatiently. 'I have no time to spare on such senseless talk,' he cried angrily. 'If you can't understand a man being on one side of the wall or the other, I won't trouble you further.'

'Doctor,' said the cleric very gently, 'we have always got on very pleasantly together. If only for the sake of old friendship, stop and tell me your fifth question.'

The impatient Simon sank into a chair by the door and said briefly: 'The head and shoulders were cut about in a queer way. It seemed to be done after death.'

'Yes,' said the motionless priest, 'it was done so as to make you assume exactly the one simple falsehood that you did assume. It was done to make you take for granted that the head belonged to the body.'

The borderland of the brain, where all the monsters are made, moved horribly in the Gaelic O'Brien. He felt the chaotic presence of all the horse-men and fish-women that man's unnatural fancy has begotten. A voice older than his first fathers seemed saying in his ear: 'Keep out of the monstrous garden where grows the tree with double fruit. Avoid the evil garden where died the man with two heads.' Yet, while these shameful symbolic shapes passed across the ancient mirror of his Irish soul, his Frenchified intellect was quite alert, and was watching the odd priest as closely and incredulously as all the rest.

Father Brown had turned round at last, and stood against the window with his face in dense shadow; but even in that shadow they could see it was pale as ashes. Nevertheless, he spoke quite sensibly, as if there were no Gaelic souls on earth.

'Gentlemen,' he said;. 'you did not find the strange body of Becker in the garden. You did not find any strange body in the garden. In face of Dr. Simon's rationalism, I still affirm that Becker was only partly present. Look here!' (pointing to the black bulk of the mysterious corpse); 'you never saw that man in your lives. Did you ever see this man?'

He rapidly rolled away the bald-yellow head of the unknown, and put in its place the white-maned head beside it. And there, complete, unified, unmistakable, lay Julius K. Brayne.

'The murderer,' went on Brown quietly, 'hacked off his enemy's head and flung the sword far over the wall. But he was too clever to fling the sword only. He flung the *head* over the wall also. Then he had only to clap on another head to the corpse, and (as he insisted on a private inquest) you all imagined a totally new man.'

'Clap on another head!' said O'Brien, staring. 'What other head? Heads don't grow on garden bushes, do they?'

'No,' said Father Brown huskily, and looking at his boots; 'there is only one place where they grow. They grow in the basket of the guillotine, beside which the Chief of Police, Aristide Valentin, was standing not an hour before the murder. Oh, my friends, hear me a minute more before you tear me in pieces. Valentin is an honest man, if being mad for an arguable cause is honesty. But did you ever see in that cold, grey eye of his that he is mad? He would do anything, *anything*, to break what he calls the superstition of the Cross. He has fought for it and starved for it, and now he has murdered for it. Brayne's crazy millions had hitherto been scattered among so many sects that they did little to alter the balance of things. But Valentin heard a whisper that Brayne, like so many scatter-brained sceptics, was drifting to us; and that was quite a different thing. Brayne would pour supplies into the impoverished and pugnacious Church of France; he would support six Nationalist newspapers like *The Guillotine*. The battle was already balanced on a point, and the

fanatic took flame at the risk. He resolved to destroy
the millionaire, and he did it as one would expect the
greatest of detectives to commit his only crime. He
abstracted the severed head of Becker on some crimino-
logical excuse, and took it home in his official box. He
had that last argument with Brayne, that Lord Galloway
did not hear the end of; that failing, he led him out into
the sealed garden, talked about swordsmanship, used
twigs and a sabre for illustration, and——'

Ivan of the Scar sprang up. 'You lunatic,' he yelled;
'you 'll go to my master now, if I take you by——'

'Why, I was going there,' said Brown heavily; 'I
must ask him to confess, and all that.'

Driving the unhappy Brown before them like a hostage
or sacrifice, they rushed together into the sudden
stillness of Valentin's study.

The great detective sat at his desk apparently too
occupied to hear their turbulent entrance. They
paused a moment, and then something in the look of
that upright and elegant back made the doctor run
forward suddenly. A touch and a glance showed him
that there was a small box of pills at Valentin's elbow,
and that Valentin was dead in his chair; and on the
blind face of the suicide was more than the pride of Cato.

THE QUEER FEET

IF you meet a member of that select club, 'The Twelve
True Fishermen,' entering the Vernon Hotel for the
annual club dinner, you will observe, as he takes off his
overcoat, that his evening coat is green and not black.
If (supposing that you have the star-defying audacity
to address such a being) you ask him why, he will
probably answer that he does it to avoid being mistaken
for a waiter. You will then retire crushed. But you
will leave behind you a mystery as yet unsolved and a
tale worth telling.

If (to pursue the same vein of improbable conjecture)
you were to meet a mild, hard-working little priest,
named Father Brown, and were to ask him what he
thought was the most singular luck of his life, he would
probably reply that upon the whole his best stroke was
at the Vernon Hotel, where he had averted a crime and,
perhaps, saved a soul, merely by listening to a few footsteps in a passage. He is perhaps a little proud of this
wild and wonderful guess of his, and it is possible that
he might refer to it. But since it is immeasurably unlikely that you will ever rise high enough in the social
world to find 'The Twelve True Fishermen,' or that you
will ever sink low enough among slums and criminals to
find Father Brown, I fear you will never hear the story
at all unless you hear it from me.

The Vernon Hotel, at which The Twelve True Fishermen held their annual dinners, was an institution such
as can only exist in an oligarchical society which has
almost gone mad on good manners. It was that topsy-
turvy product—an 'exclusive' commercial enterprise.
That is, it was a thing which paid, not by attracting
people, but actually by turning people away. In the
heart of a plutocracy tradesmen become cunning enough
to be more fastidious than their customers. They

positively create difficulties so that their wealthy and
weary clients may spend money and diplomacy in over-
coming them.   If there were a fashionable hotel in
London which no man could enter who was under six
foot, society would meekly make up parties of six-foot
men to dine in it.   If there were an expensive restaurant
which by a mere caprice of its proprietor was only open
on Thursday afternoon, it would be crowded on Thursday afternoon.   The Vernon Hotel stood, as if by
accident, in the corner of a square in Belgravia.   It
was a small hotel; and a very inconvenient one.   But
its very inconveniences were considered as walls protecting a particular class.   One inconvenience, in particular, was held to be of vital importance: the fact that
practically only twenty-four people could dine in the
place at once.   The only big dinner table was the
celebrated terrace table, which stood open to the air on
a sort of veranda overlooking one of the most exquisite
old gardens in London.   Thus it happened that even
the twenty-four seats at this table could only be enjoyed
in warm weather; and this making the enjoyment yet
more difficult made it yet more desired.   The existing
owner of the hotel was a Jew named Lever; and he made
nearly a million out of it, by making it difficult to get
into.   Of course he combined with this limitation in
the scope of his enterprise the most careful polish in
its performance.   The wines and cooking were really as
good as any in Europe, and the demeanour of the
attendants exactly mirrored the fixed mood of the
English upper class.   The proprietor knew all his waiters
like the fingers on his hand; there were only fifteen of
them all told.   It was much easier to become a Member
of Parliament than to become a waiter in that hotel.
Each waiter was trained in terrible silence and smoothness, as if he were a gentleman's servant.   And, indeed,
there was generally at least one waiter to every gentleman
who dined.
   The club of The Twelve True Fishermen would not
have consented to dine anywhere but in such a place,
for it insisted on a luxurious privacy; and would have

been quite upset by the mere thought that any other
club was even dining in the same building. On the
occasion of their annual dinner the Fishermen were in
the habit of exposing all their treasures, as if they were
in a private house, especially the celebrated set of fish
knives and forks which were, as it were, the insignia of
the society, each being exquisitely wrought in silver in
the form of a fish, and each loaded at the hilt with one
large pearl. These were always laid out for the fish
course, and the fish course was always the most magnificent in that magnificent repast. The society had a
vast number of ceremonies and observances, but it had
no history and no object; that was where it was so very
aristocratic. You did not have to be anything in order
to be one of the Twelve Fishers; unless you were already
a certain sort of person, you never even heard of them.
It had been in existence twelve years. Its president was
Mr. Audley. Its vice-president was the Duke of Chester.

If I have in any degree conveyed the atmosphere of
this appalling hotel, the reader may feel a natural
wonder as to how I came to know anything about it,
and may even speculate as to how so ordinary a person
as my friend Father Brown came to find himself in that
golden gallery. As far as that is concerned, my story
is simple, or even vulgar. There is in the world a very
aged rioter and demagogue who breaks into the most
refined retreats with the dreadful information that all
men are brothers, and wherever this leveller went on his
pale horse it was Father Brown's trade to follow. One
of the waiters, an Italian, had been struck down with a
paralytic stroke that afternoon; and his Jewish employer,
marvelling mildly at such superstitions, had consented
to send for the nearest Popish priest. With what the
waiter confessed to Father Brown we are not concerned,
for the excellent reason that the cleric kept it to himself;
but apparently it involved him in writing out a note or
statement for the conveying of some message or the
righting of some wrong. Father Brown, therefore, with
a meek impudence which he would have shown equally
in Buckingham Palace, asked to be provided with a

room and writing materials. Mr. Lever was torn in
two. He was a kind man, and had also that bad
imitation of kindness, the dislike of any difficulty or
scene. At the same time the presence of one unusual
stranger in his hotel that evening was like a speck of
dirt on something just cleaned. There was never any
borderland or ante-room in the Vernon Hotel, no people
waiting in the hall, no customers coming in on chance.
There were fifteen waiters. There were twelve guests.
It would be as startling to find a new guest in the hotel
that night as to find a new brother taking breakfast or
tea in one's own family. Moreover, the priest's appearance was second-rate and his clothes muddy; a mere
glimpse of him afar off might precipitate a crisis in the
club. Mr. Lever at last hit on a plan to cover, since he
might not obliterate, the disgrace. When you enter (as
you never will) the Vernon Hotel, you pass down a short
passage decorated with a few dingy but important
pictures, and come to the main vestibule and lounge
which opens on your right into passages leading to the
public rooms, and on your left to a similar passage
pointing to the kitchens and offices of the hotel. Immediately on your left hand is the corner of a glass office,
which abuts upon the lounge—a house within a house,
so to speak, like the old hotel bar which probably once
occupied its place.
In this office sat the representative of the proprietor
(nobody in this place ever appeared in person if he
could help it), and just beyond the office, on the way
to the servants' quarters, was the gentlemen's cloak-
room, the last boundary of the gentlemen's domain.
But between the office and the cloak-room was a small
private room without other outlet, sometimes used by
the proprietor for delicate and important matters, such
as lending a duke a thousand pounds or declining to
lend him sixpence. It is a mark of the magnificent
tolerance of Mr. Lever that he permitted this holy place
to be for about half an hour profaned by a mere priest,
scribbling away on a piece of paper. The story which
Father Brown was writing down was very likely a much

better story than this one, only it will never be known. I can merely state that it was very nearly as long, and that the last two or three paragraphs of it were the least exciting and absorbing.

For it was by the time that he had reached these that the priest began a little to allow his thoughts to wander and his animal senses, which were commonly keen, to awaken. The time of darkness and dinner was drawing on; his own forgotten little room was without a light, and perhaps the gathering gloom, as occasionally happens, sharpened the sense of sound. As Father Brown wrote the last and least essential part of his document, he caught himself writing to the rhythm of a recurrent noise outside, just as one sometimes thinks to the tune of a railway train. When he became conscious of the thing he found what it was: only the ordinary patter of feet passing the door, which in an hotel was no very unlikely matter. Nevertheless, he stared at the darkened ceiling, and listened to the sound. After he had listened for a few seconds dreamily, he got to his feet and listened intently, with his head a little on one side. Then he sat down again and buried his brow in his hands, now not merely listening, but listening and thinking also.

The footsteps outside at any given moment were such as one might hear in any hotel; and yet, taken as a whole, there was something very strange about them. There were no other footsteps. It was always a very silent house, for the few familiar guests went at once to their own apartments, and the well-trained waiters were told to be almost invisible until they were wanted. One could not conceive any place where there was less reason to apprehend anything irregular. But these footsteps were so odd that one could not decide to call them regular or irregular. Father Brown followed them with his finger on the edge of the table, like a man trying to learn a tune on the piano.

First, there came a long rush of rapid little steps, such as a light man might make in winning a walking race. At a certain point they stopped and changed to

a sort of slow, swinging stamp, numbering not a quarter
of the steps, but occupying about the same time. The
moment the last echoing stamp had died away would
come again the run or ripple of light, hurrying feet, and
then again the thud of the heavier walking. It was
certainly the same pair of boots, partly because (as has
been said) there were no other boots about, and partly
because they had a small but unmistakable creak in
them. Father Brown had the kind of head that cannot
help asking questions; and on this apparently trivial
question his head almost split. He had seen men run
in order to jump. He had seen men run in order to
slide. But why on earth should a man run in order to
walk? Or, again, why should he walk in order to run?
Yet no other description would cover the antics of this
invisible pair of legs. The man was either walking very
fast down one half of the corridor in order to walk very
slow down the other half; or he was walking very slow
at one end to have the rapture of walking fast at the
other. Neither suggestion seemed to make much sense.
His brain was growing darker and darker, like his
room.

Yet, as he began to think steadily, the very blackness
of his cell seemed to make his thoughts more vivid; he
began to see as in a kind of vision the fantastic feet
capering along the corridor in unnatural or symbolic
attitudes. Was it a heathen religious dance? Or some
entirely new kind of scientific exercise? Father Brown
began to ask himself with more exactness what the steps
suggested. Taking the slow step first; it certainly was
not the step of the proprietor. Men of his type walk
with a rapid waddle, or they sit still. It could not be
any servant or messenger waiting for directions. It did
not sound like it. The poorer orders (in an oligarchy)
sometimes lurch about when they are slightly drunk,
but generally, and especially in such gorgeous scenes,
they stand or sit in constrained attitudes. No; that
heavy yet springy step, with a kind of careless emphasis,
not specially noisy, yet not caring what noise it made,
belonged to only one of the animals of this earth. It

was a gentleman of western Europe, and probably one
who had never worked for his living.

Just as he came to this solid certainty, the step
changed to the quicker one, and ran past the door as
feverishly as a rat. The listener remarked that though
this step was much swifter it was also much more
noiseless, almost as if the man were walking on tiptoe.
Yet it was not associated in his mind with secrecy, but
with something else — something that he could not
remember. He was maddened by one of those half-
memories that make a man feel half-witted. Surely he
had heard that strange, swift walking somewhere.
Suddenly he sprang to his feet with a new idea in his
head, and walked to the door. His room had no direct
outlet on the passage, but let on one side into the glass
office, and on the other into the cloak-room beyond.
He tried the door into the office, and found it locked.
Then he looked at the window, now a square pane full
of purple cloud cleft by livid sunset, and for an instant
he smelt evil as a dog smells rats.

The rational part of him (whether the wiser or not)
regained its supremacy. He remembered that the proprietor had told him that he should lock the door, and
would come later to release him. He told himself that
twenty things he had not thought of might explain the
eccentric sounds outside; he reminded himself that there
was just enough light left to finish his own proper work.
Bringing his paper to the window so as to catch the last
stormy evening light, he resolutely plunged once more
into the almost completed record. He had written for
about twenty minutes, bending closer and closer to
his paper in the lessening light; then suddenly he
sat upright. He had heard the strange feet once
more.

This time they had a third oddity. Previously the
unknown man had walked, with levity indeed and
lightning quickness, but he had walked. This time he
ran. One could hear the swift, soft, bounding steps
coming along the corridor, like the pads of a fleeing and
leaping panther. Whoever was coming was a very

strong, active man, in still yet tearing excitement. Yet, when the sound had swept up to the office like a sort of whispering whirlwind, it suddenly changed again to the old slow, swaggering stamp.

Father Brown flung down his paper, and, knowing the office door to be locked, went at once into the cloak-room on the other side. The attendant of this place was temporarily absent, probably because the only guests were at dinner, and his office was a sinecure. After groping through a grey forest of overcoats, he found that the dim cloak-room opened on the lighted corridor in the form of a sort of counter or half-door, like most of the counters across which we have all handed umbrellas and received tickets. There was a light immediately above the semicircular arch of this opening. It threw little illumination on Father Brown himself, who seemed a mere dark outline against the dim sunset window behind him. But it threw an almost theatrical light on the man who stood outside the cloak-room in the corridor.

He was an elegant man in very plain evening-dress; tall, but with an air of not taking up much room; one felt that he could have slid along like a shadow where many smaller men would have been obvious and obstructive. His face, now flung back in the lamplight, was swarthy and vivacious, the face of a foreigner. His figure was good, his manners good-humoured and confident; a critic could only say that his black coat was a shade below his figure and manners, and even bulged and bagged in an odd way. The moment he caught sight of Brown's black silhouette against the sunset, he tossed down a scrap of paper with a number and called out with amiable authority: 'I want my hat and coat, please; I find I have to go away at once.'

Father Brown took the paper without a word, and obediently went to look for the coat; it was not the first menial work he had done in his life. He brought it and laid it on the counter; meanwhile, the strange gentleman, who had been feeling in his waistcoat pocket, said, laughing: 'I haven't got any silver; you can keep this.' And he threw down half a sovereign, and caught up his coat.

Father Brown's figure remained quite dark and still; but in that instant he had lost his head. His head was always most valuable when he had lost it. In such moments he put two and two together and made four million. Often the Catholic Church (which is wedded to common sense) did not approve of it. Often he did not approve of it himself. But it was a real inspiration —important at rare crises—when whosoever shall lose his head the same shall save it.

'I think, sir,' he said civilly, 'that you have some silver in your pocket.'

The tall gentleman stared. '.Hang it,' he cried. 'If I give you gold, why should you complain?'

'Because silver is sometimes more valuable than gold,' said the priest mildly; 'that is, in large quantities.'

The stranger looked at him curiously. Then he looked still more curiously up the passage towards the main entrance. Then he looked back at Brown again, and then he looked very carefully at the window beyond Brown's head, still coloured with the afterglow of the storm. Then he seemed to make up his mind. He put one hand on the counter, vaulted over as easily as an acrobat and towered above the priest, putting one tremendous hand upon his collar.

'Stand still,' he said, in a hacking whisper. 'I don't want to threaten you, but——'

'I do want to threaten you,' said Father Brown, in a voice like a rolling drum. 'I want to threaten you with the worm that dieth not, and the fire that is not quenched.'

'You 're a rum sort of cloak-room clerk,' said the other.

'I am a priest, Monsieur Flambeau,' said Brown, 'and I am ready to hear your confession.'

The other stood gasping for a few moments, and then staggered back into a chair.

The first two courses of the dinner of The Twelve

True Fishermen had proceeded with placid success. I
do not possess a copy of the menu; and if I did it would
not convey anything to anybody. It was written in a
sort of super-French employed by cooks, but quite un-
intelligible to Frenchmen. There was a tradition in the
club that the *hors d'œuvres* should be various and manifold
to the point of madness. They were taken seriously
because they were avowedly useless extras, like the
whole dinner and the whole club. There was also a
tradition that the soup course should be light and
unpretending—a sort of simple and austere vigil for the
feast of fish that was to come. The talk was that
strange, slight talk which governs the British Empire,
which governs it in secret, and yet would scarcely
enlighten an ordinary Englishman even if he could
overhear it. Cabinet Ministers on both sides were
alluded to by their Christian names with a sort of bored
benignity. The Radical Chancellor of the Exchequer,
whom the whole Tory party was supposed to be cursing
for his extortions, was praised for his minor poetry, or
his saddle in the hunting-field. The Tory leader, whom
all Liberals were supposed to hate as a tyrant, was discussed and, on the whole, praised—as a Liberal. It
seemed somehow that politicians were very important.
And yet, anything seemed important about them except their politics. Mr. Audley, the chairman, was an
amiable, elderly man who still wore Gladstone collars;
he was a kind of symbol of all that phantasmal and yet
fixed society. He had never done anything—not even
anything wrong. He was not fast; he was not even
particularly rich. He was simply in the thing; and there
was an end of it. No party could ignore him, and if
he had wished to be in the Cabinet he certainly would
have been put there. The Duke of Chester, the vice-
president, was a young and rising politician. That is to
say, he was a pleasant youth, with flat, fair hair and a
freckled face, with moderate intelligence and enormous
estates. In public his appearances were always successful and his principle was simple enough. When he
thought of a joke he made it, and was called brilliant.

When he could not think of a joke he said that this was no time for trifling, and was called able. In private, in a club of his own class, he was simply quite pleasantly frank and silly, like a schoolboy. Mr. Audley, never having been in politics, treated them a little more seriously. Sometimes he even embarrassed the company by phrases suggesting that there was some difference between a Liberal and a Conservative. He himself was a Conservative, even in private life. He had a roll of grey hair over the back of his collar like certain old-fashioned statesmen, and seen from behind he looked like the man the empire wants. Seen from the front he looked like a mild, self-indulgent bachelor, with rooms in the Albany—which he was.

As has been remarked, there were twenty-four seats at the terrace table, and only twelve members of the club. Thus they could occupy the terrace in the most luxurious style of all, being ranged along the inner side of the table, with no one opposite, commanding an uninterrupted view of the garden, the colours of which were still vivid, though evening was closing in somewhat luridly for the time of year. The chairman sat in the centre of the line, and the vice-president at the right-hand end of it. When the twelve guests first trooped into their seats it was the custom (for some unknown reason) for all the fifteen waiters to stand lining the wall like troops presenting arms to the king, while the fat proprietor stood and bowed to the club with radiant surprise, as if he had never heard of them before. But before the first chink of knife and fork this army of retainers had vanished, only the one or two required to collect and distribute the plates darting about in deathly silence. Mr. Lever, the proprietor, of course had disappeared in convulsions of courtesy long before. It would be exaggerative, indeed irreverent, to say that he ever positively appeared again. But when the important course, the fish course, was being brought on, there was—how shall I put it?—a vivid shadow, a projection of his personality, which told that he was hovering near. The sacred fish course consisted (to the eyes of the vulgar) in a sort of monstrous pudding, about the size and shape of a wedding cake, in which some considerable number of interesting fishes had finally lost the shapes which God had given to them. The Twelve True Fishermen took up their celebrated fish knives and fish forks, and approached it as gravely as if every inch of the pudding cost as much as the silver fork it was eaten with. So it did, for all I know. This course was dealt with in eager and devouring silence; and it was only when his plate was nearly empty that the young duke made the ritual remark: 'They can't do this anywhere but here.'

'Nowhere,' said Mr. Audley, in a deep bass voice, turning to the speaker and nodding his venerable head a number of times. 'Nowhere, assuredly, except here. It was represented to me that at the Café Anglais——'

Here he was interrupted and even agitated for a moment by the removal of his plate, but he recaptured the valuable thread of his thoughts. 'It was represented to me that the same could be done at the Café Anglais. Nothing like it, sir,' he said, shaking his head ruthlessly, like a hanging judge. 'Nothing like it.'

'Overrated place,' said a certain Colonel Pound, speaking (by the look of him) for the first time for some months.

'Oh, I don't know,' said the Duke of Chester, who was an optimist, 'it's jolly good for some things. You can't beat it at——'

A waiter came swiftly along the room, and then stopped dead. His stoppage was as silent as his tread; but all those vague and kindly gentlemen were so used to the utter smoothness of the unseen machinery which surrounded and supported their lives, that a waiter doing anything unexpected was a start and a jar. They felt as you and I would feel if the inanimate world disobeyed—if a chair ran away from us.

The waiter stood staring a few seconds, while there deepened on every face at table a strange shame which is wholly the product of our time. It is the combination of modern humanitarianism with the horrible modern abyss between the souls of the rich and poor. A genuine historic aristocrat would have thrown things at the waiter, beginning with empty bottles, and very probably ending with money. A genuine democrat would have asked him, with a comrade-like clearness of speech, what the devil he was doing. But these modern plutocrats could not bear a poor man near to them, either as a slave or as a friend. That something had gone wrong with the servants was merely a dull, hot embarrassment. They did not want to be brutal, and they dreaded the need to be benevolent. They wanted the thing, whatever it was, to be over. · It was over. The waiter, after standing for some seconds rigid, like a cataleptic, turned round and ran madly out of the room.

When he reappeared in the room, or rather in the doorway, it was in company with another waiter, with whom he whispered and gesticulated with southern fierceness. Then the first waiter went away, leaving the second waiter, and reappeared with a third waiter. By the time a fourth waiter had joined this hurried synod, Mr. Audley felt it necessary to break the silence in the interests of Tact. He used a very loud cough, instead of a presidential hammer, and said: 'Splendid work young Moocher's doing in Burmah. Now, no other nation in the world could have——'

A fifth waiter had sped towards him like an arrow, and was whispering in his ear: 'So sorry. Important! Might the proprietor speak to you?'

The chairman turned in disorder, and with a dazed stare saw Mr. Lever coming towards them with his lumbering quickness. The gait of the good proprietor was indeed his usual gait, but his face was by no means usual. Generally it was a genial copper-brown; now it was a sickly yellow.

'You will pardon me, Mr. Audley,' he said, with asthmatic breathlessness. 'I have great apprehensions. Your fish plates, they are cleared away with the knife and fork on them!'

'Well, I hope so,' said the chairman, with some warmth.

'You see him?' panted the excited hotel-keeper; 'you see the waiter who took them away? You know him?'

'Know the waiter?' answered Mr. Audley indignantly. 'Certainly not!'

Mr. Lever opened his hands with a gesture of agony. 'I never send him,' he said. 'I know not when or why he come. I send my waiter to take away the plates, and he find them already away.'

Mr. Audley still looked rather too bewildered to be really the man the empire wants; none of the company could say anything except the man of wood—Colonel Pound—who seemed galvanized into an unnatural life. He rose rigidly from his chair, leaving all the rest sitting, screwed his eyeglass into his eye, and spoke in a raucous undertone as if he had half-forgotten how to speak. 'Do you mean,' he said, 'that somebody has stolen our silver fish service?'

The proprietor repeated the open-handed gesture with even greater helplessness; and in a flash all the men at the table were on their feet.

'Are all your waiters here?' demanded the colonel, in his low, harsh accent.

'Yes; they 're all here. I noticed it myself,' cried the young duke, pushing his boyish face into the inmost ring. 'Always count 'em as I come in; they look so queer standing up against the wall.'

'But surely one cannot exactly remember,' began Mr. Audley, with heavy hesitation.

'I remember exactly, I tell you,' cried the duke excitedly. 'There never have been more than fifteen waiters at this place, and there were no more than fifteen to-night, I 'll swear; no more and no less.'

The proprietor turned upon him, quaking in a kind of palsy of surprise. 'You say—you say,' he stammered, 'that you see all my fifteen waiters?'

'As usual,' assented the duke. 'What is the matter with that?'

'Nothing,' said Lever, with a deepening accent, 'only you did not. For one of zem is dead upstairs.'

There was a shocking stillness for an instant in that

room. It may be (so supernatural is the word death)
that each of those idle men looked for a second at his
soul, and saw it as a small dried pea. One of them—
the duke, I think—even said with the idiotic kindness
of wealth: 'Is there anything we can do?'

'He has had a priest,' said the Jew, not untouched.

Then, as to the clang of doom, they awoke to their own
position. For a few weird seconds they had really felt
as if the fifteenth waiter might be the ghost of the dead
man upstairs. They had been dumb under that oppression, for ghosts were to them an embarrassment,
like beggars. But the remembrance of the silver broke
the spell of the miraculous; broke it abruptly and with
a brutal reaction. The colonel flung over his chair and
strode to the door. 'If there was a fifteenth man here,
friends,' he said, 'that fifteenth fellow was a thief.
Down at once to the front and back doors and secure
everything; then we'll talk. The twenty-four pearls
are worth recovering.'

Mr. Audley seemed at first to hesitate about whether
it was gentlemanly to be in such a hurry about anything;
but, seeing the duke dash down the stairs with youthful
energy, he followed with a more mature motion.

At the same instant a sixth waiter ran into the room,
and declared that he had found the pile of fish plates on
a sideboard, with no trace of the silver.

The crowd of diners and attendants that tumbled
helter-skelter down the passages divided into two groups.
Most of the Fishermen followed the proprietor to the
front room to demand news of any exit. Colonel
Pound, with the chairman, the vice-president, and one
or two others, darted down the corridor leading to the
servants' quarters, as the more likely line of escape.
As they did so they passed the dim alcove or cavern of
the cloak-room, and saw a short, black-coated figure,
presumably an attendant, standing a little way back in
the shadow of it.

'Hallo, there!' called out the duke. 'Have you seen
any one pass?'

The short figure did not answer the question directly,

but merely said: 'Perhaps I have got what you are
looking for, gentlemen.'

They paused, wavering and wondering, while he
quietly went to the back of the cloak-room, and came
back with both hands full of shining silver, which he
laid out on the counter as calmly as a salesman. It
took the form of a dozen quaintly shaped forks and
knives.

'You—you——' began the colonel, quite thrown off
his balance at last. Then he peered into the dim little
room and saw two things: first, that the short, black-clad
man was dressed like a clergyman; and, second, that the
window of the room behind him was burst, as if someone
had passed violently through.

'Valuable things to deposit in a cloak-room, aren't
they?' remarked the clergyman, with cheerful com-
posure.

'Did—did you steal those things?' stammered Mr.
Audley, with staring eyes.

'If I did,' said the cleric pleasantly, 'at least I am
bringing them back again.'

'But you didn't,' said Colonel Pound, still staring at
the broken window.

'To make a clean breast of it, I didn't,' said the other,
with some humour. And he seated himself quite gravely
on a stool.

'But you know who did,' said the colonel.

'I don't know his real name,' said the priest placidly;
'but I know something of his fighting weight, and a
great deal about his spiritual difficulties. I formed the
physical estimate when he was trying to throttle me,
and the moral estimate when he repented.'

'Oh, I say—repented!' cried young Chester, with a
sort of crow of laughter.

Father Brown got to his feet, putting his hands
behind him. 'Odd, isn't it,' he said, 'that a thief and
a vagabond should repent, when so many who are rich
and secure remain hard and frivolous, and without
fruit for God or man? But there, if you will excuse
me, you trespass a little upon my province. If you

doubt the penitence as a practical fact, there are your knives and forks. You are The Twelve True Fishers, and there are all your silver fish. But He has made me a fisher of men.'

'Did you catch this man?' asked the colonel, frowning.

Father Brown looked him full in his frowning face. 'Yes,' he said, 'I caught him, with an unseen hook and an invisible line which is long enough to let him wander to the ends of the world, and still to bring him back with a twitch upon the thread.'

There was a long silence. All the other men present drifted away to carry the recovered silver to their comrades, or to consult the proprietor about the queer condition of affairs. But the grim-faced colonel still sat sideways on the counter, swinging his long, lank legs and biting his dark moustache.

At last he said quietly to the priest: 'He must have been a clever fellow, but I think I know a cleverer.'

'He was a clever fellow,' answered the other, 'but I am not quite sure of what other you mean.'

'I mean you,' said the colonel, with a short laugh. 'I don't want to get the fellow jailed; make yourself easy about that. But I'd give a good many silver forks to know exactly how you fell into this affair, and how you got the stuff out of him. I reckon you're the most up-to-date devil of the present company.'

Father Brown seemed rather to like the saturnine candour of the soldier. 'Well,' he said, smiling, 'I mustn't tell you anything of the man's identity, or his own story, of course; but there's no particular reason why I shouldn't tell you of the mere outside facts which I found out for myself.'

He hopped over the barrier with unexpected activity, and sat beside Colonel Pound, kicking his short legs like a little boy on a gate. He began to tell the story as easily as if he were telling it to an old friend by a Christmas fire.

'You see, colonel,' he said, 'I was shut up in that small room there doing some writing, when I heard a pair of feet in this passage doing a dance that was as queer as the dance of death. First came quick, funny little steps, like a man walking on tiptoe for a wager; then came slow, careless, creaking steps, as of a big man walking about with a cigar. But they were both made by the same feet, I swear, and they came in rotation; first the run and then the walk, and then the run again. I wondered, at first idly, and then wildly, why a man should act these two parts at once. One walk I knew; it was just like yours, colonel. It was the walk of a well-fed gentleman waiting for something, who strolls about rather because he is physically alert than because he is mentally impatient. I knew that I knew the other walk, too, but I could not remember what it was. What wild creature had I met on my travels that tore along on tiptoe in that extraordinary style? Then I heard a clink of plates somewhere; and the answer stood up as plain as St. Peter's. It was the walk of a waiter— that walk with the body slanted forward, the eyes looking down, the ball of the toe spurning away the ground, the coat-tails and napkin flying. Then I thought for a minute and a half more. And I believe I saw the manner of the crime, as clearly as if I were going to commit it.'

Colonel Pound looked at him keenly, but the speaker's mild grey eyes were fixed upon the ceiling with almost empty wistfulness.

'A crime,' he said slowly, 'is like any other work of art. Don't look surprised; crimes are by no means the only works of art that come from an infernal workshop. But every work of art, divine or diabolic, has one indispensable mark—I mean, that the centre of it is simple, however much the fulfilment may be complicated. Thus, in *Hamlet*, let us say, the grotesqueness of the grave-digger, the flowers of the mad girl, the fantastic finery of Osric, the pallor of the ghost, and the grin of the skull are all oddities in a sort of tangled wreath round one plain tragic figure of a man in black. Well, this also,' he said, getting slowly down from his seat with a smile, 'this also is the plain tragedy of a man in black. Yes,' he went on, seeing the colonel look up in

some wonder, 'the whole of this tale turns on a black
coat. In this, as in *Hamlet*, there are the rococo ex-
crescences—yourselves, let us say. There is the dead
waiter, who was there when he could not be there.
There is the invisible hand that swept your table clear
of silver and melted into air. But every clever crime is
founded ultimately on some one quite simple fact—
some fact that is not itself mysterious. The mystification comes in covering it up, in leading men's thoughts
away from it. This large and subtle and (in the ordinary
course) most profitable crime, was built on the plain
fact that a gentleman's evening-dress is the same as
a waiter's. All the rest was acting, and thundering
good acting, too.'

'Still,' said the colonel, getting up and frowning at his
boots. 'I am not sure that I understand.'

'Colonel,' said Father Brown, 'I tell you that this
archangel of impudence who stole your forks walked
up and down this passage twenty times in the blaze of
all the lamps, in the glare of all the eyes. He did not go
and hide in dim corners where suspicion might have
searched for him. He kept constantly on the move in
the lighted corridors, and everywhere that he went he
seemed to be there by right. Don't ask me what he was
like; you have seen him yourself six or seven times
to-night. You were waiting with all the other grand
people in the reception-room at the end of the passage
there, with the terrace just beyond. Whenever he came
among you gentlemen, he came in the lightning style of
a waiter, with bent head, flapping napkin, and flying
feet. He shot out on to the terrace, did something to
the tablecloth, and shot back again towards the office
and the waiters' quarters. By the time he had come
under the eye of the office clerk and the waiters he had
become another man in every inch of his body, in every
instinctive gesture. He strolled among the servants
with the absent-minded insolence which they have all
seen in their patrons. It was no new thing to them that
a swell from the dinner-party should pace all parts of
the house like an animal at the Zoo; they know that

nothing marks the Smart Set more than a habit of walking where one chooses. When he was magnificently weary of walking down that particular passage he would wheel round and pace back past the office; in the shadow of the arch just beyond he was altered as by a blast of magic, and went hurrying forward again among the Twelve Fishermen, an obsequious attendant. Why should the gentlemen look at a chance waiter? Why should the waiters suspect a first-rate walking gentleman? Once or twice he played the coolest tricks. In the proprietor's private quarters he called out breezily for a siphon of soda-water, saying he was thirsty. He said genially that he would carry it himself, and he did; he carried it quickly and correctly through the thick of you, a waiter with an obvious errand. Of course, it could not have been kept up long, but it only had to be kept up till the end of the fish course.

'His worst moment was when the waiters stood in a row; but even then he contrived to lean against the wall just around the corner in such a way that for that important instant the waiters thought him a gentleman, while the gentlemen thought him a waiter. The rest went like winking. If any waiter caught him away from the table, that waiter caught a languid aristocrat. He had only to time himself two minutes before the fish was cleared, become a swift servant, and clear it himself. He put the plates down on a sideboard, stuffed the silver in his breast pocket, giving it a bulgy look, and ran like a hare (I heard him coming) till he came to the cloak-room. There he had only to be a plutocrat again—a plutocrat called away suddenly on business. He had only to give his ticket to the cloak-room attendant, and go out again elegantly as he had come in. Only—only I happened to be the cloak-room attendant.'

'What did you do to him?' cried the colonel, with unusual intensity. 'What did he tell you?'

'I beg your pardon,' said the priest immovably, 'that is where the story ends.'

'And the interesting story begins,' muttered Pound.

'I think I understand his professional trick. But I don't seem to have got hold of yours.'

'I must be going,' said Father Brown.

They walked together along the passage to the entrance hall, where they saw the fresh, freckled face of the Duke of Chester, who was bounding buoyantly along towards them.

'Come along, Pound,' he cried breathlessly. 'I've been looking for you everywhere. The dinner's going again in spanking style, and old Audley has got to make a speech in honour of the forks being saved. We want to start some new ceremony, don't you know, to commemorate the occasion. I say, you really got the goods back, what do you suggest?'

'Why,' said the colonel, eyeing him with a certain sardonic approval. 'I should suggest that henceforward we wear green coats instead of black. One never knows what mistakes may arise when one looks so like a waiter.'

'Oh, hang it all!' said the young man; 'a gentleman never looks like a waiter.'

'Nor a waiter like a gentleman, I suppose,' said Colonel Pound, with the same lowering laughter on his face. 'Reverend sir, your friend must have been very smart to act the gentleman.'

Father Brown buttoned up his commonplace overcoat to the neck, for the night was stormy, and took his commonplace umbrella from the stand.

'Yes,' he said; 'it must be very hard work to be a gentleman; but, do you know, I have sometimes thought that it may be almost as laborious to be a waiter.'

And saying 'Good evening,' he pushed open the heavy doors of that palace of pleasures. The golden gates closed behind him, and he went at a brisk walk through the damp, dark streets in search of a penny omnibus.

THE CURSE OF THE GOLDEN CROSS

SIX people sat round a small table, seeming almost as incongruous and accidental as if they had been ship-wrecked separately on the same small desert island. At least the sea surrounded them; for in one sense their island was enclosed in another island, a large and flying island like Laputa. For the little table was one of many little tables dotted about in the dining-saloon of that monstrous ship the *Moravia*, speeding through the night and the everlasting emptiness of the Atlantic. The little company had nothing in common except that all were travelling from America to England. Two of them at least might be called celebrities; others might be called obscure, and in one or two cases even dubious.

The first was the famous Professor Smaill, an authority on certain archaeological studies touching the later Byzantine Empire. His lectures, delivered in an American university, were accepted as of the first authority even in the most authoritative seats of learning in Europe. His literary works were so steeped in a mellow and imaginative sympathy with the European past, that it often gave strangers a start to hear him speak with an American accent. Yet he was, in his way, very American; he had long, fair hair brushed back from a big square forehead, long, straight features, and a curious mixture of preoccupation with a poise of potential swiftness, like a lion pondering absent-mindedly on his next leap.

There was only one lady in the group; and she was (as the journalists often said of her) a host in herself; being quite prepared to play hostess, not to say empress, at that or any other table. She was Lady Diana Wales, the celebrated lady traveller in tropical and other countries; but there was nothing rugged or masculine

67

about her appearance at dinner. She was herself handsome in an almost tropical fashion, with a mass of hot and heavy red hair; she was dressed in what the journalists call a daring fashion, but her face was intelligent and her eyes had that bright and rather prominent appearance which belongs to the eyes of ladies who ask questions at political meetings.

The other four figures seemed at first like shadows in this shining presence; but they showed differences on a closer view. One of them was a young man entered on the ship's register as Paul T. Tarrant. He was an American type which might be more truly called an American antitype. Every nation probably has an antitype; a sort of extreme exception that proves the national rule. Americans really respect work, rather as Europeans respect war. There is a halo of heroism about it; and he who shrinks from it is less than a man. The antitype is evident through being exceedingly rare. He is the dandy or dude: the wealthy waster who makes a weak villain for so many American novels. Paul Tarrant seemed to have nothing whatever to do but to change his clothes, which he did about six times a day; passing into paler or richer shades of his suit of exquisite light grey, like the delicate silver changes of the twilight. Unlike most Americans, he cultivated very carefully a short, curly beard; and unlike most dandies, even of his own type, he seemed rather sulky than showy. Perhaps there was something almost Byronic about his silence and his gloom.

The next two travellers were naturally classed together; merely because they were both English lecturers returning from an American tour. One of them was described as Leonard Smyth, apparently a minor poet, but something of a major journalist; long-headed, light-haired, perfectly dressed and perfectly capable of looking after himself. The other was a rather comic contrast, being short and broad, with a black, walrus moustache, and as taciturn as the other was talkative. But as he had been both charged with robbing and praised for rescuing a Roumanian princess threatened by a jaguar in his travelling menagerie, and had thus figured in a fashionable case, it was naturally felt that his views on God, progress, his own early life, and the future of Anglo-American relations would be of great interest and value to the inhabitants of Minneapolis and Omaha. The sixth and most insignificant figure was that of a little English priest going by the name of Brown. He listened to the conversation with respectful attention, and he was at that moment forming the impression that there was one rather curious thing about it.

'I suppose those Byzantine studies of yours, Professor,' Leonard Smyth was saying, 'would throw some light on this story of a tomb found somewhere on the south coast; near Brighton, isn't it? Brighton's a long way from Byzantium, of course. But I read something about the style of burying or embalming or something being supposed to be Byzantine.'

'Byzantine studies certainly have to reach a long way,' replied the Professor dryly. 'They talk about specialists; but I think the hardest thing on earth is to specialize. In this case, for instance: how can a man know anything about Byzantium till he knows everything about Rome before it and about Islam after it? Most Arab arts were old Byzantine arts. Why, take algebra——'

'But I won't take algebra,' cried the lady decisively. 'I never did, and I never do. But I'm awfully interested in embalming. I was with Gatton, you know, when he opened the Babylonian tombs. Ever since then I found mummies and preserved bodies and all that perfectly thrilling. Do tell us about this one.'

'Gatton was an interesting man,' said the Professor. 'They were an interesting family. That brother of his who went into Parliament was much more than an ordinary politician. I never understood the Fascisti till he made that speech about Italy.'

'Well, we're not going to Italy on this trip,' said Lady Diana persistently, 'and I believe you're going to that little place where they've found the tomb. In Sussex, isn't it?'

'Sussex is pretty large, as these little English sections go,' replied the Professor. 'One might wander about in it for a goodish time; and it's a good place to wander in. It's wonderful how large those low hills seem when you're on them.'

There was an abrupt accidental silence; and then the lady said: 'Oh, I'm going on deck,' and rose, the men rising with her. But the Professor lingered and the little priest was the last to leave the table, carefully folding up his napkin. And as they were thus left alone together the Professor said suddenly to his companion:

'What would you say was the point of that little talk?'

'Well,' said Father Brown, smiling, 'since you ask me, there was something that amused me a little. I may be wrong; but it seemed to me that the company made three attempts to get you to talk about an embalmed body said to be found in Sussex. And you, on your side, very courteously offered to talk—first about algebra, and then about the Fascisti, and then about the landscape of the downs.'

'In short,' replied the Professor, 'you thought I was ready to talk about any subject but that one. You were quite right.'

The Professor was silent for a little time, looking down at the table-cloth; then he looked up and spoke with that swift impulsiveness that suggested the lion's leap.

'See here, Father Brown,' he said, 'I consider you about the wisest and whitest man I ever met.'

Father Brown was very English. He had all the normal national helplessness about what to do with a serious and sincere compliment suddenly handed to him to his face in the American manner. His reply was a meaningless murmur; and it was the Professor who proceeded, with the same staccato earnestness:

'You see, up to a point it's all simple enough. A Christian tomb of the Dark Ages, apparently that of a bishop, has been found under a little church at Dulham on the Sussex coast. The vicar happens to be a good bit of an archaeologist himself and has been able to find out a good deal more than I know yet. There was a rumour of the corpse being embalmed in a way peculiar to Greeks and Egyptians but unknown in the West, especially at that date. So Mr. Walters (that is the vicar) naturally wonders about Byzantine influences. But he also mentions something else, that is of even more personal interest to me.'

His long, grave face seemed to grow even longer and graver as he frowned down at the table-cloth. His long finger seemed to be tracing patterns on it like the plans of dead cities and their temples and tombs.

'So I 'm going to tell you, and nobody else, why it is I have to be careful about mentioning that matter in mixed company; and why, the more eager they are to talk about it, the more cautious I have to be. It is also stated that in the coffin is a chain with a cross, common enough to look at, but with a certain secret symbol on the back found on only one other cross in the world. It is from the arcana of the very earliest Church, and is supposed to indicate St. Peter setting up his see at Antioch before he came to Rome. Anyhow, I believe there is but one other like it, and it belongs to me. I hear there is some story about a curse on it; but I take no notice of that. But whether or no there is a curse, there really is, in one sense, a conspiracy; though the conspiracy should only consist of one man.'

'Of one man?' repeated Father Brown, almost mechanically.

'Of one madman, for all I know,' said Professor Smaill. 'It 's a long story and in some ways a silly one.'

He paused again, tracing plans like architectural drawings with his finger on the cloth, and then resumed:

'Perhaps I had better tell you about it from the beginning, in case you see some little point in the story that is meaningless to me. It began years and years ago, when I was conducting some investigations on my own account in the antiquities of Crete and the Greek islands. I did a great deal of it practically single-handed; sometimes with the most rude and temporary help from the inhabitants of the place, and sometimes literally alone. It was under the latter circumstances that I found a maze of subterranean passages which led at last to a heap of rich refuse, broken ornaments, and scattered gems which I took to be the ruins of some sunken altar, and in which I found the curious gold cross. I turned it over, and on the back of it I saw the Ichthus, or fish, which was an early Christian symbol, but of a shape and pattern rather different from that commonly found; and, as it seemed to me, more realistic—more as if the archaic designer had meant it to be not merely a conventional enclosure or nimbus, but to look a little more like a real fish. It seemed to me that there was a flattening towards one end of it that was not like mere mathematical decoration, but rather like a sort of rude or even savage zoology.

'In order to explain very briefly why I thought this find important, I must tell you the point of the excavation. For one thing, it had something of the nature of an excavation of an excavation. We were on the track not only of antiquities, but of the antiquarians of antiquity. We had reason to believe, or some of us thought we had reason to believe, that these underground passages, mostly of the Minoan period, like that famous one which is actually identified with the labyrinth of the Minotaur, had not really been lost and left undisturbed for all the ages between the Minotaur and the modern explorer. We believed that these underground places, I might almost say these underground towns and villages, had already been penetrated during the intervening period by some persons prompted by some motive. About the motive there were different schools of thought: some holding that the emperors had ordered an official exploration out of mere scientific curiosity; others that the furious fashion in the later Roman Empire for all sorts of lurid Asiatic superstitions had started some nameless Manichaean sect or other rioting in the caverns in orgies that had to be hidden from the face of the sun. I belong to the group which believed that these caverns had been used in the same way as the catacombs. That is, we believed that, during some of

the persecutions which spread like a fire over the whole
empire, the Christians had concealed themselves in
these ancient pagan labyrinths of stone. It was therefore with a thrill as sharp as a thunderclap that I found
and picked up the fallen golden cross and saw the design
upon it; and it was with still more of a shock of felicity
that, on turning to make my way once more outwards
and upwards into the light of day, I looked up at the
walls of bare rock that extended endlessly along the
low passages, and saw scratched in yet ruder outline, but
if possible more unmistakable, the shape of the Fish.

'Something about it made it seem as if it might be a
fossil fish or some rudimentary organism fixed for ever
in a frozen sea. I could not analyse this analogy, otherwise unconnected with a mere drawing scratched upon
the stone, till I realized that I was saying in my subconscious mind that the first Christians must have
seemed something like fish, dumb and dwelling in a
fallen world of twilight and silence, dropped far below
the feet of men and moving in dark and twilight and
a soundless world.

'Every one walking along stone passages knows what
it is to be followed by phantom feet. The echo follows
flapping or clapping behind or in front, so that it is
almost impossible for the man who is really lonely to
believe in his loneliness. I had got used to the effects
of this echo and had not noticed it much for some time
past, when I caught sight of the symbolical shape
scrawled on the wall of rock. I stopped, and at the
same instant it seemed as if my heart stopped, too; for
my own feet had halted, but the echo went marching on.

'I ran forward, and it seemed as if the ghostly footsteps ran also, but not with that exact imitation which
marks the material reverberation of a sound. I stopped
again, and the steps stopped also; but I could have
sworn they stopped an instant too late; I called out a
question; and my cry was answered; but the voice was
not my own.

'It came round the corner of a rock just in front of
me; and throughout that uncanny chase I noticed that

it was always at some such angle of the crooked path that it paused and spoke. The little space in front of me that could be illuminated by my small electric torch was always as empty as an empty room. Under these conditions I had a conversation with I know not whom, which lasted all the way to the first white gleam of daylight, and even there I could not see in what fashion he vanished into the light of day. But the mouth of the labyrinth was full of many openings and cracks and chasms, and it would not have been difficult for him to have somehow darted back and disappeared again into the underworld of the caves. I only know that I came out on the lonely steps of a great mountain like a marble terrace, varied only with a green vegetation that seemed somehow more tropical than the purity of the rock, like the Oriental invasion that has spread sporadically over the fall of classic Hellas. I looked out on a sea of stainless blue, and the sun shone steadily on utter loneliness and silence; and there was not a blade of grass stirred with a whisper of flight nor the shadow of a shadow of man.

'It had been a terrible conversation; so intimate and so individual and in a sense so casual. This being, bodiless, faceless, nameless, and yet calling me by my name, had talked to me in those crypts and cracks where we were buried alive with no more passion or melodrama than if we had been sitting in two arm-chairs at a club. But he had told me also that he would unquestionably kill me or any other man who came into the possession of the cross with the mark of the fish. He told me frankly he was not fool enough to attack me there in the labyrinth, knowing I had a loaded revolver, and that he ran as much risk as I. But he told me, equally calmly, that he would plan my murder with the certainty of success, with every detail developed and every danger warded off, with the sort of artistic perfection that a Chinese craftsman or an Indian embroiderer gives to the artistic work of a lifetime. Yet he was no Oriental; I am certain he was a white man. I suspect that he was a countryman of my own.

'Since then I have received from time to time signs

and symbols and queer impersonal messages that have
made me certain, at least, that if the man is a maniac
he is a monomaniac. He is always telling me, in this
airy and detached way, that the preparations for my
death and burial are proceeding satisfactorily; and that
the only way in which I can prevent their being crowned
with a comfortable success is to give up the relic in my
possession—the unique cross that I found in the cavern.
He does not seem to have any religious sentiment or
fanaticism on the point; he seems to have no passion but
the passion of a collector of curiosities. That is one of
the things that makes me feel sure he is a man of the
West and not of the East. But this particular curiosity
seems to have driven him quite crazy.

'And then came this report, as yet unsubstantiated,
about the duplicate relic found on an embalmed body
in a Sussex tomb. If he had been a maniac before, this
news turned him into a demoniac possessed of seven
devils. That there should be one of them belonging to
another man was bad enough, but that there should be
two of them and neither belonging to him was a torture
not to be borne. His mad messages began to come thick
and fast like showers of poisoned arrows; and each cried
out more confidently than the last that death would
strike me at the moment when I stretched out my
unworthy hand towards the cross in the tomb.

'"You will never know me," he wrote, "you will never
say my name; you will never see my face; you will die,
and never know who has killed you. I may be in any
form among those about you; but I shall be in that
alone at which you have forgotten to look."

'From those threats I deduce that he is quite likely
to shadow me on this expedition; and try to steal the
relic or do me some mischief for possessing it. But as
I never saw the man in my life, he may be almost any
man I meet. Logically speaking, he may be any of the
waiters who wait on me at table. He may be any of
the passengers who sit with me at table.'

'He may be me,' said Father Brown, with cheerful
contempt for grammar.

'He may be anybody else,' answered Smaill seriously.
'That is what I meant by what I said just now. You
are the only man I feel sure is not the enemy.'

Father Brown again looked embarrassed; then he
smiled and said: 'Well, oddly enough, I 'm not. What
we have to consider is any chance of finding out if
he really is here before he—before he makes himself
unpleasant.'

'There is one chance of finding out, I think,' remarked
the Professor rather grimly. 'When we get to South-
ampton I shall take a car at once along the coast; I
should be glad if you would come with me, but in the
ordinary sense, of course, our little party will break up.
If any one of them turns up again in that little churchyard on the Sussex coast, we shall know who he really is.'

The Professor's programme was duly carried out, at
least to the extent of the car and its cargo in the form of
Father Brown. They coasted along the road with the
sea on one side and the hills of Hampshire and Sussex
on the other; nor was there visible to the eye any
shadow of pursuit. As they approached the village of
Dulham only one man crossed their path who had any
connection with the matter in hand: a journalist who had
just visited the church and been courteously escorted
by the vicar through the new-excavated chapel; but his
remarks and notes seemed to be of the ordinary newspaper sort. But Professor Smaill was perhaps a little
fanciful, and could not dismiss the sense of something
odd and discouraging in the attitude and appearance of
the man, who was tall and shabby, hook-nosed and
hollow-eyed, with moustaches that drooped with depression. He seemed anything but enlivened by his
late experiment as a sightseer; indeed, he seemed to be
striding as fast as possible from the sight, when they
stopped him with a question.

'It 's all about a curse,' he said; 'a curse on the place,
according to the guide-book or the parson, or the oldest
inhabitant or whoever is the authority; and really, it
feels jolly like it. Curse or no curse, I 'm glad to have
got out of it.'

'Do you believe in curses?' asked Smaill curiously.

'I don't believe in anything; I'm a journalist,' answered the melancholy being—'Boon, of the *Daily Wire*. But there's a something creepy about that crypt; and I'll never deny I felt a chill.' And he strode on towards the railway station with a further accelerated pace.

'Looks like a raven or a crow, that fellow,' observed Smaill as they turned towards the churchyard. 'What is it they say about a bird of ill omen?'

They entered the churchyard slowly, the eyes of the American antiquary lingering luxuriantly over the isolated roof of the lych-gate and the large unfathomable black growth of the yew looking like night itself defying the broad daylight. The path climbed up amid heaving levels of turf in which the gravestones were tilted at all angles like stone rafts tossed on a green sea, till it came to the ridge beyond which the great grey sea itself ran like an iron bar, with pale lights in it like steel. Almost at their feet the tough, rank grass turned into a tuft of sea-holly and ended in grey and yellow sand; and a foot or two from the holly, and outlined darkly against the steely sea, stood a motionless figure. But for its dark-grey clothing it might almost have been the statue on some sepulchral monument. But Father Brown instantly recognized something in the elegant stoop of the shoulders and the rather sullen outward thrust of the short beard.

'Gee!' exclaimed the professor of archaeology; 'it's that man Tarrant, if you call him a man. Did you think, when I spoke on the boat, that I should ever get so quick an answer to my question?'

'I thought you might get too many answers to it,' answered Father Brown.

'Why, how do you mean?' inquired the Professor, darting a look at him over his shoulder.

'I mean,' answered the other mildly, 'that I thought I heard voices behind the yew-tree. I don't think Mr. Tarrant is so solitary as he looks; I might even venture to say, so solitary as he likes to look.'

Even as Tarrant turned slowly round in his moody manner, the confirmation came. Another voice, high and rather hard, but none the less feminine, was saying with experienced raillery:

'And how was I to know he would be here?'

It was borne in upon Professor Smaill that this gay observation was not addressed to him; so he was forced to conclude, in some bewilderment, that yet a third person was present. As Lady Diana Wales came out, radiant and resolute as ever, from the shadow of the yew, he noted grimly that she had a living shadow of her own. The lean, dapper figure of Leonard Smyth, that insinuating man of letters, appeared immediately behind her own flamboyant form, smiling, his head a little on one side like a dog's.

'Snakes!' muttered Smaill; 'why, they 're all here! Or all except that little showman with the walrus whiskers.'

He heard Father Brown laughing softly beside him; and indeed the situation was becoming something more than laughable. It seemed to be turning topsy-turvy and tumbling about their ears like a pantomime trick; for even while the Professor had been speaking, his words had received the most comical contradiction. The round head with the grotesque black crescent of moustache had appeared suddenly and seemingly out of a hole in the ground. An instant afterwards they realized that the hole was in fact a very large hole, leading to a ladder which descended into the bowels of the earth; that it was in fact the entrance to the subterranean scene they had come to visit. The little man had been the first to find the entrance and had already descended a rung or two of the ladder before he put his head out again to address his fellow-travellers. He looked like some particularly preposterous grave-digger in a burlesque of *Hamlet*. He only said thickly behind his thick moustaches: 'It is down here.' But it came to the rest of the company with a start of realization that, though they had sat opposite him at meal-times for a week, they had hardly ever heard him speak before;

and that though he was supposed to be an English
lecturer, he spoke with a rather occult foreign accent.

'You see, my dear Professor,' cried Lady Diana with
trenchant cheerfulness, 'your Byzantine mummy was
simply too exciting to be missed. I simply had to come
along and see it; and I'm sure the gentlemen felt just
the same. Now you must tell us all about it.'

'I do not know all about it,' said the Professor gravely,
not to say grimly. 'In some respects I don't even know
what it's all about. It certainly seems odd that we
should have all met again so soon; but I suppose there
are no limits to the modern thirst for information. But
if we are all to visit the place it must be done in a
responsible way, and, if you will forgive me, under
responsible leadership. We must notify whoever is in
charge of the excavations; we shall probably at least
have to put our names in a book.'

Something rather like a wrangle followed on this
collision between the impatience of the lady and the
suspicions of the archaeologist; but the latter's insistence
on the official rights of the vicar and the local investigation ultimately prevailed; the little man with the
moustaches came reluctantly out of his grave again and
silently acquiesced in a less impetuous descent. Fortunately, the clergyman himself appeared at this stage
—a grey-haired, good-looking gentleman with a droop
accentuated by double eyeglasses; and while rapidly
establishing sympathetic relations with the Professor
as a fellow-antiquarian, he did not seem to regard his
rather motley group of companions with anything more
hostile than amusement.

'I hope you are none of you superstitious,' he said
pleasantly. 'I ought to tell you, to start with, that
there are supposed to be all sorts of bad omens and curses
hanging over our devoted heads in this business. I
have just been deciphering a Latin inscription which
was found over the entrance to the chapel; and it would
seem that there are no less than three curses involved:
a curse for entering the sealed chamber, a double curse
for opening the coffin, and a triple and most terrible·

curse for touching the gold relic found inside it. The
two first maledictions I have already incurred myself,'
he added with a smile; 'but I fear that even you will
have to incur the first and mildest of them if you are to
see anything at all. According to the story, the curses
descend in a rather lingering fashion, at long intervals
and on later occasions. I don't know whether that is
any comfort to you.' And the Reverend Mr. Walters
smiled once more in his drooping and benevolent manner.

'Story,' repeated Professor Smaill, 'why, what story
is that?'

'It is rather a long story and varies, like other local
legends,' answered the vicar. 'But it is undoubtedly
contemporary with the time of the tomb; and the
substance of it is embodied in the inscription and is
roughly this: Guy de Gisors, a lord of the manor here
early in the thirteenth century, had set his heart on a
beautiful black horse in the possession of an envoy
from Genoa, which that practical merchant prince
would not sell except for a huge price. Guy was driven
by avarice to the crime of pillaging the shrine and,
according to one story, even killing the bishop, who was
then resident there. Anyhow, the bishop uttered a
curse which was to fall on anybody who should continue to withhold the gold cross from its resting-place in
his tomb, or should take steps to disturb it when it had
returned there. The feudal lord raised the money for
the horse by selling the gold relic to a goldsmith in the
town; but on the first day he mounted the horse the
animal reared and threw him in front of the church
porch, breaking his neck. Meanwhile the goldsmith,
hitherto wealthy and prosperous, was ruined by a series
of inexplicable accidents, and fell into the power of a
Jew money-lender living in the manor. Eventually the
unfortunate goldsmith, faced with nothing but starvation, hanged himself on an apple-tree. The gold cross,
with all his other goods, his house, shop, and tools, had
long ago passed into the possession of the money-lender.
Meanwhile, the son and heir of the feudal lord, shocked
by the judgment on his blasphemous sire, had become a

religious devotee in the dark and stern spirit of those
times, and conceived it his duty to persecute all heresy
and unbelief among his vassals. Thus the Jew, in his
turn, who had been cynically tolerated by the father,
was ruthlessly burnt by order of the son; so that he, in
his turn, suffered for the possession of the relic; and
after these three judgments, it was returned to the
bishop's tomb; since when no eye has seen and no hand
has touched it.'

Lady Diana Wales seemed to be more impressed than
might have been expected.

'It really gives one rather a shiver,' she said, 'to think
that we are going to be the first, except the vicar.'

The pioneer with the big moustaches and the broken
English did not descend after all by his favourite ladder,
which indeed had only been used by some of the workmen conducting the excavation; for the clergyman led
them round to a larger and more convenient entrance
about a hundred yards away, out of which he himself
had just emerged from his investigations underground.
Here the descent was by a fairly gradual slope with no
difficulties save the increasing darkness; for they soon
found themselves moving in single file down a tunnel as
black as pitch, and it was some little time before they
saw a glimmer of light ahead of them. Once during
that silent march there was a sound like a catch in somebody's breath, it was impossible to say whose; and once
there was an oath like a dull explosion, and it was in
an unknown tongue.

They came out in a circular chamber like a basilica
in a ring of round arches; for that chapel had been built
before the first pointed arch of the Gothic had pierced
our civilization like a spear. A glimmer of greenish
light between some of the pillars marked the place of
the other opening into the world above, and gave a
vague sense of being under the sea, which was intensified
by one or two other incidental and perhaps fanciful
resemblances. For the dog-tooth pattern of the Norman
was faintly traceable round all the arches, giving them,
above the cavernous darkness, something of the look

of the mouths of monstrous sharks. And in the centre the dark bulk of the tomb itself, with its lifted lid of stone, might almost have been the jaws of some such leviathan.

Whether out of a sense of fitness or from the lack of more modern appliances, the clerical antiquary had arranged for the illumination of the chapel only by four tall candles in big wooden candlesticks standing on the floor. Of these only one was alight when they entered, casting a faint glimmer over the mighty architectural forms. When they had all assembled, the clergyman proceeded to light the three others, and the appearance and contents of the great sarcophagus came more clearly into view.

All eyes went first to the face of the dead, preserved across all those ages in the lines of life by some secret Eastern process, it was said, inherited from heathen antiquity and unknown to the simple graveyards of our own island. The Professor could hardly repress an exclamation of wonder; for, though the face was as pale as a mask of wax, it looked otherwise like a sleeping man who had but that moment closed his eyes. The face was of the ascetic, perhaps even the fanatical type, with a high framework of bones; the figure was clad in a golden cope and gorgeous vestments, and high up on the breast, at the base of the throat, glittered the famous gold cross upon a short gold chain, or rather necklace. The stone coffin had been opened by lifting the lid of it at the head and propping it aloft upon two strong wooden shafts or poles, hitched above under the edge of the upper slab and wedged below into the corners of the coffin behind the head of the corpse. Less could therefore be seen of the feet or the lower part of the figure, but the candlelight shone full on the face; and in contrast with its tones of dead ivory the cross of gold seemed to stir and sparkle like a fire.

Professor Smaill's big forehead had carried a big furrow of reflection, or possibly of worry, ever since the clergyman had told the story of the curse. But feminine intuition, not untouched by feminine hysteria, under-

stood the meaning of his brooding immobility better
than did the men around him. In the silence of that
candlelit cavern Lady Diana cried out suddenly:

'Don't touch it, I tell you!'

But the man had already made one of his swift
leonine movements, leaning forward over the body.
The next instant they all darted, some forward and
some backward, but all with a dreadful ducking motion
as if the sky were falling.

As the Professor laid a finger on the gold cross, the
wooden props, that bent very slightly in supporting the
lifted lid of stone, seemed to jump and straighten themselves with a jerk. The lip of the stone slab slipped
from its wooden perch; and in all their souls and
stomachs came a sickening sense of down-rushing ruin,
as if they had all been flung off a precipice. Smaill had
withdrawn his head swiftly, but not in time; and he
lay senseless beside the coffin, in a red puddle of blood
from scalp or skull. And the old stone coffin was once
more closed as it had been for centuries; save that one
or two sticks or splinters stuck in the crevice, horribly
suggestive of bones crunched by an ogre. The leviathan
had snapped its jaws of stone.

Lady Diana was looking at the wreck with eyes that
had an electric glare as of lunacy; her red hair looked
scarlet against the pallor of her face in the greenish
twilight. Smyth was looking at her, still with something doglike in the turn of his head; but it was the
expression of a dog who looks at a master whose
catastrophe he can only partly understand. Tarrant
and the foreigner had stiffened in their usual sullen
attitudes, but their faces had turned the colour of clay.
The vicar seemed to have fainted. Father Brown was
kneeling beside the fallen figure, trying to test its
condition.

Rather to the general surprise, the Byronic lounger,
Paul Tarrant, came forward to help him.

'He'd better be carried up into the air,' he said. 'I
suppose there's just a chance for him.'

'He isn't dead,' said Father Brown in a low voice,

'but I think it's pretty bad; you aren't a doctor by any chance?'

'No; but I've had to pick up a good many things in my time,' said the other. 'But never mind about me just now. My real profession would probably surprise you.'

'I don't think so,' replied Father Brown, with a slight smile. 'I thought of it about half-way through the voyage. You are a detective shadowing somebody. Well, the cross is safe from thieves now, anyhow.'

While they were speaking Tarrant had lifted the frail figure of the fallen man with easy strength and dexterity, and was carefully carrying him towards the exit. He answered over his shoulder: 'Yes, the cross is safe enough.'

'You mean that nobody else is,' replied Brown. 'Are you thinking of the curse, too?'

Father Brown went about for the next hour or two under a burden of frowning perplexity that was something beyond the shock of the tragic accident. He assisted in carrying the victim to the little inn opposite the church, interviewed the doctor, who reported the injury as serious and threatening, though not certainly fatal, and carried the news to the little group of travellers who had gathered round the table in the inn parlour. But wherever he went the cloud of mystification rested on him and seemed to grow darker the more deeply he pondered. For the central mystery was growing more and more mysterious, actually in proportion as many of the minor mysteries began to clear themselves up in his mind. Exactly in proportion as the meaning of individual figures in that motley group began to explain itself, the thing that had happened grew more and more difficult to explain. Leonard Smyth had come merely because Lady Diana had come; and Lady Diana had come merely because she chose. They were engaged in one of those floating Society flirtations that are all the more silly for being semi-intellectual. But the lady's romanticism had a superstitious side to it; and she was pretty well prostrated by the terrible end of her adventure. Paul Tarrant was a private detective, possibly watching the flirtation for some wife or husband; possibly shadowing the foreign lecturer with the moustaches, who had much the air of an undesirable alien. But if he or anybody else had intended to steal the relic, the intention had been finally frustrated. And to all mortal appearance, what had frustrated it was either an incredible coincidence or the intervention of the ancient curse.

As he stood in unusual perplexity in the middle of the village street, between the inn and the church, he felt a mild shock of surprise at seeing a recently familiar but rather unexpected figure advancing up the street. Mr. Boon, the journalist, looking very haggard in the sunshine, which showed up his shabby raiment like that of a scarecrow, had his dark and deep-set eyes (rather close together on either side of the long drooping nose) fixed on the priest. The latter looked twice before he realized that the heavy dark moustache hid something like a grin or at least a grim smile.

'I thought you were going away,' said Father Brown a little sharply. 'I thought you left by that train two hours ago.'

'Well, you see I didn't,' said Boon.

'Why have you come back?' asked the priest almost sternly.

'This is not the sort of little rural paradise for a journalist to leave in a hurry,' replied the other. 'Things happen too fast here to make it worth while to go back to a dull place like London. Besides, they can't keep me out of the affair—I mean this second affair. It was I that found the body, or at any rate the clothes. Quite suspicious conduct on my part, wasn't it? Perhaps you think I wanted to dress up in his clothes. Shouldn't I make a lovely parson?'

And the lean and long-nosed mountebank suddenly made an extravagant gesture in the middle of the market-place, stretching out his arms and spreading out his dark-gloved hands in a sort of burlesque benediction and saying: 'Oh, my dear brethren and sisters, for I would embrace you all . . .'

D 9¹³

'What on earth are you talking about?' cried Father Brown, and rapped the stones slightly with his stumpy umbrella, for he was a little less patient than usual.

'Oh, you'll find out all about it if you ask that picnic party of yours at the inn,' replied Boon scornfully. 'That man Tarrant seems to suspect me merely because I found the clothes; though he only came up a minute too late to find them himself. But there are all sorts of mysteries in this business. The little man with the big moustaches may have more in him than meets the eye. For that matter I don't see why you shouldn't have killed the poor fellow yourself.'

Father Brown did not seem in the least annoyed at the suggestion, but he seemed exceedingly bothered and bewildered by the remark.

'Do you mean,' he asked with simplicity, 'that it was I who tried to kill Professor Smaill?'

'Not at all,' said the other, waving his hand with the air of one making a handsome concession. 'Plenty of dead people for you to choose among. Not limited to Professor Smaill. Why, didn't you know somebody else had turned up, a good deal deader than Professor Smaill? And I don't see why you shouldn't have done him in, in a quiet way. Religious differences, you know . . . lamentable disunion of Christendom. . . . I suppose you've always wanted to get the English parishes back.'

'I'm going back to the inn,' said the priest quietly; 'you say the people there know what you mean, and perhaps *they* may be able to say it.'

In truth, just afterwards his private perplexities suffered a momentary dispersal at the news of a new calamity. The moment he entered the little parlour where the rest of the company were collected, something in their pale faces told him they were shaken by something yet more recent than the accident at the tomb. Even as he entered, Leonard Smyth was saying: 'Where is all this going to end?'

'It will never end, I tell you,' repeated Lady Diana, gazing into vacancy with glassy eyes; 'it will never end till we all end. One after another the curse will take us; perhaps slowly, as the poor vicar said; but it will take us all as it has taken him.'

'What in the world has happened now?' asked Father Brown.

There was a silence, and then Tarrant said in a voice that sounded a little hollow:

'Mr. Walters, the vicar, has committed suicide. I suppose it was the shock unhinged him. But I fear there can be no doubt about it. We 've just found his black hat and clothes on a rock jutting out from the shore. He seems to have jumped into the sea. I thought he looked as if it had knocked him half-witted, and perhaps we ought to have looked after him; but there was so much to look after.'

'You could have done nothing,' said the lady. 'Don't you see the thing is dealing doom in a sort of dreadful order? The Professor touched the cross, and he went first; the vicar had opened the tomb, and he went second; we only entered the chapel, and we——'

'Hold on,' said Father Brown, in a sharp voice he very seldom used; 'this has got to stop.'

He still wore a heavy though unconscious frown, but in his eyes was no longer the cloud of mystification, but a light of almost terrible understanding.

'What a fool I am!' he muttered. 'I ought to have seen it long ago. The tale of the curse ought to have told me.'

'Do you mean to say,' demanded Tarrant, 'that we can really be killed now by something that happened in the thirteenth century?'

Father Brown shook his head and answered with quiet emphasis:

'I won't discuss whether we can be killed by something that happened in the thirteenth century; but I 'm jolly certain that we can't be killed by something that *never* happened in the thirteenth century, something that never happened at all.'

'Well,' said Tarrant, 'it 's refreshing to find a priest so sceptical of the supernatural as all that.'

'Not at all,' replied the priest calmly; 'it 's not the

supernatural part I doubt. It 's the natural part. I 'm exactly in the position of the man who said: "I can believe the impossible, but not the improbable."'

'That 's what you call a paradox, isn't it?' asked the other.

'It 's what I call common sense, properly understood,' replied Father Brown. 'It really is more natural to believe a preternatural story, that deals with things we don't understand, than a natural story that contradicts things we do understand. Tell me that the great Mr. Gladstone, in his last hours, was haunted by the ghost of Parnell, and I will be agnostic about it. But tell me that Mr. Gladstone, when first presented to Queen Victoria, wore his hat in her drawing-room and slapped her on the back and offered her a cigar, and I am not agnostic at all. That is not impossible; it 's only incredible. But I 'm much more certain it didn't happen than that Parnell's ghost didn't appear; because it violates the laws of the world I do understand. So it is with that tale of the curse. It isn't the legend that I disbelieve—it 's the history.'

Lady Diana had recovered a little from her trance of Cassandra, and her perennial curiosity about new things began to peer once more out of her bright and prominent eyes.

'What a curious man you are!' she said. 'Why should you disbelieve the history?'

'I disbelieve the history because it isn't history,' answered Father Brown. 'To anybody who happens to know a little about the Middle Ages, the whole story was about as probable as Gladstone offering Queen Victoria a cigar. But does anybody know anything about the Middle Ages? Do you know what a Guild was? Have you ever heard of *salvo managio suo*? Do you know what sort of people were *Servi Regis*?'

'No, of course I don't,' said the lady, rather crossly. 'What a lot of Latin words!'

'No, of course,' said Father Brown. 'If it had been Tutankhamen and a set of dried-up Africans preserved, Heaven knows why, at the other end of the world; if it had been Babylonia or China; if it had been some race as remote and mysterious as the Man in the Moon, your newspapers would have told you all about it, down to the last discovery of a toothbrush or a collar-stud. But the men who built your own parish churches, and gave the names to your own towns and trades, and the very roads you walk on—it has never occurred to you to know anything about them. I don't claim to know a lot myself; but I know enough to see that story is stuff and nonsense from beginning to end. It was illegal for a money-lender to distrain on a man's shop and tools. It's exceedingly unlikely that the Guild would not have saved a man from such utter ruin, especially if he were ruined by a Jew. Those people had vices and tragedies of their own; they sometimes tortured and burned people. But that idea of a man, without God or hope in the world, crawling away to die because nobody cared whether he lived—that isn't a medieval idea. That's a product of our economic science and progress. The Jew wouldn't have been a vassal of the feudal lord. The Jews normally had a special position as servants of the King. Above all, the Jew couldn't possibly have been burned for his religion.'

'The paradoxes are multiplying,' observed Tarrant; 'but surely you won't deny that Jews were persecuted in the Middle Ages?'

'It would be nearer the truth,' said Father Brown, 'to say they were the only people who weren't persecuted in the Middle Ages. If you want to satirize medievalism, you could make a good case by saying that some poor Christian might be burned alive for making a mistake about the Homoousian, while a rich Jew might walk down the street openly sneering at Christ and the Mother of God. Well, that's what the story is like. It was never a story of the Middle Ages; it was never even a legend about the Middle Ages. It was made up by somebody whose notions came from novels and newspapers, and probably made up on the spur of the moment.'

The others seemed a little dazed by the historical

digression, and seemed to wonder vaguely why the priest emphasized it and made it so important a part of the puzzle. But Tarrant, whose trade it was to pick the practical detail out of many tangles of digression, had suddenly become alert. His bearded chin was thrust forward farther than ever, but his sullen eyes were wide awake.

'Ah,' he said; 'made up on the spur of the moment!'

'Perhaps that is an exaggeration,' admitted Father Brown calmly. 'I should rather say made up more casually and carelessly than the rest of an uncommonly careful plot. But the plotter did not think the details of medieval history would matter much to anybody. And his calculation in a general way was pretty nearly right, like most of his other calculations.'

'Whose calculations? Who was right?' demanded the lady with a sudden passion of impatience. 'Who is this person you are talking about? Haven't we gone through enough, without your making our flesh creep with your he's and him's?'

'I am talking about the murderer,' said Father Brown.

'What murderer?' she asked sharply. 'Do you mean that the poor Professor was murdered?'

'Well,' said the staring Tarrant gruffly into his beard, 'we can't say "murdered," for we don't know he's killed.'

'The murderer killed somebody else, who was not Professor Smaill,' said the priest gravely.

'Why, whom else could he kill?' asked the other.

'He killed the Reverend John Walters, the Vicar of Dulham,' replied Father Brown with precision. 'He only wanted to kill those two, because they both had got hold of relics of one rare pattern. The murderer was a sort of monomaniac on the point.'

'It all sounds very strange,' muttered Tarrant. 'Of course we can't swear that the vicar's really dead either. We haven't seen his body.'

'Oh, yes, you have,' said Father Brown.

There was a silence as sudden as the stroke of a gong; a silence in which that subconscious guesswork that was so active and accurate in the woman moved her almost to a shriek.

'That is exactly what you have seen,' went on the priest. 'You have seen his body. You haven't seen him—the real living man; but you have seen his body all right. You have stared at it hard by the light of four great candles; and it was not tossing suicidally in the sea, but lying in state like a Prince of the Church in a shrine built before the Crusade.'

'In plain words,' said Tarrant, 'you actually ask us to believe that the embalmed body was really the corpse of a murdered man.'

Father Brown was silent for a moment; then he said almost with an air of irrelevance:

'The first thing I noticed about it was the cross; or rather the string suspending the cross. Naturally, for most of you, it was only a string of beads and nothing else in particular; but, naturally also, it was rather more in my line than yours. You remember it lay close up to the chin, with only a few beads showing, as if the whole necklet were quite short. But the beads that showed were arranged in a special way, first one and then three, and so on; in fact, I knew at a glance that it was a rosary, an ordinary rosary with a cross at the end of it. But a rosary has at least five decades and additional beads as well; and I naturally wondered where all the rest of it was. It would go much more than once round the old man's neck. I couldn't understand it at the time; and it was only afterwards I guessed where the extra length had gone to. It was coiled round and round the foot of the wooden prop that was fixed in the corner of the coffin, holding up the lid. So that when poor Smaill merely plucked at the cross it jerked the prop out of its place and the lid fell on his skull like a club of stone.'

'By George!' said Tarrant; 'I'm beginning to think there's something in what you say. This is a queer story if it's true.'

'When I realized that,' went on Father Brown, 'I could manage more or less to guess the rest. Remember, first of all, that there never was any responsible archaeological authority for anything more than investigation. Poor old Walters was an honest antiquary, who was engaged in opening the tomb to *find out* if there was any truth in the legend about embalmed bodies. The rest was all rumour, of the sort that often anticipates or exaggerates such finds. As a fact, he found the body had not been embalmed, but had fallen into dust long ago. Only while he was working there by the light of his lonely candle in that sunken chapel, the candle-light threw another shadow that was not his own.'

'Ah!' cried Lady Diana with a catch in her breath; 'and I know what you mean now. You mean to tell us we have met the murderer, talked and joked with the murderer, let him tell us a romantic tale, and let him depart untouched.'

'Leaving his clerical disguise on a rock,' assented Brown. 'It is all dreadfully simple. This man got ahead of the Professor in the race to the churchyard and chapel, possibly while the Professor was talking to that lugubrious journalist. He came on the old clergyman beside the empty coffin and killed him. Then he dressed himself in the black clothes from the corpse, wrapped it in an old cope which had been among the real finds of the exploration, and put it in the coffin, arranging the rosary and the wooden support as I have described. Then, having thus set the trap for his second enemy, he went up into the daylight and greeted us all with the most amiable politeness of a country clergyman.'

'He ran a considerable risk,' objected Tarrant, 'of somebody knowing Walters by sight.'

'I admit he was half-mad,' agreed Father Brown; 'and I think you will admit that the risk was worth taking, for he has got off, after all.'

'I 'll admit he was very lucky,' growled Tarrant. 'And who the devil was he?'

'As you say, he was very lucky,' answered Father Brown, 'and not least in that respect. For that is the one thing we may never know.'

He frowned at the table for a moment and then went on: 'This fellow has been hovering round and threatening for years, but the one thing he was careful of was to keep the secret of who he was; and he has kept it still. But if poor Smaill recovers, as I think he will, it is pretty safe to say that you will hear more of it.'

'Why, what will Professor Smaill do, do you think?' asked Lady Diana.

'I should think the first thing he would do,' said Tarrant, 'would be to put the detectives on like dogs after this murdering devil. I should like to have a go at him myself.'

'Well,' said Father Brown, smiling suddenly after his long fit of frowning perplexity, 'I think I know the very first thing he ought to do.'

'And what is that?' asked Lady Diana with graceful eagerness.

'He ought to apologize to all of you,' said Father Brown.

It was not upon this point, however, that Father Brown found himself talking to Professor Smaill as he sat by the bedside during the slow convalescence of that eminent archaeologist. Nor, indeed, was it chiefly Father Brown who did the talking; for though the Professor was limited to small doses of the stimulant of conversation, he concentrated most of it upon these interviews with his clerical friend. Father Brown had a talent for being silent in an encouraging way; and Smaill was encouraged by it to talk about many strange things not always easy to talk about; such as the morbid phases of recovery and the monstrous dreams that often accompany delirium. It is often rather an unbalancing business to recover slowly from a bad knock on the head; and when the head is as interesting a head as that of Professor Smaill, even its disturbances and distortions are apt to be original and curious. His dreams were like bold and big designs rather out of drawing, as they can be seen in the strong but stiff archaic arts that he had studied; they were full of strange saints with square and triangular haloes, of golden outstanding

crowns and glories round dark and flattened faces, of
eagles out of the East and the high head-dresses of
bearded men with their hair bound like women. Only,
as he told his friend, there was one much simpler
and less entangled type, that continually recurred to
his imaginative memory. Again and again all these
Byzantine patterns would fade away like the fading
gold on which they were traced as upon fire; and nothing
remained but the dark, bare wall of rock on which the
shining shape of the fish was traced as with a finger
dipped in the phosphorescence of fishes. For that was
the sign which he once looked up and saw, in the moment
when he first heard round the corner of the dark passage
the voice of his enemy.

'And at last,' he said, 'I think I have seen a meaning
in the picture and the voice; and one that I never
understood before. Why should I worry because one
madman among a million of sane men, leagued in a
great society against him, chooses to brag of persecuting
me or pursuing me to death? The man who drew in
the dark catacomb the secret symbol of Christ was persecuted in a very different fashion. He was the solitary
madman; the whole sane society was leagued together
not to save but to slay him. I have sometimes fussed
and fidgeted and wondered whether this or that man
was my persecutor; whether it was Tarrant; whether it
was Leonard Smyth; whether it was any one of them.
Suppose it had been all of them! Suppose it had been
all the men on the boat and the men on the train and
the men in the village. Suppose, so far as I was concerned, they were all murderers. I thought I had a
right to be alarmed because I was creeping through the
bowels of the earth in the dark and there was a man
who would destroy me. What would it have been like,
if the destroyer had been up in the daylight and had
owned all the earth and commanded all the armies and
the crowds? How if he had been able to stop all the
earths or smoke me out of my hole, or kill me the
moment I put my nose out in the daylight? What was
it like to deal with murder on that scale? The world

has forgotten these things, as until a little while ago it had forgotten war.'

'Yes,' said Father Brown, 'but the war came. The fish may be driven underground again, but it will come up into the daylight once more. As St. Antony of Padua humorously remarked, "it is only fishes who survive the Deluge."'

THE SWORD OF WOOD

Down in the little village of Grayling-Abbot, in Somerset, men did not know that the world we live in had begun. They did not know that all we have come to call 'modern' had silently entered England, and changed the air of it. Well, they did not know it very clearly even in London: though one or two shrewd men like my Lord Clarendon, and perhaps Prince Rupert, with his chemicals and his sad eyes, may have had a glimmer of it.

On the contrary, by the theory of the thing, the old world had returned. Christmas could be kept again; the terrible army was disbanded; the swarthy young man with the sour, humorous face, who had been cheered from Dover to Whitehall, brought back in him the blood of kings. Every one was saying (especially in Grayling-Abbot) that now it would be Merry England again. But the swarthy young man knew better. The Merry Monarch knew he was not meant to make Merry England. If he treated his own life as a comedy, it was for a philosophical reason; because comedy is the only poetry of compromise. And he was a compromise; and he knew it. Therefore he turned, like Prince Rupert, to the chemicals; and played with the little toys that were to become the terrible engines of modern science. So he might have played with tiger-cubs, so long as they were as small as his spaniels.

But down in Grayling-Abbot it was much easier to believe that old England had been restored, because it had never, in any serious sense, been disturbed. The fierce religious quarrels of the seventeenth century had only stirred that rustic neighbourhood to occasional panics of witch-burning. And these, though much rarer in the medieval society, were not inconsistent with it.

The squire, Sir Guy Griffin, was famous as a fighter quite in the medieval style. Though he had commanded a troop under Newcastle in the Civil Wars with conspicuous success, the local legend of his bodily prowess eclipsed any national chronicle of his military capacity. Through two or three counties round Grayling-Abbot, his reputation for swordsmanship had quite eclipsed his reputation for generalship. So, in the Middle Ages, it happened that Cœur-de-Lion's hand could keep his head: it happened that Bruce's hand could keep his head. And in both cases the head has suffered unfairly from the glorification of the hand.

The same almost unbroken medieval tradition even clung round the young schoolmaster, Dennis Tryon, who was just locking up his little school for the last time; having been transferred to a private post at Sir Guy's own house, to teach Sir Guy's six hulking sons, who had learned their father's skill with the sword, and hitherto declined to learn anything else. In numberless and nameless ways, Tryon expressed the old traditions. He was not a Puritan, yet he wore black clothes because he might have been a priest. Though he had learned to fence and dance at College, like Milton, he was plainly dressed and weaponless; because the vague legend remained that a student was a sort of clerk, and a clerk was a sort of clergyman. He wore his brown hair long, like a Cavalier. But as it was his own hair, it was long and straight: while the Cavaliers were already beginning to wear other people's hair, which was long and curly. In that strict brown frame, his face had the boyish, frank, rather round appearance that may be seen in old miniatures of Falkland or the Duke of Monmouth. His favourite authors were George Herbert and Sir Thomas Browne; and he was very young.

He was addressing a last word to a last pupil, who happened to be lingering outside the school—a minute boy of seven, playing with one of those wooden swords, made of two lengths of lath nailed across each other, which boys have played with in all centuries.

'Jeremy Bunt,' said Tryon, with a rather melancholy playfulness, 'your sword is, as it seems to me, much an improvement on most we have lately looked on. I observe its end is something blunt; doubtless for that gallant reason that led Orlando to blunt his sword when fighting the lady, whose name, in the ingenious romance, escapes me. Let it suffice you, little one. It will kill the Giants, like Master Jack's sword of sharpness, at least as well as the swords of a standing army ever will. If you be minded to save the Lady Angelica from the ogre, it will turn the dragon to stone as quick as any sword of steel would do. And, oh, Jeremy, if the fable be false, the moral is not false. If a little boy be good and brave, he should be great, and he may be. If he be bad and base, he should be beaten with a staff'— here Tryon tapped him very softly on the shoulders with a long black walking-cane that was commonly his only ferule—'but in either way, to my thinking, your sword is as good as any other. Only, dear Jeremy'— and he bent over the child swiftly, with a sudden tenderness—'always remember your kind of sword is stronger if one holds it by the wrong end.'

He reversed the little sword in the child's hand, making it a wooden cross, and then went striding up the road like the wind, leaving the staring boy behind.

When he became conscious that human feet were following him, he knew they could not possibly be the feet of the boy. He looked round; and Jeremy was still hovering in the distance; but the rush of feet came from a far different cause.

A young lady was hurrying by close under the high hedge that was nearly as old as the Plantagenets. Her costume was like his own, in the sense that it had the quietude of the Puritan with the cut of the Cavalier. Her dress was as dark as Barebones could have asked; but the ringlets under her hood were yellow and curly, for the same reason that his own hair was brown and straight: because they were her own. Nothing else was notable about her, except that she was pretty and seemed rather in a hurry; and that her delicate profile

was pointed resolutely up the road. The face was a
little pale.

Tryon turned again to look back on his tracks; and
this time saw another figure more formidable than
Jeremy with the wooden sword.

A tall, swaggering figure, almost black against the
sunlight, was coming down the road with a rapidity that
almost amounted to a run. He had a wide hat with
feathers, and long, luxuriant hair, in the latest London
manner; but it was not any such feathers or flourishes
that arrested Tryon's attention. He had seen old Sir
Guy Griffin, who still wore his wild, white hair half-way
down his back, to show (very unnecessarily) that he
was not a Puritan. He had seen Sir Guy stick in his
hat the most startling cock's feathers, but that was
because he had no other feathers. But Tryon knew at
a glance that Sir Guy would never have come forward
in such extraordinary attitudes. The tall, fantastic
man actually drew his sword as he rushed forward; and
offered it like a lance to be splintered as from the end
of a long tilting-yard. Such frolics may have happened
a hundred times round the 'Cock' of Buckingham and
Dorset. But it was an action utterly unknown to the
gentry round Grayling-Abbot, when they settled affairs
of honour.

While he was still looking up the road at the advancing
figure, he found himself breathlessly addressed by the
escaping girl.

'You must not fight him,' she said, 'he has beaten
everybody. He has beaten even Sir Guy, and all his
sons.' She cast her eyes about him and cried out in
horror: 'And where is your sword?'

'With my spurs, mistress,' replied the schoolmaster,
in the best style of Ariosto. 'I have to win them both.'

She looked at him rather wildly and said: 'But he
has never been beaten in swordsmanship.'

Tryon, with a smile, made a salute with his black
walking-stick. 'A man with no sword,' he said, 'can
never be beaten in swordsmanship.'

The girl stood for one moment staring at him as if,

even in that scene of scurry and chase, time were
suspended for a flash. Then she seemed to leap again
like a hunted thing and plunged on: and it was only
some hundred yards higher up the road that she again
halted, hesitated, and looked back. In much the same
manner Master Jeremy Bunt, who had not the faintest
intention of deserting the delightful school in which he
was no longer required to do any work, actually ran
forward. Perhaps their curiosity ought to be excused.
For they were certainly looking at the most astounding
duel the world had ever seen. It was the duel of the
naked sword and the walking-stick: probably the only
merely defensive battle ever fought on this earth.

The day was full of sun and wind, the two chief
ingredients of a glorious day; but till that moment even
Mr. Tryon, though of a pastoral and poetical turn, had
not noticed anything specially splendid in the sky or
landscape. Now the beauty of this world came upon
him with the violence of a supernatural vision; for he
was very certain it was a vision that he soon must lose.
He was a good fencer with the foil in the Collegiate
manner. But it was not to be expected that any human
being could emerge victorious from a prolonged fight in
which he had no means of retaliation; and especially as
his opponent, whether from drink or devilry, was clearly
fighting to the death. Tryon could not be certain that
the wild creature even knew that his sword only struck
against wood.

Dennis Tryon took in every glory of the good English
land, and the still more glorious English climate, with the
corner of his eye; he took it in with that same swift,
indirect and casual, yet absolutely substantial way in
which Nature is noticed in the old English poets that
he loved. For the great poets of England, from Chaucer
to Dryden, had a trick that has since been lost, the trick
of implying the nature of a scene without apparently
even attempting to describe it. Thus, any one reading
the line 'Pack, clouds, away,' knows at once it is the
kind of clouds called *cumuli*, and could not possibly be
meant for level or streaky clouds. Or any one reading

Milton's line about the princess's turret 'bosomed high
in tufted trees' knows it means partly leafless trees, as
in early spring or autumn, when the edge of the forest
shows soft against the sky, like a brush or broom, sweeping heaven.   With the same sort of subconscious solidity,
Tryon realized the rounded and half-rosy morning clouds
that curled or huddled in the blue above the downs; and
the mute mercy of the forests, that faded from grey to
purple before they mixed with heaven.   Death, in a hat
with black plumes, was shooting a thousand shining
arrows at him every instant; and he had never loved the
world so much before.

For indeed that one streak of white steel came at him
like a shower of shining arrows.   He had to make a new
parry for every new lunge; and, with each, perversely
remembered some episode of College fencing.   When
the bright point of death missed his heart and slid past
his elbow, he saw suddenly a meadow beside the Thames.
When he seemed blinded, by the very light on that
lightning blade, leaping at his eyes, but passing over
his shoulder, he saw the old lawn at Merton as if its grass
had sprung out of the road around him.   But he began
more and more to realize something else.   He realized
that if he had held a real sword, he could have killed
his enemy six times over with the *riposte*.   When the
heart-thrust was turned, he could have put his sword
like a carving-knife into a pudding—if it had been a
sword.   When the parry protected his eyes, nothing
else could have protected his opponent, except the
unpenetrating quality of a walking-stick.   His brain was
of the very clear kind that can play two games of chess
at once.   While still whirling his black walking-stick in
a complicated but impromptu clockwork of fence, he
saw quite clearly a logical alternative.   Either the man
thought he was fighting someone with a sword: in which
case he was a very bad fencer.   Or else he knew he
was fighting someone with a stick, in which case he was
a very bad man: or (as the more timid modern phrase
goes) a very bad sportsman.

He acted suddenly in a way adapted to either case.

He introduced into his swordplay a stroke of single-stick, also learned at College, jerking his stick up so as to strike and jar the man's elbow; and then, before the arm could recover its nerve, smote the sword clean out of the hand. A look at the man's black, bewildered expression was enough. Tryon was now quite certain the man's advantage had only been in his sword. He was also quite certain the man knew it. With all the rush of his released romanticism, which roared like the wind, and rolled like the clouds, and blazed like the sun which he had thought to see no more, he sprang forward and pinned the man by the throat, with a shout of laughter. Then he said, with more restrained humour, what he had said to the little boy up the road.

'If he be bad and base,' said Tryon, 'he should be beaten with a staff.' And whirling the walking-stick round his head, he laid three thundering and echoing thwacks across the shoulders of his disarmed enemy, and walked off up the road again like the wind.

He did not notice further what his murderous enemy might attempt, but he was honestly puzzled about the conduct of the crowd. For, by this time, there was a very considerable crowd. The sword-bearing Jeremy was quite prominent in the throng behind him; the lady with the golden curls and the sensitive profile was herself pausing a moment on the outskirts of the throng in front.

As he started up the road again, the mob set up a roar, redoubled and quadrupled, and several gentlemen present whirled their plumed hats and shouted observations he could not hear. What was even more extraordinary, a great part of the crowd (including the young lady, who vanished early) appeared to be disappearing up the road, as if bringing news of some great victory like Agincourt.

By the time he came from Grayling-Abbot to Grayling-le-Griffin, the next village, there were ten heads at every cottage window; and girls threw flowers, that missed him and fell on the road. By the time he came to the outskirts of the Park, with the stone griffins, there were triumphal arches.

'It seems that I was not a little hasty with Master Bunt,' said Tryon to himself, with a puzzled smile. 'It is plain I have fallen into the Kingdom of Queen Mab. It is I, and not Master Jeremy, who have, in some sense, saved Angelica from the dragon. I was rather more embarrassed in the matter of arms, and she rather less embarrassed in the matter of attire, and there, truly, the difference seems to end. But the strangest thing of all is that, whatever I have done, I have done it with a sword of wood, like little Jeremy's.'

In his academic reflections, he lifted his long black stick to look at it; and, as he did so, the cry of many crowds broke about him like a cannonade. For he had come to the very doors of Griffin Grange, to which he had been summoned on his much milder tutorial errand. And the great Sir Guy himself came out at the entrance. He might even have justified his mythic name, allowing for certain alterations of accident. For a griffin was supposed to be a mixture of the lion and the eagle; and certainly Sir Guy's mane might have been a lion's, but that it was largely white; and his nose might have been an eagle's, but that it was partly red.

His face had at first a dangerous and even dissipated look, and Tryon had one momentary doubt about the reason of his defeat. But when he looked again at Sir Guy's erect figure and animated eye; when he rather timidly accepted his decisive handshake and received congratulations in his clear and comfortable voice, the doubt vanished. And the young schoolmaster felt even more bewildered in receiving the equally adoring, though rather more gaping, congratulations of the six strenuous sons. At the first glance, Tryon felt something like despair about their Greek and Latin. But he also felt an increasing conviction that any of them could have knocked him anywhere with a cudgel. His own triumph began to seem as fantastic and incredible as his triumphal arches.

'Assuredly it is a strange matter,' he said to himself in his simplicity. 'I was a tolerable good fencer at Merton, but not excellent. Not so good as Wilton or

Smith or old King of Christ Church. It is not to be
believed that men like these could not beat him with
their great swords, when I could beat him with a stick.
This is some jest of the great gentry, as in the ingenious
tale of Master Cervantes.'

He therefore received the uproarious plaudits of old
Griffin and his sons with some reserve; but, after a little
time, it was hard for one so simple not to perceive their
simplicity. They really did regard him, as little Jeremy
would have regarded him, as a fairy-tale hero who had
freed their valley from an ogre. The people at the
windows had not been conspirators. The triumphal
arches had not been practical jokes. He was really the
god of the countryside and he had not a notion why.

Three things convinced him finally of the reality of
his reputation. One was the mysterious fact that the
young Griffins (that brood of mythic monsters) really
made some attempt to learn. Humphrey, the eldest
and biggest, got the genitive of *quis* right the third
time, though wrong again the fourth, fifth, and sixth.
The attempts of Geoffrey to distinguish between *fingo*
and *figo* would have moved a heart of stone: and Miles,
the youngest, was really interested in the verb *ferre*;
though (being a waterside character) he had some tendency to end it with a 'y.' Underneath all this excep-
tional mental ambition, Tryon could see the huge, silent
respect which savages and schoolboys feel everywhere
for one who has 'done' something in the bodily way.
The old rural and real aristocracy of England had not
that rather cold and clumsy class-consciousness we now
call the public-school spirit; and they enjoyed sports
instead of worshipping them. But boys are the same
in all ages, and one of their sports is hero-worship.

The next and yet more fascinating fact was Sir Guy.
He was not, it was clear, in the common sense an amiable
man. Just as the slash he had at the battle of Newbury
made his eagle face almost as ugly as it was handsome,
so the neglects and disappointments of his once promising military career had made his tongue and temper
as bitter as they were sincere. Yet Tryon felt he owed

the very knowledge of such an attitude to a confidence
the old man would not have reposed in other people.

'The King hath his own again,' old Griffin would say
gloomily. 'But I think it is too late. Indeed it might
nigh as well be the King of France come to rule us as
the King of England. He hath brought back with him
French women that act in stage plays as if they were
boys; and tricks fit for pothecaries or conjurers at a fair,
and tricks like this fellow's that twitched away my sword,
and every one else's—till he met his master, thank
God.' And he smiled at Tryon, sourly, but with respect.

'Is the gentleman I met,' asked Tryon, rather timidly,
'one from the Court?'

'Yes,' answered the old man. 'Did you look at his
face?'

'Only his eyes,' said the fencer, smiling; 'they are
black.'

'His face is painted,' said Griffin. 'That is the sort
of thing they do in London. And he wears a pile of
false hair out of a barber's; and walks about in it, like
the house of a Jack-in-the Green. But his was the best
sword, as old Noll's was the best army. And what
could we do?'

The third fact, which affected Dennis Tryon most
deeply of all, was a glimpse or two of the girl he had
saved from the obstreperous courtier. It appeared she
was the parson's daughter, one Dorothy Hood, who was
often in and out of the Grange, but always avoided
him. He had every sort of delicacy himself; and a com-
prehension of her attitude made him finally certain of
his own inexplicable importance. If this had been, as
he first thought, a trick played on him in the style of
the Duke and the Tinker, so charming a girl (and he
thought her more charming every time she flashed down
a corridor or disappeared through a door) would certainly have been set to draw him on. If there was a
conspiracy, she must be in it; and her part in it would
be plain. But she was not playing the part. He caught
himself rather wishing she were.

The last stroke came when he heard her saying to

Sir Guy, by the accident of two open doors: 'All say, 'twas witchcraft; and that God helped the young gentleman only because he was good, and——'

He walked wildly away. He was the kind of academic cavalier, who had learnt all worldly manners in an unworldly cloister. To him, therefore, eavesdropping was in all cases, horrible; in her case, damnable.

On one occasion he plucked up his courage to stop and thank her for having warned him of the danger of the duel.

Her delicate, pale face, always tremulous, became positively troubled. 'But then I did not know,' she said. 'I knew you were not afraid. But I did not know then you were fighting the devils.'

'Truly, and I do not know it now,' he answered. 'By my thinking, I was fighting one man, and no such great fighting at that.'

'Everybody says it was the devils,' she said with a beautiful simplicity. 'My father says so.'

When she had slipped away, Dennis was left meditating: and a new and rather grim impression grew stronger and stronger upon him. The more he heard from servants or strangers, the clearer it was that the local legend was hardening into a tale of himself as exorcist breaking the spell of a warlock.

The youngest boy, Miles, who had been (as usual) down by the river, said the villagers were walking along the bank, looking for the old pool where witches were drowned. Humphrey said it would be no good if they found it, for the tall man with the painted face had gone back to London. But an hour later, Geoffrey came in with other news: the wicked wizard had gone out of Grayling, but the mob had stopped him on the road to Salisbury.

When Tryon bestirred himself with curiosity and alarm and looked out of the Grange gates he found fearful confirmation, almost in the image of a place of pestilence or a city of the dead. The whole population of the two villages of Grayling (save for such non-combatants as the wooden-sworded Bunt) had vanished from their streets and houses. They returned in the dark hour before dawn; and they brought with them the man with the magic sword.

Men in modern England, who have never seen a revolution, who have never seen even a real mob, cannot imagine what the capture of a witch was like. It was for all the populace of that valley a vast rising against an emperor and oppressor, a being taller, more terrible, more universal, than any one would have called either Charles I or Cromwell, even in jest. It was not, as the modern people say, the worrying of some silly old woman. It was for them a revolt against Kehama, the Almighty Man. It was for them a rebellion of the good angels after the victory of Satan. Dorothy Hood was sufficiently frightened of the mob to take Tryon's hand in the crowd, and hold it in a way that made them understand each other with an intimate tenderness never afterwards dissolved. But it never occurred to her to be sorry for the warlock.

He was standing on the river bank, with his hands tied behind him, but the sword still at his side; no one feeling disposed to meddle with it. His peruke had been torn off; and his cropped head seemed to make more glaring and horrible the unnatural colours of his face. It was like some painted demon mask. But he was quite composed, and even contemptuous. Every now and then people threw things at him, as at one in the pillory; even little Jeremy Bunt flinging his wooden sword, with all the enthusiasm of the Children's Crusade. But most things missed him and fell into the flowing river behind, into which (there could be little doubt) he himself was to be flung at last.

Then stood up for an instant in the stormy light, that rare but real spirit, for whose sake alone men have endured aristocracy, or the division of man from man. Sir Guy's scarred face looked rather unusually sulky, or even spiteful; but he turned to his bodyguard of sons. 'We must get him back safe to the Grange,' he said sourly; 'you boys have all your swords, I think. You had best draw them.'

'Why?' asked the staring Humphrey.

'Why,' answered his father, 'because they are conquered swords, like my own.' And he drew his long blade, that took the white light of the morning.

'Boys,' he said, 'it is in the hand of God if he be warlock or no. But is it to be said of our blood that we brought crowds and clubs to kill a man who had whipped each one of us fairly with the sword? Shall men say that when Griffins met their match they whined about magic? Make a ring round him, and we will bring him alive through a thousand witch-smellers.'

Already a half-ring of naked swords had swung round the victim like a spiked necklace. In those days mobs were much bolder against their masters than they are to-day. But even that mob gave to the Griffins a military reputation beyond their mere territorial rank; and the parties were thus the more equal. There was no sword in that crowd better than a Griffin sword; except the sword that hung useless at the hip of a pinioned man.

Before the next moment, which must have been blood and destruction, the man with the useless sword spoke. 'If some gentleman,' he said with marmoreal calm, 'will but put a hand in the pocket of my doublet, I think bloodshed will be spared.'

There was a long silence; and every one looked at Dennis Tryon: the man who had not feared the wizard. Every one included Dorothy; and Dennis stepped forward. He found a folded piece of paper in the doublet, opened it and read it with more and more wonder on his round young face. At the third sentence he took his hat off. At this the crowd stared more and more: it had fallen suddenly silent and all were conscious of a change and a cooling in that intense air.

'It would appear,' he said at last, 'that this is a privy letter from His Majesty, which I will not read in entirety. But it advises and permits Sir Godfrey Skene to practise with the new Magnetic Sword which the Royal Society has for some little time attempted to manufacture in pursuance of a suggestion of Lord Verulam, the founder

of our Natural Philosophy. The whole blade is mag-
netized; and it is thought it may even pull any other
iron weapon out of the hand.'

He paused a moment, in some embarrassment, and
then said: 'It is added that only a weapon of wood or
such other material could be used against it.'

Sir Guy turned to him suddenly and said: 'Is that
what you call Natural Philosophy?'

'Yes,' replied Tryon.

'I thank you,' said Griffin. 'You need not teach it
to my sons.'

Then he strode towards the prisoner, and rent the
sword away, bursting the belt that held it.

'If it were not His Majesty's own hand,' he said, 'I
would throw you with it after all.'

The next instant the Magnetic Sword of the Royal
Society vanished from men's view for ever; and Tryon
could see nothing but Jeremy's little cross of wood
heaving with the heaving stream.

ESSAYS

A DEFENCE OF RASH VOWS

If a prosperous modern man, with a high hat and a frock-coat, were to solemnly pledge himself before all his clerks and friends to count the leaves on every third tree in Holland Walk, to hop up to the City on one leg every Thursday, to repeat the whole of Mill's *Liberty* seventy-six times, to collect three hundred dandelions in fields belonging to any one of the name of Brown, to remain for thirty-one hours holding his left ear in his right hand, to sing the names of all his aunts in order of age on the top of an omnibus, or make any such unusual undertaking, we should immediately conclude that the man was mad, or, as it is sometimes expressed, was 'an artist in life.' Yet these vows are not more extraordinary than the vows which in the Middle Ages and in similar periods were made, not by fanatics merely, but by the greatest figures in civic and national civilization —by kings, judges, poets, and priests. One man swore to chain two mountains together, and the great chain hung there, it was said, for ages as a monument of that mystical folly. Another swore that he would find his way to Jerusalem with a patch over his eyes, and died looking for it. It is not easy to see that these two exploits, judged from a strictly rational standpoint, are any saner than the acts above suggested. A mountain is commonly a stationary and reliable object which it is not necessary to chain up at night like a dog. And it is not easy at first sight to see that a man pays a very high compliment to the Holy City by setting out for it under conditions which render it to the last degree improbable that he will ever get there.

But about this there is one striking thing to be noticed. If men behaved in that way in our time, we should, as we have said, regard them as symbols of the 'decadence.' But the men who did these things were not decadent; they belonged generally to the most robust classes of what is generally regarded as a robust age. Again, it will be urged that if men essentially sane performed such insanities, it was under the capricious direction of a superstitious religious system. This, again, will not hold water; for in the purely terrestrial and even sensual departments of life, such as love and lust, the medieval princes show the same mad promises and performances, the same misshapen imagination, and the same monstrous self-sacrifice. Here we have a contradiction, to explain which it is necessary to think of the whole nature of vows from the beginning. And if we consider seriously and correctly the nature of vows, we shall, unless I am much mistaken, come to the conclusion that it is perfectly sane, and even sensible, to swear to chain mountains together, and that, if insanity is involved at all, it is a little insane not to do so.

The man who makes a vow makes an appointment with himself at some distant time or place. The danger of it is that himself should not keep the appointment. And in modern times this terror of one's self, of the weakness and mutability of one's self, has perilously increased, and is the real basis of the objection to vows of any kind. A modern man refrains from swearing to count the leaves on every third tree in Holland Walk, not because it is silly to do so (he does many sillier things), but because he has a profound conviction that before he had got to the three hundred and seventy-ninth leaf on the first tree he would be excessively tired of the subject and want to go home to tea. In other words, we fear that by that time he will be, in the common but hideously significant phrase, *another man*. Now, it is this horrible fairy tale of a man constantly changing into other men that is the soul of the decadence. That John Paterson should, with apparent calm, look forward to being a certain General Barker on Monday, Dr. Macgregor on Tuesday, Sir Walter Carstairs on Wednesday, and Sam Slugg on Thursday, may seem a nightmare; but to that nightmare we give the name of

modern culture.   One great decadent, who is now dead,
published a poem some time ago in which he powerfully
summed up the whole spirit of the movement by declaring that he could stand in the prison yard and
entirely comprehend the feelings of a man about to
be hanged:

> For he that lives more lives than one
> More deaths than one must die.

And the end of all this is that maddening horror of
unreality which descends upon the decadents, and
compared with which physical pain itself would have
the freshness of a youthful thing.   The one hell which
imagination must conceive as most hellish is to be
eternally acting a play without even the narrowest and
dirtiest greenroom in which to be human.   And this is
the condition of the decadent, of the aesthete, of the
free-lover.   To be everlastingly passing through dangers
which we know cannot scathe us, to be taking oaths
which we know cannot bind us, to be defying enemies
who we know cannot conquer us—this is the grinning
tyranny of decadence which is called freedom.

Let us turn, on the other hand, to the maker of vows.
The man who made a vow, however wild, gave a healthy
and natural expression to the greatness of a great
moment.   He vowed, for example, to chain two mountains together, perhaps a symbol of some great relief,
or love, or aspiration.   Short as the moment of his
resolve might be, it was, like all great moments, a
moment of immortality, and the desire to say of it *exegi
monumentum aere perennius* was the only sentiment that
would satisfy his mind.   The modern aesthetic man
would, of course, easily see the emotional opportunity;
he would vow to chain two mountains together.   But,
then, he would quite as cheerfully vow to chain the
earth to the moon.   And the withering consciousness
that he did not mean what he said, that he was, in truth,
saying nothing of any great import, would take from him
exactly that sense of daring actuality which is the excitement of a vow.   For what could be more maddening

than an existence in which our mother or aunt received the information that we were going to assassinate the king or build a temple on Ben Nevis with the genial composure of custom?

The revolt against vows has been carried in our day even to the extent of a revolt against the typical vow of marriage. It is most amusing to listen to the opponents of marriage on this subject. They appear to imagine that the ideal of constancy was a yoke mysteriously imposed on mankind by the devil, instead of being, as it is, a yoke consistently imposed by all lovers on themselves. They have invented a phrase, a phrase that is a black-and-white contradiction in two words—'free-love'—as if a lover ever had been, or ever could be, free. It is the nature of love to bind itself, and the institution of marriage merely paid the average man the compliment of taking him at his word. Modern sages offer to the lover, with an ill-flavoured grin, the largest liberties and the fullest irresponsibility; but they do not respect him as the old Church respected him; they do not write his oath upon the heavens, as the record of his highest moment. They give him every liberty except the liberty to sell his liberty, which is the only one that he wants.

In Mr. Bernard Shaw's brilliant play *The Philanderer* we have a vivid picture of this state of things. Charteris is a man perpetually endeavouring to be a free-lover, which is like endeavouring to be a married bachelor or a white negro. He is wandering in a hungry search for a certain exhilaration which he can only have when he has the courage to cease from wandering. Men knew better than this in old times—in the time, for example, of Shakespeare's heroes. When Shakespeare's men are really celibate they praise the undoubted advantages of celibacy, liberty, irresponsibility, a chance of continual change. But they were not such fools as to continue to talk of liberty when they were in such a condition that they could be made happy or miserable by the moving of someone else's eyebrow. Suckling classes love with debt in his praise of freedom.

And he that 's fairly out of both
Of all the world is blest.
He lives as in the golden age,
When all things made were common;
He takes his pipe, he takes his glass,
He fears no man or woman.

This is a perfectly possible, rational, and manly
position. But what have lovers to do with ridiculous
affectations of fearing no man or woman? They know
that in the turning of a hand the whole cosmic engine
to the remotest star may become an instrument of music
or an instrument of torture. They hear a song older
than Suckling's, that has survived a hundred philosophies. 'Who is this that looketh out of the window,
fair as the sun, clear as the moon, terrible as an army
with banners?'

As we have said, it is exactly this back-door, this
sense of having a retreat behind us, that is, to our
minds, the sterilizing spirit in modern pleasure. Everywhere there is the persistent and insane attempt to
obtain pleasure without paying for it. Thus, in politics,
the modern Jingoes practically say: 'Let us have the
pleasures of conquerors without the pains of soldiers:
let us sit on sofas and be a hardy race.' Thus, in religion
and morals, the decadent mystics say: 'Let us have the
fragrance of sacred purity without the sorrows of self-
restraint; let us sing hymns alternately to the Virgin
and Priapus.' Thus, in love, the free-lovers say: 'Let
us have the splendour of offering ourselves without the
peril of committing ourselves; let us see whether one
cannot commit suicide an unlimited number of times.'

Emphatically it will not work. There are thrilling
moments, doubtless, for the spectator, the amateur, and
the aesthete; but there is one thrill that is known only
to the soldier who fights for his own flag, to the ascetic
who starves himself for his own illumination, to the
lover who makes finally his own choice. And it is
this transfiguring self-discipline that makes the vow a
truly sane thing. It must have satisfied even the giant
hunger of the soul of a lover or a poet to know that in

E 913

consequence of some one instant of decision that strange chain would hang for centuries in the Alps among the silences of stars and snows.   All around us is the city of small sins, abounding in back ways and retreats, but surely, sooner or later, the towering flame will rise from the harbour announcing that the reign of the cowards is over and a man is burning his ships.

A DEFENCE OF SKELETONS

SOME little time ago I stood among immemorial English trees that seemed to take hold upon the stars like a brood of Yggdrasils. As I walked among these living pillars I became gradually aware that the rustics who lived and died in their shadow adopted a very curious conversational tone. They seemed to be constantly apologizing for the trees, as if they were a very poor show. After elaborate investigation, I discovered that their gloomy and penitent tone was traceable to the fact that it was winter and all the trees were bare. I assured them that I did not resent the fact that it was winter, that I knew the thing had happened before, and that no forethought on their part could have averted this blow of destiny. But I could not in any way reconcile them to the fact that it *was* winter. There was evidently a general feeling that I had caught the trees in a kind of disgraceful deshabille, and that they ought not to be seen until, like the first human sinners, they had covered themselves with leaves. So it is quite clear that, while very few people appear to know anything of how trees look in winter, the actual foresters know less than any one. So far from the line of the tree when it is bare appearing harsh and severe, it is luxuriantly indefinable to an unusual degree; the fringe of the forest melts away like a vignette. The tops of two or three high trees when they are leafless are so soft that they seem like the gigantic brooms of that fabulous lady who was sweeping the cobwebs off the sky. The outline of a leafy forest is in comparison hard, gross, and blotchy; the clouds of night do not more certainly obscure the moon than those green and monstrous clouds obscure the tree; the actual sight of the little wood, with its grey and silver sea of life, is entirely a winter vision. So dim and delicate is the heart of the winter woods, a kind of glittering gloaming, that a figure stepping towards us in the chequered twilight seems as if he were breaking through unfathomable depths of spiders' webs.

But surely the idea that its leaves are the chief grace of a tree is a vulgar one, on a par with the idea that his hair is the chief grace of a pianist. When winter, that healthy ascetic, carries his gigantic razor over hill and valley, and shaves all the trees like monks, we feel surely that they are all the more like trees if they are shorn, just as so many painters and musicians would be all the more like men if they were less like mops. But it does appear to be a deep and essential difficulty that men have an abiding terror of their own structure, or of the structure of things they love. This is felt dimly in the skeleton of the tree: it is felt profoundly in the skeleton of the man.

The importance of the human skeleton is very great, and the horror with which it is commonly regarded is somewhat mysterious. Without claiming for the human skeleton a wholly conventional beauty, we may assert that he is certainly not uglier than a bull-dog, whose popularity never wanes, and that he has a vastly more cheerful and ingratiating expression. But just as man is mysteriously ashamed of the skeletons of the trees in winter, so he is mysteriously ashamed of the skeleton of himself in death. It is a singular thing altogether, this horror of the architecture of things. One would think it would be most unwise in a man to be afraid of a skeleton, since Nature has set curious and quite insuperable obstacles to his running away from it.

One ground exists for this terror: a strange idea has infected humanity that the skeleton is typical of death. A man might as well say that a factory chimney was typical of bankruptcy. The factory may be left naked after ruin, the skeleton may be left naked after bodily dissolution; but both of them have had a lively and workmanlike life of their own, all the pulleys creaking, all the wheels turning, in the House of Livelihood as in the House of Life. There is no reason why this creature (new, as I fancy, to art), the living skeleton, should not become the essential symbol of life.

The truth is that man's horror of the skeleton is not horror of death at all.   It is man's eccentric glory that he has not, generally speaking, any objection to being deaf, but has a very serious objection to being undignified.   And the fundamental matter which troubles him in the skeleton is the reminder that the ground-plan of his appearance is shamelessly grotesque.   I do not know why he should object to this.   He contentedly takes his place in a world that does not pretend to be genteel—a laughing, working, jeering world.   He sees millions of animals carrying, with quite a dandified levity, the most monstrous shapes and appendages, the most preposterous horns, wings, and legs, when they are necessary to utility.   He sees the good temper of the frog, the unaccountable happiness of the hippopotamus. He sees a whole universe which is ridiculous, from the animalcule, with a head too big for its body, up to the comet, with a tail too big for its head.   But when it comes to the delightful oddity of his own inside, his sense of humour rather abruptly deserts him.

In the Middle Ages and in the Renaissance (which was, in certain times and respects, a much gloomier period) this idea of the skeleton had a vast influence in freezing the pride out of all earthly pomps and the fragrance out of all fleeting pleasures.   But it was not, surely, the mere dread of death that did this, for these were ages in which men went to meet death singing; it was the idea of the degradation of man in the grinning ugliness of his structure that withered the juvenile insolence of beauty and pride.   And in this it almost assuredly did more good than harm.   There is nothing so cold or so pitiless as youth, and youth in aristocratic stations and ages tended to an impeccable dignity, an endless summer of success which needed to be very sharply reminded of the scorn of the stars.   It was well that such flamboyant prigs should be convinced that one practical joke, at least, would bowl them over, that they would fall into one grinning man-trap, and not rise again.   That the whole structure of their existence was as wholesomely ridiculous as that of a pig or a parrot they could not be expected to realize; that birth was humorous, coming of age humorous, drinking and fighting humorous, they were far too young and solemn to know. But at least they were taught that death was humorous.

There is a peculiar idea abroad that the value and fascination of what we call Nature lie in her beauty. But the fact that Nature is beautiful in the sense that a dado or a Liberty curtain is beautiful is only one of her charms, and almost an accidental one. The highest and most valuable quality in Nature is not her beauty, but her generous and defiant ugliness. A hundred instances might be taken. The croaking noise of the rooks is, in itself, as hideous as the whole hell of sounds in a London railway tunnel. Yet it uplifts us like a trumpet with its coarse kindliness and honesty, and the lover in *Maud* could actually persuade himself that this abominable noise resembled his lady-love's name. Has the poet, for whom Nature means only roses and lilies, ever heard a pig grunting? It is a noise that does a man good—a strong, snorting, imprisoned noise, breaking its way out of unfathomable dungeons through every possible outlet and organ. It might be the voice of the earth itself, snoring in its mighty sleep. This is the deepest, the oldest, the most wholesome and religious sense of the value of Nature—the value which comes from her immense babyishness. She is as top-heavy, as grotesque, as solemn, and as happy as a child. The mood does come when we see all her shapes like shapes that a baby scrawls upon a slate—simple, rudimentary, a million years older and stronger than the whole disease that is called art. The objects of earth and heaven seem to combine into a nursery tale, and our relation to things seems for a moment so simple that a dancing lunatic would be needed to do justice to its lucidity and levity. The tree above my head is flapping like some gigantic bird standing on one leg; the moon is like the eye of a Cyclops. And, however much my face clouds with sombre vanity, or vulgar vengeance, or contemptible contempt, the bones of my skull beneath it are laughing for ever.

A DEFENCE OF NONSENSE

THERE are two equal and eternal ways of looking at this twilight world of ours: we may see it as the twilight of evening or the twilight of morning; we may think of anything, down to a fallen acorn, as a descendant or as an ancestor. There are times when we are almost crushed, not so much with the load of the evil as with the load of the goodness of humanity, when we feel that we are nothing but the inheritors of a humiliating splendour. But there are other times when everything seems primitive, when the ancient stars are only sparks blown from a boy's bonfire, when the whole earth seems so young and experimental that even the white hair of the aged, in the fine Biblical phrase, is like almond-trees that blossom, like the white hawthorn grown in May. That it is good for a man to realize that he is 'the heir of all the ages' is pretty commonly admitted; it is a less popular but equally important point that it is good for him sometimes to realize that he is not only an ancestor, but an ancestor of primal antiquity; it is good for him to wonder whether he is not a hero, and to experience ennobling doubts as to whether he is not a solar myth.

The matters which most thoroughly evoke this sense of the abiding childhood of the world are those which are really fresh, abrupt, and inventive in any age; and if we were asked what was the best proof of this adventurous youth in the nineteenth century we should say, with all respect to its portentous sciences and philosophies, that it was to be found in the rhymes of Mr. Edward Lear and in the literature of nonsense. *The Dong with the Luminous Nose*, at least, is original, as the first ship and the first plough were original.

It is true in a certain sense that some of the greatest writers the world has seen—Aristophanes, Rabelais, and

123

Sterne—have written nonsense; but unless we are mistaken, it is in a widely different sense. The nonsense of these men was satiric—that is to say, symbolic; it was a kind of exuberant capering round a discovered truth. There is all the difference in the world between the instinct of satire, which, seeing in the Kaiser's moustaches something typical of him, draws them continually larger and larger; and the instinct of nonsense which, for no reason whatever, imagines what those moustaches would look like on the present Archbishop of Canterbury if he grew them in a fit of absence of mind. We incline to think that no age except our own could have understood that the Quangle-Wangle meant absolutely nothing, and the Lands of the Jumblies were absolutely nowhere. We fancy that if the account of the Knave's trial in *Alice in Wonderland* had been published in the seventeenth century it would have been bracketed with Bunyan's *Trial of Faithful* as a parody on the State prosecutions of the time. We fancy that if *The Dong with the Luminous Nose* had appeared in the same period every one would have called it a dull satire on Oliver Cromwell.

It is altogether advisedly that we quote chiefly from Mr. Lear's *Nonsense Rhymes*. To our mind he is both chronologically and essentially the father of nonsense; we think him superior to Lewis Carroll. In one sense, indeed, Lewis Carroll has a great advantage. We know what Lewis Carroll was in daily life: he was a singularly serious and conventional don, universally respected, but very much of a pedant and something of a Philistine. Thus his strange double life in earth and in dreamland emphasizes the idea that lies at the back of nonsense— the idea of *escape*, of escape into a world where things are not fixed horribly in an eternal appropriateness, where apples grow on pear-trees, and any odd man you meet may have three legs. Lewis Carroll, living one life in which he would have thundered morally against any one who walked on the wrong plot of grass, and another life in which he would cheerfully call the sun green and the moon blue, was, by his very divided nature, his one foot on both worlds, a perfect type of

the position of modern nonsense. His Wonderland is a
country populated by insane mathematicians. We feel
the whole is an escape into a world of masquerade; we
feel that if we could pierce their disguises, we might
discover that Humpty Dumpty and the March Hare
were Professors and Doctors of Divinity enjoying a
mental holiday. This sense of escape is certainly less
emphatic in Edward Lear, because of the completeness
of his citizenship in the world of unreason. We do not
know his prosaic biography as we know Lewis Carroll's.
We accept him as a purely fabulous figure, on his own
description of himself:

> His body is perfectly spherical,
> He weareth a runcible hat.

While Lewis Carroll's Wonderland is purely intellectual, Lear introduces quite another element—the element
of the poetical and even emotional. Carroll works by
the pure reason, but this is not so strong a contrast; for,
after all, mankind in the main has always regarded
reason as a bit of a joke. Lear introduces his unmeaning
words and his amorphous creatures not with the pomp of
reason, but with the romantic prelude of rich hues and
haunting rhythms.

> Far and few, far and few,
> Are the lands where the Jumblies live,

is an entirely different type of poetry to that exhibited
in *Jabberwocky*. Carroll, with a sense of mathematical
neatness, makes his whole poem a mosaic of new and
mysterious words. But Edward Lear, with more subtle
and placid effrontery, is always introducing scraps of
his own elvish dialect into the middle of simple and
rational statements, until we are almost stunned into
admitting that we know what they mean. There is a
genial ring of common sense about such lines as:

> For his aunt Jobiska said, 'Every one knows
> That a Pobble is better without his toes,'

which is beyond the reach of Carroll. The poet seems
so easy on the matter that we are almost driven to
pretend that we see his meaning, that we know the

peculiar difficulties of a Pobble, that we are as old travellers in the 'Gromboolian Plain' as he is.

Our claim that nonsense is a new literature (we might almost say a new sense) would be quite indefensible if nonsense were nothing more than a mere aesthetic fancy. Nothing sublimely artistic has ever arisen out of mere art, any more than anything essentially reasonable has ever arisen out of the pure reason. There must always be a rich moral soil for any great aesthetic growth. The principle of *art for art's sake* is a very good principle if it means that there is a vital distinction between the earth and the tree that has its roots in the earth; but it is a very bad principle if it means that the tree could grow just as well with its roots in the air. Every great literature has always been allegorical— allegorical of some view of the whole universe. The Iliad is only great because all life is a battle, the Odyssey because all life is a journey, the Book of Job because all life is a riddle. There is one attitude in which we think that all existence is summed up in the word 'ghosts'; another, and somewhat better one, in which we think it is summed up in the words *A Midsummer Night's Dream*. Even the vulgarest melodrama or detective story can be good if it expresses something of the delight in sinister possibilities—the healthy lust for darkness and terror which may come on us any night in walking down a dark lane. If, therefore, nonsense is really to be the literature of the future, it must have its own version of the Cosmos to offer; the world must not only be the tragic, romantic, and religious, it must be nonsensical also. And here we fancy that nonsense will, in a very unexpected way, come to the aid of the spiritual view of things. Religion has for centuries been trying to make men exult in the 'wonders' of creation, but it has forgotten that a thing cannot be completely wonderful so long as it remains sensible. So long as we regard a tree as an obvious thing, naturally and reasonably created for a giraffe to eat, we cannot properly wonder at it. It is when we consider it as a prodigious wave of the living soil sprawling up to the skies for no reason in particular that we take off our hats, to the astonishment of the park-keeper. Everything has in fact another side to it, like the moon, the patroness of nonsense. Viewed from that other side, a bird is a blossom broken loose from its chain of stalk, a man a quadruped begging on its hind legs, a house a gigantesque hat to cover a man from the sun, a chair an apparatus of four wooden legs for a cripple with only two.

This is the side of things which tends most truly to spiritual wonder. It is significant that in the greatest religious poem existent, the Book of Job, the argument which convinces the infidel is not (as has been represented by the merely rational religionism of the eighteenth century) a picture of the ordered beneficence of the Creation; but, on the contrary, a picture of the huge and undecipherable unreason of it. 'Hast Thou sent the rain upon the desert where no man is?' This simple sense of wonder at the shapes of things, and at their exuberant independence of our intellectual standards and our trivial definitions, is the basis of spirituality as it is the basis of nonsense. Nonsense and faith (strange as the conjunction may seem) are the two supreme symbolic assertions of the truth that to draw out the soul of things with a syllogism is as impossible as to draw out Leviathan with a hook. The well-meaning person who, by merely studying the logical side of things, has decided that 'faith is nonsense,' does not know how truly he speaks; later it may come back to him in the form that nonsense is faith.

A DEFENCE OF CHINA SHEPHERDESSES

THERE are some things of which the world does not like
to be reminded, for they are the dead loves of the
world. One of these is that great enthusiasm for the
Arcadian life which, however much it may now lie open
to the sneers of realism, did, beyond all question, hold
sway for an enormous period of the world's history,
from the times that we describe as ancient down to
times that may fairly be called recent. The conception
of the innocent and hilarious life of shepherds and shep-
herdesses certainly covered and absorbed the time of
Theocritus, of Virgil, of Catullus, of Dante, of Cervantes,
of Ariosto, of Shakespeare, and of Pope. We are told
that the gods of the heathen were stone and brass, but
stone and brass have never endured with the long
endurance of the China Shepherdess. The Catholic
Church and the Ideal Shepherd are indeed almost the
only things that have bridged the abyss between the
ancient world and the modern. Yet, as we say, the
world does not like to be reminded of this boyish
enthusiasm.

But imagination, the function of the historian, cannot
let so great an element alone. By the cheap revolutionary it is commonly supposed that imagination is a
merely rebellious thing, that it has its chief function in
devising new and fantastic republics. But imagination
has its highest use in a retrospective realization. The
trumpet of imagination, like the trumpet of the Resurrection, calls the dead out of their graves. Imagination
sees Delphi with the eyes of a Greek, Jerusalem with the
eyes of a Crusader, Paris with the eyes of a Jacobin,
and Arcadia with the eyes of a Euphuist. The prime
function of imagination is to see our whole orderly
system of life as a pile of stratified revolutions. In spite
of all revolutionaries it must be said that the function

of imagination is not to make strange things settled, so much as to make settled things strange; not so much to make wonders facts as to make facts wonders. To the imaginative the truisms are all paradoxes, since they were paradoxes in the Stone Age; to them the ordinary copy-book blazes with blasphemy.

Let us, then, consider in this light the old pastoral or Arcadian ideal. But first certainly one thing must be definitely recognized. This Arcadian art and literature is a lost enthusiasm. To study it is like fumbling in the love-letters of a dead man. To us its flowers seem as tawdry as cockades; the lambs that dance to the shepherd's pipe seem to dance with all the artificiality of a ballet. Even our own prosaic toil seems to us more joyous than that holiday. Where its ancient exuberance passed the bounds of wisdom and even of virtue, its caperings seem frozen into the stillness of an antique frieze. In those grey old pictures a bacchanal seems as dull as an archdeacon. Their very sins seem colder than our restraints.

All this may be frankly recognized: all the barren sentimentality of the Arcadian ideal and all its insolent optimism. But when all is said and done, something else remains.

Through ages in which the most arrogant and elaborate ideals of power and civilization held otherwise undisputed sway, the ideal of the perfect and healthy peasant did undoubtedly represent in some shape or form the conception that there was a dignity in simplicity and a dignity in labour. It was good for the ancient aristocrat, even if he could not attain to innocence and the wisdom of the earth, to believe that these things were the secrets of the priesthood of the poor. It was good for him to believe that even if heaven was not above him, heaven was below him. It was well that he should have amid all his flamboyant triumphs the never-extinguished sentiment that there was something better than his triumphs, the conception that 'there remaineth a rest.'

The conception of the Ideal Shepherd seems absurd

to our modern ideas.   But, after all, it was perhaps the
only trade of the democracy which was equalized with
the trades of the aristocracy even by the aristocracy
itself.   The shepherd of pastoral poetry was, without
doubt, very different from the shepherd of actual fact.
Where one innocently piped to his lambs, the other
innocently swore at them; and their divergence in intellect and personal cleanliness was immense.   But the
difference between the ideal shepherd who danced with
Amaryllis and the real shepherd who thrashed her is not
a scrap greater than the difference between the ideal
soldier who dies to capture the colours and the real
soldier who lives to clean his accoutrements, between
the ideal priest who is everlastingly by someone's bed
and the real priest who is as glad as any one else to get
to his own.   There are ideal conceptions and real men
in every calling; yet there are few who object to the
ideal conceptions, and not many, after all, who object
to the real men.

The fact, then, is this: So far from resenting the
existence in art and literature of an ideal shepherd, I
genuinely regret that the shepherd is the only democratic calling that has ever been raised to the level of
the heroic callings conceived by an aristocratic age.   So
far from objecting to the Ideal Shepherd, I wish there
were an Ideal Postman, an Ideal Grocer, and an Ideal
Plumber.   It is undoubtedly true that we should laugh
at the idea of an Ideal Postman; it is true, and it proves
that we are not genuine democrats.

Undoubtedly the modern grocer, if called upon to act
in an Arcadian manner, if desired to oblige with a
symbolic dance expressive of the delights of grocery, or
to perform on some simple instrument while his assistants
skipped around him, would be embarrassed, and perhaps
even reluctant.   But it may be questioned whether this
temporary reluctance of the grocer is a good thing, or
evidence of a good condition of poetic feeling in the
grocery business as a whole.   There certainly should be
an ideal image of health and happiness in any trade, and
its remoteness from the reality is not the only important

question. No one supposes that the mass of traditional
conceptions of duty and glory are always operative, for
example, in the mind of a soldier or a doctor; that
the Battle of Waterloo actually makes a private enjoy
pipeclaying his trousers, or that the 'health of humanity'
softens the momentary phraseology of a physician called
out of bed at two o'clock in the morning. But although
no ideal obliterates the ugly drudgery and detail of any
calling, that ideal does, in the case of the soldier or the
doctor, exist definitely in the background and makes
that drudgery worth while as a whole. It is a serious
calamity that no such ideal exists in the case of the
vast number of honourable trades and crafts on which
the existence of a modern city depends. It is a pity
that current thought and sentiment offer nothing corre-
sponding to the old conception of patron saints. If they
did there would be a Patron Saint of Plumbers, and this
would alone be a revolution, for it would force the
individual craftsman to believe that there was once a
perfect being who did actually plumb.

When all is said and done, then, we think it much
open to question whether the world has not lost something in the complete disappearance of the ideal of the
happy peasant. It is foolish enough to suppose that the
rustic went about all over ribbons, but it is better than
knowing that he goes about all over rags and being
indifferent to the fact. The modern realistic study of
the poor does in reality lead the student further astray
than the old idyllic notion. For we cannot get the
chiaroscuro of humble life so long as its virtues seem to
us as gross as its vices and its joys as sullen as its
sorrows. Probably at the very moment that we can
see nothing but a dull-faced man smoking and drinking
heavily with his friend in a pot-house, the man himself
is on his soul's holiday, crowned with the flowers of
a passionate idleness, and far more like the Happy
Peasant than the world will ever know.

THE FALLACY OF SUCCESS

THERE has appeared in our time a particular class of books and articles which I sincerely and solemnly think may be called the silliest ever known among men. They are much more wild than the wildest romances of chivalry and much more dull than the dullest religious tract. Moreover, the romances of chivalry were at least about chivalry; the religious tracts are about religion. But these things are about nothing; they are about what is called Success. On every bookstall, in every magazine, you may find works telling people how to succeed. They are books showing men how to succeed in everything; they are written by men who cannot even succeed in writing books. To begin with, of course, there is no such thing as Success. Or, if you like to put it so, there is nothing that is not successful. That a thing is successful merely means that it is; a millionaire is successful in being a millionaire and a donkey in being a donkey. Any live man has succeeded in living; any dead man may have succeeded in committing suicide. But, passing over the bad logic and bad philosophy in the phrase, we may take it, as these writers do, in the ordinary sense of success in obtaining money or worldly position. These writers profess to tell the ordinary man how he may succeed in his trade or speculation—how, if he is a builder, he may succeed as a builder; how, if he is a stockbroker, he may succeed as a stockbroker. They profess to show him how, if he is a grocer, he may become a sporting yachtsman; how, if he is a tenth-rate journalist, he may become a peer; and how, if he is a German Jew, he may become an Anglo-Saxon. This is a definite and business-like proposal, and I really think that the people who buy these books (if any people do buy them) have a moral, if not a legal, right to ask for their money

back. Nobody would dare to publish a book about
electricity which literally told one nothing about
electricity; no one would dare to publish an article on
botany which showed that the writer did not know
which end of a plant grew in the earth. Yet our modern
world is full of books about Success and successful people
which literally contain no kind of idea, and scarcely any
kind of verbal sense.

It is perfectly obvious that in any decent occupation
(such as bricklaying or writing books) there are only
two ways (in any special sense) of succeeding. One is
by doing very good work, the other is by cheating.
Both are much too simple to require any literary
explanation. If you are in for the high jump, either
jump higher than any one else, or manage somehow to
pretend that you have done so. If you want to succeed
at whist, either be a good whist-player, or play with
marked cards. You may want a book about jumping;
you may want a book about whist; you may want a
book about cheating at whist. But you cannot want
a book about Success. Especially you cannot want a
book about Success such as those which you can now
find scattered by the hundred about the book-market.
You may want to jump or to play cards; but you do
not want to read wandering statements to the effect
that jumping is jumping, or that games are won by
winners. If these writers, for instance, said anything
about success in jumping it would be something like
this: 'The jumper must have a clear aim before him.
He must desire definitely to jump higher than the other
men who are in for the same competition. He must let
no feeble feelings of mercy (sneaked from the sickening
Little Englanders and Pro-Boers) prevent him from
trying to *do his best*. He must remember that a competition in jumping is distinctly competitive, and that,
as Darwin has gloriously demonstrated, THE WEAKEST
GO TO THE WALL.' That is the kind of thing the book
would say, and very useful it would be, no doubt, if
read out in a low and tense voice to a young man just
about to take the high jump. Or suppose that in the

course of his intellectual rambles the philosopher of Success dropped upon our other case, that of playing cards, his bracing advice would run: 'In playing cards it is very necessary to avoid the mistake (commonly made by maudlin humanitarians and Free Traders) of permitting your opponent to win the game. You must have grit and snap and *go in to win*. The days of idealism and superstition are over. We live in a time of science and hard common sense, and it has now been definitely proved that in any game where two are playing IF ONE DOES NOT WIN THE OTHER WILL.' It is all very stirring, of course; but I confess that if I were playing cards I would rather have some decent little book which told me the rules of the game. Beyond the rules of the game it is all a question either of talent or dishonesty; and I will undertake to provide either one or the other —which, it is not for me to say.

Turning over a popular magazine, I find a queer and amusing example. There is an article called 'The Instinct that Makes People Rich.' It is decorated in front with a formidable portrait of Lord Rothschild. There are many definite methods, honest and dishonest, which make people rich; the only 'instinct' I know of which does it is that instinct which theological Christianity crudely describes as 'the sin of avarice.' That, however, is beside the present point. I wish to quote the following exquisite paragraphs as a piece of typical advice as to how to succeed. It is so practical; it leaves so little doubt about what should be our next step:

'The name of Vanderbilt is synonymous with wealth gained by modern enterprise. "Cornelius," the founder of the family, was the first of the great American magnates of commerce. He started as the son of a poor farmer; he ended as a millionaire twenty times over.

'He had the money-making instinct. He seized his opportunities, the opportunities that were given by the application of the steam-engine to ocean traffic, and by the birth of railway locomotion in the wealthy but undeveloped United States of America, and consequently he amassed an immense fortune.

'Now it is, of course, obvious that we cannot all follow exactly in the footsteps of this great railway monarch. The precise opportunities that fell to him do not occur to us. Circumstances have changed. But, although this is so, still, in our own sphere and in our own circumstances, we *can* follow his general methods; we can seize those opportunities that are given us, and give ourselves a very fair chance of attaining riches.'

In such strange utterances we see quite clearly what is really at the bottom of all these articles and books. It is not mere business; it is not even mere cynicism. It is mysticism; the horrible mysticism of money. The writer of that passage did not really have the remotest notion of how Vanderbilt made his money, or of how anybody else is to make his. He does, indeed, conclude his remarks by advocating some scheme; but it has nothing in the world to do with Vanderbilt. He merely wished to prostrate himself before the mystery of a millionaire. For when we really worship anything, we love not only its clearness but its obscurity. We exult in its very invisibility. Thus, for instance, when a man is in love with a woman he takes special pleasure in the fact that a woman is unreasonable. Thus, again, the very pious poet, celebrating his Creator, takes pleasure in saying that God moves in a mysterious way. Now, the writer of the paragraph which I have quoted does not seem to have had anything to do with a god, and I should not think (judging by his extreme unpracticality) that he had ever been really in love with a woman. But the thing he does worship—Vanderbilt—he treats in exactly this mystical manner. He really revels in the fact his deity Vanderbilt is keeping a secret from him. And it fills his soul with a sort of transport of cunning, an ecstasy of priestcraft, that he should pretend to be telling to the multitude that terrible secret which he does not know.

Speaking about the instinct that makes people rich, the same writer remarks:

'In olden days its existence was fully understood. The Greeks enshrined it in the story of Midas, of the

"Golden Touch." Here was a man who turned everything he laid his hands upon into gold. His life was a
progress amidst riches. Out of everything that came
in his way he created the precious metal. "A foolish
legend," said the wiseacres of the Victorian age. "A
truth," say we of to-day. We all know of such men.
We are ever meeting or reading about such persons who
turn everything they touch into gold. Success dogs
their very footsteps. Their life's pathway leads unerringly upwards. They cannot fail.'

Unfortunately, however, Midas could fail; he did.
His path did not lead unerringly upward. He starved
because whenever he touched a biscuit or a ham sand-
wich it turned to gold. That was the whole point of
the story, though the writer has to suppress it delicately,
writing so near to a portrait of Lord Rothschild. The
old fables of mankind are, indeed, unfathomably wise;
but we must not have them expurgated in the interests
of Mr. Vanderbilt. We must not have King Midas
represented as an example of success; he was a failure
of an unusually painful kind. Also, he had the ears of
an ass. Also (like most other prominent and wealthy
persons) he endeavoured to conceal the fact. It was
his barber (if I remember right) who had to be treated
on a confidential footing with regard to this peculiarity;
and his barber, instead of behaving like a go-ahead
person of the Succeed-at-all-costs school and trying to
blackmail King Midas, went away and whispered this
splendid piece of society scandal to the reeds, who
enjoyed it enormously. It is said that they also whispered it as the winds swayed them to and fro. I look
reverently at the portrait of Lord Rothschild; I read
reverently about the exploits of Mr. Vanderbilt. I know
that I cannot turn everything I touch to gold; but then
I also know that I have never tried, having a preference
for other substances, such as grass, and good wine. I
know that these people have certainly succeeded in
something: that they have certainly overcome somebody; I know that they are kings in a sense that no
men were ever kings before; that they create markets

and bestride continents. Yet it always seems to me that there is some small domestic fact that they are hiding, and I have sometimes thought I heard upon the wind the laughter and whisper of the reeds.

At least, let us hope that we shall all live to see these absurd books about Success covered with a proper derision and neglect. They do not teach people to be successful, but they do teach people to be snobbish; they do spread a sort of evil poetry of worldliness. The Puritans are always denouncing books that inflame lust; what shall we say of books that inflame the viler passions of avarice and pride? A hundred years ago we had the ideal of the Industrious Apprentice; boys were told that by thrift and work they would all become Lord Mayors. This was fallacious, but it was manly, and had a minimum of moral truth. In our society, temperance will not help a poor man to enrich himself, but it may help him to respect himself. Good work will not make him a rich man, but good work may make him a good workman. The Industrious Apprentice rose by virtues few and narrow indeed, but still virtues. But what shall we say of the gospel preached to the new Industrious Apprentice; the Apprentice who rises not by his virtues, but avowedly by his vices?

TOM JONES AND MORALITY

THE two hundredth anniversary of Henry Fielding is very justly celebrated, even if, as far as can be discovered, it is only celebrated by the newspapers. It would be too much to expect that any such merely chronological incident should induce the people who write about Fielding to read him; this kind of neglect is only another name for glory. A great classic means a man whom one can praise without having read. This is not in itself wholly unjust; it merely implies a certain respect for the realization and fixed conclusions of the mass of mankind. I have never read Pindar (I mean I have never read the Greek Pindar; Peter Pindar I have read all right), but the mere fact that I have not read Pindar, I think, ought not to prevent me and certainly would not prevent me from talking of 'the masterpieces of Pindar,' or of 'great poets like Pindar or Aeschylus.' The very learned men are singularly unenlightened on this as on many other subjects; and the position they take up is really quite unreasonable. If any ordinary journalist or man of general reading alludes to Villon or to Homer, they consider it a quite triumphant sneer to say to the man: 'You cannot read medieval French,' or: 'You cannot read Homeric Greek.' But it is not a triumphant sneer—or, indeed, a sneer at all. A man has got as much right to employ in his speech the established and traditional facts of human history as he has to employ any other piece of common human information. And it is as reasonable for a man who knows no French to assume that Villon was a good poet as it would be for a man who has no ear for music to assume that Beethoven was a good musician. Because he himself has no ear for music, that is no reason why he should assume that the human race has no ear for music. Because I am ignorant (as

138

I am), it does not follow that I ought to assume that I am deceived. The man who would not praise Pindar unless he had read him would be a low, distrustful fellow, the worst kind of sceptic, who doubts not only God, but man. He would be like a man who could not call Mount Everest high unless he had climbed it. He would be like a man who would not admit that the North Pole was cold until he had been there.

But I think there is a limit, and a highly legitimate limit, to this process. I think a man may praise Pindar without knowing the top of a Greek letter from the bottom. But I think that if a man is going to abuse Pindar, if he is going to denounce, refute, and utterly expose Pindar, if he is going to show Pindar up as the utter ignoramus and outrageous impostor that he is, then I think it will be just as well perhaps—I think, at any rate, it would do no harm—if he did know a little Greek, and even had read a little Pindar. And I think the same situation would be involved if the critic were concerned to point out that Pindar was scandalously immoral, pestilently cynical, or low and beastly in his views of life. When people brought such attacks against the morality of Pindar, I should regret that they could not read Greek; and when they bring such attacks against the morality of Fielding, I regret very much that they cannot read English.

There seems to be an extraordinary idea abroad that Fielding was in some way an immoral or offensive writer. I have been astounded by the number of the leading articles, literary articles, and other articles written about him just now in which there is a curious tone of apologizing for the man. One critic says that after all he couldn't help it, because he lived in the eighteenth century; another says that we must allow for the change of manners and ideas; another says that he was not altogether without generous and humane feelings; another suggests that he clung feebly, after all, to a few of the less important virtues. What on earth does all this mean? Fielding described Tom Jones as going on in a certain way, in which, most unfortu-

nately, a very large number of young men do go on.   It
is unnecessary to say that Henry Fielding knew that it
was an unfortunate way of going on.   Even Tom Jones
knew that.   He said in so many words that it was a
very unfortunate way of going on; he said, one may
almost say, that it had ruined his life; the passage is
there for the benefit of any one who may take the trouble
to read the book.   There is ample evidence (though even
this is of a mystical and indirect kind), there is ample
evidence that Fielding probably thought that it was
better to be Tom Jones than to be an utter coward and
sneak.   There is simply not one rag or thread or speck
of evidence to show that Fielding thought that it was
better to be Tom Jones than to be a good man.   All
that he is concerned with is the description of a definite
and very real type of young man; the young man whose
passions and whose selfish necessities sometimes seemed
to be stronger than anything else in him.

The practical morality of Tom Jones is bad, though
not so bad, *spiritually* speaking, as the practical morality
of Arthur Pendennis or the practical morality of Pip,
and certainly nothing like so bad as the profound
practical immorality of Daniel Deronda.   The practical
morality of Tom Jones is bad; but I cannot see any
proof that his theoretical morality was particularly bad.
There is no need to tell the majority of modern young
men even to live up to the theoretical ethics of Henry
Fielding.   They would suddenly spring into the stature
of archangels if they lived up to the theoretic ethics of
poor Tom Jones.   Tom Jones is still alive, with all his
good and all his evil; he is walking about the streets; we
meet him every day.   We meet with him, we drink
with him, we smoke with him, we talk with him, we
talk about him   The only difference is that we have no
longer the intellectual courage to write about him.   We
split up the supreme and central human being, Tom
Jones, into a number of separate aspects.   We let Mr.
J. M. Barrie write about him in his good moments, and
make him out better than he is.   We let Zola write
about him in his bad moments, and make him out much

worse than he is. We let Maeterlinck celebrate those moments of spiritual panic which he knows to be cowardly; we let Mr. Rudyard Kipling celebrate those moments of brutality which he knows to be far more cowardly. We let obscene writers write about the obscenities of this ordinary man. We let puritan writers write about the purities of this ordinary man. We look through one peephole that makes men out as devils, and we call it the new art. We look through another peephole that makes men out as angels, and we call it the New Theology. But if we pull down some dusty old books from the bookshelf, if we turn over some old mildewed leaves, and if in that obscurity and decay we find some faint traces of a tale about a complete man, such a man as is walking on the pavement outside, we suddenly pull a long face, and we call it the coarse morals of a bygone age.

The truth is that all these things mark a certain change in the general view of morals; not, I think, a change for the better. We have grown to associate morality in a book with a kind of optimism and prettiness; according to us, a moral book is a book about moral people. But the old idea was almost exactly the opposite; a moral book was a book about immoral people. A moral book was full of pictures like Hogarth's 'Gin Lane' or 'Stages of Cruelty,' or it recorded, like the popular broadsheet, 'God's dreadful judgment' against some blasphemer or murderer. There is a philosophical reason for this change. The homeless scepticism of our time has reached a subconscious feeling that morality is somehow merely a matter of human taste—an accident of psychology. And if goodness only exists in certain human minds, a man wishing to praise goodness will naturally exaggerate the amount of it that there is in human minds or the number of human minds in which it is supreme. Every confession that man is vicious is a confession that virtue is visionary. Every book which admits that evil is real is felt in some vague way to be admitting that good is unreal. The modern instinct is that if the heart of man is evil, there is nothing that remains good. But the older feeling was that if the heart of man was ever so evil, there was something that remained good — goodness remained good. An actual avenging virtue existed ouside the human race; to that men rose, or from that men fell away. Therefore, of course, this law itself was as much demonstrated in the breach as in the observance. If Tom Jones violated morality, so much the worse for Tom Jones. Fielding did not feel, as a melancholy modern would have done, that every sin of Tom Jones was in some way breaking the spell, or we may even say destroying the fiction, of morality. Men spoke of the sinner breaking the law; but it was rather the law that broke him. And what modern people call the foulness and freedom of Fielding is generally the severity and moral stringency of Fielding. He would not have thought that he was serving morality at all if he had written a book all about nice people. Fielding would have considered Mr. Ian Maclaren extremely immoral; and there is something to be said for that view. Telling the truth about the terrible struggle of the human soul is surely a very elementary part of the ethics of honesty. If the characters are not wicked, the book is.

This older and firmer conception of right as existing outside human weakness and without reference to human error can be felt in the very lightest and loosest of the works of old English literature. It is commonly unmeaning enough to call Shakespeare a great moralist; but in this particular way Shakespeare is a very typical moralist. Whenever he alludes to right and wrong it is always with this old implication. Right is right, even if nobody does it. Wrong is wrong, even if everybody is wrong about it.

FRENCH AND ENGLISH

It is obvious that there is a great deal of difference between being international and being cosmopolitan. All good men are international. Nearly all bad men are cosmopolitan. If we are to be international we must be national. And it is largely because those who call themselves the friends of peace have not dwelt sufficiently on this distinction that they do not impress the bulk of any of the nations to which they belong. International peace means a peace between nations, not a peace after the destruction of nations, like the Buddhist peace after the destruction of personality. The golden age of the good European is like the heaven of the Christian: it is a place where people will love each other; not like the heaven of the Hindu, a place where they will be each other. And in the case of national character this can be seen in a curious way. It will generally be found, I think, that the more a man really appreciates and admires the soul of another people the less he will attempt to imitate it; he will be conscious that there is something in it too deep and too unmanageable to imitate. The Englishman who has a fancy for France will try to be French; the Englishman who admires France will remain obstinately English. This is to be particularly noticed in the case of our relations with the French, because it is one of the outstanding peculiarities of the French that their vices are all on the surface, and their extraordinary virtues concealed. One might almost say that their vices are the flower of their virtues.

Thus their obscenity is the expression of their passionate love of dragging all things into the light. The avarice of their peasants means the independence of their peasants. What the English call their rudeness in the streets is a phase of their social equality. The worried look of their women is connected with the responsibility of their women; and a certain unconscious brutality of hurry and gesture in the men is related to their inexhaustible and extraordinary military courage. Of all countries, therefore, France is the worst country for a superficial fool to admire. Let a fool hate France: if the fool loves it he will soon be a knave. He will certainly admire it, not only for the things that are not creditable, but actually for the things that are not there. He will admire the grace and indolence of the most industrious people in the world. He will admire the romance and fantasy of the most determinedly respectable and commonplace people in the world. This mistake the Englishman will make if he admires France too hastily; but the mistake that he makes about France will be slight compared with the mistake that he makes about himself. An Englishman who professes really to like French realistic novels, really to be at home in a French modern theatre, really to experience no shock on first seeing the savage French caricatures, is making a mistake very dangerous for his own sincerity. He is admiring something he does not understand. He is reaping where he has not sown, and taking up where he has not laid down; he is trying to taste the fruit when he has never toiled over the tree. He is trying to pluck the exquisite fruit of French cynicism, when he has never tilled the rude but rich soil of French virtue.

The thing can only be made clear to Englishmen by turning it round. Suppose a Frenchman came out of democratic France to live in England, where the shadow of the great houses still falls everywhere, and where even freedom was, in its origin, aristocratic. If the Frenchman saw our aristocracy and liked it, if he saw our snobbishness and liked it, if he set himself to imitate it, we all know what we should feel. We all know that we should feel that that particular Frenchman was a repulsive little gnat. He would be imitating English aristocracy; he would be imitating the English vice. But he would not even understand the vice he plagiarized: especially he would not understand that

the vice is partly a virtue. He would not understand
those elements in the English which balance snobbishness and make it human: the great kindness of the
English, their hospitality, their unconscious poetry,
their sentimental conservatism, which really admires
the gentry. The French Royalist sees that the English
like their King. But he does not grasp that while it
is base to worship a King, it is almost noble to worship
a powerless King. The impotence of the Hanoverian
Sovereigns has raised the English loyal subject almost
to the chivalry and dignity of a Jacobite. The Frenchman sees that the English servant is respectful: he does
not realize that he is also disrespectful; that there is
an English legend of the humorous and faithful servant,
who is as much a personality as his master; the Caleb
Balderstone, the Sam Weller. He sees that the English
do admire a nobleman; he does not allow for the fact
that they admire a nobleman most when he does not
behave like one. They like a noble to be unconscious
and amiable: the slave may be humble, but the master
must not be proud. The master is Life, as they would
like to enjoy it; and among the joys they desire in him
there is none which they desire more sincerely than that
of generosity, of throwing money about among mankind, or, to use the noble medieval word, largesse—the
joy of largeness. That is why a cabman tells you you
are no gentleman if you give him his correct fare. Not
only his pocket, but his soul is hurt. You have wounded
his ideal. You have defaced his vision of the perfect
aristocrat. All this is really very subtle and elusive;
it is very difficult to separate what is mere slavishness
from what is a sort of vicarious nobility in the English
love of a lord. And no Frenchman could easily grasp
it at all. He would think it was mere slavishness; and
if he liked it, he would be a slave. So every Englishman must (at first) feel French candour to be mere
brutality. And if he likes it, he is a brute. These
national merits must not be understood so easily. It
requires long years of plenitude and quiet, the slow
growth of great parks, the seasoning of oaken beams,

the dark enrichment of red wine in cellars and in inns, all the leisure and the life of England through many centuries, to produce at last the generous and genial fruit of English snobbishness. And it requires battery and barricade, songs in the streets, and ragged men dead for an idea, to produce and justify the terrible flower of French indecency.

When I was in Paris a short time ago, I went with an English friend of mine to an extremely brilliant and rapid succession of French plays, each occupying about twenty minutes. They were all astonishingly effective; but there was one of them which was so effective that my friend and I fought about it outside, and had almost to be separated by the police. It was intended to indicate how men really behaved in a wreck or naval disaster, how they break down, how they scream, how they fight each other without object and in a mere hatred of everything. And then there was added, with all that horrible irony which Voltaire began, a scene in which a great statesman made a speech over their bodies, saying that they were all heroes and had died in a fraternal embrace. My friend and I came out of this theatre, and as he had lived long in Paris, he said, like a Frenchman: 'What admirable artistic arrangement! Is it not exquisite?' 'No,' I replied, assuming as far as possible the traditional attitude of John Bull in the pictures in *Punch* — 'No, it is not exquisite. Perhaps it is unmeaning; if it is unmeaning I do not mind. But if it has a meaning I know what the meaning is; it is that under all their pageant of chivalry men are not only beasts, but even hunted beasts. I do not know much of humanity, especially when humanity talks in French. But I know when a thing is meant to uplift the human soul, and when it is meant to depress it. I know that *Cyrano de Bergerac* (where the actors talked even quicker) was meant to encourage man. And I know that this was meant to discourage him.' 'These sentimental and moral views of art,' began my friend, but I broke into his words as a light broke into my mind. 'Let me say to you,' I said, 'what Jaurès

said to Liebknecht at the Socialist Conference: "You
have not died on the barricades." You are an Englishman, as I am, and you ought to be as amiable as I am.
These people have some right to be terrible in art, for
they have been terrible in politics. They may endure
mock tortures on the stage; they have seen real tortures
in the streets. They have been hurt for the idea of
Democracy. They have been hurt for the idea of
Catholicism. It is not so utterly unnatural to them
that they should be hurt for the idea of literature. But,
by blazes, it is altogether unnatural to me! And the
worst thing of all is that I, who am an Englishman,
loving comfort, should find comfort in such things as
this. The French do not seek comfort here, but rather
unrest. This restless people seeks to keep itself in a
perpetual agony of the revolutionary mood. Frenchmen, seeking revolution, may find the humiliation of
humanity inspiring. But God forbid that two pleasure-
seeking Englishmen should ever find it pleasant!'

WINE WHEN IT IS RED

I SUPPOSE that there will be some wigs on the green in connection with the recent manifesto signed by a string of very eminent doctors on the subject of what is called 'alcohol.' 'Alcohol' is, to judge by the sound of it, an Arabic word, like 'algebra' and 'Alhambra,' those two other unpleasant things. The Alhambra in Spain I have never seen; I am told that it is a low and rambling building; I allude to the far more dignified erection in Leicester Square. If it is true, as I surmise, that 'alcohol' is a word of the Arabs, it is interesting to realize that our general word for the essence of wine and beer and such things comes from a people which has made particular war upon them. I suppose that some aged Moslem chieftain sat one day at the opening of his tent and, brooding with black brows and cursing in his black beard over wine as the symbol of Christianity, racked his brains for some word ugly enough to express his racial and religious antipathy, and suddenly spat out the horrible word 'alcohol.' The fact that the doctors had to use this word for the sake of scientific clearness was really a great disadvantage to them in fairly discussing the matter. For the word really involves one of those beggings of the question which make these moral matters so difficult. It is quite a mistake to suppose that, when a man desires an alcoholic drink, he necessarily desires alcohol.

Let a man walk ten miles steadily on a hot summer's day along a dusty English road, and he will soon discover why beer was invented. The fact that beer has a very slight stimulating quality will be quite among the smallest reasons that induce him to ask for it. In short, he will not be in the least desiring alcohol; he will be desiring beer. But, of course, the question cannot be settled in such a simple way. The real difficulty which

148

confronts everybody, and which especially confronts doctors, is that the extraordinary position of man in the physical universe makes it practically impossible to treat him in either one direction or the other in a purely physical way. Man is an exception, whatever else he is. If he is not the image of God, then he is a disease of the dust. If it is not true that a divine being fell, then we can only say that one of the animals went entirely off its head. In neither case can we really argue very much from the body of man simply considered as the body of an innocent and healthy animal. His body has got too much mixed up with his soul, as we see in the supreme instance of sex. It may be worth while uttering the warning to wealthy philanthropists and idealists that this argument from the animal should not be thoughtlessly used, even against the atrocious evils of excess; it is an argument that proves too little or too much. Doubtless, it is unnatural to be drunk. But then in a real sense it is unnatural to be human. Doubtless, the intemperate workman wastes his tissues in drinking; but no one knows how much the sober workman wastes his tissues by working. No one knows how much the wealthy philanthropist wastes his tissues by talking; or, in much rarer conditions, by thinking. All the human things are more dangerous than anything that affects the beasts—sex, poetry, property, religion. The real case against drunkenness is not that it calls up the beast, but that it calls up the Devil. It does not call up the beast, and if it did it would not matter much, as a rule; the beast is a harmless and rather amiable creature, as anybody can see by watching cattle. There is nothing bestial about intoxication; and certainly there is nothing intoxicating or even particularly lively about beasts. Man is always something worse or something better than an animal; and a mere argument from animal perfection never touches him at all. Thus, in sex no animal is either chivalrous or obscene. And thus no animal ever invented anything so bad as drunkenness—or so good as drink.

The pronouncement of these particular doctors is very clear and uncompromising; in the modern atmosphere, indeed, it even deserves some credit for moral courage. The majority of modern people, of course, will probably agree with it in so far as it declares that alcoholic drinks are often of supreme value in emergencies of illness; but many people, I fear, will open their eyes at the emphatic terms in which they describe such drink as considered as a beverage; but they are not content with declaring that the drink is in moderation harmless: they distinctly declare that it is in moderation beneficial.   But I fancy that, in saying this, the doctors had in mind a truth that runs somewhat counter to the common opinion.   I fancy that it is the experience of most doctors that giving any alcohol for illness (though often necessary) is about the most morally dangerous way of giving it. Instead of giving it to a healthy person who has many other forms of life, you are giving it to a desperate person, to whom it is the only form of life.   The invalid can hardly be blamed if by some accident of his erratic and overwrought condition he comes to remember the thing as the very water of vitality and to use it as such. For in so far as drinking is really a sin it is not because drinking is wild, but because drinking is tame; not in so far as it is anarchy, but in so far as it is slavery.   Probably the worst way to drink is to drink medicinally. Certainly the safest way to drink is to drink carelessly; that is, without caring much for anything, and especially not caring for the drink.

The doctor, of course, ought to be able to do a great deal in the way of restraining those individual cases where there is plainly an evil thirst; and beyond that the only hope would seem to be in some increase, or, rather, some concentration of ordinary public opinion on the subject.   I have always held consistently my own modest theory on the subject.   I believe that if by some method the local public-house could be as definite and isolated a place as the local post office or the local railway station, if all types of people passed through it for all types of refreshment, you would have the same

safeguard against a man behaving in a disgusting way
in a tavern that you have at present against his behaving
in a disgusting way in a post office: simply the presence
of his ordinary sensible neighbours. In such a place
the kind of lunatic who wants to drink an unlimited
number of whiskies would be treated with the same
severity with which the post-office authorities would
treat an amiable lunatic who had an appetite for licking
an unlimited number of stamps. It is a small matter
whether in either case a technical refusal would be
officially employed. It is an essential matter that in
both cases the authorities could rapidly communicate
with the friends and family of the mentally afflicted
person. At least, the postmistress would not dangle
a strip of tempting sixpenny stamps before the enthu-
siast's eyes as he was being dragged away with his
tongue out. If we made drinking open and official we
might be taking one step towards making it careless.
In such things to be careless is to be sane: for neither
drunkards nor Moslems can be careless about drink.

THE GARDENER AND THE GUINEA

STRICTLY speaking, there is no such thing as an English Peasant. Indeed, the type can only exist in community, so much does it depend on co-operation and common laws. One must not think primarily of a French Peasant, any more than of a German Measle. The plural of the word is its proper form; you cannot have a Peasant till you have a peasantry. The essence of the Peasant ideal is equality; and you cannot be equal all by yourself.

Nevertheless, because human nature always craves and half creates the things necessary to its happiness, there are approximations and suggestions of the possibility of such a race even here. The nearest approach I know to the temper of a Peasant in England is that of the country gardener; not, of course, the great scientific gardener attached to the great houses; he is a rich man's servant like any other. I mean the small jobbing gardener who works for two or three moderate-sized gardens; who works on his own; who sometimes even owns his house; and who frequently owns his tools. This kind of man has really some of the characteristics of the true Peasant—especially the characteristics that people don't like. He has none of that irresponsible mirth which is the consolation of most poor men in England. The gardener is even disliked sometimes by the owners of the shrubs and flowers; because (like Micaiah) he prophesies not good concerning them, but evil. The English gardener is grim, critical, self-respecting; sometimes even economical. Nor is this (as the reader's lightning wit will flash back at me) merely because the English gardener is always a Scotch gardener. The type does exist in pure South England blood and speech; I have spoken to the type. I was speaking to the type only the other evening, when a rather odd little incident occurred.

.　　.　　.　　.　　.　　.

It was one of those wonderful evenings in which the sky was warm and radiant while the earth was still comparatively cold and wet. But it is of the essence of Spring to be unexpected; as in that heroic and hackneyed line about coming 'before the swallow dares.' Spring never is Spring unless it comes too soon. And on a day like that one might pray, without any profanity, that Spring might come on earth, as it was in heaven. The gardener was gardening. I was not gardening. It is needless to explain the causes of this difference; it would be to tell the tremendous history of two souls. It is needless because there is a more immediate explanation of the case: the gardener and I, if not equal in agreement, were at least equal in difference. It is quite certain that he would not have allowed me to touch the garden if I had gone down on my knees to him. And it is by no means certain that I should have consented to touch the garden if he had gone down on his knees to me. His activity and my idleness, therefore, went on steadily side by side through the long sunset hours.

And all the time I was thinking what a shame it was that he was not sticking his spade into his own garden, instead of mine: he knew about the earth and the underworld of seeds, the resurrection of Spring and the flowers that appear in order like a procession marshalled by a herald. He possessed the garden intellectually and spiritually, while I only possessed it politically. I know more about flowers than coal-owners know about coal; for at least I pay them honour when they are brought above the surface of the earth. I know more about gardens than railway shareholders seem to know about railways: for at least I know that it needs a man to make a garden; a man whose name is Adam. But as I walked on that grass my ignorance overwhelmed me—and yet that phrase is false, because it suggests something like a storm from the sky above. It is truer to say that my ignorance exploded underneath me, like a mine dug long before; and indeed it was dug before the beginning of the ages. Green bombs of bulbs and seeds were bursting underneath me everywhere; and, so far as my knowledge went, they had been laid by a conspirator. I trod quite uneasily on this uprush of the earth; the Spring is always only a fruitful earthquake. With the land all alive under me I began to wonder more and more why this man, who had made the garden, did not own the garden. If I stuck a spade into the ground, I should be astonished at what I found there . . . and just as I thought this I saw that the gardener was astonished too.

Just as I was wondering why the man who used the spade did not profit by the spade, he brought me something he had found actually in my soil. It was a thin worn gold piece of the Georges, of the sort which are called, I believe, Spade Guineas. Anyhow, a piece of gold.

.   .   .   .   .   .

If you do not see the parable as I saw it just then, I doubt if I can explain it just now. He could make a hundred other round yellow fruits: and this flat yellow one is the only sort that I can make. How it came there I have not a notion—unless Edmund Burke dropped it in his hurry to get back to Butler's Court. But there it was: this is a cold recital of facts. There may be a whole pirate's treasure lying under the earth there, for all I know or care; for there is no interest in a treasure without a Treasure Island to sail to. If there is a treasure it will never be found, for I am not interested in wealth beyond the dreams of avarice—since I know that avarice has no dreams, but only insomnia. And, for the other party, my gardener would never consent to dig up the garden.

Nevertheless, I was overwhelmed with intellectual emotions when I saw that answer to my question: the question of why the garden did not belong to the

gardener. No better epigram could be put in reply
than simply putting the Spade Guinea beside the Spade.
This was the only underground seed that I could understand. Only by having a little more of that dull,
battered yellow substance could I manage to be idle
while he was active. I am not altogether idle myself;
but the fact remains that the power is in the thin slip
of metal we call the Spade Guinea, not in the strong
square and curve of metal which we call the Spade.
And then I suddenly remembered that as I had found
gold on my ground by accident, so richer men in the
north and west counties had found coal in their ground,
also by accident.

I told the gardener that as he had found the thing
he ought to keep it, but that if he cared to sell it to me
it could be valued properly, and then sold. He said,
at first with characteristic independence, that he would
like to keep it. He said it would make a brooch for his
wife. But a little later he brought it back to me without
explanation. I could not get a ray of light on the reason
of his refusal; but he looked lowering and unhappy.
Had he some mystical instinct that it is just such
accidental and irrational wealth that is the doom of all
peasantries? Perhaps he dimly felt that the boy's
pirate tales are true; and that buried treasure is a thing
for robbers and not for producers. Perhaps he thought
there was a curse on such capital: on the coal of the
coal-owners, on the gold of the gold-seekers. Perhaps
there is.

THE MAD OFFICIAL

GOING mad is the slowest and dullest business in the world. I have very nearly done it more than once in my boyhood, and so have nearly all my friends, born under the general doom of mortals, but especially of moderns; I mean the doom that makes a man come almost to the end of thinking before he comes to the first chance of living.

But the process of going mad is dull, for the simple reason that a man does not know that it is going on. Routine and literalism and a certain dry-throated earnestness and mental thirst, these are the very atmosphere of morbidity. If once the man could become conscious of his madness, he would cease to be mad. He studies certain texts in Daniel or cryptograms in Shakespeare through monstrously magnifying spectacles, which are on his nose night and day. If once he could take off the spectacles he would smash them. He deduces all his fantasies about the Sixth Seal or the Anglo-Saxon Race from one unexamined and invisible first principle. If he could once see the first principle, he would see that it is not there.

This slow and awful self-hypnotism of error is a process that can occur not only with individuals, but also with whole societies. It is hard to pick out and prove; that is why it is hard to cure. But this mental degeneration may be brought to one test, which I truly believe to be a real test. A nation is not going mad when it does extravagant things, so long as it does them in an extravagant spirit. Crusaders not cutting their beards till they found Jerusalem, Jacobins calling each other Harmodius and Epaminondas when their names were Jacques and Jules: these are wild things, but they were done in wild spirits at a wild moment.

. . . .

But whenever we see things done wildly, but taken tamely, then the State is growing insane. For instance, I have a gun licence. For all I know, this would logically allow me to fire off fifty-nine enormous field-guns day and night in my back garden. I should not be surprised at a man doing it; for it would be great fun. But I should be surprised at the neighbours putting up with it, and regarding it as an ordinary thing merely because it might happen to fulfil the letter of my licence.

Or, again, I have a dog licence; and I may have the right (for all I know) to turn ten thousand wild dogs loose in Buckinghamshire. I should not be surprised if the law were like that; because in modern England there is practically no law to be surprised at. I should not be surprised even at the man who did it; for a certain kind of man, if he lived long under the English landlord system, might do anything. But I should be surprised at the people who consented to stand it. I should, in other words, think the world a little mad if the incident were received in silence.

.   .   .   .   .   .

Now things every bit as wild as this are being received in silence every day. All strokes slip on the smoothness of a polished wall. All blows fall soundless on the soft-ness of a padded cell. For madness is a passive as well as an active state: it is a paralysis, a refusal of the nerves to respond to the normal stimuli, as well as an unnatural stimulation. There are commonwealths, plainly to be distinguished here and there in history, which pass from prosperity to squalor, or from glory to insignificance, or from freedom to slavery, not only in silence, but with serenity. The face still smiles while the limbs, literally and loathsomely, are dropping from the body. There are peoples that have lost the power of astonishment at their own actions. When they give birth to a fantastic fashion or a foolish law, they do not start or stare at the monster they have brought forth. They have grown used to their own unreason; chaos is their cosmos; and the whirlwind is the breath of their

nostrils. These nations are really in danger of going
off their heads *en masse*; of becoming one vast vision of
imbecility, with toppling cities and crazy country-sides,
all dotted with industrious lunatics. One of these
countries is modern England.

.   .   .   .   .   .

Now here is an actual instance, a small case of how
our social conscience really works: tame in spirit, wild
in result, blank in realization; a thing without the light
of mind in it. I take this paragraph from a daily paper:
'At Epping, yesterday, Thomas Woolbourne, a Lam-
bourne labourer, and his wife were summoned for
neglecting their five children. Dr. Alpin said he was
invited by the inspector of the N.S.P.C.C. to visit
defendants' cottage. Both the cottage and the children
were dirty. The children looked exceedingly well in
health, but the conditions would be serious in case of
illness. Defendants were stated to be sober. The man
was discharged. The woman, who said she was hampered by the cottage having no water supply and that
she was ill, was sentenced to six weeks' imprisonment.
The sentence caused surprise, and the woman was
removed crying: "Lord, save me!"'
I know no name for this but Chinese. It calls up
the mental picture of some archaic and changeless
Eastern Court, in which men with dried faces and stiff
ceremonial costumes perform some atrocious cruelty to
the accompaniment of formal proverbs and sentences of
which the very meaning has been forgotten. In both
cases the only thing in the whole farrago that can be
called real is the wrong. If we apply the lightest touch
of reason to the whole Epping prosecution it dissolves
into nothing.
I here challenge any person in his five wits to tell me
what that woman was sent to prison for. Either it was
for being poor, or it was for being ill. Nobody could
suggest, nobody will suggest, nobody, as a matter of
fact, did suggest, that she had committed any other
crime. The doctor was called in by a Society for the

Prevention of Cruelty to Children. Was this woman guilty of cruelty to children? Not in the least. Did the doctor say she was guilty of cruelty to children? Not in the least. Was there any evidence even remotely bearing on the sin of cruelty? Not a rap. The worst that the doctor could work himself up to saying was that though the children were 'exceedingly' well, the conditions would be serious in case of illness. If the doctor will tell me any conditions that would be comic in case of illness, I shall attach more weight to his argument.

Now this is the worst effect of modern worry. The mad doctor has gone mad. He is literally and practically mad; and still he is quite literally and practically a doctor. The only question is the old one: *Quis docebit ipsum doctorem ?* Now cruelty to children is an utterly unnatural thing; instinctively accursed of earth and heaven. But neglect of children is a natural thing; like neglect of any other duty. It is a mere difference of degree that divides extending arms and legs in callisthenics and extending them on the rack. It is a mere difference of degree that separates any operation from any torture. The thumb-screw can easily be called Manicure. Being pulled about by wild horses can easily be called Massage. The modern problem is not so much what people will endure as what they will not endure. But I fear I interrupt. . . . The boiling oil is boiling; and the Tenth Mandarin is already reciting the 'Seventeen Serious Principles and the Fifty-three Virtues of the Sacred Emperor.'

THE PRIEST OF SPRING

THE sun has strengthened and the air softened just before Easter Day. But it is a troubled brightness which has a breath not only of novelty but of revolution. There are two great armies of the human intellect who will fight till the end on this vital point, whether Easter is to be congratulated on fitting in with the Spring—or the Spring on fitting in with Easter.

The only two things that can satisfy the soul are a person and a story; and even a story must be about a person. There are indeed very voluptuous appetites and enjoyments in mere abstractions—like mathematics, logic, or chess. But these mere pleasures of the mind are like mere pleasures of the body. That is, they are mere pleasures, though they may be gigantic pleasures; they can never by a mere increase of themselves amount to happiness. A man just about to be hanged may enjoy his breakfast, especially if it be his favourite breakfast; and in the same way he may enjoy an argument with the chaplain about heresy, especially if it is his favourite heresy. But whether he can enjoy either of them does not depend on either of them; it depends upon his spiritual attitude towards a subsequent event. And that event is really interesting to the soul; because it is the end of a story and (as some hold) the end of a person.

.　　.　　.　　.　　.　　.

Now it is this simple truth which, like many others, is too simple for our scientists to see. This is where they go wrong, not only about true religion, but about false religions too; so that their account of mythology is more mythical than the myth itself. I do not confine myself to saying that they are quite incorrect when they

160

state (for instance) that Christ was a legend of dying and
reviving vegetation, like Adonis or Persephone. I say
that even if Adonis was a god of vegetation, they have
got the whole notion of him wrong. Nobody, to begin
with, is sufficiently interested in decaying vegetables, as
such, to make any particular mystery or disguise about
them; and certainly not enough to disguise them under
the image of a very handsome young man, which is a
vastly more interesting thing. If Adonis was connected with the fall of leaves in autumn and the return
of flowers in spring, the process of thought was quite
different. It is a process of thought which springs up
spontaneously in all children and young artists; it
springs up spontaneously in all healthy societies. It is
very difficult to explain in a diseased society.

The brain of man is subject to short and strange
snatches of sleep. A cloud seals the city of reason or
rests upon the sea of imagination; a dream that darkens
as much, whether it is a nightmare of atheism or a day-
dream of idolatry. And just as we have all sprung from
sleep with a start and found ourselves saying some
sentence that has no meaning, save in the mad tongues
of the midnight, so the human mind starts from its
trances of stupidity with some complete phrase upon its
lips: a complete phrase which is a complete folly. Unfortunately it is not like the dream sentence, generally
forgotten in the putting on of boots or the putting in
of breakfast. This senseless aphorism, invented when
man's mind was asleep, still hangs on his tongue and
entangles all his relations to rational and daylight
things. All our controversies are confused by certain
kinds of phrases which are not merely untrue, but were
always unmeaning; which are not merely inapplicable,
but were always intrinsically useless. We recognize
them wherever a man talks of 'the survival of the
fittest,' meaning only the survival of the survivors; or
wherever a man says that the rich 'have a stake in the
country,' as if the poor could not suffer from misgovern-
ment or military defeat; or where a man talks about
'going on towards Progress,' which only means going

on towards going on; or when a man talks about 'government by the wise few,' as if they could be picked out
by their pantaloons. 'The wise few' must mean either
the few whom the foolish think wise or the very foolish
who think themselves wise.

There is one piece of nonsense that modern people
still find themselves saying, even after they are more or
less awake, by which I am particularly irritated. It
arose in the popularized science of the nineteenth
century, especially in connection with the study of
myths and religions. The fragment of gibberish to
which I refer generally takes the form of saying: 'This
god or hero really represents the sun.' Or: 'Apollo
killing the Python *means* that the summer drives out
the winter.' Or: 'The King dying in a western battle
is a *symbol* of the sun setting in the west.' Now I should
really have thought that even the sceptical professors,
whose skulls are as shallow as frying-pans, might have
reflected that human beings never think or feel like this.
Consider what is involved in this supposition. It pre-
sumes that primitive man went out for a walk and saw
with great interest a big burning spot on the sky. He
then said to primitive woman: 'My dear, we had better
keep this quiet. We mustn't let it get about. The
children and the slaves are so very sharp. They might
discover the sun any day, unless we are very careful.
So we won't call it "the sun," but I will draw a picture
of a man killing a snake; and whenever I do that you
will know what I mean. The sun doesn't look at all
like a man killing a snake; so nobody can possibly know.
It will be a little secret between us; and while the slaves
and the children fancy I am quite excited with a grand
tale of a writhing dragon and a wrestling demigod, I
shall really *mean* this delicious little discovery, that
there is a round yellow disk up in the air.' One does
not need to know much mythology to know that this is
a myth. It is commonly called the Solar Myth.

Quite plainly, of course, the case was just the other
way. The god was never a symbol or hieroglyph
representing the sun. The sun was a hieroglyph repre-

senting the god. Primitive man (with whom my friend Dombey is no doubt well acquainted) went out with his head full of gods and heroes, because that is the chief use of having a head. Then he saw the sun in some glorious crisis of the dominance of noon or the distress of nightfall, and he said: 'That is how the face of the god would shine when he had slain the dragon,' or: 'That is how the whole world would bleed to westward, if the god were slain at last.'

No human being was ever really so unnatural as to worship Nature. No man, however indulgent (as I am) to corpulency, ever worshipped a man as round as the sun or a woman as round as the moon. No man, however attracted to an artistic attenuation, ever really believed that the Dryad was as lean and stiff as the tree. We human beings have never worshipped Nature; and indeed, the reason is very simple. It is that all human beings are superhuman beings. We have printed our own image upon Nature, as God has printed His image upon us. We have told the enormous sun to stand still; we have fixed him on our shields, caring no more for a star than for a starfish. And when there were powers of Nature we could not for the time control, we have conceived great beings in human shape controlling them. Jupiter does not mean thunder. Thunder means the march and victory of Jupiter. Neptune does not mean the sea; the sea is his, and he made it. In other words, what the savage really said about the sea was: 'Only my fetish Mumbo could raise such mountains out of mere water.' What the savage really said about the sun was: 'Only my great-great-grandfather Jumbo could deserve such a blazing crown.'

About all these myths my own position is utterly and even sadly simple. I say you cannot really understand any myths till you have found that one of them is not a myth. Turnip ghosts mean nothing if there are no real ghosts. Forged bank-notes mean nothing if there are no real bank-notes. Heathen gods mean nothing, and must always mean nothing, to those of us that deny the Christian God. When once a god is admitted,

even a false god, the Cosmos begins to know its place:
which is the second place. When once it is the real
God the Cosmos falls down before Him, offering flowers
in spring as flames in winter. 'My love is like a red, red
rose' does not mean that the poet is praising roses under
the allegory of a young lady. 'My love is an arbutus'
does not mean that the author was a botanist so pleased
with a particular arbutus-tree that he said he loved it.
'Who art the moon and regent of my sky' does not
mean that Juliet invented Romeo to account for the
roundness of the moon. 'Christ is the Sun of Easter'
does not mean that the worshipper is praising the sun
under the emblem of Christ. Goddess or god can clothe
themselves with the spring or summer; but the body is
more than raiment. Religion takes almost disdainfully
the dress of Nature; and indeed Christianity has done as
well with the snows of Christmas as with the snowdrops
of spring. And when I look across the sun-struck fields,
I know in my inmost bones that my joy is not solely in
the spring: for spring alone, being always returning,
would be always sad. There is somebody or something
walking there, to be crowned with flowers: and my
pleasure is in some promise yet possible and in the
resurrection of the dead.

THE FOOL

FOR many years I had sought him, and at last I found him in a club. I had been told that he was everywhere; but I had almost begun to think that he was nowhere. I had been assured that there were millions of him; but before my late discovery I inclined to think that there were none of him. After my late discovery I am sure that there is one; and I incline to think that there are several, say, a few hundreds, but unfortunately most of them occupying important positions. When I say 'him,' I mean the entire idiot.

I have never been able to discover that 'stupid public' of which so many literary men complain. The people one actually meets in trains or at tea-parties seem to me quite bright and interesting; certainly quite enough so to call for the full exertion of one's own wits. And even when I have heard brilliant 'conversationalists' conversing with other people, the conversation had much more equality and give and take than this age of intellectual snobs will admit. I have sometimes felt tired, like other people; but rather tired with men's talk and variety than with their stolidity or sameness; therefore it was that I sometimes longed to find the refreshment of a single fool.

But it was denied me. Turn where I would I found this monotonous brilliancy of the general intelligence, this ruthless, ceaseless sparkle of humour and good sense. The 'mostly fools' theory has been used in an anti-democratic sense; but when I found at last my priceless ass, I did not find him in what is commonly called the democracy; nor in the aristocracy either. The man of the democracy generally talks quite rationally, sometimes on the anti-democratic side, but always with an idea of giving reasons for what he says and referring to the realities of his experience. Nor is it

165

the aristocracy that is stupid; at least, not that section of the aristocracy which represents it in politics. They are often cynical, especially about money, but even their boredom tends to make them a little eager for any real information or originality. If a man like Mr. Winston Churchill or Mr. Wyndham[1] made up his mind for any reason to attack Syndicalism he would find out what it was first. Not so the man I found in the club.

.   .   .   .   .   .

He was very well dressed; he had a heavy but handsome face; his black clothes suggested the City and his grey moustaches the Army; but the whole suggested that he did not really belong to either, but was one of those who dabble in shares and who play at soldiers. There was some third element about him that was neither mercantile nor military. His manners were a shade too gentlemanly to be quite those of a gentleman. They involved an unction and over-emphasis of the club-man: and I suddenly remembered feeling the same thing in some old actors or old playgoers who had modelled themselves on actors. As I came in he said: 'If I was the Government,' and then put a cigar in his mouth which he lit carefully with long intakes of breath. Then he took the cigar out of his mouth again and said: 'I 'd give it 'em,' as if it were quite a separate sentence. But even while his mouth was stopped with the cigar his companion or interlocutor leaped to his feet and said with great heartiness, snatching up a hat: 'Well, I must be off. Tuesday!' I dislike these dark suspicions, but I certainly fancied I recognized the sudden geniality with which one takes leave of a bore.

When, therefore, he removed the narcotic stopper from his mouth it was to me that he addressed the belated epigram: 'I 'd give it 'em.'

'What would you give them,' I asked—'the minimum wage?'

'I 'd give them beans,' he said. 'I 'd shoot 'em down —shoot 'em down, every man Jack of them. I lost my best train yesterday, and here 's the whole country

[1] George Wyndham (1863–1913)

paralysed, and here 's a handful of obstinate fellows standing between the country and coal. I 'd shoot 'em down!'

'That would surely be a little harsh,' I pleaded. 'After all, they are not under martial law, though I suppose two or three of them have commissions in the Yeomanry.'

'Commissions in the Yeomanry!' he repeated, and his eyes and face, which became startling and separate, like those of a boiled lobster, made me feel sure that he had something of the kind himself.

'Besides,' I continued, 'wouldn't it be quite enough to confiscate their money?'

'Well, I 'd send them all to penal servitude, anyhow,' he said, 'and I 'd confiscate their funds as well.'

'The policy is daring and full of difficulty,' I replied, 'but I do not say that it is wholly outside the extreme rights of the republic. But you must remember that though the facts of property have become quite fantastic, yet the sentiment of property still exists. These coal-owners, though they have not earned the mines, though they could not work the mines, do' quite honestly feel that they own the mines. Hence your suggestion of shooting them down, or even of confiscating their property, raises very——'

'What do you mean?' asked the man with the cigar, with a bullying eye. 'Who yer talking about?'

'I 'm talking about what you were talking about,' I replied; 'as you put it so perfectly, about the handful of obstinate fellows who are standing between the country and the coal. I mean the men who are selling their own coal for fancy prices, and who, as long as they can get those prices, care as little for national starvation as most merchant princes and pirates have cared for the provinces that were wasted or the peoples that were enslaved just before their ships came home. But though I am a bit of a revolutionist myself, I cannot quite go with you in the extreme violence you suggest. You say——'

'I say,' he cried, bursting through my speech with a

really splendid energy like that of some noble beast,
'I say I'd take all these blasted miners and——'

I had risen slowly to my feet, for I was profoundly
moved; and I stood staring at that mental monster.

'Oh,' I said, 'so it is the *miners* who are all to be sent
to penal servitude, so that we may get more coal. It
is the *miners* who are to be shot dead, every man Jack
of them; for if once they are all shot dead they will
start mining again. . . . You must forgive me, sir; I
know I seem somewhat moved. . . . The fact is, I have
just found something . . . something I have been
looking for for years.'

'Well,' he asked, with no unfriendly stare, 'and what
have you found?'

'No,' I answered, shaking my head sadly, 'I do not
think it would be quite kind to tell you what I have
found.'

He had a hundred virtues, including the capital
virtue of good humour, and we had no difficulty in
changing the subject and forgetting the disagreement.
He talked about society, his town friends, and his
country sports, and I discovered in the course of it that
he was a county magistrate, a Member of Parliament,
and a director of several important companies. He
was also that other thing, which I did not tell him.

.　　.　　.　　.　　.　　.

The moral is that a certain sort of person does exist,
to whose glory this article is dedicated. He is not the
ordinary man. He is not the miner, who is sharp
enough to ask for the necessities of existence. He is
not the mine-owner, who is sharp enough to get a great
deal more, by selling his coal at the best possible moment.
He is not the aristocratic politician, who has a cynical
but a fair sympathy with both economic opportunities.
But he is the man who appears in scores of public places
open to the upper middle class or (that less known but
more powerful section) the lower upper class. Men like
this all over the country are really saying whatever
comes into their heads in their capacities of justice of

the peace, candidate for Parliament, Colonel of the Yeomanry. old family doctor, Poor Law guardian, coroner, or, above all, arbiter in trade disputes. He suffers, in the literal sense, from softening of the brain; he has softened it by always taking the view of everything most comfortable for his country, his class, and his private personality. He is a deadly public danger. But as I have given him his name at the beginning of this article there is no need for me to repeat it at the end.

THE SENTIMENTAL SCOT

OF all the great nations of Christendom, the Scotch are by far the most romantic. I have just enough Scotch experience and just enough Scotch blood to know this in the only way in which a thing can really be known; that is, when the outer world and the inner world are at one. I know it is always said that the Scotch are practical, prosaic, and puritan; that they have an eye to business.

I like that phrase 'an eye' to business. Polyphemus had an eye for business; it was in the middle of his forehead. It served him admirably for the only two duties which are demanded in a modern financier and captain of industry: the two duties of counting sheep and of eating men. But when that one eye was put out he was done for. But the Scotch are not one-eyed practical men, though their best friends must admit that they are occasionally business-like. They are, quite fundamentally, romantic and sentimental, and this is proved by the very economic argument that is used to prove their harshness and hunger for the material. The mass of Scots have accepted the industrial civilization, with its factory chimneys and its famine prices, with its steam and smoke and steel—and strikes. The mass of the Irish have not accepted it. The mass of the Irish have clung to agriculture with claws of iron; and have succeeded in keeping it. That is because the Irish, though far inferior to the Scotch in art and literature, are hugely superior to them in practical politics. You do need to be very romantic to accept the industrial civilization. It does really require all the old Gaelic glamour to make men think that Glasgow is a grand place. Yet the miracle is achieved and while I was in Glasgow I shared the illusion. I have never had the faintest illusion about Leeds or

Birmingham. The industrial dream suited the Scots. Here was a really romantic vista, suited to a romantic people; a vision of higher and higher chimneys taking hold upon the heavens, of fiercer and fiercer fires in which adamant could evaporate like dew. Here were taller and taller engines that began already to shriek and gesticulate like giants. Here were thunderbolts of communication which already flashed to and fro like thoughts. It was unreasonable to expect the rapt, dreamy, romantic Scot to stand still in such a whirl of wizardry to ask whether he, the ordinary Scot, would be any the richer.

   .   .   .   .   .

He, the ordinary Scot, is very much the poorer. Glasgow is not a rich city. It is a particularly poor city ruled by a few particularly rich men. It is not, perhaps, quite so poor a city as Liverpool, London, Manchester, Birmingham, or Bolton. It is vastly poorer than Rome, Rouen, Munich, or Cologne. A certain civic vitality notable in Glasgow may, perhaps, be due to the fact that the high poetic patriotism of the Scots has there been reinforced by the cutting common sense and independence of the Irish. In any case, I think there can be no doubt of the main historical fact. The Scotch were tempted by the enormous but unequal opportunities of industrialism, because the Scotch are romantic. The Irish refused those enormous and unequal opportunities, because the Irish are clear-sighted. They would not need very clear sight by this time to see that in England and Scotland the temptation has been a betrayal. The industrial system has failed.

   .   .   .   .   .

I was coming the other day along a great valley road that strikes out of the westland counties about Glasgow, more or less towards the east and the widening of the Forth. It may, for all I know (I amused myself with the fancy), be the way along which Wallace came with

his crude army, when he gave battle before Stirling
Brig; and, in the midst of medieval diplomacies, made
a new nation possible. Anyhow, the romantic quality
of Scotland rolled all about me, as much in the last
reek of Glasgow as in the first rain upon the hills. The
tall factory chimneys seemed trying to be taller than
the mountain peaks; as if this landscape were full (as
its history has been full) of the very madness of ambition.
The wage-slavery we live in is a wicked thing. But
there is nothing in which the Scotch are more piercing
and poetical, I might say more perfect, than in their
Scotch wickedness. It is what makes the Master of
Ballantrae the most thrilling of all fictitious villains.
It is what makes the Master of Lovat the most thrilling
of all historical villains. It is poetry. It is an intensity
which is on the edge of madness—or (what is worse)
magic. Well, the Scotch have managed to apply something of this fierce romanticism even to the lowest of all
lordships and serfdoms; the proletarian inequality of
to-day. You do meet now and then, in Scotland, the
man you never meet anywhere else but in novels; I
mean the self-made man; the hard, insatiable man,
merciless to himself as well as to others. It is not
'enterprise'; it is kleptomania. He is quite mad, and
a much more obvious public pest than any other kind
of kleptomaniac; but though he is a cheat, he is not
an illusion. He does exist; I have met quite two of
him. Him alone among modern merchants we do not
weakly flatter when we call him a bandit. Something
of the irresponsibility of the true Dark Ages really clings
about him. Our scientific civilization is not a civilization; it is a smoke nuisance. Like smoke it is choking
us; like smoke it will pass away. Only of one or two
Scotsmen, in my experience, was it true that where
there is smoke there is fire.

. . . . . .

But there are other kinds of fire; and better. The
one great advantage of this strange national temper is
that, from the beginning of all chronicles, it has provided

resistance as well as cruelty.   In Scotland nearly everything has always been in revolt—especially loyalty.   If
these people are capable of making Glasgow, they are
also capable of wrecking it; and the thought of my
many good friends in that city makes me really doubtful
about which would figure in human memories as the
more huge calamity of the two.   In Scotland there are
many rich men so weak as to call themselves strong.
But there are not so many poor men weak enough to
believe them.

As I came out of Glasgow I saw men standing about
the road.   They had little lanterns tied to the fronts of
their caps, like the fairies who used to dance in the old
fairy pantomimes.   They were not, however, strictly
speaking, fairies.   They might have been called gnomes,
since they worked in the chasms of those purple and
chaotic hills.   They worked in the mines from whence
comes the fuel of our fires.   Just at the moment when
I saw them, moreover, they were not dancing; nor were
they working.   They were doing nothing.   Which, in
my opinion (and I trust yours), was the finest thing
they could do.

THE ROMANTIC IN THE RAIN

THE middle classes of modern England are quite fanatic-
ally fond of washing; and are often enthusiastic for
teetotalism. I cannot therefore comprehend why it is
that they exhibit a mysterious dislike of rain. Rain,
that inspiring and delightful thing, surely combines the
qualities of these two ideals with quite a curious perfection. Our philanthropists are eager to establish
public baths everywhere. Rain surely is a public bath;
it might almost be called mixed bathing. The appearance of persons coming fresh from this great natural
lustration is not perhaps polished or dignified; but for
the matter of that, few people are dignified when
coming out of a bath. But the scheme of rain in itself
is one of an enormous purification. It realizes the
dream of some insane hygienist: it scrubs the sky. Its
giant brooms and mops seem to reach the starry rafters
and starless corners of the cosmos; it is a cosmic spring-
cleaning.

If the Englishman is really fond of cold baths, he ought
not to grumble at the English climate for being a cold
bath. In these days we are constantly told that we
should leave our little special possessions and join in the
enjoyment of common social institutions and a common
social machinery. I offer the rain as a thoroughly
Socialistic institution. It disregards that degraded
delicacy which has hitherto led each gentleman to take
his shower-bath in private. It is a better shower-bath,
because it is public and communal; and, best of all,
because somebody else pulls the string.

. . . . . .

As for the fascination of rain for the water drinker, it
is a fact the neglect of which I simply cannot comprehend. The enthusiastic water drinker must regard a

rainstorm as a sort of universal banquet and debauch of his own favourite beverage. Think of the imaginative intoxication of the wine drinker if the crimson clouds sent down claret or the golden clouds hock. Paint upon primitive darkness some such scenes of apocalypse, towering and gorgeous skyscapes in which champagne falls like fire from heaven or the dark skies grow purple and tawny with the terrible colours of port. All this must the wild abstainer feel, as he rolls in the long soaking grass, kicks his ecstatic heels to heaven, and listens to the roaring rain. It is he, the water drinker, who ought to be the true bacchanal of the forests; for all the forests are drinking water. Moreover, the forests are apparently enjoying it: the trees rave and reel to and fro like drunken giants; they clash boughs as revellers clash cups; they roar undying thirst and howl the health of the world.

All around me as I write is a noise of Nature drinking: and Nature makes a noise when she is drinking, being by no means refined. If I count it Christian mercy to give a cup of cold water to a sufferer, shall I complain of these multitudinous cups of cold water handed round to all living things; a cup of water for every shrub; a cup of water for every weed? I would be ashamed to grumble at it. As Sir Philip Sidney said, their need is greater than mine—especially for water.

.   .   .   .   .   .

There is a wild garment that still carries nobly the name of a wild Highland clan: a clan come from those hills where rain is not so much an incident as an atmosphere. Surely every man of imagination must feel a tempestuous flame of Celtic romance spring up within him whenever he puts on a mackintosh. I could never reconcile myself to carrying an umbrella; it is a pompous Eastern business, carried over the heads of despots in the dry, hot lands. Shut up, an umbrella is an unmanageable walking-stick; open, it is an inadequate tent. For my part, I have no taste for pretending to be a walking pavilion; I think nothing of my hat, and precious little of my head. If I am to be protected against wet, it must be by some closer and more careless protection, something that I can forget altogether. It might be a Highland plaid. It might be that yet more Highland thing, a mackintosh.

And there is really something in the mackintosh of the military qualities of the Highlander. The proper cheap mackintosh has a blue and white sheen as of steel or iron; it gleams like armour. I like to think of it·as the uniform of that ancient clan in some of its old and misty raids. I like to think of all the Macintoshes, in their mackintoshes, descending on some doomed Lowland village, their wet waterproofs flashing in the sun or moon. For indeed this is one of the real beauties of rainy weather, that while the amount of original and direct light is commonly lessened, the number of things that reflect light is unquestionably increased. There is less sunshine; but there are more shiny things, such beautifully shiny things as pools and puddles and mackintoshes. It is like moving in a world of mirrors.

.   .   .   .   .   .

And indeed this is the last and not the least gracious of the casual works of magic wrought by rain: that while it decreases light, yet it doubles it. If it dims the sky, it brightens the earth. It gives the roads (to the sympathetic eye) something of the beauty of Venice. Shallow lakes of water reiterate every detail of earth and sky; we dwell in a double universe. Sometimes walking upon bare and lustrous pavements, wet under numerous lamps, a man seems a black blot on all that golden looking-glass and could fancy he was flying in a yellow sky. But wherever trees and towns hang head downwards in a pygmy puddle, the sense of Celestial topsy-turvydom is the same. This bright, wet, dazzling confusion of shape and shadow, of reality and reflection, will appeal strongly to any one with the transcendental instinct about this dreamy and dual life of ours. It will always give a man the strange sense of looking down at the skies.

THE PERFECT GAME

WE have all met the man who says that some odd things have happened to him, but that he does not really believe that they were supernatural. My own position is the opposite of this. I believe in the supernatural as a matter of intellect and reason, not as a matter of personal experience. I do not see ghosts; I only see their inherent probability. But it is entirely a matter of the mere intelligence, not even of the emotions; my nerves and body are altogether of this earth, very earthy. But upon people of this temperament one weird incident will often leave a peculiar impression. And the weirdest circumstance that ever occurred to me occurred a little while ago. It consisted in nothing less than my playing a game, and playing it quite well for some seventeen consecutive minutes. The ghost of my grandfather would have astonished me less.

On one of these blue and burning afternoons I found myself, to my inexpressible astonishment, playing a game called croquet. I had imagined that it belonged to the epoch of Leech and Anthony Trollope, and I had neglected to provide myself with those very long and luxuriant side-whiskers which are really essential to such a scene. I played it with a man whom we will call Parkinson, and with whom I had a semi-philosophical argument which lasted through the entire contest. It is deeply implanted in my mind that I had the best of the argument; but it is certain and beyond dispute that I had the worst of the game.

'Oh, Parkinson, Parkinson!' I cried, patting him affectionately on the head with a mallet, 'how far you really are from the pure love of the sport—you who can play. It is only we who play badly who love the Game itself. You love glory; you love applause; you love the earthquake voice of victory; you do not love croquet. You do not love croquet until you love being beaten at croquet. It is we, the bunglers, who adore the occupation in the abstract. It is we to whom it is art for art's sake. If we may see the face of Croquet herself (if I may so express myself) we are content to see her face turned upon us in anger. Our play is called amateurish; and we wear proudly the name of amateur, for amateurs is but the French for Lovers. We accept all adventures from our Lady, the most disastrous or the most dreary. We wait outside her iron gates (I allude to the hoops), vainly essaying to enter. Our devoted balls, impetuous and full of chivalry, will not be confined within the pedantic boundaries of the mere croquet ground. Our balls seek honour in the ends of the earth; they turn up in the flower-beds and the conservatory; they are to be found in the front garden and the next street. No, Parkinson! The good painter loves his skill. It is the bad painter who loves his art. The good musician loves being a musician; the bad musician loves music. With such a pure and hopeless passion do I worship croquet. I love the game itself. I love the parallelogram of grass marked out with chalk or tape, as if its limits were the frontiers of my sacred fatherland, the four seas of Britain. I love the mere swing of the mallets, and the click of the balls is music. The four colours are to me sacramental and symbolic, like the red of martyrdom, or the white of Easter Day. You lose all this, my poor Parkinson. You have to solace yourself for the absence of this vision by the paltry consolation of being able to go through hoops and to hit the stick.'

And I waved my mallet in the air with a graceful gaiety.

'Don't be too sorry for me,' said Parkinson, with his simple sarcasm. 'I shall get over it in time. But it seems to me that the more a man likes a game the better he would want to play it. Suppose the pleasure in the thing itself does come first, doesn't the pleasure of success come naturally and inevitably afterwards? Or, take your own simile of the Knight and his Lady-love.

I admit the gentleman does first and foremost want to be in the lady's presence. But I never heard of a gentleman who wanted to look an utter ass when he was there.'

'Perhaps not; though he generally looks it,' I replied. 'But the truth is that there is a fallacy in the simile, although it was my own. The happiness at which the lover is aiming is an infinite happiness, which can be extended without limit. The more he is loved, normally speaking, the jollier he will be. It is definitely true that the stronger the love of both lovers, the stronger will be the happiness. But it is not true that the stronger the play of both croquet players the stronger will be the game. It is logically possible—(follow me closely here, Parkinson!)—it is logically possible to play croquet too well to enjoy it at all. If you could put this blue ball through that distant hoop as easily as you could pick it up with your hand, then you would not put it through that hoop any more than you pick it up with your hand; it would not be worth doing. If you could play unerringly you would not play at all. The moment the game is perfect the game disappears.'

'I do not think, however,' said Parkinson, 'that you are in any immediate danger of effecting that sort of destruction. I do not think your croquet will vanish through its own faultless excellence. You are safe for the present.'

I again caressed him with the mallet, knocked a ball about, wired myself, and resumed the thread of my discourse.

The long, warm evening had been gradually closing in, and by this time it was almost twilight. By the time I had delivered four more fundamental principles, and my companion had gone through five more hoops, the dusk was verging upon dark.

'We shall have to give this up,' said Parkinson, as he missed a ball almost for the first time. 'I can't see a thing.'

'Nor can I,' I answered, 'and it is a comfort to reflect that I could not hit anything if I saw it.'

With that I struck a ball smartly, and sent it away into the darkness towards where the shadowy figure of Parkinson moved in the hot haze. Parkinson immediately uttered a loud and dramatic cry. The situation, indeed, called for it. I had hit the right ball.

Stunned with astonishment, I crossed the gloomy ground, and hit my ball again. It went through a hoop. I could not see the hoop; but it was the right hoop. I shuddered from head to foot.

Words were wholly inadequate, so I slouched heavily after that impossible ball. Again I hit it away into the night, in what I supposed was the vague direction of the quite invisible stick. And in the dead silence I heard the stick rattle as the ball struck it heavily.

I threw down my mallet. 'I can't stand this,' I said. 'My ball has gone right three times. These things are not of this world.'

'Pick your mallet up,' said Parkinson; 'have another go.'

'I tell you I daren't. If I made another hoop like that I should see all the devils dancing there on the blessed grass.'

'Why devils?' asked Parkinson; 'they may be only fairies making fun of you. They are sending you the "Perfect Game," which is no game.'

I looked about me. The garden was full of a burning darkness, in which the faint glimmers had the look of fire. I stepped across the grass as if it burnt me, picked up the mallet, and hit the ball somewhere—somewhere where another ball might be. I heard the dull click of the balls touching, and ran into the house like one pursued.

THE WIND AND THE TREES

I AM sitting under tall trees, with a great wind boiling like surf about the tops of them, so that their living load of leaves rocks and roars in something that is at once exultation and agony. I feel, in fact, as if I were actually sitting at the bottom of the sea among mere anchors and ropes, while over my head and over the green twilight of water sounded the everlasting rush of waves and the toil and crash of shipwreck of tremendous ships. The wind tugs at the trees as if it might pluck them root and all out of the earth like tufts of grass. Or, to try yet another desperate figure of speech for this unspeakable energy, the trees are straining and tearing and lashing as if they were a tribe of dragons each tied by the tail.

As I look at these top-heavy giants tortured by an invisible and violent witchcraft, a phrase comes back into my mind. I remember a little boy of my acquaintance who was once walking in Battersea Park under just such torn skies and tossing trees. He did not like the wind at all; it blew in his face too much; it made him shut his eyes; and it blew off his hat, of which he was very proud. He was, as far as I remember, about four. After complaining repeatedly of the atmospheric unrest, he said at last to his mother: 'Well, why don't you take away the trees, and then it wouldn't wind?'

Nothing could be more intelligent or natural than this mistake. Any one looking for the first time at the trees might fancy that they were indeed vast and titanic fans, which by their mere waving agitated the air around them for miles. Nothing, I say, could be more human and excusable than the belief that it is the trees which make the wind. Indeed, the belief is so human and excusable that it is, as a matter of fact, the belief of about ninety-nine out of a hundred of the philosophers, reformers, sociologists, and politicians of the great age in which we live. My small friend was, in fact, very like the principal modern thinkers; only much nicer.

.   .   .   .   .   .

In the little apologue or parable which he has thus the honour of inventing, the trees stand for all visible things and the wind for the invisible. The wind is the spirit which bloweth where it listeth; the trees are the material things of the world which are blown where the spirit lists. The wind is philosophy, religion, revolution; the trees are cities and civilizations. We only know that there is a wind because the trees on some distant hill suddenly go mad. We only know that there is a real revolution because all the chimney-pots go mad on the whole skyline of the city.

Just as the ragged outline of a tree grows suddenly more ragged and rises into fantastic crests or tattered tails, so the human city rises under the wind of the spirit into toppling temples or sudden spires. No man has ever seen a revolution. Mobs pouring through the palaces, blood pouring down the gutters, the guillotine lifted higher than the throne, a prison in ruins, a people in arms—these things are not revolution, but the results of revolution.

You cannot see a wind; you can only see that there is a wind. So, also, you cannot see a revolution; you can only see that there is a revolution. And there never has been in the history of the world a real revolution, brutally active and decisive, which was not preceded by unrest and new dogma in the region of invisible things. All revolutions began by being abstract. Most revolutions began by being quite pedantically abstract.

The wind is up above the world before a twig on the tree has moved. So there must always be a battle in the sky before there is a battle on the earth. Since it is lawful to pray for the coming of the kingdom, it is lawful also to pray for the coming of the revolution that shall restore the kingdom. It is lawful to hope to hear the

wind of heaven in the trees. It is lawful to pray:
'Thine anger come on earth as it is in heaven.'

.   .   .   .   .

The great human dogma, then, is that the wind moves
the trees. The great human heresy is that the trees
move the wind. When people begin to say that the
material circumstances have alone created the moral
circumstances, then they have prevented all possibility
of serious change. For if my circumstances have made
me wholly stupid, how can I be certain even that I am
right in altering those circumstances?

The man who represents all thought as an accident
of environment is simply smashing and discrediting all
his own thoughts—including that one. To treat the
human mind as having an ultimate authority is necessary
to any kind of thinking, even free thinking. And
nothing will ever be reformed in this age or country
unless we realize that the moral fact comes first.

For example, most of us, I suppose, have seen in
print and heard in debating clubs an endless discussion
that goes on between Socialists and total abstainers.
The latter say that drink leads to poverty; the former
say that poverty leads to drink. I can only wonder at
either of them being content with such simple physical
explanations. Surely it is obvious that the thing which
among the English proletariat leads to poverty is the
same as the thing which leads to drink: the absence of
strong civic dignity, the absence of an instinct that
resists degradation.

When you have discovered why the enormous English
estates were not long ago cut up into small holdings
like the land of France, you will have discovered why
the Englishman is more drunken than the Frenchman.
The Englishman, among his million delightful virtues,
really has this quality, which may strictly be called
'hand to mouth,' because under its influence a man's
hand automatically seeks his own mouth, instead of
seeking (as it sometimes should do) his oppressor's nose.
And a man who says that the English inequality in

land is due only to economic causes, or that the drunkenness of England is due only to economic causes, is saying
something so absurd that he cannot really have thought
what he was saying.

Yet things quite as preposterous as this are said and
written under the influence of that great spectacle of
babyish helplessness, the economic theory of history.
We have people who represent that all great historic
motives were economic, and then have to howl at the
top of their voices in order to induce the modern
democracy to act on economic motives. The extreme
Marxian politicians in England exhibit themselves as a
small, heroic minority, trying vainly to induce the world
to do what, according to their theory, the world always
does. The truth is, of course, that there will be a social
revolution the moment the thing has ceased to be purely
economic. You can never have a revolution in order
to establish a democracy. You must have a democracy
in order to have a revolution.

·   ·   ·   ·   ·   ·

I get up from under the trees, for the wind and the
slight rain have ceased. The trees stand up like golden
pillars in a clear sunlight. The tossing of the trees and
the blowing of the wind have ceased simultaneously. So
I suppose there are still modern philosophers who will
maintain that the trees make the wind.

HUMANITY: AN INTERLUDE

EXCEPT for some fine works of art, which seem to be there by accident, the City of Brussels is like a bad Paris, a Paris with everything noble cut out, and everything nasty left in. No one can understand Paris and its history who does not understand that its fierceness is the balance and justification of its frivolity. It is called a city of pleasure; but it may also very specially be called a city of pain. The crown of roses is also a crown of thorns. Its people are too prone to hurt others, but quite ready also to hurt themselves. They are martyrs for religion, they are martyrs for irreligion; they are even martyrs for immorality. For the indecency of many of their books and papers is not of the sort which charms and seduces, but of the sort that horrifies and hurts; they are torturing themselves. They lash their own patriotism into life with the same whips which most men use to lash foreigners to silence. The enemies of France can never give an account of her infamy or decay which does not seem insipid and even polite compared with the things which the Nationalists of France say about their own nation. They taunt and torment themselves; sometimes they even deliberately oppress themselves. Thus, when the mob of Paris could make a government to please itself, it made a sort of sublime tyranny to order itself about. The spirit is the same from the Crusades or St. Bartholomew to the apotheosis of Zola. The old religionists tortured men physically for a moral truth. The new realists torture men morally for a physical truth.

Now Brussels is Paris without this constant purification of pain. Its indecencies are not regrettable incidents in an everlasting revolution. It has none of the things which make good Frenchmen love Paris; it has only the things which make unspeakable Englishmen

love it. It has the part which is cosmopolitan—and
narrow; not the part which is Parisian—and universal.
You can find there (as commonly happens in modern
centres) the worst thing of all nations—the *Daily Mail*
from England, the cheap philosophies from Germany,
the loose novels of France, and the drinks of America.
But there is no English broad fun, no German kindly
ceremony, no American exhilaration, and, above all,
no French tradition of fighting for an idea.   Though all
the boulevards look like Parisian boulevards, though all
the shops look like Parisian shops, you cannot look at
them steadily for two minutes without feeling the full
distance between, let us say, King Leopold and fighters
like Clemenceau and Déroulède.

.   .   .   .   .

   For all these reasons, and many more, when I had got
into Brussels I began to make all necessary arrangements
for getting out of it again; and I had impulsively got
into a tram which seemed to be going out of the city.
In this tram there were two men talking; one was a
little man with a black French beard; the other was a
baldish man with bushy whiskers, like the financial
foreign count in a three-act farce.   And about the time
that we reached the suburb of the city, and the traffic
grew thinner, and the noises more few, I began to hear
what they were saying.   Though they spoke French
quickly, their words were fairly easy to follow, because
they were all long words.   Anybody can understand
long words because they have in them all the lucidity
of Latin.
   The man with the black beard said: 'It must that we
have the Progress.'
   The man with the whiskers parried this smartly by
saying: 'It must also that we have the Consolidation
International.'
   This is the sort of discussion which I like myself, so
I listened with some care, and I think I picked up the
thread of it.   One of the Belgians was a Little Belgian,
as we speak of a Little Englander.   The other was a

Belgian Imperialist, for though Belgium is not quite
strong enough to be altogether a nation, she is quite
strong enough to be an empire.   Being a nation means
standing up to your equals, whereas being an empire
only means kicking your inferiors.   The man with
whiskers was the Imperialist, and he was saying:
'The science, behold there the new guide of humanity.'

And the man with the beard answered him: 'It
does not suffice to have progress in the science; one
must have it also in the sentiment of the human
justice.'

This remark I applauded, as if at a public meeting,
but they were much too keen on their argument to hear
me.   The views I have often heard in England, but
never uttered so lucidly, and certainly never so fast.
Though Belgian by nation they must both have been
essentially French.   Whiskers was great on education,
which, it seems, is on the march.   All the world goes
to make itself instructed.   It must that the more instructed enlighten the less instructed.   Eh, well then,
the European must impose upon the savage the science
and the light.   Also (apparently) he must impose himself on the savage while he is about it.   To-day one
travelled quickly.   The science had changed all.   For
our fathers, they were religious, and (what was worse)
dead.   To-day humanity had electricity to the hand;
the machines came from triumphing; all the lines and
limits of the globe effaced themselves.   Soon there
would not be but the great empires and confederations,
guided by the science, always the science.

Here Whiskers stopped an instant for breath; and the
man with the sentiment of human justice had 'la parole'
off him in a flash.   Without doubt Humanity was on
the march, but towards the sentiments, the ideal, the
methods moral and pacific.   Humanity directed itself
towards Humanity.   For your wars and empires on
behalf of civilization, what were they in effect?   The
war, was it not itself an affair of the barbarism?   The
Empires, were they not things savage?   The Humanity
had passed all that; she was now intellectual.   Tolstoy

had refined all human souls with the sentiments the most
delicate and just.   Man was become a spirit: the wings
pushed . . .

.   .   .   .   .   .

At this important point of evolution the tram came
to a jerky stoppage; and staring round I found, to my
stunned consternation, that it was almost dark, that
I was far away from Brussels, that I could not dream
of getting back to dinner; in short, that through
the clinging fascination of this great controversy on
Humanity and its recent complete alteration by science
or Tolstoy, I had landed myself Heaven knows where.
I dropped hastily from the suburban tram and let it
go on without me.

I was alone in flat fields out of sight of the city.   On
one side of the road was one of those small, thin woods
which are common in all countries, but of which, by
a coincidence, the mystical painters of Flanders were
very fond.   The night was closing in with cloudy purple
and grey; there was one ribbon of silver, the last rag oi
the sunset.   Through the wood went one little path,
and somehow it suggested that it might lead to some
sign of life—there was no other sign of life on the horizon.
I went along it, and soon sank into a sort of dancing
twilight of all those tiny trees.   There is something
subtle and bewildering about that sort of frail and
fantastic wood.   A forest of big trees seems like a
bodily barrier; but somehow that mist of thin lines
seems like a spiritual barrier.   It is as if one were caught
in a fairy cloud or could not pass a phantom.   When I
had well lost the last gleam of the high road a curious and
definite feeling came upon me.   I had heard a lot about
Humanity in the tram.   Now I suddenly felt something
much more practical and extraordinary—the absence of
humanity: inhuman loneliness.   Of course, there was
nothing really lost in my state; but the mood may hit
one anywhere.   I wanted men—any men; and I felt
our awful alliance over all the globe.   And at last, when
I had walked for what seemed a long time, I saw a light

too near the earth to mean anything except the image of God.

I came out on a clear space and a low, long cottage, the door of which was open, but was blocked by a big grey horse, who seemed to prefer to eat with his head inside the sitting-room. I got past him, and found he was being fed idly by a young man who was sitting down and drinking beer inside, and who saluted me with heavy rustic courtesy, but in a strange tongue. The room was full of staring faces like owls, and these I traced at length as belonging to about six small children. Their father was still working in the fields, but their mother rose when I entered. She smiled, but she and all the rest spoke some rude language, Flamand, I suppose; so that we had to be kind to each other by signs. She fetched me beer, and pointed out my way with her finger; and I drew a picture to please the children; and as it was a picture of two men hitting each other with swords, it pleased them very much. Then I gave a Belgian penny to each child, for, as I said on chance in French: 'It must be that we have the economic equality.' But they had never heard of economic equality, while all Battersea workmen have heard of economic equality, though it is true that they haven't got it.

I found my way back to the city, and some time afterwards I actually saw in the street my two men talking, no doubt still saying, one that Science had changed all in Humanity, and the other that Humanity was now pushing the wings of the purely intellectual. But for me Humanity was hooked on to an accidental picture. I thought of a low and lonely house in the flats, behind a veil or film of slight trees, a man breaking the ground as men have broken from the first morning, and a huge grey horse champing his food within a foot of a child's head, as in the stable where Christ was born.

THE LITTLE BIRDS WHO WON'T SING

On my last morning on the Flemish coast, when I knew that in a few hours I should be in England, my eye fell upon one of the details of Gothic carving of which Flanders is full. I do not know whether the thing was old, though it was certainly knocked about and inde-cipherable, but at least it was certainly in the style and tradition of the early Middle Ages. It seemed to repre-sent men bending themselves (not to say twisting them-selves) to certain primary employments. Some seemed to be sailors tugging at ropes; others, I think, were reaping; others were energetically pouring something into something else. This is entirely characteristic of the pictures and carvings of the early thirteenth century, perhaps the most purely vigorous time in all history. The great Greeks preferred to carve their gods and heroes doing nothing. Splendid and philosophic as their com-posure is, there is always about it something that marks the master of many slaves. But if there was one thing the early medievals liked it was representing people doing something—hunting or hawking, or rowing boats, or treading grapes, or making shoes, or cooking something in a pot. 'Quicquid agunt homines, votum, timor, ira, voluptas.' (I quote from memory.) The Middle Ages is full of that spirit in all its monuments and manuscripts. Chaucer retains it in his jolly insistence on everybody's type of trade and toil. It was the earliest and youngest resurrection of Europe, the time when social order was strengthening, but had not yet become oppressive; the time when religious faiths were strong, but had not yet been exasperated. For this reason the whole effect of Greek and Gothic carving is different. The figures in the Elgin Marbles, though often rearing their steeds for an instant in the air, seem frozen for ever at that perfect instant. But a mass of medieval carving seems actually a sort of bustle or hubbub in stone. Sometimes one cannot help feeling

190

that the groups actually move and mix, and the whole front of a great cathedral has the hum of a huge hive.

.   .   .   .   .   .

But about these particular figures there was a peculiarity of which I could not be sure. Those of them that had any heads had very curious heads, and it seemed to me that they had their mouths open. Whether or no this really meant anything or was an accident of nascent art I do not know; but in the course of wondering I recalled to my mind the fact that singing was connected with many of the tasks there suggested, that there were songs for reapers reaping and songs for sailors hauling ropes. I was still thinking about this small problem when I walked along the pier at Ostend; and I heard some sailors uttering a measured shout as they laboured, and I remembered that sailors still sing in chorus while they work, and even sing different songs according to what part of their work they are doing. And a little while afterwards, when my sea journey was over, the sight of men working in the English fields reminded me again that there are still songs for harvest and for many agricultural routines. And I suddenly wondered why, if this were so, it should be quite unknown for any modern trade to have a ritual poetry. How did people come to chant rude poems while pulling certain ropes or gathering certain fruit, and why did nobody do anything of the kind while producing any of the modern things? Why is a modern newspaper never printed by people singing in chorus? Why do shopmen seldom, if ever, sing?

.   .   .   .   .

If reapers sing while reaping, why should not auditors sing while auditing and bankers while banking? If there are songs for all the separate things that have to be done in a boat, why are there not songs for all the separate things that have to be done in a bank? As the train from Dover flew through the Kentish gardens, I tried to write a few songs suitable for commercial gentlemen. Thus, the work of bank clerks when casting up columns might begin with a thundering chorus in praise of Simple Addition:

Up, my lads, and lift the ledgers, sleep and ease are o'er.
    Hear the Stars of Morning shouting: 'Two and Two are Four.'
Though the creeds and realms are reeling, though the sophists roar,
    Though we weep and pawn our watches, Two and Two are Four.

And then, of course, we should need another song for times of financial crisis and courage, a song with a more fierce and panic-stricken metre, like the rushing of horses in the night:

There 's a run upon the Bank—
        Stand away!
For the Manager 's a crank and the Secretary drank, and the Upper Tooting Bank
        Turns to bay!
Stand close: there is a run
        On the Bank.
Of our ship, our royal one, let the ringing legend run, that she fired with every gun
        Ere she sank.

.   .   .   .   .   .

And as I came into the cloud of London I met a friend of mine who actually is in a bank, and submitted these suggestions in rhyme to him for use among his colleagues. But he was not very hopeful about the matter. It was not (he assured me) that he underrated the verses, or in any sense lamented their lack of polish. No; it was rather, he felt, an indefinable something in the very atmosphere of the society in which we live that makes it spiritually difficult to sing in banks. And I think he must be right; though the matter is very mysterious. I may observe here that I think there must be some mistake in the calculations of the Socialists. They put down all our distress not to a moral tone, but to the chaos of private enterprise. Now, banks are private; but post offices are Socialistic: therefore I naturally expected that the post office would fall into the collectivist idea of a chorus. Judge of my surprise when the lady in my local post office (whom I urged to sing) dismissed the idea with far more coldness than the bank clerk had done. She seemed, indeed, to be in a considerably greater state of depression than he. Should any one suppose that this was the effect of the verses themselves, it is only fair to say that the specimen verse of the Post Office Hymn ran thus:

> O'er London our letters are shaken like snow,
> Our wires o'er the world like the thunderbolts go.
> The news that may marry a maiden in Sark,
> Or kill an old lady in Finsbury Park.
>   *Chorus* (with a swing of joy and energy):
> Or kill an old lady in Finsbury Park.

And the more I thought about the matter the more painfully certain it seemed that the most important and typical modern things could not be done with a chorus. One could not, for instance, be a great financier and sing; because the essence of being a great financier is that you keep quiet. You could not even in many modern circles be a public man and sing; because in those circles the essence of being a public man is that you do nearly everything in private. Nobody would imagine a chorus of money-lenders. Every one knows the story of the solicitors' corps of volunteers who, when the Colonel on the battle-field cried: 'Charge!' all said simultaneously: 'Six - and - eightpence.' Men can sing while charging in a military, but hardly in a legal sense. And at the end of my reflections I had really got no further than the subconscious feeling of my friend the bank clerk—that there is something spiritually suffocating about our life; not about our laws merely, but about our life. Bank clerks are without songs not because they are poor, but because they are sad. Sailors are much poorer. As I passed homewards I passed a little tin building of some religious sort, which was shaken with shouting as a trumpet is torn with its own tongue. *They* were singing, anyhow; and I had for an instant a fancy I had often had before: that with us the superhuman is the only place where you can find the human. Human nature is hunted, and has fled into sanctuary.

THE BEGINNING OF THE QUARREL

I HAVE been asked to republish these notes—which appeared in a weekly paper—as a rough sketch of certain aspects of the institution of Private Property; now so completely forgotten amid the journalistic jubilations over Private Enterprise. The very fact that the publicists say so much of the latter and so little of the former is a measure of the moral tone of the times. A pickpocket is obviously a champion of private enterprise. But it would perhaps be an exaggeration to say that a pickpocket is a champion of private property. The point about Capitalism and Commercialism, as conducted of late, is that they have really preached the extension of business rather than the preservation of belongings; and have at best tried to disguise the pickpocket with some of the virtues of the pirate. The point about Communism is that it only reforms the pickpocket by forbidding pockets.

Pockets and possessions generally seem to me to have not only a more normal but a more dignified defence than the rather dirty individualism that talks about private enterprise. In the hope that it may possibly help others to understand it, I have decided to reproduce these studies as they stand, hasty and sometimes merely topical as they were. It is indeed very hard to reproduce them in this form, because they were editorial notes to a controversy largely conducted by others; but the general idea is at least present. In any case, 'private enterprise' is no very noble way of stating the truth of one of the Ten Commandments. But there was at least a time when it was more or less true. The Manchester Radicals preached a rather crude and cruel sort of competition; but at least they practised what they preached. The newspapers now praising private enterprise are preaching the very opposite of anything that anybody dreams of practising. The practical tendency of all trade and business to-day is towards big commercial combinations, often more imperial, more impersonal, more international than many a communist commonwealth—things that are at least collective if not collectivist. It is all very well to repeat distractedly: 'What are we coming to, with all this Bolshevism?' It is equally relevant to add: 'What are we coming to, even without Bolshevism?' The obvious answer is—Monopoly. It is certainly not private enterprise. The American Trust is not private enterprise. It would be truer to call the Spanish Inquisition private judgment. Monopoly is neither private nor enterprising. It exists to prevent private enterprise. And that system of trust or monopoly, that complete destruction of property, would still be the present goal of all our progress, if there were not a Bolshevist in the world.

Now I am one of those who believe that the cure for centralization is decentralization. It has been described as a paradox. There is apparently something elvish and fantastic about saying that when capital has come to be too much in the hand of the few, the right thing is to restore it into the hands of the many. The Socialist would put it in the hands of even fewer people; but those people would be politicians, who (as we know) always administer it in the interests of the many. But before I put before the reader things written in the very thick of the current controversy, I foresee it will be necessary to preface them with these few paragraphs, explaining a few of the terms and amplifying a few of the assumptions. I was in the weekly paper arguing with people who knew the shorthand of this particular argument; but to be clearly understood, we must begin with a few definitions or, at least, descriptions. I assure the reader that I use words in quite a definite sense, but it is possible that he may use them in a different sense; and a muddle and misunderstanding of that sort does not even rise to the dignity of a difference of opinion.

For instance, Capitalism is really a very unpleasant word. It is also a very unpleasant thing. Yet the thing I have in mind, when I say so, is quite definite and definable; only the name is a very unworkable word for it. But obviously we must have some word for it. When I say 'Capitalism,' I commonly mean something that may be stated thus: 'That economic condition in which there is a class of capitalists, roughly recognizable and relatively small, in whose possession so much of the capital is concentrated as to necessitate a very large majority of the citizens serving those capitalists for a wage.' This particular state of things can and does exist, and we must have some word for it, and some way of discussing it. But this is undoubtedly a very bad word, because it is used by other people to mean quite other things. Some people seem to mean merely private property. Others suppose that capitalism must mean anything involving the use of capital. But if that use is too literal, it is also too loose and even too large. If the use of capital is capitalism, then everything is capitalism. Bolshevism is capitalism and anarchist communism is capitalism; and every revolutionary scheme, however wild, is still capitalism. Lenin and Trotsky believe as much as Lloyd George and Thomas that the economic operations of to-day must leave something over for the economic operations of to-morrow. And that is all that capital means in its economic sense. In that case, the word is useless. My use of it may be arbitrary, but it is not useless. If capitalism means private property, I am capitalist. If capitalism means capital, everybody is capitalist. But if capitalism means this particular condition of capital, only paid out to the mass in the form of wages, then it does mean something, even if it ought to mean something else.

The truth is that what we call Capitalism ought to be called Proletarianism. The point of it is not that some people have capital, but that most people only have wages because they do not have capital. I have made an heroic effort in my time to walk about the world always saying Proletarianism instead of Capitalism. But my path has been a thorny one of troubles and mis-understandings. I find that when I criticize the Duke of Northumberland for his Proletarianism, my meaning does not get home. When I say I should often agree with the *Morning Post* if it were not so deplorably Proletarian, there seems to be some strange momentary impediment to the complete communion of mind with mind. Yet that would be strictly accurate; for what I complain of, in the current defence of existing capitalism, is that it is a defence of keeping most men in wage dependence; that is, keeping most men without capital. I am not the sort of precisian who prefers conveying correctly what he doesn't mean, rather than conveying incorrectly what he does. I am totally indifferent to the term as compared to the meaning. I do not care whether I call one thing or the other by this mere printed word beginning with a 'C,' so long as it is applied to one thing and not the other. I do not mind using a term as arbitrary as a mathematical sign, if it is accepted like a mathematical sign. I do not mind calling Property x and Capitalism y, so long as nobody thinks it necessary to say that $x=y$. I do not mind saying 'cat' for capitalism and 'dog' for distributism, so long as people understand that the things are different enough to fight like cat and dog. The proposal of the wider distribution of capital remains the same, whatever we call it, or whatever we call the present glaring con-tradiction of it. It is the same whether we state it by saying that there is too much capitalism in the one sense or too little capitalism in the other. And it is really quite pedantic to say that the use of capital must be capitalist. We might as fairly say that anything social must be Socialist; that Socialism can be identified with a social evening or a social glass. Which, I grieve to say, is not the case.

Nevertheless, there is enough verbal vagueness about Socialism to call for a word of definition. Socialism is a system which makes the corporate unity of society responsible for all its economic processes, or all those affecting life and essential living. If anything important is sold, the Government has sold it; if anything important is given, the Government has given it; if anything important is even tolerated, the Government is responsible for tolerating it. This is the very reverse of anarchy; it is an extreme enthusiasm for authority. It is in many ways worthy of the moral dignity of the mind; it is a collective acceptance of very complete responsibility. But it is silly of Socialists to complain of our saying that it must be a destruction of liberty. It is almost equally silly of Anti-Socialists to complain of the unnatural and unbalanced brutality of the Bolshevist Government in crushing a political opposition. A Socialist Government is one which in its nature does not tolerate any true and real opposition. For there the Government provides everything; and it is absurd to ask a Government to *provide* an opposition.

You cannot go to the Sultan and say reproachfully: 'You have made no arrangements for your brother dethroning you and seizing the Caliphate.' You cannot go to a medieval king and say: 'Kindly lend me two thousand spears and one thousand bowmen, as I wish to raise a rebellion against you.' Still less can you reproach a Government which professes to set up everything, because it has not set up anything to pull down all it has set up. Opposition and rebellion depend on property and liberty. They can only be tolerated where other rights have been allowed to strike root, besides the central right of the ruler. Those rights must be protected by a morality which even the ruler will hesitate to defy. The critic of the State can only exist where a religious sense of right protects his claims to his own bow and spear; or at least, to his own pen or his own printing-press. It is absurd to suppose that he could borrow the royal pen to advocate regicide or use the Government printing-presses to expose the corruption of the Government. Yet it is the whole point of Socialism, the whole case for Socialism, that unless all printing-presses are Government printing-presses, printers may be oppressed. Everything is staked on the State's justice; it is putting all the eggs in one basket. Many of them will be rotten eggs; but even then you will not be allowed to use them at political elections.

About fifteen years ago a few of us began to preach, in the old *New Age* and *New Witness*, a policy of small distributed property (which has since assumed the awkward but accurate name of Distributism), as we should have said then, against the two extremes of Capitalism and Communism. The first criticism we received was from the most brilliant Fabians, especially Mr. Bernard Shaw. And the form which that first criticism took was simply to tell us that our ideal was impossible. It was only a case of Catholic credulity about fairy-tales. The Law of Rent, and other economic laws, made it inevitable that the little rivulets of property should run down into the pool of plutocracy. In truth, it was the Fabian wit, and not merely the Tory fool, who confronted our vision with that venerable verbal opening: ' If it were all divided up to-morrow——"

Nevertheless, we had an answer even in those days, and though we have since found many others, it will clarify the question if I repeat this point of principle. It is true that I believe in fairy-tales—in the sense that I marvel so much at what does exist that I am the readier to admit what might. I understand the man who believes in the Sea Serpent on the ground that there are more fish in the sea than ever came out of it. But I do it the more because the other man, in his ardour for disproving the Sea Serpent, always argues that there are not only no snakes in Iceland, but none in the world. Suppose Mr. Bernard Shaw, commenting on this credulity, were to blame me for believing (on the word of some lying priest) that stones could be thrown up into the air and hang there suspended like a rainbow. Suppose he told me tenderly that I should not believe this Popish fable of the magic stones, if I had ever had the Law of Gravity scientifically explained to me. And suppose, after all this, I found he was only talking about the impossibility of building an arch. I think most of us would form two main conclusions about him and his school.   First, we should think them very ill-informed about what is really meant by recognizing a law of nature. A law of nature can be recognized by resisting it, or out-manœuvring it, or even using it against itself, as in the case of the arch.   And second, and much more strongly, we should think them astonishingly ill-informed about what has already been done upon this earth.

Similarly, the first fact in the discussion of whether small properties can exist is the fact that they do exist. It is a fact almost equally unmistakable that they not only exist but endure.   Mr. Shaw affirmed, in a sort of abstract fury, that 'small properties will not stay small.'   Now it is interesting to note here that the opponents of anything like a several proprietary bring two highly inconsistent charges against it.   They are perpetually telling us that the peasant life in Latin or other countries is monotonous, is unprogressive, is covered with weedy superstitions, and is a sort of survival of the Stone Age.   Yet even while they taunt us with its survival, they argue that it can never survive. They point to the peasant as a perennial stick-in-the-mud; and then refuse to plant him anywhere, on the specific ground that he would not stick.   Now, the first of the two types of denunciation is arguable enough; but in order to denounce peasantries, the critics must admit that there are peasantries to denounce.   And if it were true that they always tended rapidly to disappear, it would not be true that they exhibited those primitive customs and conservative opinions which they not only do, in fact, exhibit, but which the critics reproach them with exhibiting.   They cannot in common sense accuse a thing at once of being antiquated and of being ephemeral.   It is, of course, the dry fact, to be seen in broad daylight, that small peasant properties are not ephemeral.   But anyhow, Mr. Shaw and his school must not say that arches cannot be built, and then that they disfigure the landscape.   The Distributive State is not a hypothesis for him to demolish; it is a phenomenon for him to explain.

The truth is that the conception that small property *evolves* into capitalism is a precise picture of what practically never takes place. The truth is attested even by facts of geography, facts which, as it seems to me, have been strangely overlooked. Nine times out of ten, an industrial civilization of the modern capitalist type does *not* arise, wherever else it may arise, in places where there has hitherto been a distributive civilization like that of a peasantry. Capitalism is a monster that grows in deserts. Industrial servitude has almost everywhere arisen in those empty spaces where the older civilization was thin or absent. Thus it grew up easily in the North of England rather than the South; precisely because the North had been comparatively empty and barbarous through all the ages when the South had a civilization of guilds and peasantries. Thus it grew up easily in the American continent rather than the European; precisely because it had nothing to supplant in America but a few savages, while in Europe it had to supplant the culture of multitudinous farms. Everywhere it has been but one stride from the mud-hut to the manufacturing town. Everywhere the mud-hut which really turned into the free farm has never since moved an inch towards the manufacturing town. Wherever there was the mere lord and the mere serf, they could almost instantly be turned into the mere employer and the mere employee. Wherever there has been the free man, even when he was relatively less rich and powerful, his mere memory has made complete industrial capitalism impossible. It is an enemy that has sown these tares, but even as an enemy he is a coward. For he can only sow them in waste places, where no wheat can spring up and choke them.

To take up our parable again, we say first that arches exist; and not only exist but remain. A hundred Roman aqueducts and amphitheatres are there to show that they can remain as long or longer than anything else. And if a progressive person informs us that an arch always turns into a factory chimney, or even that an arch always falls down because it is weaker than a

factory chimney, or even that wherever it does fall
down people perceive that they must replace it by a
factory chimney—why, we shall be so audacious as to
cast doubts on all these three assertions. All we could
possibly admit is that the principle supporting the
chimney is simpler than the principle of the arch; and
for that very reason the factory chimney, like the feudal
tower, can rise the more easily in a howling wilderness.

But the image has yet a further application. If at
this moment the Latin countries are largely made our
model in the matter of the small property, it is only in
the sense in which they would have been, through
certain periods of history, the only exemplars of the arch.
There was a time when all arches were Roman arches;
and when a man living by the Liffey or the Thames
would know as little about them as Mr. Shaw knows
about peasant proprietors. But that does not mean
that we fight for something merely foreign, or advance
the arch as a sort of Italian ensign; any more than we
want to make the Thames as yellow as the Tiber, or
have any particular taste in macaroni or malaria. The
principle of the arch is human, and applicable to and
by all humanity. So is the principle of well-distributed
private property. That a few Roman arches stood in
ruins in Britain is not a proof that arches cannot be
built, but on the contrary, a proof that they can.

And now, to complete the coincidence or analogy,
what is the principle of the arch? You can call it, if
you like, an affront to gravitation; you will be more
correct if you call it an appeal to gravitation. The
principle asserts that by combining separate stones of
a particular shape in a particular way, we can ensure
that their very tendency to fall shall prevent them
from falling. And though my image is merely an
illustration, it does to a great extent hold even as to
the success of more equalized properties. What upholds
an arch is an equality of pressure of the separate stones
upon each other. The equality is at once mutual aid
and mutual obstruction. It is not difficult to show
that in a healthy society the moral pressure of different

private properties acts in exactly the same way. But if the other school finds the key or comparison insufficient, it must find some other. It is clear that no natural forces can frustrate the fact. To say that any law, such as that of rent, makes against it is true only in the sense that many natural laws make against all morality and the very essentials of manhood. In that sense, scientific arguments are as irrelevant to our case for property as Mr. Shaw used to say they were to his case against vivisection.

Lastly, it is not only true that the arch of property remains, it is true that the building of such arches increases, both in quantity and quality. For instance, the French peasant before the French Revolution was already indefinitely a proprietor; it has made his property more private and more absolute, not less. The French are now less than ever likely to abandon the system, when it has proved for the second, if not the hundredth time, the most stable type of prosperity in the stress of war. A revolution as heroic, and even more unconquerable, has already in Ireland disregarded alike the Socialist dream and the Capitalist reality, with a driving energy of which no one has yet dared to foresee the limits. So, when the round arch of the Romans and the Normans had remained for ages as a sort of relic, the rebirth of Christendom found for it a further application and issue. It sprang in an instant to the titanic stature of the Gothic; where man seemed to be a god who had hanged his worlds upon nothing. Then was unsealed again something of that ancient secret which had so strangely described the priest as the builder of bridges. And when I look to-day at some of the bridges which he built above the air, I can understand a man still calling them impossible, as their only possible praise.

What do we mean by that 'equality of pressure' as of the stones in an arch? More will be said of this in detail; but in general we mean that the modern passion for incessant and restless buying and selling goes along with the extreme inequality of men too rich or too poor.

The explanation of the continuity of peasantries (which their opponents are simply forced to leave unexplained) is that, where that independence exists, it is valued exactly as any other dignity is valued when it is regarded as normal to a man; as no man goes naked or is beaten with a stick for hire.

The theory that those who start reasonably equal cannot remain reasonably equal is a fallacy founded entirely on a society in which they start extremely unequal. It is quite true that when capitalism has passed a certain point, the broken fragments of property are very easily devoured. In other words, it is true when there is a small amount of small property; but it is quite untrue when there is a large amount of small property. To argue from what happened in the rush of big business and the rout of scattered small businesses to what must always happen when the parties are more on a level, is quite illogical. It is proving from Niagara that there is no such thing as a lake. Once tip up the lake and the *whole* of the water will rush one way; as the whole economic tendency of capitalist inequality rushes one way. Leave the lake as a lake, or the level as a level, and there is nothing to prevent the lake remaining until the crack of doom—as many levels of peasantry seem likely to remain until the crack of doom. This fact is proved by experience, even if it is not explained by experience; but, as a matter of fact, it is possible to suggest not only the experience but the explanation. The truth is that there is no economic tendency whatever towards the disappearance of small property, until that property becomes so very small as to cease to act as property at all. If one man has a hundred acres and another man has half an acre, it is likely enough that he will be unable to live on half an acre. Then there will be an economic tendency for him to sell his land and make the other man the proud possessor of a hundred and a half. But if one man has thirty acres and the other man has forty acres, there is no economic tendency of any kind whatever to make the first man sell to the second. It is simply false to say that the first man cannot be secure of thirty or the second man content with forty. It is sheer nonsense; like saying that any man who owns a bull terrier will be bound to sell it to somebody who owns a mastiff. It is like saying that I cannot own a horse because I have an eccentric neighbour who owns an elephant.

Needless to say, those who insist that roughly equalized ownership cannot exist, base their whole argument on the notion that it has existed. They have to suppose, in order to prove their point, that people in England, for instance, did begin as equals and rapidly reached inequality. And it only rounds off the humour of their whole position that they assume the existence of what they call an impossibility in the one case where it has really not occurred. They talk as if ten miners had run a race, and one of them became the Duke of Northumberland. They talk as if the first Rothschild was a peasant who patiently planted better cabbages than the other peasants. The truth is that England became a capitalist country because it had long been an oligarchical country. It would be much harder to point out in what way a country like Denmark need become oligarchical. But the case is even stronger when we add the ethical to the economic common sense. When there is once established a widely scattered ownership, there is a public opinion that is stronger than any law; and very often (what in modern times is even more remarkable) a law that is really an expression of public opinion. It may be very difficult for modern people to imagine a world in which men are not generally admired for covetousness and crushing their neighbours; but I assure them that such strange patches of an earthly paradise do really remain on earth.

The truth is that this first objection of impossibility in the abstract flies flat in the face of all the facts of experience and human nature. It is not true that a moral custom cannot hold most men content with a reasonable status, and careful to preserve it. It is as if we were to say that because some men are more attractive to women than others, therefore the inhabitants of Balham under Queen Victoria could not possibly have been arranged on a monogamous model, with one man one wife. Sooner or later, it might be said, all females would be found clustering round the fascinating few, and nothing but bachelorhood be left for the unattractive many. Sooner or later the suburb must consist of a hundred hermitages and three harems. But this is not the case. It is not the case at present, whatever may happen if the moral tradition of marriage is really lost in Balham. So long as that moral tradition is alive, so long as stealing other people's wives is reprobated or being faithful to a spouse is admired, there are limits to the extent to which the wildest profligate in Balham can disturb the balance of the sexes. So any land-grabber would very rapidly find that there were limits to the extent to which he could buy up land in an Irish or Spanish or Serbian village. When it is really thought hateful to take Naboth's vineyard, as it is to take Uriah's wife, there is little difficulty in finding a local prophet to pronounce the judgment of the Lord. In an atmosphere of capitalism the man who lays field to field is flattered; but in an atmosphere of property he is promptly jeered at or possibly stoned. The result is that the village has not sunk into plutocracy or the suburb into polygamy.

Property is a point of honour. The true contrary of the word 'property' is the word 'prostitution.' And it is not true that a human being will always sell what is sacred to that sense of self-ownership, whether it be the body or the boundary. A few do it in both cases; and by doing it they always become outcasts. But it is not true that a majority must do it; and anybody who says it is, is ignorant, not of our plans and proposals, not of anybody's visions and ideals, not of distributism or division of capital by this or that process, but of the facts of history and the substance of humanity. He is a barbarian who has never seen an arch.

In the notes I have here jotted down it will be obvious, of course, that the restoration of this pattern, simple as it is, is much more complicated in a complicated society.

Here I have only traced it in its simplest form as it stood, and still stands, at the beginning of our discussion. I disregard the view that such 'reaction' cannot be. I hold the old mystical dogma that what Man has done, Man can do. My critics seem to hold a still more mystical dogma: that Man cannot possibly do a thing because he has done it. That is what seems to be meant by saying that small property is 'antiquated.' It really means that all property is dead. There is nothing to be reached upon the present lines except the increasing loss of property by everybody, as something swallowed up into a system equally impersonal and inhuman, whether we call it Communism or Capitalism. If we cannot go back, it hardly seems worth while to go forward.

There is nothing in front but a flat wilderness of standardization either by Bolshevism or Big Business. But it is strange that some of us should have seen sanity, if only in a vision, while the rest go forward chained eternally to enlargement without liberty and progress without hope.

ON EVIL EUPHEMISMS

SOMEBODY has sent me a book on Companionate
Marriage; so called because the people involved are not
married and will very rapidly cease to be companions.
I have no intention of discussing here that somewhat
crude colonial project. I will merely say that it is here
accompanied with sub-titles and other statements about
the rising generation and the revolt of youth. And it
seems to me exceedingly funny that, just when the rising
generation boasts of not being sentimental, when it
talks of being very scientific and sociological—at that
very moment everybody seems to have forgotten altogether what was the social use of marriage and to be
thinking wholly and solely of the sentimental. The
practical purposes mentioned as the first two reasons
for marriage, in the Anglican marriage service, seem to
have gone completely out of sight for some people,
who talk as if there were nothing but a rather wild
version of the third, which may relatively be called
romantic. And this, if you please, is supposed to be an
emancipation from Victorian sentiment and romance.
    But I only mention this matter as one of many, and
one which illustrates a still more curious contradiction
in this modern claim. We are perpetually being told
that this rising generation is very frank and free, and
that its whole social ideal is frankness and freedom.
Now I am not at all afraid of frankness. What I am
afraid of is fickleness. And there is a truth in the old
proverbial connection between what is fickle and what is
false. There is in the very titles and terminology of
all this sort of thing a pervading element of falsehood.
Everything is to be called something that it is not;
as in the characteristic example of Companionate
Marriage. Everything is to be recommended to the
public by some sort of synonym which is really a

pseudonym. It is a talent that goes with the time of electioneering and advertisement and newspaper headlines; but whatever else such a time may be, it certainly is not specially a time of truth.

In short, these friends of frankness depend almost entirely on Euphemism. They introduce their horrible heresies under new and carefully complimentary names; as the Furies were called the Eumenides. The names are always flattery; the names are also nonsense. The name of Birth-Control, for instance, is sheer nonsense. Everybody has always exercised birth-control; even when they were so paradoxical as to permit the process to end in a birth. Everybody has always known about birth-control, even if it took the wild and unthinkable form of self-control. The question at issue concerns different forms of birth-prevention; and I am not going to debate it here. But if I did debate it, I would call it by its name. The same is true of an older piece of sentiment indulged in by the frank and free: the expression 'Free Love.' That also is a Euphemism; that is, it is a refusal of people to say what they mean. In that sense, it is impossible to prevent *love* being free, but the moral problem challenged concerns not the passions, but the will. There are a great many other examples of this sort of polite fiction; these respectable disguises adopted by those who are always railing against respectability. In the immediate future there will probably be more still. There really seems no necessary limit to the process; and however far the anarchy of ethics may go, it may always be accompanied with this curious and pompous ceremonial. The sensitive youth of the future will never be called upon to accept Forgery as Forgery. It will be easy enough to call it Homoeography or Script-Assimilation or something else that would suggest, to the simple or the superficial, that nothing was involved but a sort of socializing or unification of individual handwriting. We should not, like the more honest Mr. Fagin, teach little boys to pick pockets; for Mr. Fagin becomes far less honest when he becomes Professor Faginski, the great sociologist, of the University

of Jena. But we should call it by some name implying
the transference of something; I cannot at the moment
remember the Greek either for pocket or pocket-hand-
kerchief. As for the social justification of murder, that
has already begun; and earnest thinkers had better
begin at once to think about a nice inoffensive name
for it. The case for murder, on modern relative and
evolutionary ethics, is quite overwhelming. There is
hardly one of us who does not, in looking round his
or her social circle, recognize some chatty person or
energetic social character whose disappearance, without
undue fuss or farewell, would be a bright event for us all.
Nor is it true that such a person is dangerous only
because he wields unjust legal or social powers. The
problem is often purely psychological, and not in the
least legal; and no legal emancipations would solve
it. Nothing would solve it but the introduction of
that new form of liberty which we may agree to call,
perhaps, the practice of Social Subtraction. Or, if we
like, we can model the new name on the other names
I have mentioned. We may call it Life-Control or
Free Death; or anything else that has as little to do with
the point of it as Companionate Marriage has to do with
either marriage or companionship.

Anyhow, I respectfully refuse to be impressed by the
claim to candour and realism put forward just now for
men, women, and movements. It seems to me obvious
that this is not really the age of audacity but merely
of advertisement; which may rather be described as
caution kicking up a fuss. Much of the mistake arises
from the double sense of the word publicity. For
publicity also is a thoroughly typical euphemism or
evasive term. Publicity does not mean revealing public
life in the interests of public spirit. It means merely
flattering private enterprises in the interests of private
persons. It means paying compliments in public; but
not offering criticisms in public. We should all be very
much surprised if we walked out of our front door one
morning and saw a hoarding on one side of the road
saying: 'Use Miggle's Milk; It Is All Cream,' and a

hoarding on the other side of the road inscribed: 'Don't Use Miggle's Milk; It 's Nearly All Water.' The modern world would be much upset if I were allowed to set up a flaming sky-sign proclaiming my precise opinion of the Colonial Port Wine praised in the flaming sign opposite. All this advertisement may have something to do with the freedom of trade; but it has nothing to do with the freedom of truth. Publicity must be praise and praise must to some extent be euphemism. It must put the matter in a milder and more inoffensive form than it might be put, however much that mildness may seem to shout through megaphones or flare in headlines. And just as this sort of loud evasion is used in favour of bad wine and bad milk, so it is used in favour of bad morals. When somebody wishes to wage a social war against what all normal people have regarded as a social decency, the very first thing he does is to find some artificial term that shall sound relatively decent. He has no more of the real courage that would pit vice against virtue than the ordinary advertiser has the courage to advertise ale as arsenic. His intelligence, such as it is, is entirely a commercial intelligence and to that extent entirely conventional. He is a shopkeeper who dresses the shop-window; he is certainly the very reverse of a rebel or a rioter who breaks the shop-window. If only for this reason, I remain cold and decline the due reverence to Companionate Marriage and the book which speaks so reverentially about the Revolt of Youth. For this sort of revolt strikes me as nothing except revolting; and certainly not particularly realistic. With the passions which are natural to youth we all sympathize; with the pain that often arises from loyalty and duty we all sympathize still more; but nobody need sympathize with publicity experts picking pleasant expressions for unpleasant things; and I for one prefer the coarse language of our fathers.

ON CALLING NAMES—CHRISTIAN AND OTHERWISE

It is said that there has been a moral breakdown; but let us be comforted; it is only a mental breakdown. Indeed I only call it a breakdown, because that was the name of a nigger dance. But it is not so much like the breakdown as it is like the cake-walk. And the case against the cake-walk is that it claims to be one in which you can eat your cake and have it. In other words, the real objection to much of modern fashion is an objection based on reason, and not specially on morality. In certain respects (not all or even perhaps most), current culture seems to me to have simply fallen to a lower level of civilization, and to be now a little nearer to niggers or even to monkeys.

I will take one example of what I mean, precisely because it has nothing directly to do with morality at all. It is now the custom of most young people to shout at each other by their Christian names, or the abbreviations of their Christian names, or the most intimate substitutes for their Christian names, as soon as they know each other, or before they know each other. If (as you and I and all smart people are aware) the dashing and distinguished Miss Vernon-Vavasour was known in baptism as Gloria but among her most devoted friends as Gurgles, there is now no difference between those who call her Gurgles and those who call her Glory and those who would normally prefer, when suddenly presented to somebody they do not know from Eve, to call her Miss Vernon-Vavasour. As soon as she is seen as a distant dot on the other side of the tennis-court, a total stranger will yell at her as Gurgles, because he hears a crowd of other total strangers doing the same. He will use her nickname, because he has never known enough about her to have heard her name. Or he will use the first name, because he has not been in her company for a sufficient number of seconds to get as far as the last one.

Now all this has nothing directly to do with right and wrong. I suppose there are savage tribes in which a person only possesses one name, and so has to be addressed by it. It might be maintained that the first name is always the noblest and most sacred in a religious and moral sense. Perhaps the Bright Young Things only use Christian names to express their holy zeal for anything that is Christian. Perhaps they talk of Tom only to remind him of his solemn dedication to St. Thomas of Canterbury or St. Thomas Aquinas. Perhaps they shriek at Peter to thrill him with the thought that he is the rock on which the Church is built. Perhaps they compress into the loud and sometimes peremptory cry of 'Jack!' all the mingled mysteries of St. John the Baptist and St. John the Evangelist. Perhaps, on the other hand, they don't. But anyhow, it is quite true that Tom, Dick, and Harry are the names of saints; while Jones, Brown, and Robinson are often only the names of snobs. Therefore the practice of talking about Tom, Dick, and Harry instead of about Mr. Jones, Mr. Brown, and Mr. Robinson, might be adopted for many reasons, noble and ignoble, worldly and unworldly. I complain of it here, not because it is worldly, but on the contrary, because it shows a lack of appreciation of the world. It especially shows a lack of appreciation of the civilized world. It shows a dullness in distinguishing and tasting the arts of civilization.

Anyhow, the matter of Christian names does not itself involve Christian morals. To take another alternative possibility: some of those happy Utopias described by Mr. Wells might possibly abolish all Christian names, or even abolish all names. It might entirely deprive us of names and only provide us with numbers. We might have labels, alphabetical and numerical, as if we were motor cars; or be known by such figures as are convicts and policemen. And all this would not involve any direct question of misconduct. We might hear Gurgles

shrieking across the tennis-court: 'Play up, K.P.
7983501, old thing; we 've got to go on to M.M. 9018972's
to tea.'   Or one of her young friends would be heard
saying languidly: 'Chuck us a cig., Q.B. 9973588; I 've
left my filthy case in X.Y. 318220's car.'   And in all
this there could arise no particular criticism of morals,
whatever the crabbed and cantankerous might offer in
the way of a criticism of manners.   There is nothing
erotic or even too emotional in those alphabetical forms
of address.   There is nothing calculated to inflame the
passions in the figure 7983501.   Our criticism of it
would be that it dulled the edge of fine cultural intercourse; that it let us down to a lower level of artistic
interest and invention; or, as Gurgles would prefer to
say, that it is a bloody bore.   It takes away certain fine
shades of personal interest, of appropriateness or in-
appropriateness, which help the coloured comedy of life.
For though one Gloria differs from another Gloria in
glory, and even every Gurgles does not gurgle alike,
there is always some artistic interest, serious or humorous,
in the association of an individual person with an individual name, perhaps carrying memories of legend or
history.   But our chief objection would still remain the
same: that it is barbaric and reactionary to destroy
these cultural distinctions between one thing and
another; because it is like rubbing out all the lines of
a fine drawing.

Now there were many things in which the Victorians
were quite wrong.   But in their punctiliousness about
etiquette in things like this, they were quite right.   In
insisting that the young lady should be called at one
stage Miss Vavasour, and only at another stage Gloria,
and only in extreme and almost desperate cases of confidence Gurgles, they were a thousand times right.   They
were maintaining a wholly superior social system, by
which social actions were significant, and not (as they
are now) all of them equally insignificant.   There is a
meaning in each of those names, as there is a meaning
in a name given in baptism or a name given in religion;
there is no meaning in the name that is merely a number.

When first we are presented to Mr. Robinson, he ought to be presented as Mr. Robinson. The formal title and the family name mean that he is what he is, whatever else he is. He is a man and a free man and a fellow-citizen and a person living under the protection of a certain social order. In short, it means that he is worthy of a certain kind of respect and consideration, *before* we know anything else whatever about his worth. If we afterwards reach such a degree of spontaneous friend-ship as to wish to call him Belisarius, or whatever his first name may happen to be, we shall have done so because we have formed certain independent opinions of our own, about qualities in him which we did not know of at the beginning; and the change will therefore have an intelligent and intelligible meaning. It will be a record of something real in our minds and in his mind. The automatic adoption of his first name by everybody creates an atmosphere of utter unreality. When I was a boy there was a real symbolism, a real poetry, and in the sane sense a real romance, in the transition from being supposed to call a lady Miss Brown to being allowed to call her Mabel. I do not discuss, of course, the dark infernal underworld where she was sometimes called Miss Mabel. The transition did not mean (as the silly sentimentalists who write against the sentimentalism of their grandmothers probably imagine) that you were in love with Mabel; it did not necessarily mean that you were even flirting with Mabel; but it did mean some-thing. It meant that she felt a certain confidence in you and did not object to counting you among her par-ticular personal companions. To-day it means nothing at all. And intelligent people have a strong objection to things that mean nothing at all.

There is also this further point. The old stages of intimacy were individual, and in that sense even uncon-ventional. The new comradeship is entirely conven-tional. It is in the exact and solid sense a convention. The old admission to special friendship occurred at different stages with different people; it was an adven-ture. The new familiarity is really a formality. It is a

thing made common like the rules of a game; it is a thing
dictated by what the instinct of the people themselves
calls 'the crowd.' But the essential point about it is
that this sort of simplification merely impoverishes life.
Life is much more rich and interesting when there are
individual initiations, special favours, and different titles
for different relations of life. This is a real and serious
social criticism; and you do not get rid of it by ranting
or sentimentalizing; either by saying that Mabel by
being called Mabel is well on the road to being called
Jezebel; or by saying that in allowing half a hundred
men to call her whatever they choose, she is heroically
emancipating herself from the tyranny of Man.

I fancy that a real advance in progress and civilization
would do exactly the opposite. If I were constructing
a Utopia, which God forbid, I should describe a higher
civilization in which every human being had a hundred
names; in which each had a particular name known
only to a particular friend; in which there were more
and not less ceremonies differentiating the various kinds
of love and friendship and in which the suitor had to
go through ten names before he got to Glory. That
would be a Utopia really worth constructing; for it
would really be a question of construction. Most of the
Utopias represent only a dull sort of destruction; the
sort of destruction that we call simplification. It would
really be something like fun to invent a ritual; but since
the neglect of religion, no man has really had the courage
to invent a ritual. It would be a great lark to draw up
a code of law, decorating Tom, Dick, and Harry with
their Seven Secret Names. But these things will not
come until the modern world has realized that its cure
lies in distribution and even in differentiation; and not
in mixing up everything together in one great mess.
Comradeship has become a sort of Combine; bearing
the same relation to true friendship that a Trust does
to true trade. Nobody seems to have any notion of
improving anything except by pouring it into something
else; as if a man were to pour the tea into the coffee or
the sherry into the port. The one idea in all human

things, from friendship to finance, is to pool everything. It is a very stagnant pool.

I have taken only this one type of a general tendency, because it does not mix the matter up with gushing morality or more gushing immorality. It gives some sort of chance for a little dry light of social criticism. And on a critical consideration, I repeat that these things seem to me a mere decline in civilization; like the beginning of the Dark Ages.

THE SCEPTIC AS A CRITIC

It takes three to make a quarrel. There is needed a peacemaker. The full potentialities of human fury cannot be reached until a friend of both parties tactfully intervenes. I feel myself to be in some such position in the recent American debate about Mr. Mencken's *Mercury* and the Puritans; and I admit it at the beginning with an embarrassment not untinged with terror. I know that the umpire may be torn in pieces. I know that the self-appointed umpire ought to be torn in pieces. I know, above all, that this is especially the case in anything which in any way involves international relations.

Perhaps the only sound criticism is self-criticism. Perhaps this is even more true of nations than of men. And I can quite well understand that many Americans would accept suggestions from their fellow-countrymen which they would rightly refuse from a foreigner. I can only plead that I have endeavoured to carry out the excellent patriotic principle of 'See England First' in the equally patriotic paraphrase of 'Criticize England First.' I have been engaged upon it long enough to be quite well aware that there are evils present in England that are relatively absent from America; and none more conspicuously absent, as Mr. Belloc has pointed out to the surprise of many, than the real, servile, superstitious, and mystical adoration of Money.

But what makes me so objectionable on the present occasion is that I feel a considerable sympathy with both sides. This offensive attitude I will endeavour to disguise, as far as possible, by tactfully distributed abuse of such things as I really think are abuses, and a gracefully simulated disgust with this or that part of each controversial case. But the plain truth is, that if I were an American, I should very frequently rejoice at the

American Mercury's scoring off somebody or something; nor would my modest fireside be entirely without mild rejoicings when the *American Mercury* was scored off. But I do definitely think that both sides, and perhaps especially the iconoclastic side, need what the whole modern world needs—a fixed spiritual standard even for their own intellectual purposes. I might express it by saying that I am very fond of revolutionists, but not very fond of nihilists. For nihilists, as their name implies, have nothing to revolt about.

On this side of the matter there is little to be added to the admirably sane, subtle, and penetrating article by Mr. T. S. Eliot;[1] especially that vital sentence in it in which he tells Professor Irving Babbitt (who admits the need of enthusiasm) that we cannot have an enthusiasm for having an enthusiasm. I think I know, incidentally, what we must have. Professor Babbitt is a very learned man; and I myself have little Latin and less Greek. But I know enough Greek to know the meaning of the second syllable of 'enthusiasm,' and I know it to be the key to this and every other discussion.

Let me take two examples, touching my points of agreement with the two sides. I heartily admire Mr. Mencken, not only for his vivacity and wit, but for his vehemence and sometimes for his violence. I warmly applaud him for his scorn and detestation of Service; and I think he was stating a historical fact when he said, as quoted in the *Forum*: 'When a gang of real estate agents, bond salesmen, and automobile dealers gets together to sob for Service, it takes no Freudian to surmise that someone is about to be swindled.' I do not see why he should not call a spade a spade and a swindler a swindler. I do not blame him for using vulgar words for vulgar things. But I do remark upon two ways in which the fact of his philosophy being negative makes his criticism almost shallow. First of all, it is obvious that such a satire is entirely meaningless unless swindling is a sin. And it is equally obvious that we are instantly swallowed up in the abysses of 'moralism' and

[1] 'The Humanism of Irving Babbitt,' the *Forum* for July 1928.

'religionism,' if it is a sin. And the second point, if less obvious, is equally important—that his healthy instinct against greasy hypocrisy does not really enlighten him about the heart of that hypocrisy.

What is the matter with the cult of Service is that, like so many modern notions, it is an idolatry of the intermediate, to the oblivion of the ultimate. It is like the jargon of the idiots who talk about Efficiency without any criticism of Effect. The sin of Service is the sin of Satan: that of trying to be first where it can only be second. A word like Service has stolen the sacred capital letter from the thing which it was once supposed to serve. There is a sense in serving God, and an even more disputed sense in serving man; but there is no sense in serving Service. To serve God is at least to serve an ideal being. Even if he were an imaginary being, he would still be an ideal being. That ideal has definite and even dogmatic. attributes—truth, justice, pity, purity, and the rest. To serve it, however imperfectly, is to serve a particular concept of perfection. But the man who rushes down the street waving his arms and wanting something or somebody to serve, will probably fall into the first bucket-shop or den of thieves and usurers, and be found industriously serving *them*. There arises the horrible idea that industry, reliability, punctuality, and business activity are good things; that mere readiness to serve the powers of this world is a Christian virtue. That is the case against Service, as distinct from the curse against Service, so heartily and inspiringly hurled by Mr. Mencken. But the serious case cannot be stated without once more raising the real question of whether mankind ought to serve anything; and of whether they had not better try to define what they intend to serve. All these silly words like Service and Efficiency and Practicality and the rest fail because they worship the means and not the end. But it all comes back to whether we do propose to worship the end; and preferably the right end.

Two other characteristic passages from Mr. Mencken will serve to show more sharply this curious sense in

which he misses his own point. On the one hand, he
appears to state most positively the purely personal
and subjective nature of criticism; he makes it individual
and almost irresponsible. 'The critic is first and last
simply trying to express himself; he is trying to achieve
thereby for his own inner ego the grateful feeling of a
function performed, a tension relieved, a katharsis
attained, which Wagner achieved when he wrote *Die
Walküre*, and a hen achieves every time she lays an
egg.' That is all consistent enough as far as it goes;
but unfortunately Mr. Mencken appears to go on to
something quite inconsistent with it. According to the
quotation, he afterwards bursts into a song of triumph
because there is now in America not only criticism, but
controversy. 'To-day for the first time in years there
is strife in American criticism . . . ears are bitten off,
noses are bloodied. There are wallops both above
and below the belt.'
    Now, there may be something in his case for contro-
versy; but it is quite inconsistent with his case for
creative self-expression. If the critic produces the
criticism *only* to please himself, it is entirely irrelevant
that it does not please somebody else. The somebody
else has a perfect right to say the exact opposite to please
himself, and be perfectly satisfied with himself. But
they cannot controvert because they cannot compare.
They cannot compare because there is no common
standard of comparison. Neither I nor anybody else
can have a controversy about literature with Mr.
Mencken, because there is no way of criticizing the
criticism, except by asking whether the critic is satisfied.
And there the debate ends, at the beginning: for nobody
can doubt that Mr. Mencken is satisfied.
    But not to make Mr. Mencken a mere victim of the
argumentum ad hominem, I will make the experiment in a
viler body and offer myself for dissection. I dare say a
great deal of the criticism I write really is moved by a
mood of self-expression; and certainly it is true enough
that there is a satisfaction in self-expression. I can take
something or other about which I have definite feelings

—as, for instance, the philosophy of Mr. Dreiser, which has been mentioned more than once in this debate. I can achieve for my own inner ego the grateful feeling of writing as follows:

'He describes a world which appears to be a dull and discolouring illusion of indigestion, not bright enough to be called a nightmare; smelly, but not even stinking with any strength; smelling of the stale gas of ignorant chemical experiments by dirty, secretive schoolboys— the sort of boys who torture cats in corners; spineless and spiritless like a broken-backed worm; loathsomely slow and laborious like an endless slug; despairing, but not with dignity; blaspheming, but not with courage; without wit, without will, without laughter or uplifting of the heart; too old to die, too deaf to leave off talking, too blind to stop, too stupid to start afresh, too dead to be killed, and incapable even of being damned, since in all its weary centuries it has not reached the age of reason.'

That is what I feel about it; and it certainly gives me pleasure to relieve my feelings. I have got it off my chest. I have attained a katharsis. I have laid an egg. I have produced a criticism, satisfying all Mr. Mencken's definitions of the critic. I have performed a function. I feel better, thank you.

But what influence my feelings can be expected to have on Mr. Dreiser, or anybody who does not admit my standards of truth and falsehood, I do not quite see. Mr. Dreiser can hardly be expected to say that his chemistry is quackery, as I think it—quackery without the liveliness we might reasonably expect from quacks. He does not think fatalism base and servile, as I do; he does not think free will the highest truth about humanity, as I do. He does not believe that despair is itself a sin, and perhaps the worst of sins, as Catholics do. He does not think blasphemy the smallest and silliest sort of pride, as even pagans do. He naturally does not think his own picture of life a false picture, resembling real life about as much as a wilderness of linoleum would resemble the land of all the living flowers, as I do. But he would not think it falser for being like a wilderness. He would probably admit that it was dreary, but think it correct to be dreary.   He would probably own that he was hopeless, but not see any harm in being hopeless. What I advance as accusations, he would very probably accept as compliments.

Under these circumstances, I do not quite see how I, or any one with my views, could have a *controversy* with Mr. Dreiser.   There does not seem to be any way in which I could prove him wrong, because he does not accept my view of what is wrong.   There does not seem to be any way in which he could prove himself right, because I do not share his notions of what is right.   We might, indeed, meet in the street and fall on each other; and while I believe we are both heavy men, I doubt not that he is the more formidable.   The very possibility of our being reduced to this inarticulate explanation may possibly throw some light on Mr. Mencken's remarkable description of the new literary life in America. 'Ears are bitten off,' he says; and this curious form of cultural intercourse might really be the only solution, when ears are no longer organs of hearing and there are no organs except organs of self-expression.   He that hath ears to hear and will not hear may just as well have them bitten off.   Such deafness seems inevitable in the creative critic, who is as indifferent as a hen to all noises except her own cackling over her own egg. Anyhow, hens do not criticize each other's eggs, or even pelt each other with eggs, in the manner of political controversy.   We can only say that the novelist in question has undoubtedly laid a magnificently large and solid egg—something in the nature of an ostrich's egg; and after that, there is really nothing to prevent the ostrich from hiding its head in the sand, achieving thereby for its own inner ego the grateful feeling of a function performed.   But we cannot argue with it about whether the egg is a bad egg, or whether parts of it are excellent.

In all these instances, therefore, because of the absence of a standard of ultimate values, the most ordinary functions really cannot be performed. They not only cannot be performed with 'a grateful feeling,' or a katharsis, but in the long run they cannot be performed at all.   We cannot really denounce the Service-mongering bond salesman as a swindler, because we have no certain agreement that it is shameful to be a swindler. A little manipulation of some of Mr. Mencken's own individualistic theories about mentality as superior to moralism might present the swindler as a superman. We cannot really argue for or against the mere ideal of Service, because neither side has really considered what is to be served or how we are to arrive at the right rules for serving it.   Consequently, in practice, it may turn out that the State of Service is merely the Servile State. And finally, we cannot really argue about that or any-thing else, because there are no rules of the game of argument.   There is nothing to prove who has scored a point and who has not.   There cannot be 'strife in American criticism'; the professors cannot be 'forced to make some defence.'   That would require plaintiffs and defendants to appear before some tribunal and give evidence according to some tests of truth.   There can be a disturbance, but there cannot be a discussion.

In plain words, the normal functions of man—effort, protest, judgment, persuasion, and proof—are found in fact to be hampered and hamstrung by these negations of the sceptic even when the sceptic seems at first to be only denying some distant vision or some miraculous tale.   Each function is found in fact to refer to some end, to some test, to some way of distinguishing between use and misuse, which the mere sceptic destroys as completely as he could destroy any myth or superstition. If the function is only performed for the satisfaction of the performer, as in the parable of the critic and the egg, it becomes futile to discuss whether it is an addled egg.   It becomes futile to consider whether eggs will produce chickens or provide breakfasts.   But even to be certain of our own sanity in applying the tests, we do really have to go back to some aboriginal problem, like that of the old riddle of the priority of egg or chicken;

we do really, like the great religions, have to begin *ab
ovo.* If those primordial sanities can be disturbed, the
whole of practical life can be disturbed with them. Men
can be frozen by fatalism, or crazed by anarchism, or
driven to death by pessimism; for men will not go on
indefinitely acting on what they feel to be a fable. And
it is in this organic and almost muscular sense that
religion is really the help of man—in the sense that
without it he is ultimately helpless, almost motionless.

Mr. Mencken and Mr. Sinclair Lewis and the other
critics in the *Mercury* movement are so spirited and
sincere, they attack so vigorously so many things that
ought to be attacked, they expose so brilliantly many
things that really are impostures, that in discussing
matters with them a man will have every impulse to
put his cards on the table. It would be affectation and
almost hypocrisy in me to ignore, in this place, the fact
that I do myself believe in a special spiritual solution
of this problem, a special spiritual authority above this
chaos. Nor, indeed, is the idea altogether absent, as
an idea, from many other minds besides my own.
The Catholic philosophy is mentioned in terms of respect,
and even a sort of hope, both by Professor Babbitt [1] and
Mr. T. S. Eliot. I do not misunderstand their courtesies,
or seek to lure them a step further than they desire to
go. But, as a matter of fact, by a series of faultlessly
logical steps, Mr. Eliot led Professor Babbitt so near to
the very gates of the Catholic Church that in the end
I felt quite nervous, so to speak, for fear they should
both take another unintentional step and fall into it
by accident.

I have a particular reason for mentioning this matter
in conclusion—a reason that is directly related to this
curious effect of scepticism in weakening the normal
functions of the human being. In one of the most
brilliant and amusing of Mr. Sinclair Lewis's recent books
there is a passage which I quote from memory, but I
think more or less correctly. He said that the Catholic
Faith differs from current Puritanism in that it does not

[1] 'The Critic and American Life,' the *Forum* for February 1928.

ask a man to give up his sense of beauty, or his sense of humour, or his pleasant vices (by which he probably meant smoking and drinking, which are not vices at all), but that it does ask a man to give up his life and soul, his mind, body, reason, and all the rest. I ask the reader to consider, as quietly and impartially as possible, the statement thus made; and put it side by side with all those other facts about the gradual fossilizing of human function by the fundamental doubts of our day.

It would be far truer to say that the Faith gives a man back his body and his soul and his reason and his will and his very life. It would be far truer to say that the man who has received it receives all the old human functions which all the other philosophies are already taking away. It would be nearer to reality to say that he alone will have freedom, that he alone will have will, because he alone will believe in free will; that he alone will have reason, since ultimate doubt denies reason as well as authority; that he alone will truly act, because action is performed to an end. It is at least a less unlikely vision that all this hardening and hopeless despair of the intellect will leave him at last the only walking and talking citizen in a city of paralytics.

PROTESTANTISM: A PROBLEM NOVEL

I HAVE been looking at the little book on Protestantism which Dean Inge has contributed to the sixpenny series of Sir Ernest Benn; and though I suppose it has already been adequately criticized, it may be well to jot down a few notes on it before it is entirely forgotten. The book, which is called 'Protestantism,' obviously ought to be called 'Catholicism.' What the Dean has to say about any real thing recognizable as Protestantism is extraordinarily patchy, contradictory, and inconclusive. It is only what he has to say about Catholicism that is clear, consistent, and to the point. It is warmed and quickened by the human and hearty motive of hatred; and it makes everything else in the book look timid and tortuous by comparison. I am not going to annotate the work considered as history. There are some curious, if not conscious, falsifications of fact, especially in the form of suppressions of fact. He begins by interpreting Protestantism as a mere 'inwardness and sincerity' in religion; which none of the Protestant reformers would have admitted to be Protestantism, and which any number of Catholic reformers have made the very heart and soul of their reforms inside Catholicism. It might be suggested that self-examination is now more often urged and practised among Catholics than among Protestants. But whether or no the champions of sincerity examine themselves, they might well examine their statements. Some of the statements here might especially be the subject of second thoughts. It is really a startling suppression and falsification to say that Henry the Eighth had only a few household troops; so that his people must have favoured his policy, or they would have risen against it. It seems enough to reply that they did rise against it. And *because* Henry had only a few household troops, he brought in bands of ferocious mercenaries from abroad to put down the religious revolt of his own people. It is an effort of charity to concede even complete candour to the story-teller, who can actually use such an argument, and then keep silent upon such a sequel. Or again, it is outrageously misleading to suggest that the Catholic victims of Tudor and other tyranny were justly executed as traitors and not as martyrs to a religion. Every persecutor alleges social and secular necessity; so did Caiaphas and Annas; so did Nero and Diocletian; from the first the Christians were suppressed as enemies of the Empire; to the last the heretics were handed over to the secular arm with secular justifications. But when, in point of plain fact, a man can be hanged, drawn and quartered merely for saying Mass, or sometimes for helping somebody who has said Mass, it is simply raving nonsense to say that a religion is not being persecuted. To mention only one of many minor falsifications of this kind, it is quite true to say that Milton was in many ways more of a Humanist than a Puritan; but it is quite false to suggest that the Milton family was a typical Puritan family, in its taste for music and letters. The very simple explanation is that the Milton family was largely a Catholic family; and it was the celebrated John who specially separated himself from its creed but retained its culture. Countless other details as definitely false could be quoted; but I am much more interested in the general scope of the work—which allows itself to be so curiously pointless about Protestantism, merely in order to make a point against Catholicism.

Here is the Dean's attempt at a definition. 'What is the main function of Protestantism? It is essentially an attempt to check the tendency to corruption and degradation which attacks every institutional religion.' So far, so good. In that case St. Charles Borromeo, for instance, was obviously a leading Protestant. St. Dominic and St. Francis, who purged the congested conventionalism of much of the monasticism around them, were obviously leading Protestants. The Jesuits

who sifted legend by the learning of Bollandism, were
obviously leading Protestants. But most living Protestant leaders are not leading Protestants. If degradation
drags down *every* institutional religion, it has presumably dragged down Protestant institutional religion.
Protestants might possibly appear to purge Protestantism; but so did Catholics appear to purge Catholicism.
Plainly this definition is perfectly useless as a *distinction*
between Protestantism and Catholicism. For it is not
a description of any belief or system or body of thought;
but simply of a good intention, which all men of all
Churches would profess and a few men in some Churches
practise—especially in ours. But the Dean not only
proves that modern Protestant institutions ought to
be corrupt, he says that their primitive founders ought
to be repudiated. He distinctly holds that we cannot
follow Luther and Calvin.

Very well—let us go on and see whom we are to
follow. I will take one typical passage towards the end
of the book. The Dean first remarks: 'The Roman
Church has declared that there can be no reconciliation
between Rome and modern Liberalism or Progress.'
One would like to see the encyclical or decree in which
this declaration was made. Liberalism might mean
many things, from the special thing which Newman de-
nounced (and defined) to the intention of voting at a
by-election for Sir John Simon. Progress generally
means something which the Pope has never, so far as
I know, found it necessary to deny; but which the Dean
himself has repeatedly and most furiously denied. He
then goes on: 'Protestantism is entirely free from this
uncompromising preference for the Dark Ages.' 'The
Dark Ages,' of course, is cant and claptrap; we need take
no notice of that. But we may perhaps notice, not
without interest and amusement, that about twenty-
five lines before, the Dean himself has described the
popular Protestantism of America as if it were a barbarism and belated obscurantism. From which one
may infer that the Dark Ages are still going on, exactly
where there is Protestantism to preserve them. And

considering that he says at least five times that the appeal of Protestants to the letter of Scripture is narrow and superstitious, it surely seems a little astonishing that he should sum up by declaring Protestantism, as such, to be '*entirely* free' from this sort of darkness. Then, on top of all this welter of wordy contradictions, we have this marvellous and mysterious conclusion: 'It is in this direction that Protestants may look for the beginning of what may really be a new Reformation, a resumption of the unfinished work of Sir Thomas More, Giordano Bruno, and Erasmus.'

In short, Protestants may look forward to a Reformation modelled on the work of two Catholics and one obscure mystic, who was not a Protestant and of whose tenets they and the world know practically nothing. One hardly knows where to begin, in criticizing this very new Reformation, two-thirds of which was apparently started by men of the Old Religion. We might meekly suggest that, if it be regrettable that the work of Sir Thomas More was 'unfinished,' some portion of the blame may perhaps attach to the movement that cut off his head. Is it possible, I wonder, that what the Dean really means is that we want a new Reformation to undo all the harm that was done by the old Reformation? In this we certainly have no reason to quarrel with him. We should be delighted also to have a new Reformation, of ourselves as well as of Protestants and other people; though it is only fair to say that Catholics did, within an incredibly short space of time, contrive to make something very like a new Reformation; which is commonly called the Counter-Reformation. St. Vincent de Paul and St. Francis of Sales have at least as good a right to call themselves inheritors of the courtesy and charity of More as has the present Dean of St. Paul's. But putting that seventeenth-century reform on one side, there is surely something rather stupendous about the reform that the Dean proposes for the twentieth century, and the patron saints he selects for it out of the sixteenth century.

For this, it seems, is how we stand. We are not to

follow Luther and Calvin. But we are to follow More
and Erasmus. And that, if you please, is the true
Protestantism and the promise of a second Reformation.
We are to copy the views and virtues of the men who
found they *could* remain under the Pope, and especially
of one who actually died for the supremacy of the Pope.
We are to throw away practically every rag of thought
or theory that was held by the people who did not remain under the supremacy of the Pope. And we are to
bind up all these views in a little popular pamphlet
with an orange cover and call them 'Protestantism.'
The truth is that Dean Inge had an impossible title and
an impossible task. He had to present Protestantism as
Progress; when he is far too acute and cultivated a man
not to suspect that it was (as it was) a relapse into
barbarism and a break away from all that was central
in civilization. Even by the test of the Humanist, it
·made religion inhuman. Even by the test of the liberal,
it substituted literalism for liberalism. Even if the
goal had been mere Modernism, it led its followers to
it by a long, dreary, and straggling detour, a wandering
in the wilderness, that did not even discover Modernism
till it had first discovered Mormonism. Even if the goal
had been logical scepticism, Voltaire could reach it more
rapidly from the school of the Jesuits than the poor
Protestant provincial brought up among the Jezreelites.
Every mental process, even the process of going wrong,
is clearer in the Catholic atmosphere. Protestantism
has done nothing for Dean Inge, except give him a
Deanery which rather hampers his mental activity. It
has done nothing for his real talent or scholarship or
sense of ideas. It has not in history defended any of
the ideas he defends, or helped any of the liberties in
which he hopes. But it has done one thing: it has hurt
something he hates. It has done some temporary or
apparent harm to the heritage of St. Peter. It once
made something that looked like a little crack in the wall
of Rome. And because of *that*, the Dean can pardon
anything to the Protestants—even Protestantism.
For this is the strange passion of his life; and he toils

through all these pages of doubts and distinctions only
for the moment when he can liberate his soul in one wild
roar of monomaniac absurdity: 'Let the innocent Dreyfus die in prison; let the Irishman who has committed
a treacherous murder be told to leave "politics" out of
his confession; let the lucrative imposture of Lourdes...'
That is the way to talk! It is so tiring, pretending to
talk sense.

THE PROTESTANT SUPERSTITIONS

THAT delightful guessing game, which has long caused innocent merriment in so many Catholic families, the game of guessing at exactly which line of an article, say on Landscape or Latin Elegiacs, we shall find the Dean of St. Paul's introducing the Antidote to Antichrist; or the Popish Plot Revealed—that most familiar of our Catholic parlour games happened to be entertaining me some time ago, as a sort of substitute for a crossword puzzle, when I found I had hit on a very lucky example. I wrote above about 'Catholic families,' and had almost, by force of associations, written 'Catholic firesides.' And I imagine that the Dean really does think that even in this weather we keep the home-fires burning, like the fire of Vesta, in permanent expectation of relighting the fires of Smithfield. Anyhow, this sort of guessing game or crossword puzzle is seldom disappointing. The Dean must by this time have tried quite a hundred ways of leading up to his beloved topic; and even concealing it, like a masked battery, until he can let loose the cannonade in a perfect tornado of temper. Then the crossword puzzle is no longer a puzzle, though the crosswords are apparent and appropriate enough; especially those devoted to the great historical process of crossing out the Cross.

In the case of this particular article, it was only towards the end of it that the real subject was allowed to leap out from an ambush upon the reader. I think it was a general article on Superstition; and, being a journalistic article of the modern type, it was of course devoted to discussing superstition without defining superstition. In an article of that enlightened sort, it seemed enough for the writer to suggest that superstition is anything that he does not happen to like. Some of

the things are also things that I do not happen to like.
But such a writer is not reasonable even when he is
right. A man ought to have some more philosophical
objection to stories of ill luck than merely calling them
credulity; as certainly as a man ought to have some more
philosophical objection to Mass than to call it Magic.
It is hardly a final refutation of Spiritualists to prove
that they believe in Spirits; any more than a refutation
of Deists to prove that they believe in Deity. Creed
and credence and credulity are words of the same origin
and can be juggled backwards and forwards to any
extent. But when a man assumes the absurdity of
anything that anybody else believes, we wish first to
know what he believes; on what principle he believes
and, above all, upon what principle he disbelieves.
There is no trace of anything so rational in the Dean's
piece of metaphysical journalism. If he had stopped to
define his terms, or in other words to tell us what he was
talking about, such an abstract analysis would of course
have filled up some space in the article. There might
have been no room for the Alarum Against the Pope.

The Dean of St. Paul's got to business, in a paragraph
in the second half of his article, in which he unveiled to
his readers all the horrors of a quotation from Newman:
a very shocking and shameful passage in which the
degraded apostate says that he is happy in his religion,
and in being surrounded by the things of his religion;
that he likes to have objects that have been blessed by
the holy and beloved, that there is a sense of being protected by prayers, sacramentals and so on; and that
happiness of this sort satisfies the soul. The Dean,
having given us this one ghastly glimpse of the Cardinal's
spiritual condition, drops the curtain with a groan and
says it is Paganism. How different from the Christian
orthodoxy of Plotinus!

Now it was exactly that little glimpse that interested
me in this matter; not so much a glimpse into the soul
of the Cardinal as into the mind of the Dean. I suddenly seemed to see, in much simpler form than I had
yet realized, the real issue between him and us. And the

curious thing about the issue is this; that what he thinks about us is exactly what we think about him. What I for one feel most strongly, in considering a case like that of the Dean and his quotation from the Cardinal, is that the Dean is a man of distinguished intelligence and culture, that he is always interesting, that he is sometimes even just, or at least justified or justifiable; but that he is first and last the champion of a Superstition; the man who is really and truly defending a Superstition, as it would be understood by people who could define a Superstition. What makes it all the more amusing is that it is in a rather special sense a Pagan Superstition. But what makes it most intensely interesting, so far as I am concerned, is that the Dean is devoted to what may be called *par excellence* a superstitious Superstition. I mean that it is in a special sense a *local* superstition.

Dean Inge is a superstitious person because he is worshipping a relic; a relic in the sense of a remnant. He is idolatrously adoring the broken fragment of something; simply because that something happens to have lingered out of the past in the place called England; in the rather battered form called Protestant Christianity. It is as if a local patriot were to venerate the statue of Our Lady of Walsingham *only* because she was in Walsingham and without even remembering that she was in Heaven. It is still more as if he venerated a fragment chipped from the toe of the statue and forgot where it came from and ignored Our Lady altogether. I do not think it superstitious to respect the chip in relation to the statue, or the statue in relation to the saint, or the saint in relation to the scheme of theology and philosophy. But I do think it superstitious to venerate, or even to accept, the fragment because it happens to be there. And Dean Inge does accept the fragment called Protestantism because it happens to be there.

Let us for a moment consider the whole matter as philosophers should: in a universal air above all local superstitions like the Dean's. It is quite obvious that there are three or four philosophies or views of life possible to reasonable men; and to a great extent these are embodied in the great religions or in the wide field of irreligion. There is the atheist, the materialist or monist or whatever he calls himself, who believes that all is ultimately material, and all that is material is mechanical. That is emphatically a view of life; not a very bright or breezy view, but one into which it is quite possible to fit many facts of existence. Then there is the normal man with the natural religion, which accepts the general idea that the world has a design and therefore a designer; but feels the Architect of the Universe to be inscrutable and remote, as remote from men as from microbes. That sort of theism is perfectly sane; and is really the ancient basis of the solid if somewhat stagnant sanity of Islam. There is again the man who feels the burden of life so bitterly that he wishes to renounce all desire and all division, and rejoin a sort of spiritual unity and peace from which (as he thinks) our separate selves should never have broken away. That is the mood answered by Buddhism and by many metaphysicians and mystics. Then there is a fourth sort of man, sometimes called a mystic and perhaps more properly to be called a poet; in practice he can very often be called a pagan. His position is this: it is a twilight world and we know not where it ends. If we do not know enough for monotheism, neither do we know enough for monism. There may be a borderland and a world beyond; but we can only catch hints of it as they come; we may meet a nymph in the forest; we may see the fairies on the mountains. We do not know enough about the natural to *deny* the preternatural. That was, in ancient times, the healthiest aspect of Paganism. That is, in modern times, the rational part of Spiritualism. All these are possible as general views of life; and there is a fourth that is at least equally possible, though certainly more positive.

The whole point of this last position might be expressed in the line of M. Cammaerts's beautiful little poem about bluebells; *le ciel est tombé par terre*. Heaven has *descended* into the world of matter; the supreme spiritual power is now operating by the machinery of matter, dealing miraculously with the bodies and souls of men. It

blesses all the five senses; as the senses of the baby
are blessed at a Catholic christening. It blesses even
material gifts and keepsakes, as with relics or rosaries.
It works through water or oil or bread or wine. Now
that sort of mystical materialism may please or dis-
please the Dean, or anybody else. But I cannot for the
life of me understand why the Dean, or anybody else,
does not *see* that the Incarnation is as much a part of
that idea as the Mass; and that the Mass is as much a
part of that idea as the Incarnation. A Puritan may
think it blasphemous that God should become a wafer.
A Moslem thinks it blasphemous that God should become a workman in Galilee. And he is perfectly right,
from his point of view; and given his primary principle.
But if the Moslem has a principle, the Protestant has only
a prejudice. That is, he has only a fragment; a relic; a
superstition. If it be profane that the miraculous should
descend to the plane of matter, then certainly Catholicism is profane; and Protestantism is profane; and
Christianity is profane. Of all human creeds or concepts,
in that sense, Christianity is the most utterly profane.
But why a man should accept a Creator who was a carpenter, and then worry about holy water, why he should
accept a local Protestant tradition that God was born
in some particular place mentioned in the Bible, merely
because the Bible had been left lying about in England,
and then say it is incredible that a blessing should linger
on the bones of a saint, why he should accept the first and
most stupendous part of the story of Heaven on Earth,
and then furiously deny a few small but obvious deduc-
tions from it—that is a thing I do not understand; I never
could understand; I have come to the conclusion that
I shall never understand. I can only attribute it to
Superstition.

PICKWICK PAPERS

THERE are those who deny with enthusiasm the existence of a God and are happy in a hobby which they call the Mistakes of Moses. I have not studied their labours in detail, but it seems that the chief mistake of Moses was that he neglected to write the Pentateuch. The lesser errors, apparently, were not made by Moses, but by another person equally unknown. These controversialists cover the very widest field, and their attacks upon Scripture are varied to the point of wildness. They range from the proposition that the unexpurgated Bible is almost as unfit for an American girls' school as is an unexpurgated Shakespeare; they descend to the proposition that kissing the Book is almost as hygienically dangerous as kissing the babies of the poor. A superficial critic might well imagine that there was not one single sentence left of the Hebrew or Christian Scriptures which this school had not marked with some ingenious and uneducated comment. But there is one passage at least upon which they have never pounced, at least to my knowledge; and in pointing it out to them I feel that I am, or ought to be, providing material for quite a multitude of Hyde Park orations. I mean that singular arrangement in the mystical account of the Creation by which light is created first and all the luminous bodies afterwards. One could not imagine a process more open to the elephantine logic of the Bible-smasher than this: that the sun should be created after the sunlight. The conception that lies at the back of the phrase is indeed profoundly antagonistic to much of the modern point of view. To many modern people it would sound like saying that foliage existed before the first leaf; it would sound like saying that childhood existed before a baby was born. The idea is, as I have

said, alien to most modern thought, and like many other
ideas which are alien to most modern thought, it is a
very subtle and a very sound idea. Whatever be the
meaning of the passage in the actual primeval poem,
there is a very real metaphysical meaning in the idea
that light existed before the sun and stars. It is not
barbaric; it is rather Platonic. The idea existed before
any of the machinery which made manifest the idea.
Justice existed when there was no need of judges, and
mercy existed before any man was oppressed.

However this may be in the matter of religion and
philosophy, it can be said with little exaggeration that
this truth is the very key of literature. The whole
difference between co struction and creation is exactly
this: that a thing constructed can only be loved after
it is constructed; but a thing created is loved before
it exists, as the mother can love the unborn child. In
creative art the essence of a book exists before the
book or before even the details or main features of
the book; the author enjoys it and lives in it with a
kind of prophetic rapture. He wishes to write a comic
story before he has thought of a single comic incident.
He desires to write a sad story before he has thought of
anything sad. He knows the atmosphere before he
knows anything. There is a low priggish maxim sometimes uttered by men so frivolous as to take humour
seriously—a maxim that a man should not laugh at his
own jokes. But the great artist not only laughs at
his own jokes; he laughs at his own jokes before he has
made them. In the case of a man really humorous
we can see humour in his eye before he has thought
of any amusing words at all. So the creative writer
laughs at his comedy before he creates it, and he has
tears for his tragedy before he knows what it is. When
the symbols and the fulfilling facts do come to him,
they come generally in a manner very fragmentary and
inverted, mostly in irrational glimpses of crisis or con-
summation. The last page comes before the first;
before his romance has begun, he knows that it has
ended well. He sees the wedding before the wooing;

he sees the death before the duel. But most of all he sees the colour and character of the whole story prior to any possible events in it. This is the real argument for art and style, only that the artists and the stylists have not the sense to use it. In one very real sense style is far more important than either character or narrative. For a man knows what style of book he wants to write when he knows nothing else about it.

Pickwick is in Dickens's career the mere mass of light before the creation of sun or moon. It is the splendid, shapeless substance of which all his stars were ultimately made. You might split up *Pickwick* into innumerable novels as you could split up that primeval light into innumerable solar systems. The *Pickwick Papers* constitute first and foremost a kind of wild promise, a pre-natal vision of all the children of Dickens. He had not yet settled down into the plain, professional habit of picking out a plot and characters, of attending to one thing at a time, of writing a separate, sensible novel and sending it off to his publishers. He is still in the youthful whirl of the kind of world that he would like to create. He has not yet really settled what story he will write, but only what sort of story he will write. He tries to tell ten stories at once; he pours into the pot all the chaotic fancies and crude experiences of his boyhood; he sticks in irrelevant short stories shamelessly, as into a scrap-book; he adopts designs and abandons them, begins episodes and leaves them unfinished; but from the first page to the last there is a nameless and elemental ecstasy—that of the man who is doing the kind of thing that he can do. Dickens, like every other honest and effective writer, came at last to some degree of care and self-restraint. He learned how to make his dramatis personae assist his drama; he learned how to write stories which were full of rambling and perversity, but which were stories. But before he wrote a single real story, he had a kind of vision. It was a vision of the Dickens world—a maze of white roads, a map full of fantastic towns, thundering coaches, clamorous market-places, uproarious inns,

strange and swaggering figures. That vision was
Pickwick.

It must be remembered that this is true even in connection with the man's contemporaneous biography.
Apart from anything else about it, *Pickwick* was his
first great chance. It was a big commission given in
some sense to an untried man, that he might show what
he could do. It was in a strict sense a sample. And
just as a sample of leather can be only a piece of leather,
or a sample of coal a lump of coal, so this book may
most properly be regarded as simply a lump of Dickens.
He was anxious to show all that was in him. He was
more concerned to prove that he could write well than
to prove that he could write this particular book well.
And he did prove this, at any rate. No one ever sent
such a sample as the sample of Dickens. His roll of
leather blocked up the street; his lump of coal set the
Thames on fire.

The book originated in the suggestion of a publisher;
as many more good books have done than the arrogance
of the man of letters is commonly inclined to admit.
Very much is said in our time about Apollo and Admetus,
and the impossibility of asking genius to work within
prescribed limits or assist an alien design. But after
all, as a matter of fact, some of the greatest geniuses
have done it, from Shakespeare botching up bad comedies
and dramatizing bad novels down to Dickens writing a
masterpiece as the mere framework for a Mr. Seymour's
sketches. Nor is the true explanation irrelevant to the
spirit and power of Dickens. Very delicate, slender,
and bizarre talents are indeed incapable of being used
for an outside purpose, whether of public good or of
private gain. But about very great and rich talent
there goes a certain disdainful generosity which can
turn its hand to anything. Minor poets cannot write
to order; but very great poets can write to order. The
larger the man's mind, the wider his scope of vision,
the more likely it will be that anything suggested to
him will seem significant and promising; the more he
has a grasp of everything the more ready he will be to

write anything. It is very hard (if that is the question) to throw a brick at a man and ask him to write an epic; but the more he is a great man the more able he will be to write about the brick. It is very unjust (if that is all) to point to a hoarding of Colman's mustard and demand a flood of philosophical eloquence; but the greater the man is the more likely he will be to give it to you. So it was proved, not for the first time, in this great experiment of the early employment of Dickens. Messrs. Chapman and Hall came to him with a scheme for a string of sporting stories to serve as the context, and one might almost say the excuse, for a string of sketches by Seymour, the sporting artist. Dickens made some modifications in the plan, but he adopted its main feature; and its main feature was Mr. Winkle. To think of what Mr. Winkle might have been in the hands of a dull *farceur*, and then to think of what he is, is to experience the feeling that Dickens made a man out of rags and refuse. Dickens was to work splendidly and successfully in many fields, and to send forth many brilliant books and brave figures. He was destined to have the applause of continents like a statesman, and to dictate to his publishers like a despot; but perhaps he never worked again so supremely well as here, where he worked in chains. It may well be questioned whether his one hack book is not his masterpiece.

Of course it is true that as he went on his independence increased, and he kicked quite free of the influences that had suggested his story. So Shakespeare declared his independence of the original chronicle of Hamlet, Prince of Denmark, eliminating altogether (with some wisdom) another uncle called Wiglerus. At the start the Nimrod Club of Chapman and Hall may have even had equal chances with the Pickwick Club of young Mr. Dickens; but the Pickwick Club became something much better than any publisher had dared to dream of. Some of the old links were indeed severed by accident or extraneous trouble; Seymour, for whose sake the whole had perhaps been planned, blew his brains out before he had drawn ten pictures. But such things

were trifles compared to *Pickwick* itself. It mattered
little now whether Seymour blew his brains out, so long
as Charles Dickens blew his brains in. The work
became systematically and progressively more powerful
and masterly. Many critics have commented on the
somewhat discordant and inartistic change between the
earlier part of *Pickwick* and the later; they have pointed
out, not without good sense, that the character of Mr.
Pickwick changes from that of a silly buffoon to that
of a solid merchant. But the case, if these critics had
noticed it, is much stronger in the minor characters of
the great company. Mr. Winkle, who has been an idiot
(even, perhaps, as Mr. Pickwick says, 'an impostor'),
suddenly becomes a romantic and even reckless lover,
scaling a forbidden wall and planning a bold elopement.
Mr. Snodgrass, who has behaved in a ridiculous manner
in all serious positions, suddenly finds himself in a
ridiculous position—that of a gentleman surprised in
a secret love affair—and behaves in a manner perfectly
manly, serious, and honourable. Mr. Tupman alone
has no serious emotional development, and for this
reason it is, presumably, that we hear less and less of
Mr. Tupman towards the end of the book. Dickens has
by this time got into a thoroughly serious mood—a
mood expressed indeed by extravagant incidents, but
none the less serious for that; and into this Winkle and
Snodgrass, in the character of romantic lovers, could be
made to fit. Mr. Tupman had to be left out of the love
affairs; therefore Mr. Tupman is left out of the book.

Much of the change was due to the entrance of the
greatest character in the story. It may seem strange
at the first glance to say that Sam Weller helped to
make the story serious. Nevertheless, this is strictly
true. The introduction of Sam Weller had, to begin
with, some merely accidental and superficial effects.
When Samuel Weller had appeared, Samuel Pickwick
was no longer the chief farcical character. Weller
became the joker and Pickwick in some sense the butt
of his jokes. Thus it was obvious that the more simple,
solemn, and really respectable this butt could be made

the better. Mr. Pickwick had been the figure capering before the footlights. But with the advent of Sam, Mr. Pickwick had become a sort of black background and had to behave as such. But this explanation, though true as far as it goes, is a mean and unsatisfactory one, leaving the great elements unexplained. For a much deeper and more righteous reason Sam Weller introduces the more serious tone of Pickwick. He introduces it because he introduces something which it was the chief business of Dickens to preach throughout his life—something which he never preached so well as when he preached it unconsciously. Sam Weller introduces the English People.

Sam Weller is the great symbol in English literature of the populace peculiar to England. His incessant stream of sane nonsense is a wonderful achievement of Dickens: but it is no great falsification of the incessant stream of sane nonsense as it really exists among the English poor. The English poor live in an atmosphere of humour; they think in humour. Irony is the very air that they breathe. A joke comes suddenly from time to time into the head of a politician or a gentleman, and then as a rule he makes the most of it; but when a serious word comes into the mind of a coster it is almost as startling as a joke. The word 'chaff' was, I suppose, originally applied to badinage to express its barren and unsustaining character; but to the English poor chaff is as sustaining as grain. The phrase that leaps to their lips is the ironical phrase. I remember once being driven in a hansom cab down a street that turned out to be a cul-de-sac, and brought us bang up against a wall. The driver and I simultaneously said something. But I said: 'This 'll never do!' and he said: 'This is all right!' Even in the act of pulling back his horse's nose from a brick wall, that confirmed satirist thought in terms of his highly trained and traditional satire; while I, belonging to a duller and simpler class, expressed my feelings in words as innocent and literal as those of a rustic or a child.

This eternal output of divine derision has never been

so truly typified as by the character of Sam; he is a grotesque fountain which gushes the living waters for ever. Dickens is accused of exaggeration and he is often guilty of exaggeration; but here he does not exaggerate: he merely symbolizes and sublimates like any other great artist. Sam Weller does not exaggerate the wit of the London street arab one atom more than Colonel Newcome, let us say, exaggerates the stateliness of an ordinary soldier and gentleman, or than Mr. Collins exaggerates the fatuity of a certain kind of country clergyman. And this breath from the boisterous brotherhood of the poor lent a special seriousness and smell of reality to the whole story. The unconscious follies of Winkle and Tupman are blown away like leaves before the solid and conscious folly of Sam Weller. Moreover, the relations between Pickwick and his servant Sam are in some ways new and valuable in literature. Many comic writers had described the clever rascal and his ridiculous dupe; but here, in a fresh and very human atmosphere, we have a clever servant who was not a rascal and a dupe and who was not ridiculous. Sam Weller stands in some ways for a cheerful knowledge of the world; Mr. Pickwick stands for a still more cheerful ignorance of the world. And Dickens responded to a profound human sentiment (the sentiment that has made saints and the sanctity of children) when he made the gentler and less-travelled type—the type which moderates and controls. Knowledge and innocence are both excellent things, and they are both very funny. But it is right that knowledge should be the servant and innocence the master.

The sincerity of this study of Sam Weller has produced one particular effect in the book which I wonder that critics of Dickens have never noticed or discussed. Because it has no Dickens 'pathos,' certain parts of it are truly pathetic. Dickens, realizing rightly that the whole tone of the book was fun, felt that he ought to keep out of it any great experiments in sadness and keep within limits those that he put in. He used this restraint in order not to spoil the humour; but (if he had known himself better) he might well have used it in order not to spoil the pathos. This is the one book in which Dickens was, as it were, forced to trample down his tender feelings; and for that very reason it is the one book where all the tenderness there is is quite unquestionably true. An admirable example of what I mean may be found in the scene in which Sam Weller goes down to see his bereaved father after the death of his stepmother. The most loyal admirer of Dickens can hardly prevent himself from giving a slight shudder when he thinks of what Dickens might have made of that scene in some of his more expansive and maudlin moments. For all I know old Mrs. Weller might have asked what the wild waves were saying; and for all I know old Mr. Weller might have told her. As it is, Dickens, being forced to keep the tale taut and humorous, gives a picture of humble respect and decency which is manly, dignified, and really sad. There is no attempt made by these simple and honest men, the father and son, to pretend that the dead woman was anything greatly other than she was; their respect is for death, and for the human weakness and mystery which it must finally cover. Old Tony Weller does not tell his shrewish wife that she is already a white-winged angel; he speaks to her with an admirable good nature and good sense:

'"Susan," I says, "you 've been a wery good vife to me altogether: keep a good heart, my dear, and you 'll live to see me punch that 'ere Stiggins's 'ead yet." She smiled at this, Samivel . . . but she died arter all.'

That is perhaps the first and the last time that Dickens ever touched the extreme dignity of pathos. He is restraining his compassion, and afterwards he let it go. Now laughter is a thing that can be let go; laughter has in it a quality of liberty. But sorrow has in it by its very nature a quality of confinement; pathos by its very nature fights with itself. Humour is expansive; it bursts outwards; the fact is attested by the common expression, 'holding one's sides.' But sorrow is not expansive; and it was afterwards the mistake of

Dickens that he tried to make it expansive. It is the
one great weakness of Dickens as a great writer, that
he did try to make that sudden sadness, that abrupt
pity, which we call pathos, a thing quite obvious,
infectious, public, as if it were journalism or the measles.
It is pleasant to think that in this supreme masterpiece,
done in the dawn of his career, there is not even this
faint fleck upon the sun of his just splendour. Pickwick
will always be remembered as the great example of everything that made Dickens great; of the solemn con-
viviality of great friendships, of the erratic adventures
of old English roads, of the hospitality of old English
inns, of the great fundamental kindliness and honour
of old English manners. First of all, however, it will
always be remembered for its laughter, or, if you will,
for its folly. A good joke is the one ultimate and sacred
thing which cannot be criticized. Our relations with
a good joke are direct and even divine relations. We
speak of 'seeing' a joke just as we speak of 'seeing' a
ghost or a vision. If we have seen it, it is futile to
argue with us; and we have seen the vision of *Pickwick*.
Pickwick may be the top of Dickens's humour; I think
upon the whole it is. But the broad humour of *Pickwick*
he broadened over many wonderful kingdoms; the
narrow pathos of *Pickwick* he never found again.

OLIVER TWIST

In considering Dickens, as we almost always must consider him, as a man of rich originality, we may possibly miss the forces from which he drew even his original energy. It is not well for man to be alone. We, in the modern world, are ready enough to admit that when it is applied to some problem of monasticism or of an ecstatic life. But we will not admit that our modern artistic claim to absolute originality is really a claim to absolute unsociability; a claim to absolute loneliness. The anarchist is at least as solitary as the ascetic. And the men of very vivid vigour in literature, the men such as Dickens, have generally displayed a large sociability towards the society of letters, always expressed in the happy pursuit of pre-existent themes, sometimes expressed, as in the case of Molière or Sterne, in downright plagiarism. For even theft is a confession of our dependence on society. In Dickens, however, this element of the original foundations on which he worked is quite especially difficult to determine. This is partly due to the fact that for the present reading public he is practically the only one of his long line that is read at all. He sums up Smollett and Goldsmith, but he also destroys them. This one giant, being closest to us, cuts off from our view even the giants that begat him. But much more is this difficulty due to the fact that Dickens mixed up with the old material, materials so subtly modern, so made of the French Revolution, that the whole is transformed. If we want the best example of this, the best example is *Oliver Twist*.

Relatively to the other works of Dickens *Oliver Twist* is not of great value, but it is of great importance. Some parts of it are so crude and of so clumsy a melodrama, that one is almost tempted to say that Dickens would have been greater without it. But even if he had been greater without it he would still have been incomplete without it. With the exception of some gorgeous passages, both of humour and horror, the interest of the book lies not so much in its revelation of Dickens's literary genius as in its revelation of those moral, personal, and political instincts which were the make-up of his character and the permanent support of that literary genius. It is by far the most depressing of all his books; it is in some ways the most irritating; yet its ugliness gives the last touch of honesty to all that spontaneous and splendid output. Without this one discordant note all his merriment might have seemed like levity.

Dickens had just appeared upon the stage and set the whole world laughing with his first great story, *Pickwick*. *Oliver Twist* was his encore. It was the second opportunity given to him by those who had rolled about with laughter over Tupman and Jingle, Weller and Dowler. Under such circumstances a stagy reciter will sometimes take care to give a pathetic piece after his humorous one; and with all his many moral merits there was much that was stagy about Dickens. But this explanation alone is altogether inadequate and unworthy. There was in Dickens this other kind of energy, horrible, uncanny, barbaric, capable in another age of coarseness, greedy for the emblems of established ugliness, the coffin, the gibbet, the bones, the bloody knife. Dickens liked these things and he was all the more of a man for liking them; especially he was all the more of a boy. We can all recall with pleasure the fact that Miss Petowker (afterwards Mrs. Lillyvick) was in the habit of reciting a poem called *The Blood Drinker's Burial*. I cannot express my regret that the words of this poem are not given; for Dickens would have been quite as capable of writing *The Blood Drinker's Burial* as Miss Petowker was of reciting it. This strain existed in Dickens alongside of his happy laughter; both were allied to the same robust romance. Here as elsewhere Dickens is

close to all the permanent human things. He is close
to religion, which has never allowed the thousand devils
on its churches to stop the dancing of its bells. He is
allied to the people, to the real poor, who love nothing
so much as to take a cheerful glass and to talk about
funerals. The extremes of his gloom and gaiety are
the mark of religion and democracy; they mark him off
from the moderate happiness of philosophers, and from
that stoicism which is the virtue and the creed of
aristocrats. There is nothing odd in the fact that the
same man who conceived the humane hospitalities of
Pickwick should also have imagined the inhuman
laughter of Fagin's den. They are both genuine and
they are both exaggerated. And the whole human
tradition has tied up together in a strange knot these
strands of festivity and fear. It is over the cups of
Christmas Eve that men have always competed in
telling ghost stories.

This first element was present in Dickens, and it is
very powerfully present in *Oliver Twist*. It had not
been present with sufficient consistency or continuity
in *Pickwick* to make it remain on the reader's memory
at all, for the tale of 'Gabriel Grubb' is grotesque rather
than horrible, and the two gloomy stories of the 'Madman' and the 'Queer Client' are so utterly irrelevant
to the tale, that even if the reader remember them he
probably does not remember that they occur in *Pickwick*.
Critics have complained of Shakespeare and others for
putting comic episodes into a tragedy. It required a
man with the courage and coarseness of Dickens actually
to put tragic episodes into a farce. But they are not
caught up into the story at all. In *Oliver Twist*, however, the thing broke out with an almost brutal inspiration, and those who had fallen in love with Dickens for
his generous buffoonery may very likely have been
startled at receiving such very different fare at the next
helping. When you have bought a man's book because
you like his writing about Mr. Wardle's punch-bowl and
Mr. Winkle's skates, it may very well be surprising to
open it and read about the sickening thuds that beat

out the life of Nancy, or that mysterious villain whose face was blasted with disease.

As a nightmare, the work is really admirable. Characters which are not very clearly conceived as regards their own psychology are yet, at certain moments, managed so as to shake to its foundations our own psychology. Bill Sikes is not exactly a real man, but for all that he is a real murderer. Nancy is not really impressive as a living woman; but (as the phrase goes) she makes a lovely corpse. Something quite childish and eternal in us, something which is shocked with the mere simplicity of death, quivers when we read of those repeated blows or see Sikes cursing the tell-tale cur who will follow his bloody footprints. And this strange, sublime, vulgar melodrama, which is melodrama and yet is painfully real, reaches its hideous height in that fine scene of the death of Sikes, the besieged house, the boy screaming within, the crowd screaming without, the murderer turned almost a maniac and dragging his victim uselessly up and down the room, the escape over the roof, the rope swiftly running taut, and death sudden, startling, and symbolic; a man hanged. There is in this and similar scenes something of the quality of Hogarth and many other English moralists of the early eighteenth century. It is not easy to define this Hogarthian quality in words, beyond saying that it is a sort of alphabetical realism, like the cruel candour of children. But it has about it these two special principles which separate it from all that we call realism in our time. First, that with us a moral story means a story about moral people; with them a moral story meant more often a story about immoral people. Second, that with us realism is always associated with some subtle view of morals; with them realism was always associated with some simple view of morals. The end of Bill Sikes exactly in the way that the law would have killed him—this is a Hogarthian incident; it carries on that tradition of startling and shocking platitude.

All this element in the book was a sincere thing in the

author, but none the less it came from old soils, from the graveyard and the gallows, and the lane where the ghost walked. Dickens was always attracted to such things, and (as Forster says with inimitable simplicity) 'but for his strong sense might have fallen into the follies of spiritualism.' As a matter of fact, like most of the men of strong sense in his tradition, Dickens was left with a half-belief in spirits which became in practice a belief in bad spirits. The great disadvantage of those who have too much strong sense to believe in supernaturalism is that they keep last the low and little forms of the supernatural, such as omens, curses, spectres, and retributions, but find a high and happy supernaturalism quite incredible. Thus the Puritans denied the sacraments, but went on burning witches. This shadow does rest, to some extent, upon the rational English writers like Dickens; supernaturalism was dying, but its ugliest roots died last. Dickens would have found it easier to believe in a ghost than in a vision of the Virgin with angels. There, for good or evil, however, was the root of the old diablerie in Dickens, and there it is in *Oliver Twist*. But this was only the first of the new Dickens elements which must have surprised those Dickensians who eagerly bought his second book. The second of the new Dickens elements is equally indisputable and separate. It swelled afterwards to enormous proportions in Dickens's work; but it really has its rise here. Again, as in the case of the element of diablerie, it would be possible to make technical exceptions in favour of *Pickwick*. Just as there were quite inappropriate scraps of the gruesome element in *Pickwick*, so there are quite inappropriate allusions to this other topic in *Pickwick*. But nobody by merely reading *Pickwick* would even remember this topic; no one by merely reading *Pickwick* would know what this topic is; this third great subject of Dickens; this second great subject of the Dickens of *Oliver Twist*.

This subject is social oppression. It is surely fair to say that no one could have gathered from *Pickwick* how this question boiled in the blood of the author of

Pickwick. There are, indeed, passages, particularly in connection with Mr. Pickwick in the debtor's prison, which prove to us, looking back on a whole public career, that Dickens had been from the beginning bitter and inquisitive about the problem of our civilization. No one could have imagined at the time that this bitterness ran in an unbroken river under all the surges of that superb gaiety and exuberance. With *Oliver Twist* this sterner side of Dickens was suddenly revealed. For the very first pages of *Oliver Twist* are stern even when they are funny. They amuse, but they cannot be enjoyed, as can the passages about the follies of Mr. Snodgrass or the humiliations of Mr. Winkle. The difference between the old easy humour and this new harsh humour is a difference not of degree but of kind. Dickens makes game of Mr. Bumble because he wants to kill Mr. Bumble; he made game of Mr. Winkle because he wanted him to live for ever. Dickens has taken the sword in hand; against what is he declaring war?

It is just here that the greatness of Dickens comes in; it is just here that the difference lies between the pedant and the poet. Dickens enters the social and political war, and the first stroke he deals is not only significant but even startling. Fully to see this we must appreciate the national situation. It was an age of reform, and even of radical reform; the world was full of radicals and reformers; but only too many of them took the line of attacking everything and anything that was opposed to some particular theory among the many political theories that possessed the end of the eighteenth century. Some had so much perfected the perfect theory of republicanism that they almost lay awake at night because Queen Victoria had a crown on her head. Others were so certain that mankind had hitherto been merely strangled in the bonds of the State that they saw truth only in the destruction of tariffs or of by-laws. The greater part of that generation held that clearness, economy, and a hard common sense, would soon destroy the errors that had been erected by the superstitions and sentimentalities of the past. In pursuance of this idea many of the new men of the new century, quite confident that they were invigorating the new age, sought to destroy the old sentimental clericalism, the old sentimental feudalism, the old-world belief in priests, the old-world belief in patrons, and among other things the old-world belief in beggars. They sought among other things to clear away the old visionary kindliness on the subject of vagrants. Hence those reformers enacted not only a new reform bill but also a new poor law. In creating many other modern things they created the modern workhouse, and when Dickens came out to fight it was the first thing that he broke with his battle-axe.

This is where Dickens's social revolt is of more value than mere politics and avoids the vulgarity of the novel with a purpose. His revolt is not a revolt of the commercialist against the feudalist, of the Nonconformist against the Churchman, of the Free-trader against the Protectionist, of the Liberal against the Tory. If he were among us now his revolt would not be the revolt of the Socialist against the Individualist, or of the Anarchist against the Socialist. His revolt was simply and solely the eternal revolt; it was the revolt of the weak against the strong. He did not dislike this or that argument for oppression; he disliked oppression. He disliked a certain look on the face of a man when he looks down on another man. And that look on the face is, indeed, the only thing in the world that we have really to fight between here and the fires of Hell. That which pedants of that time and this time would have called the sentimentalism of Dickens was really simply the detached sanity of Dickens. He cared nothing for the fugitive explanations of the Constitutional Conservatives; he cared nothing for the fugitive explanations of the Manchester School. He would have cared quite as little for the fugitive explanations of the Fabian Society or of the modern scientific Socialist. . He saw that under many forms there was one fact, the tyranny of man over man; and he struck at it when he saw it,

whether it was old or new.   When he found that foot-
men and rustics were too much afraid of Sir Leicester
Dedlock, he attacked Sir Leicester Dedlock; he did
not care whether Sir Leicester Dedlock said he was
attacking England or whether Mr. Rouncewell, the
Ironmaster, said he was attacking an effete oligarchy.
In that case he pleased Mr. Rouncewell, the Ironmaster,
and displeased Sir Leicester Dedlock, the Aristocrat.
But when he found that Mr. Rouncewell's workmen
were much too frightened of Mr. Rouncewell, then he
displeased Mr. Rouncewell in turn; he displeased Mr.
Rouncewell very much by calling him Mr. Bounderby.
When he imagined himself to be fighting old laws he
gave a sort of vague and general approval to new laws.
But when he came to the new laws they had a bad
time.   When Dickens found that after a hundred
economic arguments and granting a hundred economic
considerations, the fact remained that paupers in modern
workhouses were much too afraid of the beadle, just as
vassals in ancient castles were much too afraid of the
Dedlocks, then he struck suddenly and at once.   This
is what makes the opening chapters of *Oliver Twist* so
curious and important.   The very fact of Dickens's
distance from, and independence of, the elaborate
financial arguments of his time, makes more definite
and dazzling his sudden assertion that he sees the old
human tyranny in front of him as plain as the sun at
noonday.   Dickens attacks the modern workhouse with
a sort of inspired simplicity as of a boy in a fairy-tale
who had wandered about, sword in hand, looking for
ogres and who had found an indisputable ogre.   All the
other people of his time are attacking things because
they are bad economics or because they are bad politics,
or because they are bad science; he alone is attacking
things because they are bad.   All the others are Radicals
with a large R; he alone is radical with a small one.
He encounters evil with that beautiful surprise which,
as it is the beginning of all real pleasure, is also the
beginning of all righteous indignation.   He enters the
workhouse just as Oliver Twist enters it, as a little child.

This is the real power and pathos of that celebrated passage in the book which has passed into a proverb; but which has not lost its terrible humour even in being hackneyed. I mean, of course, the everlasting quotation about Oliver Twist asking for more. The real poignancy that there is in this idea is a very good study in that strong school of social criticism which Dickens represented. A modern realist describing the dreary workhouse would have made all the children utterly crushed, not daring to speak at all, not expecting anything, not hoping anything, past all possibility of affording even an ironical contrast or a protest of despair. A modern, in short, would have made all the boys in the workhouse pathetic by making them all pessimists. But Oliver Twist is not pathetic because he is a pessimist. Oliver Twist is pathetic because he is an optimist. The whole tragedy of that incident is in the fact that he does expect the universe to be kind to him, that he does believe that he is living in a just world. He comes before the Guardians as the ragged peasants of the French Revolution came before the Kings and Parliaments of Europe. That is to say, he comes, indeed, with gloomy experiences, but he comes with a happy philosophy. He knows that there are wrongs of man to be reviled; but he believes also that there are rights of man to be demanded. It has often been remarked as a singular fact that the French poor, who stand in historic tradition as typical of all the desperate men who have dragged down tyranny, were, as a matter of fact, by no means worse off than the poor of many other European countries before the Revolution. The truth is that the French were tragic because they were better off. The others had known the sorrowful experiences; but they alone had known the splendid expectation and the original claims. It was just here that Dickens was so true a child of them and of that happy theory so bitterly applied. They were the one oppressed people that simply asked for justice; they were the one Parish Boy who innocently asked for more.

GREAT EXPECTATIONS

Great Expectations, which was written in the afternoon of Dickens's life and fame, has a quality of serene irony and even sadness, which puts it quite alone among his other works. At no time could Dickens possibly be called cynical, he had too much vitality; but relatively to the other books this book is cynical; but it has the soft and gentle cynicism of old age, not the hard cynicism of youth. To be a young cynic is to be a young brute; but Dickens, who had been so perfectly romantic and sentimental in his youth, could afford to admit this touch of doubt into the mixed experience of his middle age. At no time could any books by Dickens have been called Thackerayan. Both of the two men were too great for that. But relatively to the other Dickensian productions this book may be called Thackerayan. It is a study in human weakness and the slow human surrender. It describes how easily a free lad of fresh and decent instincts can be made to care more for rank and pride and the degrees of our stratified society than for old affection and for honour. It is an extra chapter to *The Book of Snobs*.

The best way of stating the change which this book marks in Dickens can be put in one phrase. In this book for the first time the hero disappears. The hero had descended to Dickens by a long line which begins with the gods, nay, perhaps if one may say so, which begins with God. First comes Deity and then the image of Deity; first comes the god and then the demi-god, the Hercules who labours and conquers before he receives his heavenly crown. That idea, with continual mystery and modification, has continued behind all romantic tales; the demi-god became the hero of paganism; the hero of paganism became the knight-errant of Christianity; the knight-errant who wandered and was foiled before he triumphed became the hero of the later prose romance, the romance in which the hero had to fight a duel with the villain but always survived, in which the hero drove desperate horses through the night in order to rescue the heroine, but always rescued her.

This heroic modern hero, this demi-god in a top-hat, may be said to reach his supreme moment and typical example about the time when Dickens was writing that thundering and thrilling and highly unlikely scene in *Nicholas Nickleby*, the scene where Nicholas hopelessly denounces the atrocious Gride in his hour of grinning triumph, and a thud upon the floor above tells them that the heroine's tyrannical father has died just in time to set her free.   That is the apotheosis of the pure heroic as Dickens found it, and as Dickens in some sense continued it.   It may be that it does not appear with quite so much unmistakable youth, beauty, valour, and virtue as it does in Nicholas Nickleby.   Walter Gay is a simpler and more careless hero, but when he is doing any of the business of the story he is purely heroic.   Kit Nubbles is a humbler hero, but he is a hero; when he is good he is very good.   Even David Copperfield, who confesses to boyish tremors and boyish evasions in his account of his boyhood, acts the strict stiff part of the chivalrous gentleman in all the active and determining scenes of the tale.   But *Great Expectations* may be called, like *Vanity Fair*, a novel without a hero.   Almost all Thackeray's novels except *Esmond* are novels without a hero, but only one of Dickens's novels can be so described.   I do not mean that it is a novel without a *jeune premier*, a young man to make love; *Pickwick* is that and *Oliver Twist*, and, perhaps, *The Old Curiosity Shop*.   I mean that it is a novel without a hero in the same far deeper and more deadly sense in which *Pendennis* is also a novel without a hero.   I mean that it is a novel which aims chiefly at showing that the hero is unheroic.

All such phrases as these must appear of course to overstate the case.   Pip is a much more delightful

person than Nicholas Nickleby. Or to take a stronger
case for the purpose of our argument, Pip is a much
more delightful person than Sydney Carton. Still the
fact remains. Most of Nicholas Nickleby's personal
actions are meant to show that he is heroic. Most of
Pip's actions are meant to show that he is not heroic.
The study of Sydney Carton is meant to indicate that
with all his vices Sydney Carton was a hero. The study
of Pip is meant to indicate that with all his virtues Pip
was a snob. The motive of the literary explanation
is different. Pip and Pendennis are meant to show
how circumstances can corrupt men. Sam Weller and
Hercules are meant to show how heroes can subdue
circumstances.

This is the preliminary view of the book which is
necessary if we are to regard it as a real and separate
fact in the life of Dickens. Dickens had many moods
because he was an artist; but he had one great mood,
because he was a great artist. Any real difference
therefore from the general drift, or rather (I apologize
to Dickens) the general drive of his creation is very
important. This is the one place in his work in which
he does, I will not say feel like Thackeray, far less
think like Thackeray, less still write like Thackeray, but
this is the one of his works in which he understands
Thackeray. He puts himself in some sense in the same
place; he considers mankind at somewhat the same
angle as mankind is considered in one of the sociable
and sarcastic novels of Thackeray. When he deals
with Pip he sets out not to show his strength like the
strength of Hercules, but to show his weakness like the
weakness of Pendennis. When he sets out to describe
Pip's great expectations he does not set out, as in a fairy
tale, with the idea that these great expectations will be
fulfilled; he sets out from the first with the idea that
these great expectations will be disappointing. We
might very well, as I have remarked elsewhere, apply
to all Dickens's books the title *Great Expectations*. All
his books are full of an airy and yet ardent expectation
of everything; of the next person who shall happen to

speak, of the next chimney that shall happen to smoke, of the next event, of the next ecstasy; of the next fulfilment of any eager human fancy. All his books might be called *Great Expectations*. But the only book to which he gave the name of *Great Expectations* was the only book in which the expectation was never realized. It was so with the whole of that splendid and unconscious generation to which he belonged. The whole glory of that old English middle class was that it was unconscious; its excellence was entirely in that, that it was the culture of the nation, and that it did not know it. If Dickens had ever known that he was optimistic, he would have ceased to be happy.

It is necessary to make this first point clear: that in *Great Expectations* Dickens was really trying to be a quiet, a detached, and even a cynical observer of human life. Dickens was trying to be Thackeray. And the final and startling triumph of Dickens is this: that even to this moderate and modern story, he gives an incomparable energy which is not moderate and which is not modern. He is trying to be reasonable; but in spite of himself he is inspired. He is trying to be detailed, but in spite of himself he is gigantic. Compared to the rest of Dickens this is Thackeray; but compared to the whole of Thackeray we can only say in supreme praise of it that it is Dickens.

Take, for example, the one question of snobbishness. Dickens has achieved admirably the description of the doubts and vanities of the wretched Pip as he walks down the street in his new gentlemanly clothes, the clothes of which he is so proud and so ashamed. Nothing could be so exquisitely human, nothing especially could be so exquisitely masculine as that combination of self-love and self-assertion and even insolence with a naked and helpless sensibility to the slightest breath of ridicule. Pip thinks himself better than every one else, and yet anybody can snub him; that is the everlasting male, and perhaps the everlasting gentleman. Dickens has described perfectly this quivering and defenceless dignity. Dickens has described perfectly how ill-armed it is against the coarse humour of real humanity—the real humanity which Dickens loved, but which idealists and philanthropists do not love, the humanity of cabmen and costermongers and men singing in a third-class carriage; the humanity of Trabb's boy. In describing Pip's weakness Dickens is as true and as delicate as Thackeray. But Thackeray might have been easily as true and as delicate as Dickens. This quick and quiet eye for the tremors of mankind is a thing which Dickens possessed, but which others possessed also. George Eliot or Thackeray could have described the weakness of Pip. Exactly what George Eliot and Thackeray could not have described was the vigour of Trabb's boy. There would have been admirable humour and observation in their accounts of that intolerable urchin. Thackeray would have given us little light touches of Trabb's boy, absolutely true to the quality and colour of the humour, just as in his novels of the eighteenth century, the glimpses of Steele or Bolingbroke or Doctor Johnson are exactly and perfectly true to the colour and quality of their humour. George Eliot in her earlier books would have given us shrewd authentic scraps of the real dialect of Trabb's boy, just as she gave us shrewd and authentic scraps of the real talk in a Midland country town. In her later books she would have given us highly rationalistic explanations of Trabb's boy; which we should not have read. But exactly what they could never have given, and exactly what Dickens does give, is the *bounce* of Trabb's boy. It is the real unconquerable rush and energy in a character which was the supreme and quite indescribable greatness of Dickens. He conquered by rushes; he attacked in masses; he carried things at the spear point in a charge of spears; he was the Rupert of Fiction. The thing about any figure of Dickens, about Sam Weller or Dick Swiveller, or Micawber, or Bagstock, or Trabb's boy—the thing about each one of these persons is that he cannot be exhausted. A Dickens character hits you first on the nose and then in the waistcoat, and then in the eye and then in the waistcoat again, with the blinding rapidity of some battering engine. The scene in which Trabb's boy continually overtakes Pip in order to reel and stagger as at a first encounter is a thing quite within the real competence of such a character; it might have been suggested by Thackeray, or George Eliot, or any realist. But the point with Dickens is that there is a rush in the boy's rushings; the writer and the reader rush with him. They start with him, they stare with him, they stagger with him, they share an inexpressible vitality in the air which emanates from this violent and capering satirist. Trabb's boy is among other things a boy; he has a physical rapture in hurling himself like a boomerang and in bouncing to the sky like a ball. It is just exactly in describing this quality that Dickens is Dickens and that no one else comes near him. No one feels in his bones that Felix Holt was strong as he feels in his bones that little Quilp was strong. No one can feel that even Rawdon Crawley's splendid smack across the face of Lord Steyne is quite so living and life-giving as the 'kick after kick' which old Mr. Weller dealt the dancing and quivering Stiggins as he drove him towards the trough. This quality, whether expressed intellectually or physically, is the profoundly popular and eternal quality in Dickens; it is the thing that no one else could do. This quality is the quality which has always given its continuous power and poetry to the common people everywhere. It is life; it is the joy of life felt by those who have nothing else but life. It is the thing that all aristocrats have always hated and dreaded in the people. And it is the thing which poor Pip really hates and dreads in Trabb's boy.

A great man of letters or any great artist is symbolic without knowing it. The things he describes are types because they are truths. Shakespeare may, or may not, have ever put it to himself that Richard the Second was a philosophical symbol; but all good criticism must necessarily see him so. It may be a reasonable question whether the artist should be allegorical. There can be no doubt among sane men that the critic should be allegorical. Spenser may have lost by being less realistic than Fielding. But any good criticism of *Tom Jones* must be as mystical as the *Faerie Queene*. Hence it is unavoidable in speaking of a fine book like *Great Expectations* that we should give even to its unpretentious and realistic figures a certain massive mysticism. Pip is Pip, but he is also the well-meaning snob. And this is even more true of those two great figures in the tale which stand for the English democracy. For, indeed, the first and last word upon the English democracy is said in Joe Gargery and Trabb's boy. The actual English populace, as distinct from the French populace or the Scotch or Irish populace, may be said to lie between those two types. The first is the poor man who does not assert himself at all, and the second is the poor man who asserts himself entirely with the weapon of sarcasm. The only way in which the English now ever rise in revolution is under the symbol and leadership of Trabb's boy. What pikes and shillelahs were to the Irish populace, what guns and barricades were to the French populace, that chaff is to the English populace. It is their weapon, the use of which they really understand. It is the one way in which they can make a rich man feel uncomfortable, and they use it very justifiably for all it is worth. If they do not cut off the heads of tyrants at least they sometimes do their best to make the tyrants lose their heads. The gutter boys of the great towns carry the art of personal criticism to so rich and delicate a degree that some well-dressed persons when they walk past a file of them feel as if they were walking past a row of omniscient critics or judges with a power of life and death. Here and there only is some ordinary human custom, some natural human pleasure suppressed in deference to the fastidiousness of the rich. But all the rich tremble before the fastidiousness of the poor.

Of the other type of democracy it is far more difficult to speak. It is always hard to speak of good things or good people, for in satisfying the soul they take away a certain spur to speech. Dickens was often called a

sentimentalist. In one sense he sometimes **was a**
sentimentalist. But if sentimentalism be held to mean
something artificial or theatrical, then in the core and
reality of his character Dickens was the very reverse
of a sentimentalist. He seriously and definitely loved
goodness. To see sincerity and charity satisfied him
like a meal. What some critics call his love of sweét
stuff is really his love of plain beef and bread. Sometimes one is tempted to wish that in the long Dickens
dinner the sweet courses could be left out; but this does
not make the whole banquet other than a banquet
singularly solid and simple. The critics complain of the
sweet things, but not because they are so strong as to
like simple things. They complain of the sweet things
because they are so sophisticated as to like sour things;
their tongues are tainted with the bitterness of absinthe.
Yet because of the very simplicity of Dickens's moral
tastes it is impossible to speak adequately of them; and
Joe Gargery must stand as he stands in the book, a thing
too obvious to be understood. But this may be said
of him in one of his minor aspects, that he stands for
a certain long-suffering in the English poor, a certain
weary patience and politeness which almost breaks the
heart. One cannot help wondering whether that great
mass of silent virtue will ever achieve anything on
this earth.

HARD TIMES

I HAVE heard that in some debating clubs there is a rule that the members may discuss anything except religion and politics. I cannot imagine what they do discuss; but it is quite evident that they have ruled out the only two subjects which are either important or amusing. The thing is a part of a certain modern tendency to avoid things because they lead to warmth; whereas, obviously, we ought, even in a social sense, to seek those things specially. The warmth of the discussion is as much a part of hospitality as the warmth of the fire. And it is singularly suggestive that in English literature the two things have died together. The very people who would blame Dickens for his sentimental hospitality are the very people who would also blame him for his narrow political conviction. The very people who would mock him for his narrow radicalism are those who would mock him for his broad fireside. Real conviction and real charity are much nearer than people suppose. Dickens was capable of loving all men; but he refused to love all opinions. The modern humanitarian can love all opinions, but he cannot love all men; he seems, sometimes, in the ecstasy of his humanitarianism, even to hate them all. He can love all opinions, including the opinion that men are unlovable.

In feeling Dickens as a lover we must never forget him as a fighter, and a fighter for a creed; but indeed there is no other kind of fighter. The geniality which he spread over all his creations was geniality spread from one centre, from one flaming peak. He was willing to excuse Mr. Micawber for being extravagant; but Dickens and Dickens's doctrine were strictly to decide how far he was to be excused. He was willing to like Mr. Twemlow in spite of his snobbishness, but

Dickens and Dickens's doctrine were alone to be judges of how far he was snobbish. There was never a more didactic writer: hence there was never one more amusing. He had no mean modern notion of keeping the moral doubtful. He would have regarded this as a mere piece of slovenliness, like leaving the last page illegible.

Everywhere in Dickens's work these angles of his absolute opinion stood up out of the confusion of his general kindness, just as sharp and splintered peaks stand up out of the soft confusion of the forests. Dickens is always generous, he is generally kind-hearted, he is often sentimental, he is sometimes intolerably maudlin; but you never know when you will not come upon one of the convictions of Dickens; and when you do come upon it you do know it. It is as hard and as high as any precipice or peak of the mountains. The highest and hardest of these peaks is *Hard Times*.

It is here more than anywhere else that the sternness of Dickens emerges as separate from his softness; it is here, most obviously, so to speak, that his bones stick out. There are indeed many other books of his which are written better and written in a sadder tone. *Great Expectations* is melancholy in a sense; but it is doubtful of everything, even of its own melancholy. *The Tale of Two Cities* is a great tragedy, but it is still a sentimental tragedy. It is a great drama, but it is still a melodrama. But this tale of *Hard Times* is in some way harsher than all these. For it is the expression of a righteous indignation which cannot condescend to humour and which cannot even condescend to pathos. Twenty times we have taken Dickens's hand and it has been sometimes hot with revelry and sometimes weak with weariness; but this time we start a little, for it is inhumanly cold; and then we realize that we have touched his gauntlet of steel.

One cannot express the real value of this book without being irrelevant. It is true that one cannot express the real value of anything without being irrelevant. If we take a thing frivolously we can take it separately, but the moment we take a thing seriously, if it were

only an old umbrella, it is obvious that that umbrella
opens above us into the immensity of the whole universe.
But there are rather particular reasons why the value
of the book called *Hard Times* should be referred back
to great historic and theoretic matters with which it
may appear superficially to have little or nothing to
do. The chief reason can perhaps be stated thus—
that English politics had for more than a hundred years
been getting into more and more of a hopeless tangle
(a tangle which, of course, has since become even worse)
and that Dickens did in some extraordinary way see
what was wrong, even if he did not see what was right.

The Liberalism which Dickens and nearly all of his
contemporaries professed had begun in the American
and the French Revolutions. Almost all modern
English criticism upon those revolutions has been
vitiated by the assumption that those revolutions burst
upon a world which was unprepared for their ideas—a
world ignorant of the possibility of such ideas. Somewhat the same mistake is made by those who suggest
that Christianity was adopted by a world incapable
of criticizing it; whereas obviously it was adopted by
a world that was tired of criticizing everything. The
vital mistake that is made about the French Revolution
is merely this—that every one talks about it as the
introduction of a new idea. It was not the introduction
of a new idea; there are no new ideas. Or if there are
new ideas, they would not cause the least irritation if
they were introduced into political society; because the
world having never got used to them there would be no
mass of men ready to fight for them at a moment's
notice. That which was irritating about the French
Revolution was this—that it was not the introduction
of a new ideal, but the practical fulfilment of an old one.
From the time of the first fairy tales men had always
believed ideally in equality; they had always thought
that something ought to be done, if anything could be
done, to redress the balance between Cinderella and the
ugly sisters. The irritating thing about the French was
not that they said this ought to be done; everybody

said that. The irritating thing about the French was that they did it. They proposed to carry out into a positive scheme what had been the vision of humanity; and humanity was naturally annoyed. The kings of Europe did not make war upon the Revolution because it was a blasphemy, but because it was a copy-book maxim which had been just too accurately copied. It was a platitude which they had always held in theory unexpectedly put into practice. The tyrants did not hate democracy because it was a paradox; they hated it because it was a truism which seemed in some danger of coming true.

Now it happens to be hugely important to have this right view of the Revolution in considering its political effects upon England. For the English, being a deeply and indeed excessively romantic people, could never be quite content with this quality of cold and bald obviousness about the republican formula. The republican formula was merely this—that the State must consist of its citizens ruling equally, however unequally they may do anything else. In their capacity of members of the State they are all equally interested in its preservation. But the English soon began to be romantically restless about this eternal truism; they were perpetually trying to turn it into something else, into something more picturesque — progress perhaps, or anarchy. At last they turned it into the highly exciting and highly unsound system of politics, which was known as the Manchester School, and which was expressed with a sort of logical flightiness, more excusable in literature, by Mr. Herbert Spencer. Of course Danton or Washington or any of the original republicans would have thought these people were mad. They would never have admitted for a moment that the State must not interfere with commerce or competition; they would merely have insisted that if the State did interfere, it must really be the State—that is, the whole people. But the distance between the common sense of Danton and the mere ecstasy of Herbert Spencer marks the English way of colouring and altering the revolutionary idea. The English people as a body went blind, as the saying is, for interpreting democracy entirely in terms of liberty. They said in substance that if they had more and more liberty it did not matter whether they had any equality or any fraternity. But this was violating the sacred trinity of true politics; they confounded the persons and they divided the substance.

Now the really odd thing about England in the nineteenth century is this—that there was one Englishman who happened to keep his head. The men who lost their heads lost highly scientific and philosophical heads; · they were great cosmic systematizers like Spencer, great social philosophers like Bentham, great practical politicians like Bright, great political economists like Mill. The man who kept his head kept a head full of fantastic nonsense; he was a writer of rowdy farces, a demagogue of fiction, a man without education in any serious sense whatever, a man whose whole business was to turn ordinary cockneys into extraordinary caricatures. Yet when all these other children of the revolution went wrong he, by a mystical something in his bones, went right. He knew nothing of the Revolution; yet he struck the note of it. He returned to the original sentimental commonplace upon which it is for ever founded, as the Church is founded on a rock. In an England gone mad about a minor theory he reasserted the original idea—the idea that no one in the State must be too weak to influence the State.

This man was Dickens. He did this work much more genuinely than it was done by Carlyle or Ruskin; for they were simply Tories making out a romantic case for the return of Toryism. But Dickens was a real Liberal demanding the return of real Liberalism. Dickens was there to remind people that England had rubbed out two words of the revolutionary motto, had left only Liberty and destroyed Equality and Fraternity. In this book, *Hard Times*, he specially champions equality. In all his books he champions fraternity.

The atmosphere of this book and what it stands for

can be very adequately conveyed in the note on the book by Lord Macaulay, who may stand as a very good example of the spirit of England in those years of eager emancipation and expanding wealth—the years in which Liberalism was turned from an omnipotent truth to a weak scientific system. Macaulay's private comment on *Hard Times* runs: 'One or two passages of exquisite pathos and the rest sullen Socialism.' That is not an unfair and certainly not a specially hostile criticism, but it exactly shows how the book struck those people who were mad on political liberty and dead about everything else. Macaulay mistook for a new formula called Socialism what was, in truth, only the old formula· called political democracy. He and his Whigs had so thoroughly mauled and modified the original idea of Rousseau or Jefferson that when they saw it again they positively thought that it was something quite new and eccentric. But the truth was that Dickens was not a Socialist, but an unspoilt Liberal; he was not sullen; nay, rather, he had remained strangely hopeful. They called him a sullen Socialist only to disguise their astonishment at finding still loose about the London streets a happy republican.

Dickens is the one living link between the old kindness and the new, between the good will of the past and the good works of the future. He links May Day with Bank Holiday, and he does it almost alone. All the men around him, great and good as they were, were in comparison puritanical, and never so puritanical as when they were also atheistic. He is a sort of solitary pipe down which pours to the twentieth century the original river of Merry England. And although this *Hard Times* is, as its name implies, the hardest of his works, although there is less in it perhaps than in any of the others of the *abandon* and the buffoonery of Dickens, this only emphasizes the more clearly the fact that he stood almost alone for a more humane and hilarious view of democracy. None of his great and much more highly educated contemporaries could help him in this. Carlyle was as gloomy on the one side as

Herbert Spencer on the other. He protested against the commercial oppression simply and solely because. It was not only an oppression but a depression. And this protest of his was made specially in the case of the book before us. It may be bitter, but it was a protest against bitterness. It may be dark, but it is the darkness of the subject and not of the author. He is by his own account dealing with hard times, but not with a hard eternity, not with a hard philosophy of the universe. Nevertheless, this is the one place in his work where he does not make us remember human happiness by example as well as by precept. This is, as I have said, not the saddest, but certainly the harshest of his stories. It is perhaps the only place where Dickens, in defending happiness, for a moment forgets to be happy.

He describes Bounderby and Gradgrind with a degree of grimness and sombre hatred very different from the half-affectionate derision which he directed against the old tyrants or humbugs of the earlier nineteenth century —the pompous Dedlock or the fatuous Nupkins, the grotesque Bumble or the inane Tigg. In those old books his very abuse was benignant; in *Hard Times* even his sympathy is hard. And the reason is again to be found in the political facts of the century. Dickens could be half genial with the older generation of oppressors because it was a dying generation. It was evident, or at least it seemed evident then, that Nupkins could not go on much longer making up the law of England to suit himself; that Sir Leicester Dedlock could not go on much longer being kind to his tenants as if they were dogs and cats. And some of these evils the nineteenth century did really eliminate or improve. For the first half of the century Dickens and all his friends were justified in feeling that the chains were falling from mankind. At any rate, the chains did fall from Mr. Rouncewell the Ironmaster. And when they fell from him he picked them up and put them upon the poor.

POEMS

PREFATORY NOTE
TO
'THE WILD KNIGHT' AND OTHER POEMS

I LEAVE these verses as they stand, although they contain innumerable examples of what I now see to be errors of literature, and one or two examples of what I have come to think errors of opinion. But they never had any great merit beyond genuineness, and I do not wish to spoil that by mixing up two periods of my life. On two definite matters here embodied in verse I have altered my opinion; and if I mention what they are I really do not mean it for egoism, but only for honesty.

In the matter of the 'Anglo-American Alliance,'[1] I have come to see that our hopes of brotherhood with America are the same in kind as our hopes of brotherhood with any other of the great independent nations of Christendom. And a very small study of history was sufficient to show me that the American nation, which is a hundred years old, is at least fifty years older than the Anglo-Saxon race.

And in the matter of the Dreyfus[2] case, while not having been able to reach any final conclusion about the proper verdict on the individual, I have come largely to attribute the difficulty of doing so to the acrid and irrational unanimity of the English press. My position may be roughly stated thus: There may have been a fog of injustice in the French courts; I know that there was a fog of injustice in the English newspapers. For the rest, there are verses which I cannot take so seriously as to alter them. The man who wrote them was honest; and he had the same basic views as myself. Besides, nobody need read the book: I certainly beg to be excused.

G. K. C.

BATTERSEA, 1905.

[1] 'An Alliance,' p. 303.
[2] 'To a Certain Nation,' p. 310,

275

NOTE

My thanks are due to the Editors of the *Outlook* and the *Speaker* for the kind permission they have given me to reprint a considerable number of the following poems. They have been selected and arranged rather with a view to unity of spirit than to unity of time or value; many of them being juvenile.

Another tattered rhymester in the ring,
  With but the old plea to the sneering schools,
That on him too, some secret night in spring,
  Came the old frenzy of a hundred fools

To make some thing : the old want dark and deep,
  The thirst of men, the hunger of the stars,
Since first it tinged even the Eternal's sleep,
  With monstrous dreams of trees and towns and
      wars.

When all He made for the first time He saw,
  Scattering stars as misers shake their pelf.
Then in the last strange wrath broke His own law,
  And made a graven image of Himself.

BY THE BABE UNBORN

IF trees were tall and grasses short,
  As in some crazy tale,
If here and there a sea were blue
  Beyond the breaking pale,

If a fixed fire hung in the air
  To warm me one day through,
If deep green hair grew on great hills,
  I know what I should do.

In dark I lie: dreaming that there
  Are great eyes cold or kind,
And twisted streets and silent doors,
  And living men behind.

Let storm-clouds come: better an hour,
  And leave to weep and fight,
Than all the ages I have ruled
  The empires of the night.

I think that if they gave me leave
  Within that world to stand,
I would be good through all the day
  I spent in fairyland.

They should not hear a word from me
  Of selfishness or scorn,
If only I could find the door,
  If only I were born.

THE WORLD'S LOVER

My eyes are full of lonely mirth:
  Reeling with want and worn with scars,
For pride of every stone on earth,
  I shake my spear at all the stars.

A live bat beats my crest above,
  Lean foxes nose where I have trod,
And on my naked face the love
  Which is the loneliness of God.

Outlawed: since that great day gone by—
  When before prince and pope and queen
I stood and spoke a blasphemy—
  'Behold the summer leaves are green.'

They cursed me: what was that to me
  Who in that summer darkness furled,
With but an owl and snail to see,
  Had blessed and conquered all the world?

They bound me to the scourging-stake,
  They laid their whips of thorn on me;
I wept to see the green rods break,
  Though blood be beautiful to see.

Beneath the gallows' foot abhorred
  The crowds cry 'Crucify!' and 'Kill!'
Higher the priests sing: 'Praise the Lord,
  The warlock dies'; and higher still

Shall heaven and earth hear one cry sent
  Even from the hideous gibbet height:
'Praise to the Lord Omnipotent,
  The vultures have a feast to-night.'

THE SKELETON

CHATTERING finch and water-fly
Are not merrier than I;
Here among the flowers I lie
Laughing everlastingly.
No: I may not tell the best;
Surely, friends, I might have guessed
Death was but the good King's jest,
    It was hid so carefully.

A CHORD OF COLOUR

My Lady clad herself in grey,
    That caught and clung about her throat;
Then all the long grey winter day
    On me a living splendour smote;
And why grey palmers holy are,
    And why grey minsters great in story,
And grey skies ring the morning star,
    And grey hairs are a crown of glory.

My Lady clad herself in green,
    Like meadows where the wind-waves pass;
Then round my spirit spread, I ween,
    A splendour of forgotten grass.
Then all that dropped of stem or sod,
    Hoarded as emeralds might be,
I bowed to every bush, and trod
    Amid the live grass fearfully.

My Lady clad herself in blue,
    Then on me, like the seer long gone,
The likeness of a sapphire grew,
    The throne of him that sat thereon.

Then knew I why the Fashioner
    Splashed reckless blue on sky and sea;
And ere 'twas good enough for her,
    He tried it on Eternity.

Beneath the gnarled old Knowledge-tree
    Sat, like an owl, the evil sage:
'The World 's a bubble,' solemnly
    He read, and turned a second page.
'A bubble, then, old crow,' I cried,
    'God keep you in your weary wit!
A bubble—have you ever spied
    The colours I have seen on it?'

THE HAPPY MAN

To teach the grey earth like a child,
    To bid the heavens repent,
I only ask from Fate the gift
    Of one man well content.

Him will I find: though when in vain
    I search the feast and mart,
The fading flowers of liberty,
    The painted masks of art.

I only find him at the last,
    On one old hill where nod
Golgotha's ghastly trinity—
    Three persons and one god.

THE UNPARDONABLE SIN

I DO not cry, beloved, neither curse.
    Silence and strength, these two at least are good.
    He gave me sun and stars and aught He could,
But not a woman's love; for that is hers.

He sealed her heart from sage and questioner—
  Yea, with seven seals, as he has sealed the grave.
  And if she give it to a drunken slave,
The Day of Judgment shall not challenge her.

Only this much: if one, deserving well,
  Touching your thin young hands and making suit,
  Feel not himself a crawling thing, a brute,
Buried and bricked in a forgotten hell;

Prophet and poet be he over sod,
  Prince among angels in the highest place,
  God help me, I will smite him on the face,
Before the glory of the face of God.

A NOVELTY

Why should I care for the Ages
  Because they are old and grey?
To me, like sudden laughter,
  The stars are fresh and gay;
The world is a daring fancy,
  And finished yesterday.

Why should I bow to the Ages
  Because they were drear and dry?
Slow trees and ripening meadows
  For me go roaring by,
A living charge, a struggle
  To escalade the sky.

The eternal suns and systems,
  Solid and silent all,
To me are stars of an instant,
  Only the fires that fall
From God's good rocket, rising
  On this night of carnival.

ULTIMATE

THE vision of a haloed host
   That weep around an empty throne;
And, aureoles dark and angels dead,
   Man with his own life stands alone.

'I am,' he says his bankrupt creed;
   'I am,' and is again a clod:
The sparrow starts, the grasses stir,
   For he has said the name of God.

THE DONKEY

WHEN fishes flew and forests walked
   And figs grew upon thorn,
Some moment when the moon was blood
   Then surely I was born;

With monstrous head and sickening cry
   And ears like errant wings,
The devil's walking parody
   On all four-footed things.

The tattered outlaw of the earth,
   Of ancient crooked will;
Starve, scourge, deride me: I am dumb,
   I keep my secret still.

Fools! For I also had my hour;
   One far fierce hour and sweet:
There was a shout about my ears,
   And palms before my feet.

THE BEATIFIC VISION

THROUGH what fierce incarnations, furled
    In fire and darkness, did I go,
Ere I was worthy in the world
    To see a dandelion grow?

Well, if in any woes or wars
    I bought my naked right to be,
Grew worthy of the grass, nor gave
    The wren, my brother, shame for me.

But what shall God not ask of him
    In the last time when all is told,
Who saw her stand beside the hearth,
    The firelight garbing her in gold?

THE HOPE OF THE STREETS

THE still sweet meadows shimmered: and I stood
    And cursed them, bloom of hedge and bird of tree,
And bright and high beyond the hunch-backed wood
    The thunder and the splendour of the sea.

Give back the Babylon where I was born,
    The lips that gape give back, the hands that grope,
And noise and blood and suffocating scorn
    And eddy of fierce faces—and a hope

That 'mid those myriad heads one head find place,
    With brown hair curled like breakers of the sea,
And two eyes set so strangely in the face
    That all things else are nothing suddenly.

ECCLESIASTES

THERE is one sin: to call a green leaf grey,
    Whereat the sun in heaven shuddereth.
There is one blasphemy: for death to pray,
    For God alone knoweth the praise of death.

There is one creed: 'neath no world-terror's wing
    Apples forget to grow on apple-trees.
There is one thing is needful—everything—
    The rest is vanity of vanities.

THE SONG OF THE CHILDREN

THE World is ours till sunset,
    Holly and fire and snow,
And the name of our dead brother
    Who loved us long ago.

The grown folk mighty and cunning,
    They write his name in gold;
But we can tell a little
    Of the million tales he told.

He taught them laws and watchwords,
    To preach and struggle and pray;
But he taught us deep in the hayfield
    The games that the angels play.

Had he stayed here for ever,
    Their world would be wise as ours—
And the king be cutting capers,
    And the priest be picking flowers.

But the dark day came: they gathered:
    On their faces we could see
They had taken and slain our brother,
    And hanged him on a tree.

*K 913

THE FISH

DARK the sea was: but I saw him,
  One great head with goggle eyes,
Like a diabolic cherub
  Flying in those fallen skies.

I have heard the hoarse deniers,
  I have known the wordy wars;
I have seen a man, by shouting,
  Seek to orphan all the stars.

I have seen a fool half-fashioned
  Borrow from the heavens a tongue,
So to curse them more at leisure—
  —And I trod him not as dung.

For I saw that finny goblin
  Hidden in the abyss untrod;
And I knew there can be laughter
  On the secret face of God.

Blow the trumpets, crown the sages,
  Bring the age by reason fed!
('He that sitteth in the heavens,
  He shall laugh'—the prophet said.)

GOLD LEAVES

Lo! I am come to autumn,
  When all the leaves are gold;
Grey hairs and golden leaves cry out
  The year and I are old.

In youth I sought the prince of men,
  Captain in cosmic wars,
Our Titan, even the weeds would show
  Defiant, to the stars.

But now a great thing in the street
  Seems any human nod,
Where shift in strange democracy
  The million masks of God.

In youth I sought the golden flower
  Hidden in wood or wold,
But I am come to autumn,
  When all the leaves are gold.

THOU SHALT NOT KILL

I HAD grown weary of him; of his breath
And hands and features I was sick to death.
Each day I heard the same dull voice and tread;
I did not hate him: but I wished him dead.
And he must with his blank face fill my life—
Then my brain blackened, and I snatched a knife.

But ere I struck, my soul's grey deserts through
A voice cried: 'Know at least what thing you do.
This is a common man: knowest thou, O soul,
What this thing is? somewhere where seasons roll
There is some living thing for whom this man
Is as seven heavens girt into a span,
For some one soul you take the world away—
Now know you well your deed and purpose. Slay!'

Then I cast down the knife upon the ground
And saw that mean man for one moment crowned.
I turned and laughed: for there was no one by—
The man that I had sought to slay was I.

A CERTAIN EVENING

THAT night the whole world mingled,
The souls were babes at play,
And angel danced with devil,
And God cried, 'Holiday!'

The sea had climbed the mountain peaks,
And shouted to the stars
To come to play: and down they came
Splashing in happy wars.

The pine grew apples for a whim,
The cart-horse built a nest;
The oxen flew, the flowers sang,
The sun rose in the west.

And 'neath the load of many worlds,
The lowest life God made
Lifted his huge and heavy limbs
And into heaven strayed.

To where the highest life God made
Before His presence stands;
But God Himself cried, 'Holiday!'
And she gave me both her hands.

A MAN AND HIS IMAGE

ALL day the nations climb and crawl and pray
In one long pilgrimage to one white shrine,
Where sleeps a saint whose pardon, like his peace,
Is wide as death, as common, as divine.

His statue in an aureole fills the shrine,
The reckless nightingale, the roaming fawn,
Share the broad blessing of his lifted hands,
Under the canopy, above the lawn.

But one strange night, a night of gale and flood,
  A sound came louder than the wild wind's tone;
The grave-gates shook and opened: and one stood
  Blue in the moonlight, rotten to the bone.

Then on the statue, graven with holy smiles,
  There came another smile—tremendous—one
Of an Egyptian god. 'Why should you rise?
  Do I not guard your secret from the sun?

'The nations come; they kneel among the flowers
  Sprung from your blood, blossoms of May and June.
Which do not poison them—is it not strange?
  Speak!' And the dead man shuddered in the moon.

'Shall I not cry the truth?'—the dead man cowered—
  'Is it not sad, with life so tame and cold,
That earth should fade into the sun's white fires
  With the best jest in all its tales untold?

'If I should cry that in this shrine lie hid
  Stories that Satan from his mouth would spew;
Wild tales that men in hell tell hoarsely—speak!
  Saint and Deliverer! Should I slander you?'

Slowly the cowering corse reared up its head:
  'Nay, I am vile . . . but when for all to see,
You stand there, pure and painless—death of life!
  Let the stars fall—I say you slander me!

'You make me perfect, public, colourless;
  You make my virtues sit at ease—you lie!
For mine were never easy—lost or saved,
  I had a soul—I was. And where am I?

'Where is my good? the little real hoard,
  The secret tears, the sudden chivalries;
The tragic love, the futile triumph—where?
  Thief, dog, and son of devils—where are these?

'I will lift up my head: in leprous loves
    Lost, and the soul's dishonourable scars—
By God, I was a better man than This
    That stands and slanders me to all the stars.

'Come down!' And with an awful cry, the corse
    Sprang on the sacred tomb of many tales,
And stone and bone, locked in a loathsome strife,
    Swayed to the singing of the nightingales.

Then one was thrown: and where the statue stood
    Under the canopy, above the lawn,
The corse stood; grey and lean, with lifted hands
    Raised in tremendous welcome to the dawn.

'Now let all nations climb and crawl and pray;
    Though I be basest of my old red clan,
They shall not scale, with cries or sacrifice,
    The stature of the spirit of a man.'

THE MARINER

THE violet scent is sacred
    Like dreams of angels bright;
The hawthorn smells of passion
    Told in a moonless night.

But the smell is in my nostrils,
    Through blossoms red or gold,
Of my own green flower unfading,
    A bitter smell and bold.

The lily smells of pardon,
    The rose of mirth; but mine
Smells shrewd of death and honour,
    And the doom of Adam's line.

The heavy scent of wine-shops
  Floats as I pass them by,
But never a cup I quaff from,
  And never a house have I.

Till dropped down forty fathoms,
  I lie eternally;
And drink from God's own goblet
  The green wine of the sea.

THE TRIUMPH OF MAN

I PLOD and peer amid mean sounds and shapes,
  I hunt for dusty gain and dreary praise,
  And slowly pass the dismal grinning days,
Monkeying each other like a line of apes.

What care?   There was one hour amid all these
  When I had stripped off like a tawdry glove
  My starriest hopes and wants, for very love
Of time and desolate eternities.

Yea, for one great hour's triumph, not in me
  Nor any hope of mine did I rejoice,
  But in a meadow game of girls and boys
Some sunset in the centuries to be.

CYCLOPEAN

A MOUNTAINOUS and mystic brute
No rein can curb, no arrow shoot,
Upon whose doomed deformèd back
I sweep the planets' scorching track.

Old is the elf, and wise, men say,
His hair grows green as ours grows grey;
He mocks the stars with myriad hands,
High as that swinging forest stands.

But though in pygmy wanderings dull
I scour the deserts of his skull,
I never find the face, eyes, teeth,
Lowering or laughing underneath.

I met my foe in an empty dell,
His face in the sun was naked hell.
I thought: 'One silent, bloody blow,
No priest would curse, no crowd would know.'

Then cowered: a daisy, half concealed,
Watched for the fame of that poor field;
And in that flower and suddenly
Earth opened its one eye on me.

JOSEPH

IF the stars fell; night's nameless dreams
  Of bliss and blasphemy came true,
If skies were green and snow were gold,
  And you loved me as I love you;

O long light hands and curled brown hair,
  And eyes where sits a naked soul;
Dare I even then draw near and burn
  My fingers in the aureole?

Yes, in the one wise foolish hour
  God gives this strange strength to a man.
He can demand, though not deserve,
  Where ask he cannot, seize he can.

But once the blood's wild wedding o'er,
  Were not dread his, half dark desire,
To see the Christ-child in the cot,
  The Virgin Mary by the fire?

MODERN ELFLAND

I CUT a staff in a churchyard copse,
   I clad myself in ragged things,
I set a feather in my cap
   That fell out of an angel's wings.

I filled my wallet with white stones,
   I took three foxgloves in my hand,
I slung my shoes across my back,
   And so I went to fairyland.

But lo, within that ancient place
   Science had reared her iron crown,
And the great cloud of steam went up
   That telleth where she takes a town.

But cowled with smoke and starred with lamps
   That strange land's light was still its own;
The word that witched the woods and hills
   Spoke in the iron and the stone.

Not Nature's hand had ever curved
   That mute unearthly porter's spine.
Like sleeping dragon's sudden eyes
   The signals leered along the line.

The chimneys thronging crooked or straight
   Were fingers signalling the sky;
The dog that strayed across the street
   Seemed four-legged by monstrosity.

'In vain,' I cried, 'though you too touch
   The new time's desecrating hand,
Through all the noises of a town
   I hear the heart of fairyland.'

I read the name above a door,
   Then through my spirit pealed and passed:
'This is the town of thine own home,
   And thou hast looked on it at last.'

ETERNITIES

I CANNOT count the pebbles in the brook.
  Well hath He spoken: 'Swear not by thy head,
  Thou knowest not the hairs,' though He, we read,
Writes that wild number in His own strange book.

I cannot count the sands or search the seas,
  Death cometh, and I leave so much untrod.
  Grant my immortal aureole, O my God,
And I will name the leaves upon the trees.

In heaven I shall stand on gold and glass,
  Still brooding earth's arithmetic to spell;
  Or see the fading of the fires of hell
Ere I have thanked my God for all the grass.

A CHRISTMAS CAROL

THE Christ-child lay on Mary's lap,
  His hair was like a light.
(O weary, weary were the world,
  But here is all aright.)

The Christ-child lay on Mary's breast,
  His hair was like a star.
(O stern and cunning are the kings,
  But here the true hearts are.)

The Christ-child lay on Mary's heart,
  His hair was like a fire.
(O weary, weary is the world,
  But here the world's desire.)

The Christ-child stood at Mary's knee,
  His hair was like a crown,
And all the flowers looked up at Him,
  And all the stars looked down.

ALONE

BLESSINGS there are of cradle and of clan,
  Blessings that fall of priests' and princes' hands;
  But never blessing full of lives and lands,
Broad as the blessing of a lonely man.

Though that old king fell from his primal throne,
  And ate among the cattle, yet this pride
  Had found him in the deepest grass, and cried
An 'Ecce Homo' with the trumpets blown.

And no mad tyrant, with almighty ban,
  Who in strong madness dreams himself divine,
  But hears through fumes of flattery and of wine
The thunder of this blessing name him man.

Let all earth rot past saints' and seraphs' plea,
  Yet shall a Voice cry through its last lost war:
  'This is the world, this red wreck of a star,
That a man blessed beneath an alder-tree.'

KING'S CROSS STATION

THIS circled cosmos whereof man is god
  Has suns and stars of green and gold and red,
And cloudlands of great smoke, that range o'er range
  Far floating, hide its iron heavens o'erhead.

God! shall we ever honour what we are,
  And see one moment ere the age expire,
The vision of man shouting and erect,
  Whirled by the shrieking steeds of flood and fire?

Or must Fate act the same grey farce again,
  And wait, till one, amid Time's wrecks and scars,
Speaks to a ruin here: 'What poet-race
  Shot such cyclopean arches at the stars?'

THE HUMAN TREE

MANY have Earth's lovers been,
Tried in seas and wars, I ween;
Yet the mightiest have I seen·
 Yea, the best saw I.
One that in a field alone
Stood up stiller than a stone
 Lest a moth should fly.

Birds had nested in his hair,
On his shoon were mosses rare,
Insect empires flourished there,
 Worms in ancient wars;
But his eyes burn like a glass,
Hearing a great sea of grass
 Roar towards the stars.

From them to the human tree
Rose a cry continually:
'Thou art still, our Father, we
 Fain would have thee nod.
Make the skies as blood below thee,
Though thou slay us, we shall know thee.
 Answer us, O God!

'Show thine ancient fame and thunder,
Split the stillness once asunder,
Lest we whisper, lest we wonder
 Art thou there at all?'
But I saw him there alone,
Standing stiller than a stone
 Lest a moth should fall.

TO THEM THAT MOURN

(W. E. G., May 1898)

LIFT up your heads: in life, in death,
  God knoweth his head was high.
Quit we the coward's broken breath
  Who watched a strong man die.

If we must say: 'No more his peer
  Cometh; the flag is furled,'
Stand not too near him, lest he hear
  That slander on the world.

The good green earth he loved and trod
  Is still, with many a scar,
Writ in the chronicles of God,
  A giant-bearing star.

He fell: but Britain's banner swings
  Above his sunken crown.
Black death shall have his toll of kings
  Before that cross goes down.

Once more shall move with mighty things
  His house of ancient tale,
Where kings whose hands were kissed of kings
  Went in: and came out pale.

O young ones of a darker day,
  In art's wan colours clad,
Whose very love and hate are grey—
  Whose very sin is sad,

Pass on: one agony long-drawn
  Was merrier than your mirth,
When hand-in-hand came death and dawn,
  And spring was on the earth.

THE OUTLAW

PRIEST, is any song-bird stricken?
  Is one leaf less on the tree?
Is this wine less red and royal
  That the hangman waits for me?

He upon your cross that hangeth,
  It is writ of priestly pen,
On the night they built His gibbet,
  Drank red wine among His men.

Quaff, like a brave man, as He did,
  Wine and death as heaven pours—
This is my fate: O ye rulers,
  O ye pontiffs, what is yours?

To wait trembling, lest yon loathly
  Gallows-shape whereon I die,
In strange temples yet unbuilded,
  Blaze upon an altar high.

BEHIND

I SAW an old man like a child,
His blue eyes bright, his white hair wild,
Who turned for ever, and might not stop,
Round and round like an urchin's top.

'Fool,' I cried, 'while you spin round,
Others grow wise, are praised, are crowned.'
Ever the same round road he trod,
'This is better: I seek for God.

'We see the whole world, left and right,
Yet at the blind back hides from sight
The unseen Master that drives us forth
To East and West, to South and North.

'Over my shoulder for eighty years
I have looked for the gleam of the sphere of spheres.
'In all your turning, what have you found?'
'At least, I know why the world goes round.'

THE END OF FEAR

THOUGH the whole heaven be one-eyed with the moon,
  Though the dead landscape seem a thing possessed,
  Yet I go singing through that land oppressed
As one that singeth through the flowers of June.

No more, with forest-fingers crawling free
  O'er dark flint wall that seems a wall of eyes,
  Shall evil break my soul with mysteries
Of some world-poison maddening bush and tree.

No more shall leering ghosts of pimp and king
  With bloody secrets veiled before me stand.
  Last night I held all evil in my hand
Closed: and behold it was a little thing.

I broke the infernal gates and looked on him
  Who fronts the strong creation with a curse;
  Even the god of a lost universe,
Smiling above his hideous cherubim.

And pierced far down in his soul's crypt unriven
  The last black crooked sympathy and shame,
  And hailed him with that ringing rainbow name
Erased upon the oldest book in heaven.

Like emptied idiot masks, sin's loves and wars
  Stare at me now: for in the night I broke
  The bubble of a great world's jest, and woke
Laughing with laughter such as shakes the stars.

THE HOLY OF HOLIES

'ELDER father, though thine eyes
Shine with hoary mysteries,
Canst thou tell what in the heart
Of a cowslip blossom lies?

'Smaller than all lives that be,
Secret as the deepest sea,
Stands a little house of seeds,
Like an elfin's granary.

'Speller of the stones and weeds,
Skilled in Nature's crafts and creeds,
Tell me what is in the heart
Of the smallest of the seeds.'

'God Almighty, and with Him
Cherubim and Seraphim,
Filling all eternity—
Adonai Elohim.'

THE MIRROR OF MADMEN

I DREAMED a dream of heaven, white as frost,
The splendid stillness of a living host;
Vast choirs of upturned faces, line o'er line.
Then my blood froze; for every face was mine.

Spirits with sunset plumage throng and pass,
Glassed darkly in the sea of gold and glass.
But still on every side, in every spot,
I saw a million selves, who saw me not.

I fled to quiet wastes, where on a stone,
Perchance, I found a saint, who sat alore;
I came behind: he turned with slow, sweet grace,
And faced me with my happy, hateful face.

I cowered like one that in a tower doth bide,
Shut in by mirrors upon every side;
Then I saw, islanded in skies alone
And silent, one that sat upon a throne.

His robe was bordered with rich rose and gold,
Green, purple, silver out of sunsets old;
But o'er his face a great cloud edged with fire,
Because it covereth the world's desire.

But as I gazed, a silent worshipper,
Methought the cloud began to faintly stir;
Then I fell flat, and screamed with grovelling head:
'If thou hast any lightning, strike me dead!

'But spare a brow where the clean sunlight fell,
The crown of a new sin that sickens hell.
Let me not look aloft and see mine own
Feature and form upon the Judgment-throne.'

Then my dream snapped: and with a heart that
    leapt
I saw across the tavern where I slept,
The sight of all my life most full of grace,
A gin-damned drunkard's wan half-witted face.

E. C. B.

BEFORE the grass grew over me,
   I knew one good man through and through,
And knew a soul and body joined
   Are stronger than the heavens are blue.

A wisdom worthy of thy joy,
   O great heart, read I as I ran;
Now, though men smite me on the face,
   I cannot curse the face of man.

I loved the man I saw yestreen
  Hanged with his babe's blood on his palms.
I loved the man I saw to-day
  Who knocked not when he came with alms.

Hush!—for thy sake I even faced
  The knowledge that is worse than hell;
And loved the man I saw but now
  Hanging head downwards in the well.

THE DESECRATERS

Witness all: that unrepenting,
  Feathers flying, music high,
I go down to death unshaken
  By your mean philosophy.

For your wages, take my body,
  That at least to you I leave;
Set the sulky plumes upon it,
  Bid the grinning mummers grieve.

Stand in silence: steep your raiment
  In the night that hath no star;
Don the mortal dress of devils,
  Blacker than their spirits are.

Since ye may not, of your mercy,
  Ere I lie on such a hearse,
Hurl me to the living jackals
  God hath built for sepulchres.

AN ALLIANCE

THIS is the weird of a world-old folk,
  That not till the last link breaks,
Not till the night is blackest,
  The blood of Hengist wakes.
When the sun is black in heaven,
  The moon as blood above,
And the earth is full of hatred,
  This people tells its love.

In change, eclipse, and peril,
  Under the whole world's scorn,
By blood and death and darkness
  The Saxon peace is sworn;
That all our fruit be gathered,
  And all our race take hands,
And the sea be a Saxon river
  That runs through Saxon lands.

Lo! not in vain we bore him;
  Behold it! not in vain,
Four centuries' dooms of torture
  Choked in the throat of Spain,
Ere priest or tyrant triumph—
  We know how well—we know—
Bone of that bone can whiten,
  Blood of that blood can flow.

Deep grows the hate of kindred,
  Its roots take hold on hell;
No peace or praise can heal it,
  But a stranger heals it well.
Seas shall be red as sunsets,
  And kings' bones float as foam,
And heaven be dark with vultures,
  The night our son comes home.

THE ANCIENT OF DAYS

A CHILD sits in a sunny place,
  Too happy for a smile,
And plays through one long holiday
  With balls to roll and pile;
A painted windmill by his side
  Runs like a merry tune,
But the sails are the four great winds of heaven,
  And the balls are the sun and moon.

A staring doll's-house shows to him
  Green floors and starry rafter,
And many-coloured graven dolls
  Live for his lonely laughter.
The dolls have crowns and aureoles,
  Helmets and horns and wings,
For they are the saints and seraphim,
  The prophets and the kings.

THE LAST MASQUERADE

A WAN new garment of young green
  Touched, as you turned your soft brown hair;
  And in me surged the strangest prayer
Ever in lover's heart hath been.

That I who saw your youth's bright page,
  A rainbow change from robe to robe,
  Might see you on this earthly globe,
Crowned with the silver crown of age.

Your dear hair powdered in strange guise,
  Your dear face touched with colours pale;
  And gazing through the mask and veil
The mirth of your immortal eyes.

THE EARTH'S SHAME

NAME not his deed: in shuddering and in haste
  We dragged him darkly o'er the windy fell:
That night there was a gibbet in the waste,
    And a new sin in hell.

Be his deed hid from commonwealths and kings,
  By all men born be one true tale forgot;
But three things, braver than all earthly things,
    Faced him and feared him not.

Above his head and sunken secret face
  Nested the sparrow's young and dropped not dead.
From the red blood and slime of that lost place
    Grew daisies white, not red.

And from high heaven looking upon him,
  Slowly upon the face of God did come
A smile the cherubim and seraphim
    Hid all their faces from.

VANITY

  A WAN sky greener than the lawn,
    A wan lawn paler than the sky.
She gave a flower into my hand,
    And all the hours of eve went by.

Who knows what round the corner waits
    To smite?   If shipwreck, snare, or slur
Shall leave me with a head to lift,
    Worthy of him that spoke with her.

A wan sky greener than the lawn,
    A wan lawn paler than the sky.
She gave a flower into my hand,
    And all the days of life went by.

Live ill or well, this thing is mine,
  From all I guard it, ill or well.
One tawdry, tattered, faded flower
  To show the jealous kings in hell.

THE LAMP POST

LAUGH your best, O blazoned forests,
  Me ye shall not shift or shame
With your beauty: here among you
  Man hath set his spear of flame.

Lamp to lamp we send the signal,
  For our lord goes forth to war;
Since a voice, ere stars were builded,
  Bade him colonize a star.

Laugh ye, cruel as the morning,
  Deck your heads with fruit and flower,
Though our souls be sick with pity,
  Yet our hands are hard with power.

We have read your evil stories,
  We have heard the tiny yell
Through the voiceless conflagration
  Of your green and shining hell.

And when men, with fires and shouting,
  Break your old tyrannic pales;
And where ruled a single spider
  Laugh and weep a million tales.

This shall be your best of boasting:
  That some poet, poor of spine,
Full and sated with our wisdom,
  Full and fiery with our wine,

Shall steal out and make a treaty
  With the grasses and the showers,
Rail against the grey town-mother,
  Fawn upon the scornful flowers;

Rest his head among the roses,
  Where a quiet song-bird sounds,
And no sword made sharp for traitors,
  Hack him into meat for hounds.

THE PESSIMIST

You that have snarled through the ages, take your
    answer and go—
I know your hoary question, the riddle that all men know.
You have weighed the stars in a balance, and grasped
    the skies in a span:
Take, if you must have answer, the word of a common
    man.

Deep in my life lies buried one love unhealed, unshriven,
One hunger still shall haunt me—yea, in the streets of
    heaven;
This is the burden, babbler, this is the curse shall cling,
This is the thing I bring you; this is the pleasant thing.

'Gainst you and all your sages, no joy of mine shall strive,
This one dead self shall shatter the men you call alive.
My grief I send to smite you, no pleasure, no belief,
Lord of the battered grievance, what do you know of
    grief?

I only know the praises to heaven that one man gave,
That he came on earth for an instant, to stand beside a
    grave,
The peace of a field of battle, where flowers are born of
    blood.
I only know one evil that makes the whole world good.

Beneath this single sorrow the globe of moon and sphere
Turns to a single jewel, so bright and brittle and dear
That I dread lest God should drop it, to be dashed into
    stars below.

     ·   ·   ·   ·   ·   ·

You that have snarled through the ages, take your
    answer and go.

A FAIRY TALE

ALL things grew upwards, foul and fair:
The great trees fought and beat the air
With monstrous wings that would have flown;
But the old earth clung to her own,
Holding them back from heavenly wars,
Though every flower sprang at the stars.

But he broke free: while all things ceased,
Some hour increasing, he increased.
The town beneath him seemed a map,
Above the church he cocked his cap,
Above the cross his feather flew
Above the birds: and still he grew.

The trees turned grass; the clouds were riven;
His feet were mountains lost in heaven;
Through strange new skies he rose alone,
The earth fell from him like a stone,
And his own limbs beneath him far
Seemed tapering down to touch a star.

He reared his head, shaggy and grim,
Staring among the cherubim;
The seven celestial floors he rent,
One crystal dome still o'er him bent:
Above his head, more clear than hope,
All heaven was a microscope.

A PORTRAIT

FAIR faces crowd on Christmas night
  Like seven suns a-row,
But all beyond is the wolfish wind
  And the crafty feet of the snow.

But through the rout one figure goes
  With quick and quiet tread;
Her robe is plain, her form is frail—
  Wait if she turn her head.

I say no word of line or hue,
  But if that face you see,
Your soul shall know the smile of faith's
  Awful frivolity.

Know that in this grotesque old masque
  Too loud we cannot sing,
Or dance too wild, or speak too wide
  To praise a hidden thing.

That though the jest be old as night,
  Still shaketh sun and sphere
An everlasting laughter
  Too loud for us to hear.

FEMINA CONTRA MUNDUM

THE sun was black with judgment, and the moon
      Blood: but between
I saw a man stand, saying: 'To me at least
      The grass is green.

'There was no star that I forgot to fear
      With love and wonder.
The birds have loved me'; but no answer came—
      Only the thunder.

L 913

Once more the man stood, saying: 'A cottage door,
        Wherethrough I gazed
That instant as I turned—yea, I am vile;
        Yet my eyes blazed.

'For I had weighed the mountains in a balance,
        And the skies in a scale,
I come to sell the stars—old lamps for new—
        Old stars for sale.'

Then a calm voice fell all the thunder through,
        A tone less rough:
'Thou hast begun to love one of my works
        Almost enough.'

TO A CERTAIN NATION

WE will not let thee be, for thou art ours.
    We thank thee still, though thou forget these things,
For that hour's sake when thou didst wake all powers
    With a great cry that God was sick of kings.

Leave thee there grovelling at their rusted greaves,
    These hulking cowards on a painted stage,
Who, with imperial pomp and laurel leaves,
    Show their Marengo—one man in a cage.

These, for whom stands no type or title given
    In all the squalid tales of gore and pelf;
Though cowed by crashing thunders from all heaven
    Cain never said: 'My brother slew himself.'

Tear you the truth out of your drivelling spy,
    The maniac whom you set to swing death's scythe.
Nay; torture not the torturer—let him lie:
    What need of racks to teach a worm to writhe?

TO A CERTAIN NATION 311

Bear with us, O our sister, not in pride,
  Nor any scorn we see thee spoiled of knaves,
But only shame to hear, where Danton died,
  Thy foul dead kings all laughing in their graves.

Thou hast a right to rule thyself; to be
  The thing thou wilt; to grin, to fawn, to creep;
To crown these clumsy liars; aye, and we
  Who knew thee once, we have a right to weep.

THE PRAISE OF DUST

'What of vile dust?' the preacher said.
  Methought the whole world woke,
The dead stone lived beneath my foot,
  And my whole body spoke.

'You, that play tyrant to the dust,
  And stamp its wrinkled face,
This patient star that flings you not
  Far into homeless space.

'Come down out of your dusty shrine
  The living dust to see,
The flowers that at your sermon's end
  Stand blazing silently.

'Rich white and blood-red blossom; stones,
  Lichens like fire encrust;
A gleam of blue, a glare of gold,
  The vision of the dust.

'Pass them all by: till, as you come
  Where, at a city's edge,
Under a tree—I know it well—
  Under a lattice ledge.

'The sunshine falls on one brown head.
  You, too, O cold of clay,
Eater of stones, may haply hear
  The trumpets of that day

'When God to all His paladins
  By His own splendour swore
To make a fairer face than heaven,
  Of dust and nothing more.'

THE BALLAD OF THE BATTLE OF GIBEON

FIVE kings rule o'er the Amorite,
Mighty as fear and old as night;
Swathed with unguent and gold and jewel,
Waxed they merry and fat and cruel.
Zedek of Salem, a terror and glory,
Whose face was hid while his robes were gory;
And Hoham of Hebron, whose loathly face is
Heavy and dark o'er the ruin of races;
And Piram of Jarmuth, drunk with strange wine,
Who dreamed he had fashioned all stars that shine;
And Debir of Eglon wild, without pity,
Who raged like a plague in the midst of his city;
And Japhia of Lachish, a fire that flameth,
Who did in the daylight what no man nameth.

These five kings said one to another:
'King unto king o'er the world is brother,
Seeing that now, for a sign and a wonder,
A red eclipse and a tongue of thunder,
A shape and a finger of desolation,
Is come against us a kingless nation.
Gibeon hath failed us: it were not good
That a man remember where Gibeon stood.'
Then Gibeon sent to our captain, crying:
'Son of Nun, let a shaft be flying,

For unclean birds are gathering greedily;
Slack not thy hand, but come thou speedily.
Yea, we are lost save thou maintain'st us,
For the kings of the mountains are gathered against us

Then to our people spake the Deliverer:
'Gibeon is high, yet a host may shiver her;
Gibeon hath sent to me crying for pity,
For the lords of the cities encompass the city
With chariot and banner and bowman and lancer,
And I swear by the living God I will answer.
Gird you, O Israel, quiver and javelin,
Shield and sword for the road we travel in;
Verily, as I have promised, pay I
Life unto Gibeon, death unto Ai.'

Sudden and still as a bolt shot right
Up on the city we went by night.
Never a bird of the air could say:
'This was the children of Israel's way.
Only the hosts sprang up from sleeping,
Saw from the heights a dark stream sweeping;
Sprang up straight as a great shout stung them,
And heard the Deliverer's war-cry among them,
Heard under cupola, turret, and steeple
The awful cry of the kingless people.

Started the weak of them, shouted the strong of them,
Crashed we a thunderbolt into the throng of them,
Blindly with heads bent, and shields forced before us,
We heard the dense roar of the strife closing o'er us.
And drunk with the crash of the song that it sung them,
We drove the great spear-blade in God's name among
    them.

Redder and redder the sword-flash fell,
Our eyes and our nostrils were hotter than hell;
Till full all the crest of the spear-surge shocking us,
Hoham of Hebron cried out mocking us:
'Nay, what need of the war-sword's plying,

Out of the desert the dust comes flying.
A little red dust, if the wind be blowing—
Who shall reck of its coming or going?'
Back the Deliverer spake as a clarion:
'Mock at thy slaves, thou eater of carrion!
Laughest thou at us, in thy kingly clowning,
We, that laughed upon Ramases frowning,
We that stood up proud, unpardoned,
When his face was dark and his heart was hardened?
Pharaoh we knew and his steeds, not faster
Than the word of the Lord in thine ear, O master.'
Sheer through the turban his wantons wove him,
Clean to the skull the Deliverer clove him;
And the two hosts reeled at the sign appalling,
As the great king fell like a great house falling.

Loudly we shouted, and living and dying,
Bore them all backward with strength and strong crying;
And Caleb struck Zedek hard at the throat,
And Japhia of Lachish Zebulon smote.
The war-swords and axes were clashing and groaning,
The fallen were fighting and foaming and moaning,
The war-spears were breaking, the war-horns were
      braying,
Ere the hands of the slayers were sated with slaying.
And deep in the grasses grown gory and sodden,
The treaders of all men were trampled and trodden;
And over them, routed and reeled like cattle,
High over·the turn of the tide of the battle,
High over noises that deafen and cover us,
Rang the Deliverer's voice out over us.

'Stand thou still, thou sun upon Gibeon,
Stand thou, moon, in the valley of Ajalon!
Shout thou, people, a cry like thunder,
For the kings of the earth are broken asunder.
Now we have said as the thunder says it,
Something is stronger than strength and slays it.
Now we have written for all time later,
Five kings are great, yet a law is greater.

Stare, O sun! in thine own great glory,
This is the turn of the whole world's story.
Stand thou still, thou sun upon Gibeon,
Stand thou, moon, in the valley of Ajalon!

'Smite! amid spear-blades blazing and breaking,
More than we know of is rising and making.
Stab with the javelin, crash with the car!
Cry! for we know not the thing that we are.
Stand, O sun! that in horrible patience
Smiled on the smoke and the slaughter of nations.
Thou shalt grow sad for a little crying,
Thou shalt be darkened for one man's dying—
Stand thou still, thou sun upon Gibeon,
Stand thou, moon, in the valley of Ajalon!'

After the battle was broken and spent
Up to the hill the Deliverer went,
Flung up his arms to the storm-clouds flying,
And cried unto Israel, mightily crying:
'Come up, O warriors! come up, O brothers!
Tribesmen and herdsmen, maidens and mothers;
The bondman's son and the bondman's daughter,
The hewer of wood and the drawer of water,
He that carries and he that brings,
And set your foot on the neck of kings.'

This is the story of Gibeon fight—
Where we smote the lords of the Amorite;
Where the banners of princes with slaughter were sodden,
And the beards of seers in the rank grass trodden;
Where the trees were wrecked by the wreck of cars,
And the reek of the red field blotted the stars;
Where the dead heads dropped from the swords that
   sever.
Because His mercy endureth for ever.

'VULGARIZED'

ALL round they murmur: 'O profane,
  Keep thy heart's secret hid as gold';
But I, by God, would sooner be
  Some knight in shattering wars of old,

In brown outlandish arms to ride,
  And shout my love to every star
With lungs to make a poor maid's name
  Deafen the iron ears of war.

Here, where these subtle cowards crowd,
  To stand and so to speak of love,
That the four corners of the world
  Should hear it and take heed thereof.

That to this shrine obscure there be
  One witness before all men given,
As naked as the hanging Christ,
  As shameless as the sun in heaven.

These whimperers—have they spared to us
  One dripping woe, one reeking sin?
These thieves that shatter their own graves
  To prove the soul is dead within.

They talk; by God, is it not time
  Some of Love's chosen broke the girth,
And told the good all men have known
  Since the first morning of the earth?

THE BALLAD OF GOD-MAKERS

A BIRD flew out at the break of day
  From the nest where it had curled,
And ere the eve the bird had set
  Fear on the kings of the world.

The first tree it lit upon
  Was green with leaves unshed;
The second tree it lit upon
  Was red with apples red;

The third tree it lit upon
  Was barren and was brown,
Save for a dead man nailed thereon
  On a hill above a town.

That night the kings of the earth were gay
  And filled the cup and can;
Last night the kings of the earth were chill
  For dread of a naked man.

'If he speak two more words,' they said,
  'The slave is more than the free;
If he speak three more words,' they said,
  'The stars are under the sea.'

Said the King of the East to the King of the West,
  I wot his frown was set:
'Lo, let us slay him and make him as dung,
  It is well that the world forget.'

Said the King of the West to the King of the East,
  I wot his smile was dread:
'Nay, let us slay him and make him a god,
  It is well that our god be dead.'

They set the young man on a hill,
  They nailed him to a rod;
And there in darkness and in blood
  They made themselves a god.

And the mightiest word was left unsaid,
  And the world had never a mark,
And the strongest man of the sons of men
  Went dumb into the dark.

*L913

Then hymns and harps of praise they brought,
  Incense and gold and myrrh,
And they thronged above the seraphim,
  The poor dead carpenter.

'Thou art the prince of all,' they sang,
  'Ocean and earth and air.'
Then the bird flew on to the cruel cross,
  And hid in the dead man's hair.

'Thou art the sun of the world,' they cried,
  'Speak if our prayers be heard.'
And the brown bird stirred in the dead man's hair,
  And it seemed that the dead man stirred.

Then a shriek went up like the world's last cry
  From all nations under heaven,
And a master fell before a slave
  And begged to be forgiven.

They cowered, for dread in his wakened eyes
  The ancient wrath to see;
And the bird flew out of the dead Christ's hair,
  And lit on a lemon-tree.

AT NIGHT

How many million stars there be,
That only God hath numberèd;
But this one only chosen for me
In time before her face was fled.
Shall not one mortal man alive
    Hold up his head?

THE WOOD-CUTTER

WE came behind him by the wall,
  My brethren drew their brands,
And they had strength to strike him down—
  And I to bind his hands.

Only once, to a lantern gleam,
  He turned his face from the wall,
And it was as the accusing angel's face
  On the day when the stars shall fall.

I grasped the axe with shaking hands,
  I stared at the grass I trod;
For I feared to see the whole bare heavens
  Filled with the face of God.

I struck: the serpentine slow blood
  In four arms soaked the moss—
Before me, by the living Christ,
  The blood ran in a cross.

Therefore I toil in forests here
  And pile the wood in stacks,
And take no fee from the shivering folk
  Till I have cleansed the axe.

But for a curse God cleared my sight,
  And where each tree doth grow
I see a life with awful eyes,
  And I must lay it low.

ART COLOURS

ON must we go: we search dead leaves,
  We chase the sunset's saddest flames,
The nameless hues that o'er and o'er
  In lawless wedding lost their names.

God of the daybreak! Better be
  Black savages; and grin to gird
Our limbs in gaudy rags of red,
  The laughing-stock of brute and bird;

And feel again the fierce old feast,
  Blue for seven heavens that had sufficed,
A gold like shining hoards, a red
  Like roses from the blood of Christ.

THE TWO WOMEN

Lo! very fair is she who knows the ways
  Of joy: in pleasure's mocking wisdom old,
The eyes that might be cold to flattery, kind;
  The hair that might be grey with knowledge, gold.

But thou art more than these things, O my queen,
  For thou art clad in ancient wars and tears.
And looking forth, framed in the crown of thorns,
  I saw the youngest face in all the spheres

THE WILD KNIGHT

THE wasting thistle whitens on my crest,
The barren grasses blow upon my spear,
A green, pale pennon: blazon of wild faith
And love of fruitless things: yea, of my love,
Among the golden loves of all the knights,
Alone: most hopeless, sweet, and blasphemous,
The love of God:
              I hear the crumbling creeds
Like cliffs washed down by water, change, and pass;
I hear a noise of words, age after age,
A new cold wind that blows across the plains.
And all the shrines stand empty; and to me
All these are nothing: priests and schools may doubt
Who never have believed; but I have loved.
Ah, friends, I know it passing well, the love
Wherewith I love; it shall not bring to me
Return or hire or any pleasant thing—
Aye, I have tried it: Aye, I know its roots.
Earthquake and plague have burst on it in vain
And rolled back shattered—
              Babbling neophytes!
Blind, startled fools—think you I know it not?
Think you to teach me?   Know I not His ways?
Strange-visaged blunders, mystic cruelties.
All! all! I know Him, for I love Him.   Go!

So, with the wan waste grasses on my spear,
I ride for ever, seeking after God.
My hair grows whiter than my thistle plume,
And all my limbs are loose; but in my eyes
The star of an unconquerable praise:

For in my soul one hope for ever sings,
That at the next white corner of a road
My eyes may look on Him. . . .
                          Hush—I shall know
The place when it is found: a twisted path
Under a twisted pear-tree—this I saw
In the first dream I had ere I was born,
Wherein He spoke. . . .
                          But the grey clouds come down
In hail upon the icy plains: I ride,
Burning for ever in consuming fire.

*A dark manor-house shuttered and unlighted, outlined
against a pale sunset : in front a large, but neglected,
garden.   To the right, in the foreground, the porch of a
chapel, with coloured windows lighted.   Hymns within.*
*Above the porch a grotesque carved bracket, supporting a
lantern.   Astride of it sits Captain Redfeather, a flagon
in his hand.*

REDFEATHER

I have drunk to all I know of,
To every leaf on the tree,
To the highest bird of the heavens,
To the lowest fish of the sea.
What toast, what toast remaineth,
Drunk down in the same good wine,
By the tippler's cup in the tavern,
And the priest's cup at the shrine?
        [*A Priest comes out, stick in hand, and looks right
        and left.*

VOICES WITHIN

The brawler . . .

PRIEST

He has vanished

REDFEATHER

                        To the stars.
                        [*The Priest looks up.*

PRIEST [*angrily*]

What would you there, sir?

REDFEATHER

                        Give you all a toast.
            [*Lifts his flagon.   More priests come out.*
I see my life behind me: bad enough—
Drink, duels, madness, beggary, and pride,
The life of the unfit: yet ere I drop
On Nature's rubbish heap, I weigh it all,
And give you all a toast—
                        [*Reels to his feet and stands.*

The health of God!
                    [*They all recoil from him.*
Let 's give the Devil of the Heavens His due!
He that made grass so green, and wine so red,
Is not so black as you have painted Him.   [*Drinks.*

PRIEST

Blaspheming profligate!

REDFEATHER [*hurls the flagon among them*]
                    Howl! ye dumb dogs,
I named your King—let me have one great shout,
Flutter the seraphim like startled birds;
Make God recall the good days of His youth
Ere saints had saddened Him: when He came back
Conqueror of Chaos in a six days' war,
With all the sons of God shouting for joy . . .

PRIEST

And you—what is your right, and who are you,
To praise God?

REDFEATHER

          A lost soul.   In earth or heaven
What has a better right?

PRIEST

          Go, pagan, go!
Drink, dice, and dance: take no more thought than blind
Beasts of the field. . . .

REDFEATHER

          Or . . . lilies of the field,
To quote a pagan sage.   I go my way.

PRIEST [*solemnly*]
And when Death comes . . .

REDFEATHER

          He shall not find me dead.
[*Puts on his plumed hat.   The priests go out.*

REDFEATHER

These frozen fools . . .
[*The Lady Olive comes out of the chapel.   He sees her.*
                    Oh, they were right enough,
Where shall I hide my carrion from the sun?
            [*Buries his face.   His hat drops to the ground.*

OLIVE [*looking up*]

Captain, are you from church?   I saw you not.

REDFEATHER

No, I am here.   [*Lays his hand on a gargoyle.*
            I, too, am a grotesque,
And dance with all the devils on the roof.

OLIVE [*with a strange smile*]

For Satan, also, I have often prayed.

REDFEATHER [*roughly*]

Satan may worry women if he will,
For he was but an angel ere he fell,
But I—before I fell—I was a man.

OLIVE

He too, my Master, was a man: too strong
To fear a strong man's sins: 'tis written He
Descended into hell.

REDFEATHER

            Write, then, that I
                    [*Leaps to the ground before her.*
Descended into heaven . . .
                    You are ill?

OLIVE

No, well . . .

REDFEATHER

        You speak the truth—you are the Truth—
Lady, say once again then: 'I am *well*.'

OLIVE

I—ah! God give me grace—I am nigh dead.

REDFEATHER [*quietly*]

Lord Orm?

OLIVE

Yes—yes.

REDFEATHER

Is in your father's house—
Having the title-deeds—would drive you forth,
Homeless, and with your father sick to death,
Into this winter, save on a condition
Named . . .

OLIVE

And unnameable. Even so; Lord Orm—
Ah! do you know him?

REDFEATHER

Aye, I saw him once.
The sun shone on his face, that smiled and smiled,
A sight not wholesome to the eyes of man.

OLIVE

Captain, I tell you God once fell asleep,
And in that hour the world went as it would;
Dogs brought forth cats, and poison grew in grapes,
And Orm was born . . .

REDFEATHER

Why, curse him! can he not
Be kicked or paid?

OLIVE [*feverishly*]

Hush! He is just behind
There in the house—see how the great house glares,
Glares like an ogre's mask—the whole dead house
Possessed with bestial meaning. . . .   [*Screams.*
Ah! the face!
The whole great grinning house—his face! his face!
His face!

REDFEATHER [*in a voice of thunder, pointing away from
the house*]
      Look there—look there!

OLIVE
                          What is it?   What?

REDFEATHER
I think it was a bird.

OLIVE
                    What thought you, truly?

REDFEATHER   .
I think a mighty thought is drawing near.
                              [*Enter The Wild Knight.*

THE WILD KNIGHT
That house . . .   [*Points.*

OLIVE
          Ah Christ!   [*Shudders.*]   I had forgotten it.

THE WILD KNIGHT [*still pointing*]
That house! the house at last, the house of God,
Wherein God makes an evening feast for me.
The house at last: I know the twisted path
Under the twisted pear-tree: this I saw
In the first dream I had ere I was born.
It is the house of God.   He welcomes me.
                              [*Strides forward.*

REDFEATHER
That house.   God's blood!

OLIVE [*hysterically*]
                      Is not this hell's own wit?

THE WILD KNIGHT
God grows impatient, and His wine is poured,
His bread is broken.   [*Rushes forward.*

REDFEATHER [*leaps between*]
                      Stand away, great fool,
There is a devil there!

THE WILD KNIGHT [*draws his sword, and waves it as*
                he rushes]
                      God's house!—God's house!

REDFEATHER [*plucks out his own sword*]
Better my hand than his.   [*The blades clash.*
                      God alone knows
What That within might do to you, poor fool,
I can but kill you.
                      [*They fight. Olive tries to part them.*

REDFEATHER
Olive, stand away!

OLIVE
I will not stand away!   [*Steps between the swords.*
                      Stranger, a word,
Yes—you are right—God is within that house.

REDFEATHER
Olive!

OLIVE
      But He is all too beautiful
For us who only know of stars and flowers.
The thing within is all too pure and fair,   [*Shudders.*
Too awful in its ancient innocence,
For men to look upon it and not die;
Ourselves would fade into those still white fires
Of peace and mercy.   [*Struggles with her voice.*
                      There . . . enough . . . the law—
No flesh shall look upon the Lord and live.

REDFEATHER [*sticking his sword in the ground*]
You are the bravest lady in the world.

THE WILD KNIGHT [*dazed*]
May I not go within?

REDFEATHER
> Keep you the law—
No flesh shall look upon the Lord and live.

THE WILD KNIGHT [*sadly*]
Then I will go and lay me in the flowers,
For He may haply, as in ancient time,
Walk in the garden in the cool of day.   [*He goes out.*
> [*Olive reels. Redfeather catches her.*

REDFEATHER
You are the strongest woman upon earth.
The weakest woman than the strongest man
Is stronger in her hour: this is the law.
When the hour passes—then may we be strong.

OLIVE [*wildly*]
The House . . . the Face.

REDFEATHER [*fiercely*]
> I love you.   Look at me!

OLIVE [*turns her face to him*]
I hear six birds sing in that little tree,
Say, is the old earth laughing at my fears?
I think I love you also . . .

REDFEATHER
> What I am
You know.   But I will never curse a man,
Even in a mirror.

OLIVE [*smiling at him*]
> And the Devil's dance?

REDFEATHER
The Devil plotted since the world was young
With alchemies of fire and witches' oils
And magic.   But he never made a man.

OLIVE
No, not a man.

REDFEATHER

Not even my Lord Orm.
Look at the house now— [*She starts and looks.*
Honest brick and tiles.

OLIVE

You have a strange strength in this hour.

REDFEATHER

This hour
I see with mortal eye as in one flash
The whole divine democracy of things,
And dare the stars to scorn a scavenge-heap.
Olive, I tell you every soul is great.
Weave we green crowns—how noble and how high;
Fling we white flowers—how radiant and how pure
Is he, whoe'er he be, who next shall cross
This scrap of grass . . . [*Enter Lord Orm.*

OLIVE [*screams*]
Ah!

REDFEATHER [*pointing to the chapel*]
Olive, go and pray
For a man soon to die. Good day, my Lord.
[*She goes in.*

LORD ORM

Good day.

REDFEATHER

I am a friend to Lady Olive.

LORD ORM

Sir, you are fortunate.

REDFEATHER

Most fortunate
In finding, sword on thigh and ready, one
Who is a villain and a gentleman.

LORD ORM [*picks up the flagon*]

Empty, I see.

REDFEATHER

Oh, sir, you never drink,
You dread to lose yourself before the stars—
Do you not dread to sleep?

LORD ORM [*violently*]
What would you here?

REDFEATHER

Receive from you the title-deeds you hold.

LORD ORM

You entertain me.

REDFEATHER

With a bout at foils?

LORD ORM

I will not fight.

REDFEATHER

I know you better, then.
I have seen men grow mangier than the beasts,
Eat bread with blood upon their fingers, grin
While women burned: but one last law they served.
When I say 'Coward,' is the law awake?

LORD ORM

Hear me, then, too: I have seen robbers rule,
And thieves go clad in gold—age after age—
Because, though sordid, ragged, rude, and mean,
They saw, like gods, no law above their heads.
But when they fell—then for this cause they fell,
This last mean cobweb of the fairy tales
Of good and ill: that they must stand and fight
When a man bade, though they had chose to stand
And fight not. I am stronger than the world.
[*Folds his arms.*

REDFEATHER [*lifts his hand*]
If in your body be the blood of man,   [*Strikes him.*
Now let it rush to the face—

God!   Have you sunk
Lower than anger?

LORD ORM
How I triumph now.

REDFEATHER [*stamps wildly*]
Damned, whimpering dog! vile, snivelling, sick poltroon!
Are you alive?

LORD ORM
Evil, be thou my good;
Let the sun blacken and the moon be blood:
I have said the words.

REDFEATHER [*studying him*]
And if I struck you dead,
You would turn to daisies!

LORD ORM
And you do not strike.

REDFEATHER [*dreamily*]
Indeed, poor soul, such magic would be kind
And full of pity as a fairy tale:
One touch of this bright wand [*Lifts his sword*] and
down would drop
The dark abortive blunder that is you,
And you would change, forgiven, into flowers.

LORD ORM
And yet—and yet you do not strike me dead.
I do not draw: the sword is in your hand—
Drive the blade through me where I stand.

REDFEATHER
Lord Orm,
You asked the Lady Olive (I can speak
As to a toad to you, my lord)—you asked
Olive to be your paramour: and she——

LORD ORM

Refused.

REDFEATHER

And yet her father was at stake,
And she is soft and kind.   Now look at me,
Ragged and ruined, soaked in bestial sins:
My lord, I too have my virginity—
Turn the thing round, my lord, and topside down,
You cannot spell it.   Be the fact enough,
I use no sword upon a swordless man.

LORD ORM

For her?

REDFEATHER

I too have my virginity.

LORD ORM

Now look on me: I am the lord of earth,
For I have broken the last bond of man.
I stand erect, crowned with the stars—and why?
Because I stand a coward—because you
Have mercy—on a coward.   Do I win?

REDFEATHER

Though there you stand with moving mouth and eyes,
I think, my lord, you are not possible—
God keep you from my dreams.   [Goes out.

LORD ORM

                    Alone and free.
Since first in flowery meads a child I ran,
My one long thirst—to be alone and free.
Free of all laws, creeds, codes, and common tests,
Shameless, anarchic, infinite.
                    Why, then,
I might have done in that dark liberty—
If I should say 'a good deed,' men would laugh,
But here are none to laugh.
                    The godless world
Be thanked there is no God to spy on me,

Catch me and crown me with a vulgar crown
For what I do: if I should once believe
The horror of that ancient Eavesdropper
Behind the starry arras of the skies,
I should—well, well, enough of menaces—
I should not do the thing I come to do.
What do I come to do?   Let me but try
To spell it to my soul.
                              Suppose a man
Perfectly free and utterly alone,
Free of all love of law, equally free
Of all the love of mutiny it breeds,
Free of the love of heaven, and also free
Of all the love of hell it drives us to;
Not merely void of rules, unconscious of them;
So strong that naught alive could do him hurt,
So wise that he knew all things, and so great
That none knew what he was or what he did—
A lawless giant.   [*A pause : then in a low voice.*
              Would he not be good?
Hate is the weakness of a thwarted thing,
Pride is the weakness of a thing unpraised.
But he, this man . . .
              He would be like a child
Girt with the tomes of some vast library,
Who reads romance after romance, and smiles
When every tale ends well: impersonal
As God he grows—melted in suns and stars;
So would this boundless man, whom none could spy,
Taunt him with virtue, censure him with vice,
Rejoice in all men's joys; with golden pen
Write all the live romances of the earth
To a triumphant close . . .
              Alone and free—
In this grey, cool, clean garden, washed with winds,
What do I come to do among the grass,
The daisies, and the dews?   An awful thing,
To prove I am that man.
              That while these saints
Taunt me with trembling, dare me to revenge,

I breathe an upper air of ancient good
And strong eternal laughter; send my sun
And rain upon the evil and the just,
Turn my left cheek unto the smiter.   He
That told me, sword in hand, that I had fallen
Lower than anger, knew not I had risen
Higher than pride . . .
                           Enough, the deeds are mine.
                           [*Takes out the title-deeds.*
I come to write the end of a romance.
A good romance: the characters—Lord Orm,
Type of the starvèd heart and storèd brain,
Who strives to hate and cannot; fronting him—
Redfeather, rake in process of reform,
At root a poet: I have hopes of him:
He can love virtue, for he still loves vice.
He is not all burnt out.   He beats me there
(How I beat him in owning it!); in love
He is still young, and has the joy of shame.
And for the Lady Olive—who shall speak?
A man may weigh the courage of a man,
But if there be a bottomless abyss
It is a woman's valour: such as I
Can only bow the knee and hide the face
(Thank God there is no God to spy on me
And bring his cursèd crowns).
                           No, there is none!
The old incurable hunger of the world
Surges in wolfish wars, age after age.
There was no God before me: none sees where,
Between the brute-womb and the deaf, dead grave,
Unhoping, unrecorded, unrepaid,
I make with smoke, fire, and burnt-offering
This sacrifice to Chaos. [*Lights the papers.*] None behold
Me write in fire the end of the romance.
Burn! I am God, and crown myself with stars
Upon creation day: before was night
And chaos of a blind and cruel world.
I am the first God; I will trample hell,
Fight, conquer, make the story of the stars,

Like this poor story, end like a romance:

[The paper burns.

Before was brainless night: but I am God
In this black world I rend.   Let there be light!

[The paper blazes up, illuminating the garden.

I, God . . .

THE WILD KNIGHT [*rushes forward*]

God's Light! God's Voice; yes, it is He
Walking in Eden in the cool of the day!

LORD ORM [*screams*]

Tricked!   Caught!
Damned screeching rat in a hole!

*[Stabs him again and again with his sword; stamps
on his face.*

THE WILD KNIGHT [*faintly*]

Earth grows too beautiful around me: shapes
And colours fearfully wax fair and clear,
For I have heard, as thro' a door ajar,
Scraps of the huge soliloquy of God
That moveth as a mask the lips of man,
If man be very silent: they were right,
No flesh shall look upon the Lord and live.   [*Dies.*

LORD ORM [*staggers back laughing*]

Saved, saved, my secret.

REDFEATHER [*rushing in, sword in hand*]

The drawn sword at last!
Guard, son of hell!

[They fight.   Orm falls.   Olive comes in.

He too can die.   Keep back!
Olive, keep back from him!   I did not fear
Him living, and he fell before my sword;
But dead I fear him.   All is ended now;
A man's whole life tied in a bundle there,
And no good deed.   I fear him.   Come away.

GOOD NEWS

BETWEEN a meadow and a cloud that sped
  In rain and twilight, in desire and fear,
  I heard a secret—hearken in your ear:
'Behold the daisy has a ring of red.'

That hour, with half of blessing, half of ban,
  A great voice went through heaven and earth and hell,
  Crying: 'We are tricked, my great ones, is it well?
Now is the secret stolen by a man.'

Then waxed I like the wind because of this,
  And ran, like gospel and apocalypse,
  From door to door, with new anarchic lips,
Crying the very blasphemy of bliss.

In the last wreck of Nature, dark and dread,
  Shall in eclipse's hideous hieroglyph,
  One wild form reel on the last rocking cliff,
And shout: 'The daisy has a ring of red.'

THE NEGLECTED CHILD

(Dedicated, in a glow of Christmas charity, to a
philanthropic society)

THE Teachers in the Temple
  They did not lift their eyes
For the blazing star on Bethlehem
  Or the Wise Men grown wise.

They heeded jot and tittle,
  They heeded not a jot
The rending voice of Ramah
  And the children that were not.

Or how the panic of the poor
  Choked all the field with flight,
Or how the red sword of the rich
  Ran ravening through the night.

They made their notes; while naked
  And monstrous and obscene
A tyrant bathed in all the blood
  Of men that might have been.

But they did chide Our Lady
  And tax her for this thing,
That she had lost Him for a time
  And sought Him sorrowing.

TO A TURK

WARRIOR by warriors smitten,
  Gambler whose luck has turned,
Read not the small words written,
  Who know what love you earned:
You know, and none shall tell you,
  What and how long and how
They did endure in silence
  That smite in silence now.

A Liberal may belabour
  With rods your reckless dead,
As the Tory licked your sabre
  For the blood he dared not shed;
Since from the creedless chapel
  And the cushioned prize-ring came
The men that feared your glory
  And they that praised your shame.

With us too rage against the rood
  Your devils and your swine;
A colder scorn of womanhood,
  A baser fear of wine,

TO A TURK 339

And lust without the harem,
  And Doom without the God.
Go. It is not this rabble
  Sayeth to you 'Ichabod.'

Because our sorrow has sufficed
  And what we know we know;
And because you were great, Lord Antichrist,
  In the name of Christ you go;
But you shall not turn your turban
  For the little dogs that yell,
When a man rides out of a city:
  In the name of God; farewell.

THE ARISTOCRAT

THE Devil is a gentleman, and asks you down to stay
At his little place at What'sitsname (it isn't far away).
They say the sport is splendid; there is always something
    new,
And fairy scenes, and fearful feats that none but he
    can do;
He can shoot the feathered cherubs if they fly on the
    estate,
Or fish for Father Neptune with the mermaids for a bait:
He scaled amid the staggering stars that precipice, the
    sky,
And blew his trumpet above heaven; and got by mastery
The starry crown of God Himself, and shoved it on the
    shelf;
But the Devil is a gentleman and doesn't brag himself.

O blind your eyes and break your heart and hack your
    hand away,
And lose your love and shave your head; but do not go
    to stay

At the little place in What'sitsname where folks are
    rich and clever;
The golden and the goodly house, where things grow
    worse for ever;
There are things you need not know of, though you live
    and die in vain,
There are souls more sick of pleasure than you are sick
    of pain;
There is a game of April Fool that 's played behind its
    door,
Where the fool remains for ever and the April comes
    no more,
Where the splendour of the daylight grows drearier than
    the dark,
And life droops like a vulture that once was such a lark;
And that is the Blue Devil that once was the Blue Bird;
For the Devil is a gentleman, and doesn't keep his word.

LEPANTO

WHITE founts falling in the Courts of the sun,
And the Soldan of Byzantium is smiling as they run;
There is laughter like the fountains in that face of all
    men feared,
It stirs the forest darkness, the darkness of his beard,
It curls the blood-red crescent, the crescent of his lips,
For the inmost sea of all the earth is shaken with his ships.
They have dared the white republics up the capes of
    Italy,
They have dashed the Adriatic round the Lion of the Sea,
And the Pope has cast his arms abroad for agony and loss,
And called the kings of Christendom for swords about the
    Cross.
The cold Queen of England is looking in the glass;
The shadow of the Valois is yawning at the Mass;
From evening isles fantastical rings faint the Spanish gun,
And the Lord upon the Golden Horn is laughing in the
    sun.

Dim drums throbbing, in the hills half heard,
Where only on a nameless throne a crownless prince has
    stirred,
Where, risen from a doubtful seat and half attainted stall,
The last knight of Europe takes weapons from the wall,
The last and lingering troubadour to whom the bird has
    sung,
That once went singing southward when all the world was
    young.
In that enormous silence, tiny and unafraid,
Comes up along a winding road the noise of the Crusade.
Strong gongs groaning as the guns boom far,
Don John of Austria is going to the war,
Stiff flags straining in the night-blasts cold,
In the gloom black-purple, in the glint old-gold.
Torchlight crimson on the copper kettle-drums,
Then the tuckets, then the trumpets, then the cannon,
    and he comes.
Don John laughing in the brave beard curled,
Spurning of his stirrups like the thrones of all the world,
Holding his head up for a flag of all the free.
Love-light of Spain—hurrah!
Death-light of Africa!
Don John of Austria
Is riding to the sea.

Mahound is in his paradise above the evening star,
(*Don John of Austria is going to the war.*)
He moves a mighty turban on the timeless houri's knees,
His turban that is woven of the sunsets and the seas.
He shakes the peacock gardens as he rises from his ease,
And he strides among the tree-tops and is taller than the
    trees,
And his voice through all the garden is a thunder sent to
    bring
Black Azrael and Ariel and Ammon on the wing.
Giants and the Genii,
Multiplex of wing and eye,
Whose strong obedience broke the sky
When Solomon was king.

M 913

They rush in red and purple from the red clouds of the
    morn,
From temples where the yellow gods shut up their eyes
    in scorn;
They rise in green robes roaring from the green hells of
    the sea
Where fallen skies and evil hues and eyeless creatures be;
On them the sea-valves cluster and the grey sea-forests
    curl,
Splashed with a splendid sickness, the sickness of the
    pearl;
They swell in sapphire smoke out of the blue cracks of
    the ground,—
They gather and they wonder and give worship to
    Mahound.
And he saith, 'Break up the mountains where the hermit-
    folk can hide,
And sift the red and silver sands lest bone of saint abide,
And chase the Giaours flying night and day, not giving
    rest,
For that which was our trouble comes again out of the
    west.

'We have set the seal of Solomon on all things under
    sun,
Of knowledge and of sorrow and endurance of things
    done,
But a noise is in the mountains, in the mountains, and I
    know
The voice that shook our palaces—four hundred years
    ago:
It is he that saith not "Kismet"; it is he that knows not
    Fate;
It is Richard, it is Raymond, it is Godfrey in the gate!
It is he whose loss is laughter when he counts the wager
    worth,
Put down your feet upon him, that our peace be on the
    earth.'
For he heard drums groaning and he heard guns jar,
(*Don John of Austria is going to the war.*)

Sudden and still—hurrah!
Bolt from Iberia!
Don John of Austria
Is gone by Alcalar.

St. Michael's on his Mountain in the sea-roads of the
    north,
(*Don John of Austria is girt and going forth.*)
Where the grey seas glitter and the sharp tides shift
And the sea-folk labour and the red sails lift.
He shakes his lance of iron and he claps his wings of
    stone;
The noise is gone through Normandy; the noise is gone
    alone;
The North is full of tangled things and texts and aching
    eyes
And dead is all the innocence of anger and surprise,
And Christian killeth Christian in a narrow dusty room,
And Christian dreadeth Christ that hath a newer face of
    doom,
And Christian hateth Mary that God kissed in Galilee,
But Don John of Austria is riding to the sea.
Don John calling through the blast and the eclipse,
Crying with the trumpet, with the trumpet of his lips,
Trumpet that sayeth ha!
Domino Gloria !
Don John of Austria
Is shouting to the ships.

King Philip's in his closet with the Fleece about his
    neck,
(*Don John of Austria is armed upon the deck.*)
The walls are hung with velvet that is black and soft as
    sin,
And little dwarfs creep out of it and little dwarfs creep in.
He holds a crystal phial that has colours like the moon,
He touches, and it tingles, and he trembles very soon,
And his face is as a fungus of a leprous white and grey
Like plants in the high houses that are shuttered from the
    day,

And death is in the phial and the end of noble work,
But Don John of Austria has fired upon the Turk.
Don John's hunting, and his hounds have bayed—
Booms away past Italy the rumour of his raid.
Gun upon gun, ha! ha!
Gun upon gun, hurrah!
Don John of Austria
Has loosed the cannonade.

The Pope was in his chapel before day or battle broke,
(*Don John of Austria is hidden in the smoke.*)
The hidden room in man's house where God sits all the
year,
The secret window whence the world looks small and
very dear.
He sees as in a mirror on the monstrous twilight sea
The crescent of the cruel ships whose name is mystery;
They fling great shadows foe-wards, making Cross and
Castle dark,
They veil the plumèd lions on the galleys of St. Mark;
And above the ships are palaces of brown, black-bearded
chiefs,
And below the ships are prisons, where with multitudi-
nous griefs,
Christian captives sick and sunless, all a labouring race
repines
Like a race in sunken cities, like a nation in the mines.
They are lost like slaves that swat, and in the skies of
morning hung
The stairways of the tallest gods when tyranny was
young.

They are countless, voiceless, hopeless as those fallen or
fleeing on
Before the high Kings' horses in the granite of Babylon.
And many a one grows witless in his quiet room in
hell
Where a yellow face looks inward through the lattice of
his cell,

And he finds his God forgotten, and he seeks no more a
    sign—
(But Don John of Austria has burst the battle-line !)
Don John pounding from the slaughter-painted poop,
Purpling all the ocean like a bloody pirate's sloop,
Scarlet running over on the silvers and the golds,
Breaking of the hatches up and bursting of the holds,
Thronging of the thousands up that labour under sea,
White for bliss and blind for sun and stunned for liberty.
Vivat Hispania !
Domino Gloria !
Don John of Austria
Has set his people free!

Cervantes on his galley sets the sword back in the sheath,
(Don John of Austria rides homeward with a wreath.)
And he sees across a weary land a straggling road in
    Spain,
Up which a lean and foolish knight for ever rides in vain,
And he smiles, but not as Sultans smile, and settles back
    the blade. . . .
(But Don John of Austria rides home from the Crusade.)

Printed in the United Kingdom
by Lightning Source UK Ltd.
131711UK00001B/45/A

9 781406 790214